A Ma

Also by Elise Darcy

The Living Apart Together Series:

Living Apart Together

It Takes 2 to Tango

Dear John

Love on the Rooftop

Standalone Novels

Lola & The Man

The Villa in Sicily

A Mallorcan Affair

A novel

by

ELISE DARCY

Penny Lane Press

ISBN 978-1-913147-02-0

Ever has it been that love knows not its own depth
until the hour of separation.

Kahlil Gibran

1

Southwold, Suffolk, April

Ralph had been putting off returning to England. Loneliness and despair crept over him as he approached the house. A grand property such as this deserved more than a bitter, tired old man with no idea how to move forward with his life thought Ralph. He stared at the house, devoid of life, of people and could not think of a worse homecoming.

The Gables, a detached former Gentleman's residence dating back to the eighteen-sixties, was rich in gothic revival detail. Ralph still had the agents' sales details filed away somewhere from when he'd bought the property in Southwold on the Suffolk coast. In its own grounds with gardens to the front and rear, they advertised it as "ideal for a growing family."

Ralph remembered thinking at the time that it was a large place for two. But it was his wife's dream to retire to Suffolk, and she'd fallen in love with the house the moment she set eyes on it. The previous owners renovated and restored it. When he bought it, Ralph put the finishing touches to the old detached coach house to create a triple garage and an apartment in the eaves as a studio.

The garden was overgrown just as he expected. In his absence, he'd advertised for a house-sitter through the local estate agents, but he guessed they hadn't filled the position; nobody had lived here these past few months. The house exuded an air of abandonment.

It didn't help that he'd arrived home in the dead of night. His flight was delayed coming into Heathrow so he hadn't arrived in Southwold until midnight. The taxi brought him here straight from the airport. Standing there on the gravel drive with his suitcase, he could hear the car engine turning over behind him. The taxicab was costing him, but he'd asked the driver to wait. Thank god he had. Ralph looked up at the property, unoccupied for months, and couldn't bring himself to step foot inside.

The hotel in town, with a bar in which to have a late-night drink, friendly reception staff and hot water on tap, if he fancied a bath, was much more appealing. It was two minutes by car. Ralph hoped they had vacancies. But it wasn't the friendly reception staff, the hot water, the food or the late-night drink in the bar that persuaded him to check into the hotel, it was that feeling of loneliness that would descend on him like a death shroud when he walked into the house. Ralph picked up his suitcase and returned to the waiting taxi.

2

At breakfast, Ralph noticed a seminar being held in the hotel that afternoon called Reinventing Yourself. He inquired whether they had any spaces. Aimed at his generation it sounded an interesting way to kill a few hours; what to do with yourself post-retirement. Ralph knew his motivation for attending – he was putting off going home.

❖

Ralph reached for a sandwich from the afternoon tea he'd ordered at the bar after the seminar and spotted the ring on his finger glinting in the lamplight. He stared at it for a moment like he so often did when he thought about his wife.

Several sandwiches and a scone later he gave up on being able to finish them. It was far too much, and his appetite wasn't what it once was. Maybe some company wouldn't have gone amiss but although there were plenty of single ladies of a certain generation at the seminar, he couldn't find the courage to ask one to join him for afternoon tea.

He pushed the tray aside and wiped his mouth with the serviette, reminding himself that he wasn't here to meet somebody. Although he'd much rather not return home alone, it wasn't his intention to have a fling. That would be the last thing he wanted. Besides, he couldn't take another lady back with him;

there were too many memories of his wife in that house. Perhaps that's why he was having such a hard time at the prospect of returning without her.

It's not as though they'd lived there for years. They had hardly lived there any time at all. She'd spent so much effort and thought on how she wanted to decorate and furnish the property for them both, he knew every corner of The Gables would remind him of her.

He had taken on one more post – before coming home for good and retiring on the Suffolk coast where he grew up. She'd never insisted on joining him before, but that wasn't surprising considering the destinations they often sent him to. They were often war-torn countries with poor infrastructure, ailing economies, starving people and frightening factions blowing each other to smithereens. It was no place for his wife. But this time was different. His last assignment before he consigned his camera to the darkroom, and completed the final chapter of his photojournalism career, was to Mallorca. For the first time she could go with him

She was delighted at this development. Him not so much. Mallorca, a place he didn't want to revisit for reasons he would rather not share with his wife. He would have turned down the assignment if it wasn't for one thing: he'd have to explain to her why. There had been no secrets between them – but one. He'd never talked about it. He'd never talked about *her.* That was a part of his past he wanted to remain firmly in the past. There was no point dredging all that up. What good would it do? So, he had taken the assignment, and she accompanied him to the one place he thought he'd never return. And now his wife was gone.

Sitting there staring out the window fingering his wedding ring, he edged it down his finger but couldn't bring himself to take it off. It was absurd, but he still felt she would appear any moment and join him at the table as though she'd just nipped to the powder room – as she was so fond of calling it. Perhaps it wasn't helping that the last time he visited this hotel they were together and had stayed here while they looked around for a property in which to retire.

He stared into his empty coffee cup. Who knew they would travel abroad, and he would return without her. That wasn't in fact true.

'Sir?'

'Oh,' he looked up at the young waitress. 'I'm sorry, I was miles away.'

She was standing at his table holding a pot of coffee. 'Would you like a refill?'

'No, thank you.' He got out his wallet and then had a thought. 'Can you put this on my hotel bill?'

'Of course, Sir.'

He stopped at the bar. 'May I leave a tip for the young waitress?'

'Of course, Sir.'

Ralph rolled his eyes. 'How many times have I told you…?' he replied in a friendly banter to the young man behind the bar who served him drinks in the evening and kept him entertained with stories. 'It's Ralph.' He coughed.

'Are you all right, Sir?'

Ralph waved away his concern with a flick of his hand and managed a, 'I'm fine,' between hacking coughs. He sat down on a stool at the bar. The coughing subsided. A tall glass of water appeared in front of him courtesy of the concerned young man.

He sipped the water and stared at the empty bar stool beside him. Since losing his wife he had found himself adrift in a sea of indecision. What was he going to do without her? He'd put off any thoughts of retirement; what did he think he would do all day on his own? Instead, he had launched himself back into work with a frenzy.

He worked freelance and was much in demand so nobody could make him retire. But the travel and arduous journeys over inhospitable terrain in war-torn countries had taken a toll on his health. He wasn't that young man in his twenties or thirties anymore. Ralph no longer had the stamina and health to withstand the heat, exhaustion, fear, not to mention the emotional and psychological impact of witnessing the fall-out of war on the innocent people caught up in it. All this for a photograph printed in a daily rag in Blighty.

He'd won awards for his photojournalism, but now his heart wasn't in it. And neither was his health. That's when he discovered there was somebody who *could* make him retire – his GP. He wasn't taking care of himself, and the places he was travelling to abroad could be lethal. Dysentery, dengue fever, a bout of pneumonia, and to top it all forgetting to take his malaria tablets. His doctor told him he was lucky he didn't come home in a box; an unfortunate choice of words considering his wife.

With his immune system shot to pieces, for once he had no option but to heed his doctor's advice. One more trip overseas like that might finish him off. An old-fashioned quack who Ralph reckoned should have retired twenty years ago – he'd known him since a boy – had prescribed a simple remedy: rest. His GP knew the perfect place; Ralph's house he had bought to retire with his wife by the sea – The Gables.

Ralph turned around and against his doctor's advice, checked in for another night at the hotel. One step at a time, he told himself. He'd come back – hadn't he? And he had resisted the urge to take on any more assignments. He smiled at the receptionist as she handed him back his room key.

He wasn't surprised the room was still free. Every morning for the past week he'd packed his suitcase, intending to leave. However, by the time he'd had breakfast, and whiled away the morning until check out time, he'd changed his mind. *Perhaps I'll check out tomorrow.* After a week, he guessed the hotel staff had reserved the room for him indefinitely.

They handed him the morning paper, ordered the night

before. Ralph handed it back. 'Do you mind if I pick it up on my return? I'm popping out.'

'You're going out?' the hotel receptionist blurted in surprise.

Ralph didn't bat an eyelid at that comment. They might have been wondering if the guest in room thirty-three was agoraphobic. He hadn't left the hotel since he'd arrived by taxi at midnight a week ago. It was ridiculous that someone who had spent his working life travelling the world, roughing it in some of the most hazardous and inhospitable places imaginable, and yet here he was a week since his arrival, and he had only just plucked up the courage to step foot outside. He knew the reason: he was avoiding something or, more to the point, someone.

3

Ralph handed over his room key and stepped outside the hotel. Although the sun had broken through, there was still enough cloud cover to suggest more April showers to come. It was Easter and children were on their school holidays. He stood for a moment on the pavement and let people pass by. The high street was busy. He looked up and down the street and then across the road.

He'd almost forgotten how very English Southwold was with its colourful bunting strung across the road in red, white and blue; the colours of the Union Jack. Then there were the little shops and cafes; people were sitting at tables inside sipping tea and eating scones. The flower shop was there along with the greengrocers, the bakers, the butchers, numerous charity shops, gift shops and two small supermarkets.

After years on the road, travelling and living abroad, he found it disconcerting, but comforting, that when he returned it felt like he had stepped into a time warp where in this little corner of England nothing had changed. What he hadn't told his wife when she was busy preparing the house for their retirement was whether he could live here permanently. Perhaps his GP and good friend was right: over time he would settle down and call this place home once more. That's what he promised his wife he would do. But she wasn't here anymore – not strictly speaking.

A family group holding cornets and licking ice cream as they sauntered by paused in front of a shop window. Ralph glanced at the family. If he and his wife had had children, things might have been different. Perhaps there would be grandchildren now and a reason to stay. As it was, there was nothing for him here but a vacant house full of memories.

One child looked at him standing in the entrance to the hotel and caught him frowning at them. The boy poked his tongue out. Ralph returned the compliment by being very childish and poking his tongue out too. To his surprise the boy giggled, finding it funny. Ralph exchanged a smile with the boy before he disappeared into a shop.

Ralph took a deep breath. He couldn't put it off any longer. A part of him wanted to turn around and walk back into the hotel. Instead, he found himself at the flower shop across the road purchasing a bouquet.

'Would you like to write a message on a card?'

He wasn't sure what she meant. 'Pardon me?'

'We have little message cards you can put in the bouquet.'

'Oh, I see.' Ralph declined. Where he was going no one would read their cards.

'We can have it delivered.'

'That won't be necessary.' He put his bank card back in his wallet and scooped up the large bouquet.

The young lady ran ahead and opened the door for him.

He stepped outside and turned to his left, carrying the huge bouquet down the high street wishing he'd chosen to do this later in the day when the crowds on the pavement had dissipated. Around tea time would have been better, just as the shops were closing, then he wouldn't have had the problem of trying to manoeuvre around so many people.

Ralph breathed a sigh when he turned down a quiet side street and spotted the church spire up ahead. This was the reason he hadn't ventured outside the hotel. His health still wasn't one hundred per cent and even walking a short distance left him out of breath. The large bunch of flowers and dodging passers-by was proving exhausting. But it wasn't exerting himself too much that had caused him to hide in the hotel for the past week, but this – Ralph opened the gate and stepped inside the cemetery. He'd been putting off visiting his wife.

It was the guilt more than anything. If only he hadn't insisted on taking that one last assignment then perhaps she'd still be here today. Then again, how could he have foreseen what would happen when they were abroad – and the result; she would return in a box? But the worst part was he knew at the time that he wasn't being honest with her; he had taken her on his last assignment under false pretences.

What she didn't realise was that there would always be one last assignment, and then another, and then another. The fact was he didn't want to retire from the job he loved. Now ill-health had left him with no choice. That and the fact he seemed to have lost the ability to take photographs.

He could still press a button on a camera. There was nothing wrong with his hands or his eyesight. It wasn't the physical act of taking a photograph but the intuitive side of knowing it was right: the angle, the exposure, the light, the subject – *everything*. His innate ability to take anything meaningful had died with his wife.

He shook his head. It made little sense. He'd been taking photographs long before he met her. In fact, it was the aftermath of losing his first love he felt would put an end to his passion, and his career, but it intensified it. Perhaps it was pouring all that raw emotion and loss into the subject he took that enabled him to capture something on film he couldn't quite put his finger on; something unquantifiable but moving.

Ralph stopped just inside the gate and leaned on the gatepost, catching his breath. This was neither the time nor the place to be reminiscing about his first love. He hadn't thought about her in years.

He tried to focus on his dead wife instead of daydreaming about lost loves. Turing around he closed the gate and made his way to her graveside. Ralph looked down at the headstone. 'Hello old gal, I've come bearing gifts.' He nodded his head. 'I know I shouldn't have.'

He cast a furtive glance around the cemetery before he continued the conversation with his dead wife. He didn't care what people thought. She still lived on in his subconscious. You can't live with someone for so long without knowing what they would have said. She didn't like him to make a fuss, although she'd be quick to tell him, *you know they're not my favourite.*

'I know but it's spring, and all they had were Tulips, Daffodils, and Hyacinth. Sorry.' He paused and waited for her response echoing somewhere in his consciousness. 'Yes, I knew you wouldn't mind. It's the thought that counts, isn't it, Luv? That's what you always say.' His smile faded when he told her, 'I haven't been back to the house yet.'

Ralph didn't want to tell her the real reason he hadn't been back; he couldn't return to an empty house. But it was more than that. His mind wandered to his photography studio above the garage. That was the reason he'd deposited his keys with an estate agent in town before he left on his last assignment. The last thing he wanted was the possibility of squatters moving into the empty property during his absence and discovering a treasure trove of priceless cameras and equipment. That's why he asked them to find a reliable house sitter.

They'd reassured him it would be unlikely in a sleepy Suffolk seaside town that he'd have a problem with squatters. There were many second homes and holiday lets in the area that stood unoccupied for several weeks or even months at a time and they had never experienced problems of that nature. Besides, why would they single out his property?

But it wasn't the house that bothered him but the studio. He wanted nobody messing with his photographic equipment –

that's why he'd kept his studio separate, much to his wife's chagrin. The house was for their retirement and yet he couldn't imagine not taking photographs in some capacity or other even as a hobby. He couldn't stop taking pictures any more than he could stop breathing – or so he thought.

He stood there staring at her grave. Ralph was considering whether it was time to face his demons and return home. He knelt and placed the flowers against her headstone. 'Well, I'd best be off.' He stood up and lingered for a moment before making his way along the path towards the gate.

Before he reached the gate, Ralph stopped and cast his gaze around the cemetery. He wanted to leave and just head back to the hotel, but he knew he wouldn't. Ralph sighed and took the grassy path to his right, weaving between older gravestones. He came to a halt and looked down at a weather-beaten tombstone.

He reached out and placed a hand on the gravestone. 'Hello, old friend. It's been a while.' He'd always made a point of visiting him when he was home from overseas. Unlike his wife, who was laid to rest here – he'd had her body flown back from Mallorca and repatriated – where was his best friend? It was something that had haunted him his whole life.

'What happened to you?' It was a question he asked every time he returned here. Forty years had elapsed and yet Ralph still expected him to reappear and tell everyone it had been the mother of practical jokes. Ralph sighed. Nobody disappears for that long.

4

Ralph left the cemetery and turned toward the town. The busy high street was up ahead. It was the only route back to the hotel but right now he didn't feel like returning. He wanted to be on his own. He raised an eyebrow when it occurred to him; there was one place he could go, and guarantee being on his own.

Ralph stood at the top of the familiar street, looking down the long row of terraced cottages. He saw the double wrought-iron gates that led into his property at the end of the road.

He remained there for some time debating what to do. His wife, so trusting by nature, always left a key under the flowerpot by the front door of the house. Perhaps he had been a fool to make such a fuss about it. When he went on his last assignment, he gave his own key to the estate agents. Then followed a frantic phone call from abroad when he remembered the spare key he'd forgotten to pick up before he caught his flight.

Ralph asked the estate agent to collect the key and keep it until his return and assumed they'd done as he asked. He shook his head, who did that nowadays – left a spare key lying around for any Tom, Dick or Harry just to waltz in and make themselves at home?

If there was one thing Ralph couldn't abide, it was people who helped themselves to another persons' property. He'd seen enough of that over the years in war-torn countries where nothing was sacred; people's homes, their possessions, what little they had taken with no recompense.

Ralph's shoulders slumped. He didn't fancy visiting the estate agents today. Once he walked through their doors, word would spread that the famous photojournalist was back in town. He knew one agent, a keen amateur photographer, would no doubt tell the other enthusiasts who were members of the local photography club.

Ralph smiled to himself when it occurred to him that nobody need know he'd returned. He could put off visiting the estate agent for as long as he wanted because he didn't require the keys to the main house. There was his studio. Some time ago he had taken a leaf out of his wife's book and hidden a key. He hadn't left it under a flowerpot but deposited it on the narrow ledge atop the door frame to his studio apartment.

He walked down the street towards The Gables but soon came to a halt at the thought of stepping inside the studio. His mind was racing at the prospect of opening the door and being surrounded by all his equipment almost taunting him when he was aware, he had lost the ability to take anything meaningful with a camera. Ralph didn't want to put himself through that. He wished he had a key to the main house instead. There was no way he was going to the estate agents right now. The problem was he didn't fancy returning to the hotel either.

Ralph turned on his heel and retraced his steps toward the high street. Instead of heading in the direction of The Swan Hotel, he turned down a quiet side street. He knew where he was going and already tasted the salty sea air as he made his way along the clifftop path. When he got to the track, he braced his hands on the railings and closed his eyes feeling the strong easterly wind on his face.

Ralph opened his eyes and stared at the pier. It looked busy with people sitting outside the little cafés and restaurants that ran its length. He was not inclined to join them. Instead, he headed away from the pier toward the multi-coloured beach huts in the distance. It would be quieter up that end – he hoped.

Although it was bright sunshine, the wind made him shiver. He put his hands in his blazer pockets. Everyone else he passed as he walked along the clifftop didn't seem bothered by the spring breeze; people were dressed in shorts and tee-shirts. It was a warm Easter even though the Easter break fell early this year in April.

His mother, when she was alive, would have said he didn't have enough meat on his bones. That was true. A walk like this would tire him out. If it wasn't for the bracing easterly wind, he would have liked to continue. Perhaps I'll be warmer walking down there, thought Ralph glancing down at the beach hut rooftops and the promenade below. Approaching a gap in the railings, he had a choice of continuing along the clifftop walk or taking the sloping pathway down to the beach.

Ralph would rather not continue along this path. It wasn't just to do with the wind. The problem was if he kept going he would come upon the gap in the hedgerow that led into the back garden of The Gables.

He didn't want to feel tempted to look. What if the rear garden was an overgrown mess? He hadn't thought to hire a gardener in his absence. It's not as though a house sitter might tend to the garden. From his experience no one ever did anything for nothing, and they weren't being paid to look after the garden too. In fact, they didn't have to do much of anything, just sit and mind the house.

When he'd phoned the estate agent, they had been cagey about whether they had found someone to house sit while he was away. Mind you, he had been a little cagey himself about when he intended to return. But surely they would have found someone, thought Ralph. You couldn't ask for a cushier number: sitting in someone's home by the sea for months on end – and being paid for it. But the line had been bad, and he hadn't been able to speak to them for long, just enough time to inform them the house sitter had to go.

During that last conversation with the agents before he boarded his flight, he got the impression they did not fill the vacancy – something about a rumour floating around the town that the house on the clifftop was haunted. The crowded airport terminal was noisy, and Ralph couldn't hear what they were saying at the end of the line.

He'd switched off his mobile phone and boarded the flight thinking he must have got it wrong; why would anyone imagine the house was haunted? Ralph shook his head. That was the problem with small towns; somebody heard the news that the famous photojournalist's wife died and so the rumour mill started. Ralph wasn't interested in visiting the estate agents to find out. That could wait. For now, he was content to finish his afternoon walk.

5

Ralph glanced at the brightly coloured beach huts as he walked along the promenade. Family groups were sitting on deckchairs outside, but most of them were locked. It was quieter this end of the beach. The irony was that these little wooden huts were so expensive, local families who would make more use out of them couldn't afford to buy one. He wondered where the owners were; sunning themselves in Barbados no doubt.

How things had changed. He recalled those school holidays decades ago in his youth when they were occupied by families and children enjoying endless hours of fun running in and out of the sea, eating fish paste sandwiches and warming up with hot chocolate from a thermos flask. Those were the days thought Ralph recalling one beach hut owned by the parents of his best friend.

Ralph took his hands out of his pockets and undid his blazer. He'd left that strong easterly wind behind. Down on the beach there was just a soft breeze. For the first time all day Ralph felt hot. He paused for a moment to take off his coat and roll up his shirt sleeves. He looked ahead as he did so and saw the concrete promenade ending where it gave way to sand. There were more huts further along in front of sand dunes. Thinking of one in particular, Ralph wondered if it was still there.

Since returning to Southwold and buying the house on the

clifftop he had never ventured this far, either on his own or with his wife. She preferred the other end where she could sit with a cup of tea and a slice of cake in a café on the pier. He recalled one time when she was sitting enjoying the sea views he'd mentioned taking a walk along the promenade. She'd said, "The only reason for venturing down there is if we owned a beach hut," before slipping in a joke that he could always buy her one.

They both knew that would not happen. It's not that he wouldn't have bought her one if that's what she wanted, although the price of them was extortionate even by Southwold's inflated property prices. But the truth was she wasn't a sit on the beach, with the sand between her toes, kind of gal.

Ralph reached the end of the path. If he'd been with his wife, and they ventured this far along the promenade, then this would have been their cue to turn around and head back. She wouldn't slip off her shoes and walk on the sand. "That's for the kiddies," she would have said, although he longed to do it.

There were times he'd wondered how she would have coped if they'd had children. What sort of mother would she have been? Would she have changed and done things like kick off her shoes to go play on the shingle and not cared if she'd got sand on her pristine outfit? Would life together have been different; fun and spontaneous, instead of dull and monotonous?

Ralph stopped at the end of the path and looked at the sand in front of him. He didn't want to think ill of his dead wife. It wasn't her fault she was the sort of person who wouldn't do those things. It wasn't her fault he'd married her on the rebound and then realised his mistake; two wrongs didn't make a right. By then it was too late. Marriage was for life. It was the way he'd been brought up; once he'd tied the knot, there was no going back – *Till death do us part.*

It's not as though they had a bad marriage – far from it. Like-minded and compatible they got on well together. In fact, Ralph couldn't remember a cross word passing between them.

Since she died, it was like he'd lost a close friend whom he'd loved dearly. But it wasn't the love Ralph experienced once before in his life with his teenage sweetheart. He guessed that's what falling in love felt like. And knowing the day they married that he would never experience that sort of head-over-heels love again. It wasn't as though the girl he was besotted with since the day he set eyes on her at their local primary school would walk back into his life.

He'd searched for her. Not for long though. A month after Clara left Southwold, he'd found out through her parents that she'd married. Just like that. Met someone else and forgotten him. So, he did that too. Tit for Tat. He'd moved on. Except he hadn't. Not completely. The years might have dulled the pain of that rejection, but it was still there.

Ralph sighed. He stepped on to the beach holding his shoes in one hand; the warm, soft sand between his toes. He tried to dismiss her from his mind. He'd probably never see her again, and the mystery as why she left him and went to London would remain just that – a mystery. That brought to mind the old gravestone in the cemetery and his best friend, Tommy, who also disappeared from his life years ago.

Ralph shook his head trying to dismiss him from his mind too. He focused on something else that he'd been considering since his wife died. Ralph toyed with the idea of selling The Gables.

It was his wife's choice to retire here. She couldn't understand why he was so against the idea. She was aware he'd grown up here, but he hadn't put her in the picture about the history he had with the place – in particular, two young people he knew and loved years ago. To make matters worse, of all the properties she viewed on the market she fell in love with The Gables – the house Clara grew up in.

Perhaps he should have told her about the house but then he saw the look on her face when she walked up the drive and The

Gables came into view. What was the point of dragging up the past? If she liked the house, he might as well go along with it. Rather than try to talk her out of it, he built a detached garage with a studio apartment above so he could escape the house, and those memories, whenever he needed to.

Ralph was walking along the beach when he slowed. He hadn't ventured this far in a long time – years. Up ahead he saw a young man emerge from a hut. Ralph paused watching him throw his arms wide as if stretching after a good night's sleep. He appeared to be wearing just a pair of boxer shorts. If Ralph didn't know better, it looked as though the young man may have spent the night here. He shrugged. What did it matter? It wasn't any of his business.

Ralph recalled many a time when they were teenagers, and his best friend had fallen out with his parents. On those occasions when Tommy needed to get away from the house, Ralph would find him at the beach hut. Sometimes he even stayed the night and slunk back home in the morning.

His breath caught in his throat. For a moment Ralph imagined all the years had fallen away and it *was* Tommy standing on the veranda. His pace quickened, rationality giving way to emotion – how many times had he come down here in those first few days, weeks, and months when Tommy disappeared imagining he would turn up.

Ralph slowed as he drew near and saw the young man bore no resemblance to Tommy. It was just his mind playing tricks on him. Besides, his best friend wouldn't be a young man now; he'd be old like me, approaching sixty, thought Ralph. He rubbed his temples, feeling a headache coming on. This place was stirring up memories he'd rather forget.

Ralph turned away from the beach huts, and those memories, and retraced his steps up the path to the clifftop walk. He lingered at the top, catching his breath, and before he thought about it, turned toward home. Through the gap in the hedge along the clifftop walk he appeared on the lawn at the back of his property.

To his left down a small cobbled garden path was an unused vegetable garden. The couple who owned the property before him had visions of leading the good life when they retired here. Not long after they renovated the house, he became ill and his wife diagnosed with dementia, which ended their retirement dream. Ralph shook his head at the vegetable garden they never used. It made him wonder if The Gables was cursed. In his experience, something bad seemed to happen to whoever lived here.

At the end of the path were single-story brick outhouses. Ralph walked down the cobbled pathway and arrived at the sheds. He opened the first door. The rusty hinges creaked as he entered. Boxes stacked higgledy-piggledy in one corner reminded Ralph of the funeral and the wake he'd held at the house. Afterwards he wasted no time packing up all his wife's belongings and taking them to the charity shop in town. He also boxed up all their photos and mementos so there was nothing of that nature in the house to remind him of her. He'd left the boxes here in the outhouse.

'Maybe I should have got rid of this too,' Ralph spoke out loud as he removed an old blanket covering a painting on canvas. He stood back to admire the painting his wife loved so much. Browsing in a local market in Mallorca that day, she had fallen in love with the picture. To his lasting regret, Ralph had tried to persuade her not to buy it. He'd almost succeeded, but at the last minute she insisted on returning to the market to purchase it before someone else did.

Ralph declined to return with her. That's when it happened. That's why he couldn't bring himself to get rid of the painting, the one his wife loved, the one she had just bought before the bomb blast that took her life.

As soon as the funeral was over, and he'd handed over the

keys to the estate agents to find a house sitter, he flew out on another assignment and hadn't been back since.

Ralph stood there staring at the bright, vibrant colours of the Mallorcan landscape, or what was left after the blast ripped away half of the canvas. It was a dichotomy that on the one hand the painting reminded him of one of the saddest days of his life, but also it reminded him of one of the happiest times of his life; the summer he'd spent with Clara and Tommy in Mallorca when they turned eighteen.

Suddenly the fatigue hit him. He needed to lie-down. There was an assortment of bric-a-brac in the outhouse he'd never got rid of, left by the previous owners, amongst which was an old camp bed.

He walked over and sat down. It was dusty and smelled damp, but it held his weight. Ralph swung his legs up on to the bed. He still had the old blanket in his hand that was draped over the canvas. Lying down he pulled the cover up to his chin. He turned his head and stared at the painting as he drifted off to another place in time; he was young again, walking barefoot on a Mediterranean beach in the evening. He was holding her hand. She was holding on to his arm. He could feel her soft cheek against his shoulder.

He knew she was smiling. She'd turned eighteen that day and told him it wasn't her eighteenth birthday party she would remember to her dying day, but the night she became a woman. He was her first, and so was she. Clara told him they were united forever, a bond that could never be broken. There would be nobody else.

Ralph smiled in his sleep yet to wake from a beautiful dream of a future together that would never be, blissfully unaware of what was to come; something was about to happen that would change the course of their lives forever.

6

Kensington, London, July

'It's my husband…'

Clara sighed. 'Don't tell me… he's retiring, and you will be far too busy doing things together to meet up with your old friends.'

She shook her head – no.

Clara took in her grim expression. 'Oh, God. He's ill – isn't he? I'm so sorry. I shouldn't have jumped to conclusions.'

'He's not ill – and yes he *is* retiring, but we're not doing anything together unless you count getting divorced.'

'Oh.' Clara looked at her aghast. She was completely taken aback. After all these years of marriage. 'I don't know what to say. I'm so sorry, Debbie.'

'What's there to be sorry about? We haven't been happy for quite a while. It must be hard to understand from your own perspective, being happily married to Joe.'

She wasn't sure she'd have used the word *happily*. Not now anyway. She glanced at Debbie as they walked down Kensington High Street. Her life would change – obviously. It was ridiculous considering the circumstances, but Clara was just the tiniest bit jealous. She wanted her life to change too.

It wasn't as though she wanted to do anything drastic like

divorce Joe. She just needed the record to change; her husband going out the door every morning driving his black London taxicab and coming home late, exhausted. One TV dinner later, conversation minimal, he was fit for nothing except bed and the start of the same old routine the next day.

She caught Debbie staring at her. She'd known her long enough to guess when something was on her mind. 'What?'

'Don't take offence when I say this, but I thought if anyone would end up divorced, it would be you and Joe.'

Clara looked at her in surprise. 'Why?'

Debbie sighed. 'You know why.'

'No, really, why would you think that?'

'You and Joe are… different.'

'Ah.' Clara realised what she was getting at. 'You mean I'm posh whereas Joe, well… Joe isn't.'

She nodded. 'He's a working-class East End boy.'

'So?'

'It's probably late in the day to ask, and it's none of my business but… why did you marry Joe?'

Clara stopped in the middle of the street. 'You're right. It isn't any of your business.'

'I meant nothing by it, Clara.'

'Then why ask such a stupid question? I've been married for almost forty years. Doesn't that say something?'

Debbie looked at her. 'That you were meant to be together?'

'Yes.'

'Not necessarily,' Debbie countered. 'Don't forget I've been married for the same length of time. It doesn't mean you'll stay together.'

'That's your opinion.' Clara set off, walking at a pace down the street leaving her behind but she soon caught up.

'What's got into you, Clara? I only asked—'

'Just because your marriage has gone wrong, you're trying to pry into my life and find a chink in the armour.'

'Why are you getting so defensive suddenly?'

'I don't know what you're talking about,' she replied. Debbie had hit a nerve, and it had nothing to do with Joe's long hours in his job or her own dull, empty existence of coffee mornings and shopping with friends. It went far deeper than that, to a secret Clara would rather not dwell on – much less share with her friend.

A homeless person stepped in front of Debbie, holding out his hand. 'Spare a little change, miss?'

'Change?' She barked at him. 'Why don't you earn yourself a living like everybody else?'

'What – like you, miss?'

Clara looked at her friend wondering what she would say to that.

'Are you being sarcastic?' Debbie bristled. 'How do you know I don't work for a living?'

He smiled. 'I recognise your type.'

'My *type*?'

Clara touched her arm. 'Debbie – let's go.'

'No, I want to hear what he thinks he knows about me.'

Clara nervously cast a glance at the homeless man.

The homeless man looked them up and down. 'Married yourself a well-to-do husband, had two kids, and never worked again. That is if you've ever done a day's work in your life.' He eyed the lady waiting for her to deny it.

Clara looked from Debbie to the homeless man and back again. It was a stand-off. The trouble was he'd seen right through her, but her friend wasn't the type to back down. She always had to have the last word. Clara didn't want any trouble. She fished in her purse. All she had were notes.

'I don't have to stand here and listen to your drivel,' Debbie was saying as Clara took out a five-pound note.

The homeless man nodded. 'That's right – you don't. But something tells me I've hit the nail on the head.'

Out of the corner of her eye, Clara caught people walking by, looking their way at the sound of raised voices. 'We really ought to get going,' she whispered, wishing her friend would just let it go. 'We don't want to be late,' she reminded her.

'Late for an important lunch date – are we?' He'd overheard her whispering. His eyes drifted to Clara. 'Don't let me keep you from the appointment with your next designer handbag.'

He shook his head and resumed his seat on a dirty old sleeping bag on the pavement outside a shop window. 'I might be way down the food chain,' he said as he made himself comfortable. 'You can look down on me or don't look at all. Next time just walk on by like everyone else. But let me tell you something…' He pointed a finger at them. 'Two months ago you would have passed me in the street wearing a suit on my way to work. That's right…' He noted the surprise on Clara's face. 'I've worked all my life, and this is where I've ended up because I was just two paychecks away from losing it all. Do you have any idea what percentage of the population are just two paychecks away from disaster?'

She couldn't help but think of Joe. Approaching sixty, he wasn't working long hours driving his London taxi for the fun.

'Have a care, ladies; your life could change in a heartbeat.'

'Come on, Clara. Don't listen to him. He's just some drunk who has got nothing better to do than talk a load of nonsense to anybody who will listen. He doesn't know you from Adam.'

Debbie flounced off toward Fortnum and Mason where they were meeting their friends for lunch, leaving Clara still standing in front of the homeless man. She looked in her purse, put the five-pound note back and dug out a twenty. 'Sorry.' She wasn't sure what she was apologising for; the homeless man's predicament, her friend's unsympathetic attitude, not feeling as though she could do more.

'I hope you're not giving him money,' she heard Debbie comment.

The man didn't say thank you, but she didn't expect him to. What was there to be thankful for if you found yourself homeless?

She caught up with her friend at the door to Fortnum and Mason. 'Oh, for goodness sake, Clara.' Debbie had noticed her grim expression. 'Don't let it ruin our lunch date. Most people might be two paychecks away from disaster, but we're the lucky ones with husbands we can rely on who would never allow that to happen.'

Clara managed a smile for her friend's benefit. Her smile faltered as soon as they walked through the doors into Fortnum and Mason for an expensive lunch date she could not afford. That wasn't Joe's fault. As soon as they had got married, she quit her dead-end job. Although Joe insisted, he was the breadwinner, she hadn't objected to leaving employment and being a housewife. She did voluntary work as a part-time counsellor when their only child started school – but that was it.

When they were younger, it didn't bother her in the slightest that her husband brought in all the money. However, as they approached their sixties, it felt like time had crept up on them. She often worried how she would survive if, heaven forbid, something was to happen to Joe. Her thoughts turned to the homeless man. Unlike her friends with their comfortable lifestyles and Debbie who would come out of her divorce all right – Gerald worked as a solicitor in the city – Clara knew that apart from some modest savings they probably *were* two paychecks away from disaster.

7

After luncheon and with nothing to do for the afternoon, Clara and her well-heeled friends browsed around the department store. This involved spending money she couldn't afford or, more to the point, Joe couldn't afford. When she arrived home with yet more clothes or handbags or shoes, Joe would shrug his shoulders, ask her if she'd had a nice day, and then work more overtime; he was always willing to indulge his wife in her favourite past-time – shopping.

She stared out of the car window as the cab turned down the North London street of Victorian red brick semi-detached houses where they lived. She remembered when Joe first passed The Knowledge and drove a taxi; he had no problems parking at the end of a shift because not many people owned a car. Now there were at least two per household parked nose to tail all the way down the road.

They owned two cars themselves; the taxi and Joe's pride and joy – a blue Volkswagen Golf. Joe was too busy at work, so he rarely found the time to take the car out for a spin.

Clara caught the taxi driver looking at her in his rear-view mirror. She still turned heads, even though those heads were now older and greyer. Although she would be grey herself if it weren't for the trips to an expensive London Salon with Debbie. She reached in her bag for her comb and ran it through her blonde bob, trying to straighten the kink at the ends, then fixed her large brown eyes on the man looking back at her.

The taxi driver averted his gaze. Clara smiled. Joe had always said she was a looker even now, forty years after they first met. Sometimes she would catch Joe's worried expression if another man glanced her way. Not that he had anything to worry about. As Debbie once said, she was a tease, but she'd never cheat on Joe. The idea wouldn't even cross her mind. There was only one man for her, and he walked out of her life years ago. That left dependable Joe; the steadfast man she married on the rebound. A marriage that defied all odds and lasted; she had sought the safety and security of a person who would never leave her.

Clara sighed. Perhaps that's what Debbie meant when she said she felt it would be her and Joe that ended up divorced. Not that her friend knew there had been another man in Clara's life, and guessed Debbie was referring to how different she was from Joe. He was not particularly handsome but had one quality that Clara needed all those years ago that set him apart; he made a promise that come what may he would never leave her and had stayed true to his word.

As the taxi drove up the road Clara sighed as she gazed at her neighbours' modest properties identical to her own. She wondered what the driver was thinking about the woman sitting in the back of his cab wearing an expensive fur coat; looking out of place in a street such as this.

Most of the time she did feel out of place, as though her life was all wrong. But she didn't aspire to live in a Regency house in Chelsea or some other expensive address in London.

She stared out of the taxi window reminiscing about a place she once loved that was far away from London. *If only I could go back and change one thing in my life, then maybe things would have turned out differently.* Clara shook her head. She didn't want to dredge up the past. Then something came to mind she hadn't thought about in years.

She remembered when they were newlyweds and her parents visited them soon after they moved into this house. It was the first time they'd seen their new home. It was one of the most uncomfortable experiences of her life; her well-to-do parents meeting the man she had married in a registry office in London.

This wasn't the life she had envisaged when she was growing up in the sleepy market town in Suffolk. It wasn't what her parents imagined for her either. They made no bones about the fact she'd married beneath her. He was from a different – they used the word *wrong* – social class. But Joe had given her a good life. He might not have had a private school education like Clara and her peers, but the way he had treated his wife proved he was a gentleman through and through.

Her parents were wrong when they told her, out of earshot of Joe, that she'd made a big mistake. Over the years, Joe had continued to prove them wrong even now when they were dead and gone. He always remembered her birthday and their anniversary and bought her flowers for no reason other than to see her face light up. Then there were the unexpected gifts and the odd weekend away in a nice hotel. He couldn't afford these things, but he did it anyway just to make her happy.

When their daughter arrived, he worked hard to send her to an expensive school in London. "Nothing was too good for our Tamsin," he'd always say. Clara would have been content for her to attend the local state schools. It was a struggle to pay the fees on one income, and Joe had to work a lot of overtime to pay them.

As the taxi neared the end of the street where they lived, she glanced at the shopping bags and could already feel the inevitable low coming on; it always followed the high she experienced whenever a cashier handed over the bags containing her new purchases. That high dissipated as soon as she walked out of the shop.

She avoided shopping on her own, as though by doing it

with friends it was just a social thing and not a problem, an addiction. It wasn't that at all, she tried to convince herself. A little retail therapy was just a by-product; a thing she did with friends after lunch together. *She* never suggested they go shopping afterwards, they just did. It was only a few purchases here and there, and they always had to twist her arm to join them.

Only a few purchases here and there? She shook her head with dismay when she thought of the airing cupboard on the landing Joe had turned into a walk-in closet. He'd spent hours putting up shelving and making drawers that would house all her designer shoes and handbags. He modelled it on something he'd seen on TV. Clara seemed to recall the property on the television programme wasn't a small ordinary North London Semi but a large six-bedroomed detached new-build.

"Nothing is too good for our Clara," he'd said. "When I hit on the right investment opportunity and we get The Big Payday, I'll buy you a large house that comes with a proper walk-in closet."

She winced at all the lame excuses running through her head as she tried to convince herself that she didn't have a problem. As a counsellor, she recognised the signs and helped people with these issues all the time. She'd met a fair few shopaholics over the course of her voluntary work; there was always more to it than a simple lack of self-control. Often, there was an underlying deep-seated problem. Something in their past was eating away at them. Something unresolved…

She clenched her fist and willed herself not to go down that rabbit hole. That was in the past. A lifetime ago when she was a young, carefree eighteen-year-old before her life changed overnight and she lost him forever. Unless she had a time machine, no amount of wishing would change what happened and bring him back.

Perhaps if Joe wasn't working long hours and using all his spare time dreaming up the next scheme that might give them The Big Payday to solve all their money worries, then they might do things together and she'd stop shopping. Clara shook her head. It wasn't Joe's fault. If she stopped spending his money, he might work less. And so the recriminations began as they always did not long after she'd had another shopping fix. In the aftermath, she was terribly guilty for frittering money they couldn't afford on things she didn't need.

She sighed as she gathered up her bags. The problem was, despite knowing deep down this had to stop, a few days later she'd be turning up at the house with more bags, convincing herself yet again this would be the last time she wasted money. Clara thought of Joe's life also on a loop, except his time revolved around earning it not spending it.

Clara wondered what it would take, to stop this insanity. They needed to do something more meaningful with their lives than mindless shopping and Joe pouring over his get-rich-quick schemes hoping for The Big Payday that was never going to happen.

Clara sat in the taxi outside their house. Neither of them could go on like this. She'd come to the end of the road; they weren't getting any younger. Things had to change.

Something else was on her mind. She was thinking about running into that homeless person earlier in the day. She imagined her friend didn't give him a second thought, but Clara did, throughout lunch and even while she was looking for new clothes. What did he say? *Have a care; your life could change in a heartbeat.*

Clara emptied her purse of the last of the generous spending money Joe had given her this week. Handing over her fare for the taxi ride home and feeling guilty for not catching a bus or taking the tube, she put the purse back in her handbag and thought of the homeless man's parting words. She bet his comment about life changing in a heartbeat was not meant in a nice way. It felt more like a warning; a harbinger of something unexpected waiting around the next corner.

The taxi driver caught his passenger's miserable expression as she clambered out of the back of the black cab laden with four large bags. 'Cheer up, Luv. It may never happen.'

Clara rolled her eyes at the driver before he sped off. She'd always hated that saying.

Her next thought as she looked up at the house was *it already has*. It turned out that the *something unexpected* wasn't waiting around the next corner but sitting on her doorstep glaring angrily her way.

8

Her daughter held up her mobile phone and said in an accusatory tone, 'Why does your phone keep going to voicemail?'

Before Clara apologised – she'd forgotten to recharge her phone – Tamsin continued. 'Where were you? We've been waiting outside for like half an hour!'

She looked at her daughter. Anyone would think Tamsin told her she was coming. She felt like saying she wasn't a mind-reader; Clara had no idea she'd be stopping by.

Her eyes drifted from Tamsin to her two grandchildren sitting on the doorstep either side of their mother. They looked tired and subdued. When they were little, and they visited Grandma's house, they'd run up the path and throw their arms around her. Now Sophie the eldest and almost sixteen, was busy texting on her mobile phone. Little Mia now nine, all gangly legs and arms, had her head in a paperback book. They didn't even look up when she arrived.

Clara stopped in front of them laden with her shopping bags and wondered what they were doing here. Since her son-in-law's business had taken off, she rarely saw her daughter or grandchildren. They no longer needed the services of their grandparents for babysitting and doing the school run. A few years ago, they stood in as surrogate parents while Kevin and Tamsin committed all their time and energy on their goal – to build a business, get rich, sell the business and retire at forty on the proceeds. As far as she was aware, they were on track to retire in three years.

Her attention drifted to the girls. She wondered if it was worth it. They'd missed a lot of the girls' milestones. Clara and Joe were there at Sophie and Mia's first day at school and their first school play – a Christmas production that Joe filmed so that Kevin and Tamsin could watch the video later that night after work.

However, things changed when Mia started middle school and Sophie went up to high school; those days of seeing their grandchildren were long gone. While Clara welcomed the free time to herself, she missed them terribly now that Tamsin and Kevin's social visits to their poor relations – as Clara uncharitably thought of themselves – became a rarity. They were too busy leading the jet-set lifestyle.

Every school holiday the family were off somewhere exotic, travelling first class – no expense spared. Clara wondered how they expected to retire at forty if all they did was spent money. It wasn't just the holidays, but meals out in pricey restaurants and fee-paying schools. Sometimes Clara worried that her penchant for shopping had rubbed off on Tamsin. She often wondered if they were living beyond their means and one day they would run out of cash if something happened and Kevin's business folded.

Tamsin assured her that would not happen. They had more money than they knew what to do with. Clara's reaction was to advise her daughter to save it, which she knew was a bit rich coming from someone who should take her own advice. Her daughter wouldn't listen. "What for? A rainy day?" she had scoffed. To which she added, "I can assure you, Mum, there will be no such thing as a rainy day in our household. We might as well have a good time now and get accustomed to it because there will be a lot more where that came from when we sell the business. So why wait to enjoy the rewards of our hard work?"

Joe agreed with that sentiment. But then he would, wouldn't he? They'd worked hard and their boat had come in. He was all for them spending money on living their dreams.

Clara was a lot more cautious. She was worried that they were being complacent, concerned that one day something unexpected might happen that would make them wish they'd heeded her advice and saved for a rainy day. She stared at her daughter's grim expression. Was this that rainy day?

As she approached her front door with the key to hand, Tamsin and the girls stood up. Only then did she notice the suitcases sitting on the doorstep behind them. She turned to look at her daughter in surprise. 'What's this?'

'I've moved out. I've left him.'

Behind them, Mia sniffed loudly.

'Oh, don't be such a cry-baby,' moaned Sophie. 'Parents split up all the time. It's no biggie.'

'SHUTUP!' yelled Mia at her big sister.

Clara looked from Mia to Sophie.

'Now do you believe me,' said Tamsin matter-of-factly. 'Can we go inside before the whole street finds out?'

She opened the front door and stepped inside followed by Sophie still texting her friends, Mia wiping her nose with the sleeve of her jumper, and Tamsin loading three large suitcases into the hallway. 'Where shall I put these?'

Clara dumped her bags full of new designer clothes by the front door. 'I'll help you upstairs with them.'

Sophie and Mia followed them upstairs into the bedroom they once shared. Clara kept the beds made up with fresh linen just on the off chance she got a call for a sleepover which, in recent years never materialised.

The girls walked into the room and dumped their suitcases down on the beds. Despite the circumstances, Clara smiled. It was as though they had been at Grandma and Grandad's house just the other week – not months ago.

Tamsin hovered outside her bedroom.

Clara opened the door.

Tamsin's nose wrinkled in that all too familiar fashion that said she didn't like something – or someone. 'God it's like a mausoleum in there.'

Clara frowned. She thought she'd be pleased they'd kept her bedroom just the way it was when she left at eighteen to go to university. Some of her friends turned their children's bedrooms into studies or sewing rooms. That upset their children because it spelt the end of their childhood living with Mum and Dad.

There were other friend's children who came back home after university, but Tamsin was different. She never came home to live once she left for university and stayed with her boyfriend's family during the long holidays.

That might have had something to do with her boyfriend's parents retiring to Barbados. Who would want to spend their holidays in North London when they could relax on a beautiful beach in the Caribbean? Clara guessed that's what sparked off Tamsin's love for exotic travel. The boyfriend whom she'd met when they both started college twenty years ago became her husband.

Twenty years thought Clara. She assumed if they were going to split up it would have been in the tough times when they were trying to grow his business and raise two children. She stared at Tamsin wondering what had happened.

Tamsin was still standing in the doorway wrinkling her nose at something. Was it the old posters? The décor? Her rosettes and medals she'd won for sports at school that Clara kept?

Tamsin turned to her mother. 'Couldn't you have at least redecorated? I always hated that colour on the walls.'

'I thought you liked it? You chose the colour – don't you remember?'

'I was six.' Tamsin rolled her eyes. 'Never mind. I suppose this will have to do.'

Have to do? She eyed her daughter and couldn't help the sarcastic retort, 'I know it's not The Ritz.'

'What's that supposed to mean?'

'It's not what you're accustomed to, that's what I'm saying. Don't forget I've seen your house. It's not a North London semi now is it?'

Tamsin shot her mother a look. She knew what Clara was getting at. The house she grew up in was very modest compared to the detached house she and her husband bought in a gated community. She commented, 'Money isn't everything.'

Clara was taken aback by that remark. Like her father, Tamsin always made out that money was *everything*. She placed a gentle hand on her daughter's arm. 'Do you want to talk about it or just get settled in first?'

'I think I'll just get settled in – if you don't mind.'

'All right.' Clara lingered for a moment outside the door. She watched Tamsin walk around her room staring at the posters on the wall. She picked up a trophy she'd won from a sporting event at school and stood there looking at it. Clara wondered what was going through her mind. What led her to the drastic decision to leave Kevin? But above all she wanted to know what she was doing here.

Tamsin had no shortage of friends she might have called on or booked into a hotel. They had a second home in Barbados or was it the Bahamas? She knew it was somewhere exotic beginning with *B*. It was too far away just to jump in a taxi and take the girls. But why here? Why did she come home? If they had been closer, maybe she'd understand. But they weren't. Not like mothers and daughters ought to be. Not like she was with her own mother until—

Clara cut that thought dead. Instead she focused on Tamsin. She was a Daddy's girl. Always had been. Clara would never admit it to a living soul, but it was her fault the way Tamsin always gravitated to her father. She was young, selfish and self-absorbed and not ready for motherhood. When Tamsin came along all Clara saw in her daughter was competition for Joe's affections.

She'd never let on any of this to Joe. But children sense things. As she matured, Clara realised she had been stupid to imagine a baby would usurp her in Joe's eyes, but the damage was done.

All these years later, she still caught Tamsin throwing a wary expression her way, like she used to when small as if still undecided what she meant to her. No matter what Clara said, or did she could not close the distance between them. Which begged the question: what was she doing here? Perhaps Tamsin had come home for the children's sakes. She'd just left their father. They wanted to be somewhere familiar and safe. They needed their grandparents.

Her thoughts turned to Joe. He'd hit the roof if he discovered that Kevin was having an affair. Clara had no clue if that's what happened, but it could be a possibility. Kevin was a well-respected architect. And for a man approaching forty he had not let himself go or succumbed to middle-aged spread or thinning hair. Whenever she saw his photo on the cover of an upmarket House and Home magazine, featuring individual architect-designed properties he'd completed, he looked better than ever; more handsome than when Tamsin first met him.

Was that it? Tamsin discovered he was having an affair.

Tamsin walked through the room back to the open doorway where her mother was standing.

Clara stepped forward, expecting Tamsin needed a hug, when her daughter shut the door. Clara stared at the door and sighed. She guessed she would not find out anything tonight.

9

Clara could hear Sophie and Mia bickering in their bedroom. She walked along the hall intending to look in on them and ask them if they would like something to eat when the front door opened downstairs.

'Honey, I'm home!'

Clara glanced over the bannisters to see her husband putting his car keys in the dish on the sideboard. 'You're early,' she remarked as she strolled down the stairs.

He was holding out his arms.

She smiled at him and stepped into his embrace.

He enveloped her in that big bear hug of his which always made her feel safe, but worried her when she realised he was putting on weight around his midriff. Unlike Kevin, Joe had changed over the years from that skinny East End boy who fancied himself as a rocker with his slicked-back hair and army boots.

She recalled those early days when they first met. Despite his black leather jacket and biker friends, he couldn't quite pull off the edgy persona. Joe was too laid back and a big old softie at heart to get into the spirit of punk rock and scream obscenities at passers-by. He was far too polite.

She smiled as he kissed the top of her head. If only her parents were prepared to look past that leather jacket and his

East End accent, and get to know him, they might have seen what she saw; someone who would always care for her and worshipped the ground she walked on.

'For you,' said Joe releasing her and presenting her with a bouquet.

'Oh Joe, you shouldn't have.' Although she was thinking, *yes he should have.* The bouquet was much larger and more fragrant than usual. 'To what do I owe this unexpected gift?' Clara asked smiling up at him. It was never really a surprise. She would have been more surprised if he *hadn't* bought her flowers or a box of chocolates. But she always said it anyway, to which he always replied—

'I need some help here!'

Joe's eyes went wide. He turned on his heel. 'Dot, I told you to wait in the car.'

'Dot?' Clara stepped out from behind Joe's large frame and caught sight of his eighty-four-year-old mother Dorothy, standing in the doorway holding a suitcase in each hand and glowering across the hall, not at Joe, but at Clara as though it was her fault she'd been left waiting.

Clara turned to Joe. 'Are you taking your mother somewhere?'

'Haven't you told her yet?' she growled.

Clara shifted her eyes to Joe. 'Told me what?'

'Here, let me take those,' said Joe, avoiding her question as he ran over to help Dorothy with her suitcases.

Winston yapped at Joe as soon as he came near.

Clara eyed her mother-in-law as she handed over the two old-fashioned brown leather suitcases to her son. She then bent over to scoop up the little dog at her heels. She stood up straight and made a show of reaching for her back, the expression on her round face pained as though she had pulled something. Clara knew better. She rolled her eyes at Dot as she was affectionately known to everyone else except Clara.

Ever since she'd first met Dorothy, she had been on to her.

She'd told Joe soon after they got together, but he didn't have a clue what she was talking about. What Clara was 'on' to was her theatrics to get attention, from her son. And there was the other thing. As far as Dorothy was concerned no woman was good enough for her son, especially Clara. She took an instant dislike to her because she wanted Joe to marry a nice East End girl.

Clara tried to put that thought out of her mind which was easier said than done when she was standing in her house, larger than life, and still just as intimidating even at the ripe old age of eighty-four. Whenever Dorothy came to visit, she always brought with her a litany of disparaging remarks. "What do you call this?" she'd say when Clara had slaved over the oven to produce something special for dinner, only to be told, "What's wrong with meat and two veg? Now that's a *proper* meal. None of this French nonsense."

She remembered that comment last time Dorothy came to supper because that "French nonsense" was Lasagne. But woe betide her if she contradicted her mother-in-law.

Thinking of dinner, they already had three unexpected guests staying for tea, and Clara didn't have a clue what to give *them*. She'd been so busy on the shopping expedition with her friends that she had forgotten the groceries. That wouldn't have bothered Joe this evening; there was still one ready meal left in the freezer. She was intending to make do with a sandwich.

Clara eyed Dorothy's luggage. Where was Joe taking her with those suitcases? Maybe she was going on a trip. A little holiday. That would be a first. In all the years she had known her, she had never seen her mother-in-law leave the East End of London for any length of time. But there was a first time for everything, and perhaps this was it.

Clara hoped she had just popped in for a quick cuppa before Joe took her on her way. It would solve the problem of dinner. She was sure Tamsin and the girls would make do with sandwiches this evening. Clara was going to check with Joe when

Dorothy was leaving when he strode past her carrying a suitcase in each hand.

Clara was about to ask where he was taking those old musty-smelling suitcases when Dorothy cut in with, 'Well, where is my room?'

Joe glanced over his shoulder. 'Can you manage the stairs?'

'I'm not an invalid.'

'This way.'

Clara folded her arms. She had her answer. Not only was Dorothy staying for dinner, but it looked as though she was stopping the night too before he drove her to her destination tomorrow. Clara's gaze followed him up the stairs. There was just one small problem. 'Joe, I need to have a word about—'

'I'll just be two ticks, Clara.'

'But—'

'Why don't you put the kettle on, Luv?'

Dorothy added, 'How thoughtful of you, Joe. I'm gasping for a cuppa and *nobody* has bothered to make me a cup of tea since I arrived.'

Clara scowled at Dorothy's back. She knew that remark was directed at her.

'And Winston needs feeding – don't you my sweet boy?'

'Can you manage the dog or would you like Clara to carry him up the stairs?'

Clara frowned at Dorothy cradling the dog in her arms. She treated Winston like a baby. The dog could walk up the stairs by himself, but Dorothy insisted on carrying him everywhere. A Yorkshire terrier, he looked like one of her granddaughters' teddy bears with its white, black and sable fur. He was tiny, some might say cute and cuddly, not that Clara thought that.

She lingered at the foot of the stairs, hands on hips, watching Joe heaving the two cases up the stairs. She left him to sort out where Dorothy would sleep tonight when he discovered the two spare bedrooms were already taken. Hopefully, he'd just load the cases and his mother, along with her precious dog, back in his taxi and take her to her destination tonight.

With that thought, Clara smiled and decided to put the kettle on so they could have a quick cuppa before they left. She was just turning on her heel when she heard Dorothy's dog yapping.

Clara glanced up the stairs and saw why Winston was making such a fuss. She'd forgotten about Marley. The black cat with the white paws was enjoying a quiet nap on a bed. He raced down the stairs. About half-way down the cat stopped, turned around and hissed at his pursuer. Winston must have escaped from Dorothy's arms when he spotted the cat.

Winston came to an abrupt halt and backed away from the hissing cat before turning tail and scampering back along the hall upstairs no doubt straight into Mummy's arms.

Clara watched the cat saunter down the rest of the stairs, ignoring her as he passed by. He disappeared into the kitchen. Next to appear was Joe. 'Why didn't you tell me Tamsin and the girls were staying over?'

The girls followed behind their grandfather carrying their suitcases. 'I'm not sharing the sofa bed with Mia if that's what you're thinking,' said Sophie, stalking down the stairs. She stopped in the hall in front of Clara, glaring at her as if it was her fault she was turfed out of the spare bedroom. Clara cast her gaze up at Joe. 'You didn't give me a chance to explain.'

'It will only be for one night,' said Joe, helping Mia down with her bag.

Clara breathed a sigh of relief when she heard Joe's comment about one night. For a moment there, it had crossed her mind that Dorothy was moving in! Which was ridiculous; she had her own place. Dorothy was independent. There was no way she would—

'You'll both be going home with Mum tomorrow, won't you?'

Clara frowned. Tamsin hadn't put him in the picture. Her next thought was *what about Dorothy?*

'What about Dot?' asked Sophie, taking the words right out of Clara's mouth.

'Well…'

'Has Dot got dementia? Is that why she's coming to live with you now because she can't live on her own? My friend's granny has caught it.'

Sophie rolled her eyes at her little sister. 'You don't *catch* dementia, you idio—'

'She's coming to live with *us*?!' exclaimed Clara, her head swivelling from the girls to Joe.

10

Joe glanced nervously at wife as she herded the grandchildren into the dining room. 'Clara, darling, will you sort out the sofa bed while I see to Dot?'

Clara stared at him. She knew what his game was; she wouldn't lift off in front of the girls. The grandchildren had never heard her utter a cross word. Well, there was a first time for everything thought Clara, about to do just that. There was no way on God's green earth Dorothy was coming to live with—

'Granddad, are Mummy and Daddy getting a divorce?'

Joe and Clara turned around and stared at Mia.

Sophie added matter-of-factly, 'Mum's left Dad.'

'Pardon?' said Joe in surprise before rounding on Clara. 'Is this true? Is this why Tamsin and the girls are here? She's left Kevin?'

'To be honest, I'm as much in the dark as you are.' Clara shrugged as she pulled off the seat cushions on the sofa bed. When she looked up, Joe was striding out of the room.

'Joe, where are you going? '

'Upstairs to find out what's going on?'

She rushed out of the room and caught his arm. 'When she's ready to talk I am sure she'll come down. In the meantime, why don't we give her some space and make up the sofa bed for the girls tonight.'

Joe glanced up the stairs, sighed and then relented. He followed her back into the dining room. Neither granddaughter made a move to help their grandparents. Perched on the arm of the sofa, Sophie was texting on her mobile phone and Mia was sitting crossed legged on the rug in front of the fireplace rummaging through her bag, no doubt looking for another book to read.

Clara looked at them both. 'Once we get the bed set up, then we can have something to eat. What would you like for tea?'

When they used to stay at Grandma and Grandpa's house, the question of what they wanted for dinner was met with hands shooting in the air and Mia and Sophie competing to see who could shout out their favourite food the loudest. This time, Sophie just shrugged her shoulders and said, 'Dunno.'

Mia, who was busy leafing through a book, turned to Grandma and said, 'I'm not hungry.'

'What do you mean, you're not hungry? You're *always* hungry?'

Joe caught Clara's eye and shook his head as if to say, leave her be.

Clara ignored him. 'I know – why don't I surprise you? How does that sound?' She looked from Sophie to Mia and got no response. Mia didn't even look up from her book

While Joe finished putting the bed down, Clara fetched sheets and blankets from the airing cupboard. She had to pass the spare bedroom twice on her way back and forth to the airing cupboard. The door was ajar. She paused with an armful of linen and frowned at Dorothy. Her two suitcases were open on the bed. She was busy taking out her clothes and hanging them in the empty wardrobe. She looked as though she was moving in.

Clara narrowed her eyes. If it wasn't for Tamsin in the room next door, she would have had it out with Joe before it got this far. Dorothy had only been here ten minutes and she was already making herself at home. And the dog was sitting on the bed.

Clara didn't mind Marley sleeping on the beds, but Dorothy's smelly, hairy fur ball of a mutt was a different matter.

As if he had telepathy, the dog turned his head in her direction and growled at her.

Dorothy said, 'What's the matter, my sweet boy?' As she turned toward the open doorway to find out what had caught his attention, Clara stepped past, out of sight. She paused outside Tamsin's door. The door was shut. She listened for a moment. There was no sound of Tamsin crying in her pillow as she expected.

A memory resurfaced of times gone by when she had stood outside this door after Tamsin had broken up with boyfriends when she was a teenager. Then as now she was dying to open the door and comfort her daughter. But Tamsin wouldn't open her heart. Maybe if they'd been closer. But they weren't. And whose fault is that Clara berated herself. It wasn't just that she had a lot of growing up to do herself when she had Tamsin. There was something else.

She wished she'd told Tamsin the circumstances of her birth. Joe felt it best to keep her in the dark, and Clara agreed for her own selfish reasons. Now she wondered what their relationship would have been if Tamsin had known the truth from the start. Perhaps they could have sat down and talked about it when she got older. Then Clara might have been able to share a secret from her past and as a result have had a mother-daughter relationship instead of this – Clara glared at the door. Joe might have been right: it could have made things worse.

She sighed. There were some things in life that once done can never be undone. "Let sleeping dogs lie," Joe had told her when she broached the subject of telling Tamsin the truth one day. He didn't want to discuss it any further. He didn't see the point of opening old wounds or from Tamsin's perspective creating new ones. "It's all in the past. What good would it do her now?"

Indeed, thought Clara. As Joe said, it was all in the past. But that didn't mean *he* was dead and forgotten. "Who are you referring to?" Joe had asked when she had shared her thoughts aloud. And that was the end of the conversation. She didn't want to talk about *that* either.

Clara frowned at the door and for a moment considered knocking to see if she was okay. She knew what she'd get. She tried it anyway. 'Tamsin – it's me.'

'I'm not in the mood to talk.'

Clara pursed her lips. *You mean you're not in the mood to talk to me.* She made her way downstairs and deposited the linen, blankets and spare pillows in a heap on the sofa bed. 'Where's Grandad?'

Mia looked up from her book. 'He said he was going out to get dinner.'

'A takeaway?' Clara glanced at the door and thought *what a good idea.* 'Right, come on you two, how about helping Grandma make up the bed?'

She caught the girls exchange bored glances, so she threw a pillowcase in Sophie's direction. It landed on her head. Mia laughed at her sister sitting there with a pillowcase on her head.

'That's not funny,' said Sophie taking it in her hands. She picked up a pillow, looked across at her little sister and got her own back. She threw the pillow at her.

'Hey!' Mia's book went flying out of her hands. She picked up the pillow and stalked towards Sophie.

'Oh, no.' Sophie put her phone in the back pocket of her jeans and picked up the other pillow. 'You know you can be scary when you're angry, little sis.'

'I am NOT little!'

A pillow fight ensued as they bounced around the springy sofa bed shouting and whooping with laughter.

Clara stood there watching the girls, smiling at them affectionately until she heard Dorothy's booming voice in the bedroom above them. 'Clara! Where's that cuppa you promised me? And what's that noise?'

She rolled her eyes at the ceiling and left the girls to their pillow fight.

Sophie and Mia collapsed in silly girlish fits of giggles. They lay on their backs side by side on the bed.

Mia turned to her big sister. 'Soph.'

'What?' Sophie already had her phone in her hands, checking out what her friends were up to at the weekend.

'Do you think Mum and Dad will get back together?'

Sophie glanced at her little sister and was about to come out with some offhand remark like, *how do I know,* just to shut her up when she caught the expression on her face. Her sister was so clever that sometimes she forgot how little she still was. For once, Sophie put her phone down and acted like a big sister who protected little sisters from reality. 'You know what?'

Her sister looked at her hopefully.

'Everyone has arguments. I'm sure it's nothing. I bet tomorrow we'll be going home.'

'Do you think so?'

Sophie didn't really think so. How would she know what was going on? She was just a teenager. All she could do right now was save her little sister – and herself – from a sleepless night worrying about Mum and Dad. Sophie smiled at Mia, crossed her fingers behind her back and said, 'Everything will be all right, I promise.'

'Come on, you two, off the bed so I can finish making it up,' said Clara, walking into the room. She had just returned from the kitchen where she'd put some plates in the oven to warm up after she'd taken Dorothy up a cup of tea and two digestive biscuits.

Sophie carried on texting her friends while Mia found her book, leaving Grandma to make up the bed. Clara had just finished when Joe opened the front door and stepped inside bringing with him the distinct aroma of fish and chips. The girls smelt it too. 'Fish and Chips!' they both exclaimed in unison. 'I can't remember the last time we had fish and chips,' Sophie remarked.

Clara imagined that Kevin and Tamsin preferred expensive restaurants to fish and chips from the local chippie.

'What's this?' said Dorothy, walking into the dining room.

Clara heaved a sigh. 'It's fish and chips, Dorothy.'

'I can see that. Whose idea was it?' Dorothy asked, throwing Clara a disapproving look.

Clara knew what she was thinking; you didn't bother to cook a proper meal. A nice East End girl would cook a proper meal for her husband to come into after a day at work, not send him out to fetch his own dinner.

Joe looked sheepishly at his mother. 'It was my idea. We could rustle up something else if you don't fancy—'

'Don't be silly, I love fish and chips.'

Clara frowned at her mother-in-law. If it had been *her* idea, she would have refused to eat it on principle. She rolled her eyes at Dorothy and shifted her attention to Sophie and Tamsin eating their meal like two sulky teenagers just because she'd told them not to use their phones up the dinner table.

Mia was staring at her plate, absently shifting the food around with her fork. She wasn't eating, Clara noticed. That wasn't like Mia. Normally, she wolfed down her dinner and asked for seconds.

Apart from the sound of Dorothy smacking her lips as she tucked into her meal, everyone was quiet. Clara wondered when Dorothy would put her foot in it and ask Tamsin why she was staying overnight at Mum and Dad's house. Thank goodness she hadn't got around to that – yet.

Joe broke the silence. As if reading Clara's mind, he glanced at Dorothy and then at the grandchildren. 'Well, isn't this grand, having you all round for Friday fish and chips and a sleepover?' Joe looked at Sophie and Mia attempting to lighten the mood.

He then looked at Tamsin and asked, 'Is Kevin away on another business trip this weekend?'

Tamsin looked up from her meal and, for a split second, she didn't catch his drift. The expression on her face said *what the hell are you talking about?* Then the penny dropped. Her gaze shifted to Dorothy. He was trying to forestall any awkward question. 'Uh, yes, Kevin is away on business, so I thought it would be nice to stay here with the girls.'

'But Mummy, that's not—OW!' Mia shot her big sister a filthy look. 'Mummy, Sophie kicked me under the table.'

Sophie looked at Mia. 'God, you're not going to cry again, are you?'

Mia's faced crumpled.

Clara leaned towards Mia and put an arm around her shoulders. 'Why don't you eat some of your fish and chips before it gets cold?'

Mia picked up her fork and stabbed a chip, staring crossly at her sister across the table.

Joe caught Clara's eye. 'As we're all here, I have a piece of good news to share with you all.'

11

Good news? Clara glanced around the table. They could do with a bit of good news. It's not that she didn't like having family over to dinner, or even staying the night, she just wished it was under different circumstances. Tamsin had left Kevin for reasons she had yet to divulge, on top of which she had Dorothy to contend with until tomorrow morning when she went on her merry way.

It was an uncharitable thought, but she didn't much care where Dorothy was off to tomorrow, providing she left post-haste and didn't come back.

Her attention shifted to Joe. She smiled. 'Well, don't keep us in suspense… what's this piece of good news?'

'Have you won the lottery, Granddad?' asked Mia.

'As good as,' said Joe, rubbing his hands together.

Clara eyed her husband.

'I found this great investment opportunity that's certain to provide The Big Payday.'

As soon as she heard those three words, *The Big Payday,* Clara closed her eyes, shook her head and zoned out of the rest of the details. It was all she could do not to slam her fist down on the table and have it out with Joe.

She was sick of hearing about The Big Payday. When was he going to accept that he would never get The Big Payday? All these conferences and seminars he'd attended with get-rich-schemes that turned out too good to be true. They targeted gullible or desperate people like Joe who were willing to part with their hard-earned cash for a promise of a future that never materialized.

She stared at her husband's cheery face. She'd seen that expression countless times before. When was Joe going to get real? He would not achieve The Big Payday this way. His dream of cruising around the med on a yacht in retirement would remain just that – a dream. In fact, at this rate he would never retire and do anything different with his life; he would work until he dropped.

As she cleared away the plates, leaving him sitting up the table talking about his next amazing investment opportunity, she wondered where he thought the money was coming from. His best bet was to go and buy a lottery ticket. It would cost a lot less money, be a lot less risky, but it amounted to the same thing; it was a gamble.

That's what she realised Joe had been doing all these years – gambling. Taking a punt. Over the years, he'd have had a better chance of scoring The Big Payday by taking a flutter at the bookies instead of wasting so much time, energy and money on schemes that led nowhere.

Clara walked into the dining room to collect the last plate and heard Joe say, 'It's at the weekend.'

'What's at the weekend?' asked Clara, picking up his plate.

'The seminar. Haven't you been listening?'

She frowned at him and glanced at Dorothy who had dozed off in her chair. 'Are you going with your mother?'

'Dot? Of course not. What a funny thing to ask.'

'Are you dropping your mother off on the way?'

'Dropping her off?'

'Mummy, can I get down from the table now?'

Tamsin and Sophie looked up from their phones. Tamsin glanced at her parents, sensed there was a row brewing, and said,

'Why don't we sit in the lounge?' Clara watched the three of them troop out of the kitchen. She turned back to Joe and pointed at Dorothy. 'Have you forgotten that you're taking your mother somewhere?'

'I haven't forgotten.'

Clara breathed a sigh of relief. The last thing she wanted was to be landed with Dorothy for the *entire* weekend.

'It just might take some time.'

'Some time?' She was confused. 'What are you talking about?'

Joe wiped his mouth with a napkin, got up from his seat and walked around the table to where she was standing. He took the plate out of her hand and put it back on the table, then took her hands in his. He glanced at Dorothy before turning his attention to Clara. Joe lowered his voice to a whisper. 'Her GP thinks she's got dementia.'

'Oh, Joe.' She squeezed his hands. 'I'm so sorry.'

'Yes, well she *is* getting on. I suppose it's to be expected at her age. The thing is she's been so forgetful since Dad died that they don't think she can cope living on her own. She will tell you otherwise. You know what Dot is like.'

Clara pursed her lips willing herself not to come out with a sarcastic remark. Of course she knew what Dorothy was like; she'd known her long enough.

'While we find sheltered accommodation or perhaps a nursing home, I thought we could you know, keep an eye on her.'

Clara smiled. 'That's fine by me. I'll pop round—'

'Ah, that's just it,' Joe butted in, 'wouldn't it save a whole heap of time and trouble if we didn't have to pop to her place?'

'How's that?'

'If she's living here, then we don't—'

'What?' Clara stepped back in surprise.

'I suggested it to Dot. I expected some resistance, but she didn't think twice about it. Just packed her bags and here we are.' He waved his hand at the large woman sitting in the chair snoring.

Clara's mouth dropped open.

'Talking of which…' Joe walked out of the kitchen.

She followed him from the room. 'You *are* joking. Tell me this is a wind-up and you're taking her somewhere, anywhere tomorrow morning.'

'Why would I joke about something like this?' Joe started up the stairs. 'She's got dementia and can't live on her own.'

'But… but weren't you going to discuss it with me first?' Clara said to his back as she followed him up the stairs.

'Discuss it?' Joe shook his head. 'What's there to discuss? We've got a spare bedroom.' Joe frowned as he walked past the spare bedroom. 'We *will* have a spare bedroom when Tamsin patches things up with Kevin. In the meantime, we will just have to make do.'

Clara gulped. 'How long?'

Joe walked into the bedroom. 'What do you mean, how long?'

She gritted her teeth. 'How long will she be with us? Have you investigated sheltered accommodation? What about a care home?'

Joe smiled. 'All in good time.' He turned around and opened their wardrobe.

Clara frowned and sat down on the bed. That wasn't good enough. 'When will you start looking?'

'Ah, I've got this seminar I'm attending. So, when I get back…'

'On Sunday then. We will get on the internet as soon as you get back.'

'Sunday? I'll be at the conference.'

'It's two days?'

'Uh-huh.'

'An *entire* weekend?'

'Yep.'

Clara stared at her husband. He'd never attended one of these so-called investment seminars for an entire weekend.

She had a thought. 'Are you staying in a hotel?'

'Yes. The seminar is being held at the hotel, so you stay over and attend both days.'

Clara now wished she'd paid attention when he was talking about it up the dinner table. 'Why didn't you tell me about it sooner?'

Joe looked sheepishly at his wife.

She got the impression he wasn't telling her something.

'You have not been enthusiastic about these seminars, so I went ahead and booked it before you could talk me out of it. I really want to go on this one. It will change our lives. I'm convinced of it.'

Clara sighed. If she said no, Joe would bow to her wishes. He always had. Whatever she wanted, or didn't want, he'd go along with it.

She didn't want him to go, and she didn't want to be left alone with his mother all weekend. Clara knew what he'd say. She wouldn't be alone; she had Tamsin and the girls here. But that wasn't the point. Dorothy would still be here in the house.

Joe was standing in front of the wardrobe, overnight bag at the ready, waiting for her to give him the all clear that she was okay with him going.

She sighed. 'All right, go if you must.'

Joe breathed an audible sigh of relief and packed some things into his duffel bag before she changed her mind.

'Out of interest,' said Clara, watching him pack, 'have you booked a double room at the hotel?'

'Better than that,' said Joe smiling. 'It's a suite.'

'Is it now?'

'Oh, yes. It's got a nice view of the market square.'

'Excellent.'

Joe zipped up his bag and turned around. 'Why do you ask?'

'Because I rather fancy a break away myself. A long weekend sounds just the ticket.' She hadn't been away on a short break, or any break all year. Since Joe's last venture which had gone south, they had no money for a holiday.

She didn't want to think about all those great investment opportunities that promised the earth and never delivered. Right now, she didn't even want the details of the next scam her gullible Joe was about to get them involved in. All that was on her mind was the possibility of a break away and some time to themselves to talk over what they were going to do about his mother.

Dorothy moving in with them was only a short-term solution; the sooner Joe faced up to that, and they sorted out alternative arrangements, the better. A break away together could not have come at a better time. Besides, whatever Joe was about to get himself into Clara wanted to be there.

Joe was standing there looking at her quizzically. 'I suppose we could book something when I get back.'

'Joe, you've already got a hotel room booked. A whole suite!'

'Oh. Yes. Right.'

'I don't see why we can't go together. I don't mind killing some time during the day while you're at the conference. At least we can spend the evening together.'

Joe was already shaking his head no before Clara had finished speaking.

She looked at him a moment. 'Are you saying *no*?' This was the first time in their married lives Joe had ever said no to her about anything. She always got her own way. *Always.*

'Look, it's impossible.'

'Impossible?' Clara folded her arms. 'Why?'

Joe said, 'Who will look after Dot?'

And there, in a nutshell, was just what Clara was afraid of. It was mean of her to think it, but she didn't want her latter years taken up with caring for his elderly mother. She wanted to do things with her life before she morphed into Dorothy – a dependent.

And that was the other thing: if she wasn't careful, once Dorothy settled in here, there was no telling when she would leave. Clara eyed her husband. When he didn't want to do something, he could drag his feet royally. Finding sheltered accommodation or a care home for his mother would be one of those things.

She wasn't having that, but for now she had an idea how to get away for the weekend. 'Tamsin is at home for a few days. She can keep an eye on Dorothy.'

Joe was still shaking his head. 'Look, Clara, you won't want to come along once you find out where I'm going. It won't be your idea of a fun weekend.'

Clara stood her ground. 'Try me.'

'All right,' Joe drawled. 'You know how you don't much care for the coast.'

She nodded her head. It was true. 'So, I take it this hotel is on the coast.'

'Not only that, it's old. The hotel is ancient and might be run down even.'

Clara narrowed her eyes. 'Run down, you say?'

'Oh, yes. I should imagine it's *very* rundown.'

'Rats and mice?'

Joe bobbed his head this way and that in a non-committal gesture. 'Could be.'

'I see,' said Clara flatly. Joe was trying his level best to put her off. Did he think she was stupid? She'd seen photos of the hotels where he had attended seminars in the past. She'd even gone with him occasionally and spent the day lounging around expensive lobbies while he attended his seminars.

The one thing she could guarantee was that they were not rundown. They weren't hosted in plush, expensive hotels for nothing. How else would they draw in the gullible punters but with a taste of the life of luxury they would get accustomed to if their investment paid off. Why would this be any different?

Clara made up her mind. 'I'm coming.'

'That's not a good—'

'I don't want to hear another word on the subject.'

Joe shrugged. 'Fine.' He strolled out of the bedroom with his bag. 'But don't say I didn't warn you.'

12

Clara gathered up some things in an overnight bag. Why was Joe trying to put her off tagging along, she thought? Unless he was intending to go with someone else.

She smiled at that ludicrous idea. Since the moment he saw her and pulled over in his taxi to pick up the pretty, blonde-haired girl, he had eyes for no one else. As far as she was concerned, he hadn't looked at another woman their entire marriage. So, what was the problem with her coming along? Unless he thought she had an ulterior motive, like trying to talk him out of whatever hair-brained scheme he was getting himself mixed up in.

Clara decided that must be it as she took her bag downstairs and left it by the front door. Joe was already outside loading his bag into the boot of the car. She wandered into the kitchen. Joe told her he'd left a leaflet all about the hotel stuck on the fridge door. Clara promised she would check the details before they set off. She sat down at the kitchen table with the pamphlet to see what facilities the hotel had to offer. Everything seemed perfect for a weekend break away – until she read the address at the bottom of the leaflet. 'Blast!'

'What's the matter, Grandma?'

Clara looked up to find Mia standing in front of her with a concerned expression.

'Nothing, sweetheart. Can I get you something?'

'Some juice, please.'

She left the leaflet on the kitchen table and poured Mia a glass of orange juice from the fridge. When she turned around Mia was browsing through it. 'Is this where Granddad is going tomorrow?'

'Yes.'

'It looks nice.'

Clara wasn't sure if Mia was referring to the hotel or the photos of the surrounding area.

'Is Granddad going to the seaside?'

'Yes. The hotel is in the town, but it's only a short walk from the pier.'

'There's a pier? I don't see a picture.' Mia looked at her grandma. 'Have you been here before?'

Clara sighed. Her granddaughter was too bright by half. 'Yes. It was a long time ago.'

'Did you go with Granddad?'

'No, honey.'

'Are you going with Granddad tomorrow? You can show him the pier.'

Clara shook her head. 'I'm not going.'

'Why not?'

'Because I'd much rather spend the weekend seeing my lovely granddaughters.' She took the leaflet out of Mia's hands and placed the glass of juice in front of her. 'Now drink up.'

Mia picked up the glass.

Clara watched her drink her juice feeling guilty for just telling her what amounted to a half-truth. She wanted to spend time with Mia, Sophie and Tamsin, but would still have opted for a weekend in a beautiful hotel. How unfortunate that it had to be there. Little wonder Joe was trying to put her off. She would never return to—

'Where's Southwold, Grandma?'

Clara picked up the pamphlet and stuck it back on the fridge door with a magnet. She turned to look at Mia. She must have read the address. 'It's a little town in Suffolk on the coast.'

'Near the seaside.'

'Yes. That's why it has a pier.'

'And a beach.'

'Uh-huh.'

'Will you take us there someday? I'd like to see Southwold.'

She took Mia's empty glass and put it in the dishwasher. 'I think you'll find it disappointing after the exotic beaches Mummy and Daddy take you to on holiday in The Caribbean.'

Mia frowned. 'It's always so hot, and they don't have donkey rides and piers with amusement arcades. I remember when I was little, and we went on holiday to the seaside. I don't think I've ever been on a pier. Then Daddy earned lots of money and now all we ever do is go to the airport and fly abroad.'

Clara looked at her a moment. Her youngest grandchild always had a long memory. She must have been three when she was last taken to the seaside in England.

'Will you take us to Southwold?'

'Perhaps Mummy will take you for a day trip.'

'I want you to come too. You remember where the pier is.'

'I'm sure Mummy will find it.'

'Don't you want to come with us?'

'It's not that, sweetheart.'

'Don't you like the seaside?'

Not anymore, thought Clara. She smiled at Mia. 'Someone has to look after Dorothy. You know she's not very well, don't you?'

'She's got dementia. Her mind is not very well. Perhaps she'd feel better if she came to the seaside too. That way we could all see the pier.'

Clara stared at Mia. She had an answer for everything.

'Mia! There you are.' Tamsin appeared in the doorway. 'It's bedtime. Clean your teeth.'

A look of resignation crossed her features as she slid off the kitchen chair. She walked over to Clara. 'Night, night, Grandma.'

Clara gave her a hug. 'Night, night.'

Mia walked over to her mother. 'Mummy, will you take me to Southwold?'

Tamsin put an arm around her shoulders and guided her out of the room. Clara heard her say, 'Southwold? Where's that?'

'It's in Suffolk by the seaside. Can we go someday?'

'Why would you want to go there?' her daughter replied with disdain as though Mia had just asked to spend the day in Blackpool.

'I want to see the pier and the amusement arcades and ride a donkey on the beach.'

'Who put that idea into your head?'

'Granddad is going there tomorrow.'

'That's for work, honey.'

Mia frowned.

'Besides, your Grandma and Granddad are getting on in years. They're old and old people don't want to do anything adventurous. That's why they go to places like Southwold.'

Clara stood in the kitchen doorway, hands on hips, listening to this exchange as her daughter walked Mia up the stairs to the bathroom. She bristled when she heard her say they were old and didn't want to do anything adventurous.

Tamsin continued, 'We're young. We want to do things like snorkelling on the barrier reef, don't we honey.'

'I suppose so,' Mia replied in a small voice.

'Good girl. Now come on, let's brush your teeth and get into your pyjamas.'

Clara walked out of the kitchen and saw Joe reaching for her overnight bag in the hallway. 'Don't bother with that,' she said to his back. He turned around. 'I was just putting the bags in the car tonight so we can get an early start in the morning. I must let Tamsin know she's got to keep an eye on Dot.'

Clara held up the pamphlet. 'I'm not coming. Why didn't you tell me the hotel was in Southwold? For a minute there, I thought you didn't want my company.'

Joe looked at his shoes. 'I didn't want to dredge up the past. I thought I could talk you out of it before you found out where I was going.' He looked up. 'Sorry.'

She walked over with the leaflet in her hand. 'Don't be sorry. It's not your fault they're holding the seminar there.'

Joe took the pamphlet. 'I've never been to Southwold or anywhere on the Suffolk coast. I would like to see where you grew up.'

'I know.'

Joe looked at her. 'It was a long time ago, Clara. Can't you—'

'Let it go? Is that what you were going to say?' she said bitterly.

'No, of course not. Well, not in so many words. It was a long time ago.'

'You said that already.' It made her wonder if you ever moved on from losing someone you love. That grief was ever present, weighing heavy on your heart. She put on a good front. Always had. But Joe understood how she felt and that she would never be entirely happy.

She put her hand on his cheek. 'You're a good man, Joe.' She glanced at his overnight bag. 'I just wish you were not going to another of those stupid seminars.'

'It's not stupid, Clara. I'm telling you, this time it will change our lives. I just know it.'

She sighed. It might change their lives, but was it going to change their lives for the better? That's what worried her. If their financial situation worsened, then would she have to find a job? What was she going to do? She was a grief counsellor, but she'd only ever worked in a voluntary capacity. Somehow it seemed wrong to charge people money to help them work through their grief.

'I'm off to bed,' announced Joe. 'I want to get an early start tomorrow because it's at least a two-hour drive.'

Clara nodded. It was a shame they weren't running the seminar closer to home. She watched him cross the hallway and check on the girls snuggled up in the sofa bed. She couldn't imagine they were asleep yet.

Joe closed the door. 'I said goodnight. Mia is reading a book. I think Sophie is listening to some music on her phone. Well, I'm off to bed.' He made for the stairs. 'Are you coming?'

'Soon. I'm just finishing up in the kitchen.'

'Need a hand?'

She shook her head. She would switch the dishwasher on and then head up herself. 'It's a shame they weren't holding the seminar here in London.'

Joe paused on the stairs and glanced over his shoulder. He yawned. 'I'm bushed. I think I'll go straight to sleep.'

'All right.' She could tell he was preoccupied with the seminar. She walked into the kitchen, ran a dishcloth under some warm water and wiped the kitchen surfaces before pressing the *start* button on the dishwasher. She stood there for a moment listening to the dishwasher churning into life with a low, muted rumble then turned around. Something caught her eye: it was the pamphlet advertising the conference Joe was attending at the weekend. She hadn't noticed before, but the hotel in Southwold wasn't the only venue.

She opened a drawer to find a spare pair of reading glasses and sat down at the kitchen table. She stared at the address of the other hotel where the convention was being held; it was right here in London. She took off her reading glasses and thought of Joe loading his overnight bag into the back of the car. If he attended the seminar in London, he wouldn't have had to go away for the weekend. That begged the question: why was he attending the seminar in Southwold? The obvious explanation – it was fully booked in London. Her eyes drifted to the phone.

She wanted to phone the hotel and find out. Clara shook her head. What had got into her? He wouldn't *choose* to have a weekend away in a hotel without her, which he knew would be the case when she found out where he was going.

She stuck the pamphlet back on the fridge door. She wanted to keep the phone number of the hotel handy so she could ring Joe tomorrow evening in his hotel suite and see how his first day went. More to the point, she wanted to check Joe wasn't doing anything stupid like handing over more of his hard-earned money. She didn't want to know how much the seminar had cost him already.

She still hoped she could talk him out of going but that looked unlikely. At least she could speak to him tomorrow evening and try to persuade him not to bother with the second day and come home. The problem was Joe always finished what he started, and the seminar would be no exception.

She lingered in front of the pamphlet, still in two minds whether she should ring that hotel. Perhaps if someone had dropped out at the last minute, there might be a vacancy. The hotel looked nice. In fact, if that were the case, and the seminar package included a stay at the hotel, they could still have a weekend away together.

Clara made up her mind. She'd give them a ring on the off-chance. It was for selfish reasons. Seeing those lovely hotels on the front of the pamphlet made her realise she was desperate for a break away even if it was right here in London.

She took the leaflet and made the call. Five minutes later she replaced the handset. She didn't need to inquire about a cancellation. There were still plenty of vacancies for tomorrow, but the same seminar being held in Southwold was sold out.

'Is it because it was cheaper?' she had inquired. That would explain why Joe chose to go there.

'Not at all,' replied the receptionist. 'It could turn out more expensive, especially if you were one of the last to book.'

'How come?'

'There would be only suites available.'

'Suites?' She narrowed her eyes. Didn't Joe say he had booked a suite?

'Yes, then if you factor in your travel costs to get there depending on where you are travelling from—'

She didn't need to hear any more and put the phone down. Now she wanted an explanation. Of all the places why would he choose to go to the one place he knew she could not bring herself to return to? Clara marched up the stairs and into their bedroom.

13

Clara switched on her bedside lamp and glanced at the time. She got out of bed, wandered down to the kitchen for a glass of water and looked in on her grandchildren. The girls were fast asleep. Her eyes drifted to the unused place setting at the dining room table. She had covered Joe's plate with some cling film and placed his uneaten meal in the fridge so Marley the cat couldn't get at it. She had expected Joe home for dinner. That was six hours ago. She'd tried calling his mobile phone but to no avail. It was now getting on for midnight.

Clara hadn't slept well the past two nights. She wanted to ask Joe why he had gone all the way to Southwold for the seminar when he could have attended it right here in London and saved himself an expensive overnight stay. There was no chance to pose that question before he left. Joe had been fast asleep when she went to bed on Friday evening, and to her surprise as soon as her head hit the pillow, she was out like a light.

He must have been up at the crack of dawn on Saturday morning for when she woke at six with that question still on her mind, he was gone. He'd left her a cryptic note on his pillow. Clara stared at the message in her hand. *There's something I need to tell you. I will be back in two days then all will be revealed – I promise.*

That evening she had tried phoning him in his suite, but he was out. The hotel confirmed the seminar had finished for the day at five on the dot. She'd asked what time the conference started the following morning, hoping to catch him before he left; it turned out there was no day two.

Clara stared at the note. There had been no secrets between them. Now she wanted to ask him what he had been doing in Southwold that warranted staying an extra night.

Determined to confront him, she had stayed up awaiting his return. However, she made the mistake of wandering upstairs to find the novel she was reading and had laid down on the bed just for a moment. Two hours later she had woken up only to discover Joe *still* hadn't come home. She was wondering if he had got stuck in a tailback. Maybe she should change into her nightie and go to bed.

She put her glass of water down on the sideboard in the hall and was just reaching for the phone when a loud persistent knocking at the front door startled her.

'Mum, what's going on?' Tamsin was standing at the top of the stairs in her pyjamas looking worried.

'It's okay, Tam, it's your Dad. He must have forgotten his door key.'

'It's the middle of the night!'

'I expect he got stuck in traffic on the way home.' At least she hoped that's what it was.

'Grandma…' Sophie opened the dining-room door. 'What was that noise?'

'It woke us up,' said Mia, standing beside her sister rubbing the sleep out of her eyes.

'Girls,' Tamsin shouted from upstairs, 'go back to bed.'

'What's all the commotion?' Dorothy walked out of her bedroom and came up behind Tamsin. 'What on earth is going on down there?' She cast an angry glance down the stairs in Clara's direction.

Clara groaned at the sight of Dorothy. That's all she needed. She turned to her grandchildren. 'It's all right, girls,' she said shooing them back into the room. 'It's only Granddad.'

'Do you think he bought us a present?' asked Mia.

'A present?' Sophie looked at her little sister. 'It's not your birthday, why do you think he's got you a present?'

'Granddad used to bring us back presents whenever they went away.'

Although Sophie thought her sister was being stupid as usual, she lingered by the door to see if perhaps Granddad *had* remembered to bring home a little something for them like he used to.

'Girls, are you going to bed?'

Sophie rolled her eyes. 'Yes, Mum.' She turned to Mia and put her finger to her lips.

Mia smiled up at her rebel of an older sister and stood peeping out from behind the dining-room door waiting to see Granddad.

As she opened the front door, Clara said, 'I told you not to forget your key in case you were… late.'

'Good evening, Ma'am.'

Clara knitted her brow at the two police officers – one male, one female – standing on her doorstep. Her heart skipped a beat. 'Where's Joe?' She looked past them at the police car with the blue flashing light. In an instant, she knew what had happened. He'd had a pint or two at the hotel bar before heading home. She knew what he was like. Affable Joe, he'd bought a round of drinks and was too busy talking to anybody who would listen and then lost count of how many pints he'd downed before hitting the road.

'You idiot!' said Clara out loud. 'I should have warned him to stay away from the hotel bar. I'm sorry, officer. If you just let him out of the police car….'

The two police officers exchanged a glance. 'May we come inside?'

Clara glanced at the car. 'But what about Joe?'

They repeated the question except this time she got the distinct impression it wasn't a question. 'Of course.' She stepped back and let them into the house.

The police officers walked into the hallway. 'Is this your family?'

Clara glanced over her shoulder. Tamsin was standing between Sophie and Mia with a comforting arm around each of their shoulders. All three of them were looking anxious.

'That's my daughter and granddaughters.'

'Now look here,' Dorothy was making her way down the stairs carrying Winston in her arms. 'What is the meaning of this?'

'And that's my mother-in-law.' Clara rolled her eyes at Dorothy in exasperation and turned to the two officers. 'If you just release Joe, I'm sure we can clear up—'

'Joe was arrested?' Dorothy barked.

The female officer stepped forward ignoring the large woman thundering down the stairs towards them. 'Are you Mrs Delaney, Joe Delaney's wife?' she asked Clara.

'Yes.'

The woman officer glanced around the hallway before her eyes settled on her partner with a silent question. He nodded for her to proceed. 'There's been an accident.'

Clara furrowed her brow. 'Oh. Okay. Do you need the insurance details? My husband, Joe, drives a taxi for a living. He's no stranger to the prangs you get out and about on the road. People just aren't careful these days. That's not to say my husband isn't careful,' she added. 'I'm sure it wasn't his fault. I'll fetch the paperwork—'

The female officer caught her arm. 'Your husband, Joe, has been involved in a road traffic accident.'

'Ah, you mean there was a hold up on the A12?'

The female officer shook her head. 'It was more serious than that.'

Clara swallowed hard. 'Is he… dead?'

The officers exchanged glances. 'No, he's not dead, he's—'

'Oh, thank god!' Clara let out a huge sigh of relief. For a moment there, she imagined it was serious. 'Where is he?

'He's in hospital.'

'Right. Well, I suppose we better make plans.' She turned around to look at Tamsin. 'I'll see him now. Why don't we arrange for you to pop along in the morning? Although I'll check first because he might come home in the morning and we wouldn't want you to trek all the way to the hosp—'

'Mrs Delaney.'

Clara turned around. 'Yes?'

'I believe your husband is in surgery right now.'

'Surgery?' Clara stopped short.

'It might be best if you come to the hospital.'

She looked at them askance. 'That's what I was just saying.'

The officer looked around the hallway. 'All of you.'

'You want us all to go? My mother-in-law is eighty-four. She can't possibly—'

'Mrs Delaney.' The officer looked over at the other Mrs Delaney. 'You need to see your son…'

Before it's too late, thought Clara realising the gravity of the situation. She glanced at the female officer who nodded her head.

Clara held back her tears for the sake of Tamsin and the girls. The last thing they needed was for her to fall apart. *He wasn't dead, he wasn't dead,* Clara kept repeating to herself. If he was in surgery, he would pull through. They wouldn't operate if there wasn't a chance – would they?

14

Clara grabbed a handful of coats while everyone, including Dorothy who was uncharacteristically quiet, put on their shoes. Although Clara was the only one dressed because she hadn't gone to bed yet, she got the impression there wasn't time for them to change out of their nightwear. Only Sophie protested. 'Mum, I can't go out in my pyjamas.'

'Darling, nobody will see you. It's the dead of night.'

The police officer with a teenage daughter of his own came to her rescue. 'Why don't we help Mrs Delaney out to the car while you change?'

Sophie shot into the dining room.

Tamsin helped Mia into her coat.

Clara turned to her mother-in-law. 'Dorothy, this lady is a police officer. She will show you to the police car. They will take us to the hospital to visit Joe.' Clara spoke slowly, enunciating every word hoping that Dorothy understood what was going on.

Dorothy glared at her daughter-in-law. 'The way you're talking anyone would think I've got dementia.'

Clara pursed her lips. Sometimes it was difficult to believe she had dementia.

Dorothy grabbed her coat, gave Clara a sour look, and headed out of the house. The female officer helped her into the police car and didn't object to Winston coming along too.

Clara stepped out on to the front porch. Tamsin was right behind her. 'Mum, there isn't room for all of us in the police car. I'll take Dad's car.' She pointed to Joe's pride and joy parked at the kerb. Clara looked at Joe's little sports car and thanked her lucky stars he'd driven down to Southwold in his taxicab because that's what probably saved his life. If he'd been driving that… Clara shuddered to think.

'I've picked up the keys from the sideboard in the hall,' continued Tamsin. 'Why don't you go with Dorothy and I'll take the girls.'

Mia clung to her Mum.

Sophie for once wasn't glued to her phone. 'Here, Mia,' she said to her little sister, 'I picked up your book just in case there's a bit of a wait.'

Mia managed a smile for her big sister.

'That's very thoughtful of you, Sophie,' said Tamsin in surprise.

'I'll meet you at the hospital then,' were Clara's parting words as she headed to the police car. She paused before she climbed in the back of the car, taking in Sophie and Mia's worried expressions. 'Granddad will be just fine.'

Tamsin pulled her daughters close. 'Come on, you heard what Grandma said. We better get going because Granddad will be expecting us when the doctor has finished making him all better.'

Sophie added, 'Yes, come on Mia let's find out what Granddad brought us back from his trip.'

'I don't want a present. I just want Granddad to be okay.'

Clara heard that exchange before she shut the passenger door. That's all she wanted too. She turned to look at the female police officer sitting next to her. 'Can you give me some details about his condition?'

'He suffered a head trauma. I believe he had to have surgery to relieve the pressure on his brain.'

Clara nodded. 'After surgery he will be okay, right?' It was more of a statement than a question.

'I'm afraid I'm not medically qualified to answer that question. The surgeon will tell you more when we arrive at the hospital.'

Clara sat back in her seat and stared out of the window. It wasn't long before they arrived at the hospital. She hadn't been taking much notice of their whereabouts during the brief ten minute journey. All that was on her mind was that Joe had to be okay. Just had to be. He made her a promise once that he would never leave her. She couldn't bear to be left all alone.

She closed her eyes. It was the one thing she was most afraid of. It had happened once before, years ago before she met Joe. She didn't realize she was trembling at the memory until she felt a hand on her arm to steady her. Clara looked up. The young policewoman was smiling at her sympathetically.

'We're here,' she said to Clara as the police car drew up outside the hospital entrance.

'Well, it's about time!' Dorothy exclaimed from the front seat.

'Sorry about that,' whispered Clara glancing at her mother-in-law. She watched her struggling to get her large frame out of the car.

Clara and Dorothy followed the two police officers through the main entrance and straight into a lift that took them to the wards. Trepidation swept over Clara. Suddenly this was for real; the possibility that he might not pull through hit her as she imagined what his surgeon would say to her.

Clara remembered Tamsin and the girls. She turned to the officers. 'My daughter was following us in a small sports car.'

'It's all right,' the female officer reassured her. 'One of us will pop down to the entrance and keep an eye out for them.'

Clara was nodding at the police officer when she saw the surgeon approaching. 'Mrs Delaney?'

Dorothy stepped forward. 'I'm Mrs Delaney.'

The officer said to the surgeon, 'This is Joe Delaney's mother.'

He looked over her head at Clara. 'And you are….?'

'Clara – Joe's wife. Is he going to be all right?'

A nurse appeared from a side door. 'You can see him now.'

He wasn't dead. Clara remembered to breathe. A feeling of utter relief settled over her.

Dorothy rushed past the nurse into the room.

Clara was about the follow when the surgeon said, 'May I have a word?'

'Of course,' Clara said nervously.

The surgeon took her into a small side room behind the nurse's station and closed the door. He offered her a seat.

Clara perched on the edge of a cushioned seat opposite him.

'The surgery went well. Because of the head trauma there was some internal bleeding, but we relieved the pressure on the brain.'

'That's good, right?' she said praying there wasn't a *but*…

'Yes. However…'

Clara could feel her pulse quickening.

'Your husband is in a coma.'

'A coma?'

'Yes. In some ways it's a blessing because it allows the brain time to heal.'

She nodded her head. 'Great. Well, I'll see him now.' Clara rose from her seat.

'But, under the circumstances you might consider getting his affairs in order.'

Clara looked at him blankly. 'His affairs?'

'Yes. Does your husband have a will?'

Clara was shocked. 'I don't understand. I thought you said the surgery went well…?'

'I did. It's true. But he *has* suffered a head trauma, and where the brain is concerned, there's no telling—'

'I want to see my husband now.' She opened the door and stepped out of the room.

'Grandma!'

Clara turned around to find Mia running down the corridor, her coat over her pyjamas. Tamsin and Sophie were following close behind. Mia ran into her arms. 'Where's Granddad?'

The surgeon walked out of the side room. He glanced at Mia and said to Clara, 'You'd do well to heed my advice.'

'What did the doctor say?' asked Tamsin watching him head in the other direction down the hallway.

Clara stared after him.

'Mum?'

Clara turned and looked at Mia, Sophie and Tamsin. They were hanging on her every word, she could tell. She took a moment to consider before replying. 'The doctor said the surgery went well and—'

'Did he have an operation?' asked Mia.

Clara turned to her youngest granddaughter and took both her hands. 'He did. Granddad hit his head so had to have an operation to make him better. The thing is Mia when you see Granddad, he won't be awake. The doctor said he needs plenty of rest and so he will be asleep for a while.

'Like Sleeping Beauty?'

Clara smiled at her. 'Something like that.' She caught Tamsin frowning at her.

'What do you mean he will be asleep for a while?' whispered Tamsin out of earshot of the girls. 'Is he in a coma?'

'Yes, while his brain has a chance to heal.'

She left out the part about the doctor suggesting she make sure his affairs are in order. He'd survived the car accident and the op on his brain – hadn't he? There was no need to worry Tamsin unnecessarily. Her Joe was a fighter. He would pull through, and Clara wasn't going to think otherwise.

15

Clara roused. At first, she didn't open her eyes, convinced it had all been a bad dream until she heard the familiar *beep beep beep* of the monitor. She sat up and stretched. Her neck ached from sleeping in the uncomfortable hospital chair.

She opened her eyes and stared at Joe. 'Good morning, my love.' She stifled a yawn. After two nights sleeping in a chair, she didn't know if she could face another night in the hospital. She'd sent Tamsin home with the girls and Dorothy. They'd agreed to take it in shifts, but she couldn't bring herself to leave his bedside.

She thought back to the dreadful night two days ago when she walked into this room. Joe was hooked up to all these machines, his head bandaged, his face bruised as though he had been in a bar fight. On the first night, she'd sat by his bedside wide awake. All she could think about was what if she had been with him in the car? What if she was lying in a hospital bed too or hadn't survived the accident?

It might be selfish but there were still things she wanted to do with her life. She wasn't ready to check out. Clara leaned forward and took Joe's hand. Her mind wandered to the seminar in Southwold. Over the years, Joe had made some abysmal investment decisions which cost them financially. If anyone had asked, Clara would have said, despite the lack of money, she was content. But did contentment equal happiness, fulfilment, a life well-lived? Clara shook her head willing herself not to go down that road. She'd never questioned her life with Joe before – why now when her husband was in a coma? *I'm a terrible person,* Clara silently berated herself.

'And in here we have a patient who sustained a head trauma because of a traffic accident.' She turned in her chair to see the consultant walk into the room. He was followed by four young trainee doctors. While the trainees studied Joe's medical notes, the consultant looked at Clara. 'Have you thought about getting your husband's affairs in order?'

Clara sat up with a start, surprised he brought that up again. She glanced at Joe. 'I thought he was on the mend? He no longer needs the ventilator. He's breathing on his own. That's a good sign, isn't it?' She looked at the doctor, willing him to tell her everything would be all right. All Clara wanted was for Joe to wake up so they could go home and leave this nightmare behind them.

The consultant said, 'Things are looking a lot more encouraging.' He took the medical notes and flicked through the paperwork. 'However…'

Clara frowned. She would much rather he didn't add a caveat every time he said something. 'Are you saying my husband is not out of the woods yet? He could still—' She didn't want to say the *D* word.

'I have to be blunt with you, Mrs Delaney. If he doesn't make a full recovery—'

'*Full* recovery?' She stared at Joe and then the penny dropped. 'You're talking about if this is permanent.' She'd read about people who'd had head injuries and never fully recovered. She didn't know what was worse; for them to die, or for them to live out the rest of their life lying unresponsive in a hospital bed.

She'd read about a vegetative state. It wasn't something she had considered until now. What if this *was* the worst-case scenario: Joe unable to wake up?

Clara refused to believe that. 'He *will* wake up, I know it.'

The consultant surprised her with his response, 'I have every confidence he will.'

'Great.' That's all she wanted to hear.

'However…'

Clara rolled her eyes in the consultant's direction.

'With brain injuries there's no telling when this will happen or what condition he will be in when he does.'

'Condition?'

'Yes, until he wakes up, we won't know what sort of cognitive function—' He rephrased. 'What I mean to say is we won't know what sort of brain damage if any he has sustained.'

Clara looked at him.

The consultant continued, 'The brain is a very complicated organ. He might be fine. But…'

She was getting the picture.

'Right now, I can't give you any definitive answers about what the future holds. Until Joe wakes up…' He trailed off aware there was nothing more of consequence to add.

'Fine. I'll wait until he wakes up.' She turned in her seat to stare at Joe.

'*If* he wakes up,' commented the consultant as he walked out of the room followed by his little entourage. Clara ignored that last comment. He said he had every confidence Joe *would* wake up.

She felt a hand on her shoulder. 'Are you all right, my dear?'

Clara wiped her eyes with a tissue and looked away from the nurse in embarrassment. 'Sorry.'

'No need to apologise. The consultants often have this effect on people. Sometimes their bedside manner can leave a lot to be desired.' The nurse looked at Joe. 'Ah, I see Joe is off the ventilator today. Well done, Joe.' The nurse patted his hand.

'Did you see that?' Clara jumped out of her seat. 'His little finger moved at your touch.'

The nurse looked at Clara. She took in the dark circles

around her eyes and her dishevelled clothes. Mrs Delaney didn't look as though she'd slept properly for days.

The nurse said gently, 'I think you need to take care of yourself. You want to be in a fit state to care for your husband when he wakes up.'

'When he wakes up,' repeated Clara in a daze, suddenly feeling dog-tired.

'I think it would be a good idea if you went home.'

She shook her head. 'I couldn't possibly leave.'

'There's someone here to take you home.'

She looked at the nurse in surprise. 'Is it my daughter, Tamsin?' Clara was trying to recall if she had phoned her. The trouble was her brain was so foggy from lack of sleep she was having a hard time remembering what happened five minutes ago.

At the nurse's insistence, Clara walked out of the ward to find her son-in-law standing in the corridor. 'Kevin? What are you doing here?'

'I heard about Joe. Sophie texted me. I only found out this morning, so I came straight over to your house, but nobody was answering the door. I came here instead. Are Tamsin and the girls okay?'

Clara nodded.

'Ah.' Kevin held up his phone at the sound of an incoming text. He read the text. 'It's Sophie. They've all gone shopping for some groceries.' He looked up from his phone. 'Doesn't sound as though Sophie wanted to go, she said Mum wouldn't leave her and Mia with Dorothy.' Kevin threw Clara a questioning look.

Clara rolled her eyes. 'Um, Joe's mother is living with us. She's got dementia, apparently.'

'Well, it never rains but it pours, does it?'

'Tell me about it.' She managed a smile. Kevin had met Dorothy. He was no stranger to how difficult she could be and that was without the dementia.

If it wasn't bad enough having Dorothy come to live, and

Tamsin and Kevin breaking up – now this? Joe in hospital. She was close to tears again.

Kevin stepped forward and put an arm around her shoulders. 'I said to the nurse I was here to see Joe. They told me you'd been here for two days straight. Let me take you home, Clara. Then I'll come back and sit with Joe until Tamsin arrives.' Kevin held up his phone. 'I'll text Tamsin to see if she'll let me take the girls home. As you may have gathered, I'm not in her good books.'

Clara stared at Kevin. 'What did you do?'

'Me?' said Kevin in surprise. 'What did she tell you?'

Clara sighed. 'Nothing. She didn't want to talk about it.'

'*She* left *me!*' Kevin snapped before apologizing. 'I am *so* sorry.' He glanced toward the ward. 'You've got enough on your plate right now. At least let me drive you home so you can catch up on some sleep. Then I'll return and take the next shift. I promise I will contact you if anything changes.'

Clara was too tired to argue.

16

The car drew up outside the house. The girls were back from their shopping trip. Clara saw Tamsin loading bags of grocery shopping from the back of Joe's car.

Mia was standing at the front door helping her mum with the bags when she spotted her dad's BMW. 'Daddy!' Mia rushed down the garden path before Tamsin could stop her.

Kevin got out of the car. Mia threw herself into Daddy's arms. He carried Mia up the garden path and put her down in front of Tamsin. 'Hello, Tamsin. Do you want help with the shopping?'

Clara followed behind them and stopped at the front door.

Tamsin ignored Kevin's question and looked at her mum. 'Who's with Dad?' There was a recriminating tone to her voice which said *you shouldn't have left him.*

Kevin stepped in. 'I went to see Joe and offered to bring her home to catch up on some shut-eye.'

Tamsin rounded on her husband. 'I wasn't talking to you.'

'I was just saying—'

'Well, don't!'

'Tamsin, what's got into you? Can't we talk like two civilised—'

'Mia, honey,' said Clara, taking her hand. 'Why don't we pop inside and make everyone lunch.'

Mia reluctantly let go of Daddy's hand.

She led Mia into the house, passing by the lounge on the way to the kitchen. Sophie was sitting in the room with headphones on listening to music on her phone.

Dorothy was sitting in the chair opposite reading a newspaper. She caught her trying to scoot past the open doorway unnoticed. 'Why aren't you at the hospital with Joe?'

Clara rolled her eyes. 'I'm tired, Dorothy. I haven't slept for three days. I needed to go home, freshen up, and have a lie-down.'

Dorothy glared at her daughter-in-law. 'What is it with the likes of you? It's all *me, me, me*. Can't you think about someone other than yourself for a change?'

'The likes of me?' She felt like marching in there, snatching her precious daily rag and tearing it into tiny pieces. Why did Dorothy always, *always* play the class card, making her feel as though she was a spoilt, entitled brat?

'Grandma, I'm hungry.' Mia tugged on her hand, dragging her towards the kitchen.

'You're hungry?' said Clara in surprise. Mia hadn't been hungry all weekend since she'd turned up here with Tamsin and Sophie. Now she'd seen her dad, her appetite had returned. Dorothy was all but forgotten in her haste to make Mia a bite to eat before she changed her mind.

'There.' She set a plate of sandwiches down on the kitchen table along with a glass of milk, and a slice of homemade cake.

'I want lunch,' Dorothy shouted from the lounge.

'Make it yourself,' Clara said under her breath.

'Shall I take my sandwiches into the lounge and share them with Dot?'

'That's kind of you, Mia, but I will make Dorothy and your sister lunch too.'

'What about Mummy and Daddy?'

Clara sighed. She'd forgotten about them. 'I'll see if they've finished loading the shopping into the hall.'

She whipped out of the kitchen hoping they weren't having a full-blown row on her doorstep. She wished she'd stayed at Joe's bedside. Coming home was proving far more tiring than sitting in the uncomfortable hospital chair.

She walked over to the front door, bent down to pick up two shopping bags and heard Kevin and Tamsin arguing outside.

'I don't want to go with you to the hospital,' Tamsin was saying.

'In that case, I'll look after the girls.'

'No.'

'Why not? What has got into you? First you walk out for no reason, taking the girls with you. Now, you don't want me to see them? What the hell have I done to deserve this?'

Clara hovered by the door feeling ashamed for spying on them, but she desperately wanted to know what was going on. Why *had* Tamsin left Kevin?

Tamsin said, 'I'm going to see Dad.'

The next thing Clara heard was the sound of Joe's car engine revving up. She poked her head outside as Tamsin headed off down the street.

Kevin turned around to look at Clara. He sighed. 'Guess I'm not seeing Joe today.'

'I've got the girls if you want to go after her. I mean if you want to follow her to the hospital.'

Kevin waved his hand as if to say *what's the point?* 'Here, let me help you with those.' He took the shopping bags out of her hands leaving her standing on the doorstep staring up the street. She still couldn't believe it. They had been together since they were sixteen. Why would she walk out on their marriage now?

'Where's my lunch?' Dorothy bellowed.

Clara had the impulse to phone for a taxi to return to the hospital. Instead she turned on her heel, stepped into the house and closed the front door.

When she walked into the kitchen, Kevin had just finished

making cheese sandwiches. 'I'll pop these next door,' he said striding past Clara with a tea tray laden with a platter of sandwiches and some plates. She heard Dorothy's exclaim, 'Oh, it's Kevin. I didn't know you were here. How lovely to see you.'

'You too, Dot.'

Sophie took her plate and said, 'Hi Dad,' as though the last few days hadn't happened, and Mum hadn't left their dad and taken them to their grandparents.

Clara lingered by the lounge door watching all this.

Kevin smiled at his eldest daughter before turning around. He stopped in front of Clara. 'I made you lunch too if you're hungry. I'll keep an eye on Dot if you want to have a lie-down.'

Clara smiled at Kevin. A Londoner through and through. He wasn't an East End Boy like Joe but hailed from North London – Hendon to be exact – which was where he'd met Tamsin at a friend's sixteenth birthday party. It shouldn't have surprised Clara that Dorothy hit it off with Tamsin's husband; he was from a working-class background after all. But there was one thing which, on paper, should not have endeared him to a woman like Dorothy who appeared to mistrust anybody not like her – an East Ender, working-class. And white.

Kevin's parents were Jamaican immigrants who arrived in England in the 1950s. Both Kevin's parents had passed away, but Clara recalled the laughter and joviality that used to fill a room whenever they visited. And when Dorothy got together with Kevin's parents, they were a riot. They were good friends.

'Is there anything else I can get you, Dot?' asked Kevin, squatting his six-foot frame down in front of her and putting an affectionate hand on her arm.

Dorothy said, 'I rather fancy a cup of tea.'

'A cup of tea coming up.'

Clara followed Kevin back into the kitchen. 'You know what? I will have a lie-down.'

She walked out of the kitchen passing Mia with her empty

plate and overheard Mia asking her Dad, 'Can we come home with you tonight?'

Clara stopped in the doorway wondering what Kevin would say.

Kevin said, 'I'd like that very much, sweetheart. The thing is your Grandma and Dorothy need some company while Granddad is in hospital. So, it would be really kind of you to stay here and help them out.'

'Can you stay too?'

'Well, that is a good idea, but Daddy has got clients he has to meet otherwise they might go away and see someone else. Then Daddy's firm won't get the contract to build their nice houses. We wouldn't want that, would we?'

'Mia shook her head and opened her yoghurt pot.'

Kevin glanced over at Clara with a pained expression.

Clara said, 'I'm sure things will work themselves out,' referring to Tamsin and whatever was going on.

'I hope so,' Kevin commented staring at Mia.

She left them in the kitchen and walked up the stairs thinking about her daughter. She hoped Tamsin hadn't done something stupid, like have an affair. Would Kevin be able to forgive her? Why would she jeopardise everything she had for a fling? It made little sense. Clara marched upstairs. She didn't know how she would sleep now and wanted to speak to Tamsin and find out what was going on.

She walked into her bedroom and found her mobile phone on the dressing table where she'd left it three days ago. It needed recharging. She'd left the house without it when the police arrived and took her to the hospital. She'd been keeping in touch with Tamsin through the hospital payphone.

Clara found the recharger and plugged it into the wall socket discovering six missed calls – all from Debs.

Clara kicked off her shoes and sat on the bed listening to the messages. She'd missed their usual lunch date. Then Debs contacted because the judge had completed her divorce and she wanted to celebrate. Followed by another message from a worried Debs thinking Clara was avoiding her because she didn't wish to be friends with a divorcee. "I won't be suddenly making eyes at Joe if that's what you're thinking."

'Oh Debs,' she said to the empty room. It was a ridiculous thing for Debs to say, but it happened; when people divorced, so-called friends – couples – who they might have known for years disown them. It was as though they had become social pariahs just because they were no longer married.

The trouble was Clara didn't want to talk about Joe's car accident, but if she didn't phone her, she wouldn't put it past Debs to pop round. And if talking about Joe was hard enough, there was also the subject of her mother-in-law staying in her house, and her daughter leaving Kevin. The last few days were overwhelming. She didn't know how to cope. Taking it one day at a time was all she could do.

Clara was trying to quell the impulse to run away until it had all blown over and her life was back to normal; Joe driving his taxi all the hours god sent, the girls at home with their parents where they belonged, and Dorothy… Clara frowned. She knew it was an awful thought but right now she couldn't care less where Dorothy was if it wasn't here – under her roof.

Clara lay down on her bed and stared at the ceiling. *And to think, the other day I wished our lives would change.* She thought of the homeless person they had bumped into and his prophetic words: *have a care; your life could change in a heartbeat.*

17

She sat up in bed, picked up the phone on her bedside table and dialled Deb's number. She was looking forward to a friendly chat.

'I thought something dreadful had happened.'

Clara closed her eyes. 'Well, funny you should say that…'

She told Debs about Joe going away to another of those seminars and the car accident on the way home. 'The good news was he is off the ventilator. He had a bleed on the brain. But you know Joe, he's larger than life. He'll pull through – I just know it.' Somewhere in the conversation she had slipped in about the doctor suggesting she make sure his affairs were in order.

She felt a lump in her throat as she tried to convince her friend, and herself, that everything would be okay. That's what she'd phoned Debs for: a bit of reassurance. Her friend always looked on the bright side of life. Debs would put her mind at ease and convince her she had nothing to worry about.

'Why do you think Joe attended the seminar in Southwold and not here in London?' The question threw Clara. Out of everything she'd told her, why was she focusing on that? 'That's of no consequence now.'

'Are you sure?'

'Joe has been in a car accident,' she reminded her. 'He's in a coma. I'm praying he pulls through. He *will* pull through, won't he?'

'Of course he will.'

There was silence on the phone.

'Debs?'

'Did you do what the doctor advised, Clara? Are his affairs in order?'

Clara couldn't believe she asked that question. 'You said he'd pull through.'

'Yes, I'm sure he will, but…'

Now Debs sounded like the doctor.

'It doesn't hurt to be prepared if something untoward happens.'

Debs was making her anxious. She lay down on the bed with the phone to her ear. Now she wished she hadn't phoned.

'I'll speak to Gerald. We're still on good terms despite the divorce. In fact, since we split up, we've become great friends. Sorry, I digress. Look, you will need a solicitor. I can arrange for you to stop by his office with any paperwork.'

Clara shook her head. She did not want to search for the will or instruct a solicitor. What nonsense. Besides, she didn't want to tempt fate. 'Everything will be fine, don't you worry' she reassured Debs; convinced things would get back to normal soon. She did her best to ignore the voice in her head reminding her of the last words Joe had spoken before he left home. "This trip will change our lives."

She waited for her friend to say something. 'Debs – are you still there?'

'But what if something unexpected happens? I don't mean to sound harsh, but you can't bury your head in the sand over this one. Think about the future. There's your daughter and granddaughters to consider too. What if, heaven forbid, he didn't pull through and you hadn't sorted out his estate?'

His estate. She found that laughable; it wasn't as though they were wealthy. He owned a black cab and a three-bedroom semi-detached property in North London, which he'd re-mortgaged to fund those silly get-rich-quick schemes. Her friends were in a different league with their second homes and large savings pots. One was even paying for their grandchildren to go to fee-paying schools.

She knew where this was coming from. Despite Debs remaining on good terms with her husband, she hadn't told her everything about the break-up. She found out from a mutual friend that Debbie's husband had had a fling with his legal assistant. It was so clichéd, but true. Little wonder Debs only saw the worst-case scenario.

Clara imagined she had been through a terrible time discovering her husband had cheated on her. What if that had happened to her? But she would never have to deal with that. Joe worshiped the ground she walked on – always had, always will. Perhaps that's why Debs hadn't been very forthcoming over the real nature of her marriage break-up.

Debbie said, 'Will you promise me you will think about what I said? I'd be happier knowing you had things in place if…'

Clara sighed. She realised Debs was worried about her. 'Oh, all right. '

'You promise?'

'Yes, cross my heart and hope to—' she stopped.

'I'll find out when Gerald has a free appointment and get back to you. In the meantime, if you want me to pop over with some shopping, do some housework – anything – call me.'

She heard Mia and Sophie arguing downstairs, and Dorothy shouting out for Kevin to make her another cup of tea. 'Debs, that's very kind of you to offer but…'

'You want alone time to process all this.'

Alone time? She rolled her eyes at the cacophony downstairs. *Chance would be a fine thing.* She signed off promising to contact her the moment there was any change.

As she reached over and placed the handset in the cradle, she felt a pang of guilt for not being at Joe's bedside. She rolled over on her side and put a pillow over her head trying to drown out the noise downstairs. Someone had turned on the television. It was loud. She could hear the news. She guessed it was Dorothy. She must have forgotten to switch on her hearing aid again.

She had barely slept when she heard Dorothy's dog and his annoying *yap, yap, yap* followed a moment later by an angry *hissing.*

Clara threw the pillow on the floor and opened her eyes to find Marley sitting on the bed. He meowed at her.

'What? You think it's my fault Dorothy came to stay and brought that annoying Yorkshire terrier with her?'

Marley meowed even louder.

'Well, I don't have to lie here and listen to you berating me!' She rose from the bed wondering why she had suddenly started talking to the cat. Feeling stressed, she replayed the conversation with Debs. She didn't want to face it, and now she couldn't get the question out of her mind: what if he never woke up? She shook her head. *Don't even go there.*

Clara refused to acknowledge Deb's so-called worst-case scenario. However, she decided to find the will and other financial paperwork, stuff it in an envelope and pass it on to Gerald for safekeeping. She would search for it now as she couldn't sleep. The moment she drifted off, all she saw was Joe lying in hospital and her stomach churned.

Clara got out of bed. 'I'm doing this for Debs,' she said as she walked down the stairs, trying to convince herself that going to all this trouble was unnecessary. She wandered into the kitchen to find Kevin still running around after Dorothy. 'I'm feeding the dog, then making Dorothy a cup of tea. Would you like one?' offered Kevin.

'There's something I need to do.' She walked over to a kitchen drawer and rummaged through odds and ends until she found the spare key, then stepped out the back door into the garden.

'Clara?'

'I'm popping out to the shed.'

'The shed?' Kevin glanced out the kitchen window at the large wooden structure at the bottom of the garden. 'Do you mean Joe's man cave?' It was Joe's pride and joy. Kevin helped him choose it then employed friends to erect it and install power and light.

It wasn't a shed at all but a home office with double patio doors and a view of the garden. There was also a small veranda where Joe sat on a chair with his laptop to plan his next disastrous scheme that would fail spectacularly.

Clara thought Joe's man cave was an expensive waste of money when they had a spare bedroom to use as a study. What she later discovered was he wanted a home office as far from the house as possible. It was somewhere private, away from prying eyes – away from her. He was less likely to be disturbed at the bottom of the garden than in another room in the house.

She knew why he wanted his privacy. This was where Joe researched and planned the next brilliant idea that would lead to The Big Payday. Clara sighed. Who could foresee his last oh-so-brilliant idea would lead to a trip to casualty and an extended stay in the hospital in a coma?

She put the key in the lock. She couldn't remember the last time she had ventured down here. When it was first put up, Joe had furnished it with a desk, chair, filing cabinet, and some bookshelves. They sat together inside the cosy wooden structure and he spoke about his plans for their retirement.

That's when he told her about the yacht he wanted to buy to cruise around the Mediterranean; something large enough to live on in relative comfort. They would anchor off beautiful coves surrounded by an azure blue sea, or in fishing harbours with white-washed villas under pantile roofs.

Clara paused before she opened the door. Ten years had gone by since that conversation about Joe's plans for their future.

'Ten years,' she whispered. And he was still no nearer to

achieving his dream. Thinking of Joe lying comatose in that hospital bed, she felt dreadful when she recalled her response after he'd told her what he dreamed of doing in retirement. She wanted to know how long they'd be away.

"How long?" he'd said in surprise. "However long it takes."

"*What* takes?"

"Seeing the Med – seeing the world." He'd used the term, "sailing off into the sunset." "But what will we *do* all day?" she'd replied.

"*Do*?" He'd stared at her over his glasses with a perplexed look on his face. "Relax, read, sun ourselves, maybe some snorkelling. It doesn't matter what we *do* all day? He'd got shirty at that point. 'Why – have you got a better idea?"

Clara stood outside the shed staring at the door thinking back to that conversation. She didn't have a better idea but told him she was after something a little more... adventurous.

She recalled his response. "Cruising around the med is adventurous". 'Imagine all the little towns and coves we will discover. We could be like Joan and Jack from *Romancing the Stone*."

Clara smiled when she remembered that movie – one of Joe's favourites. She also remembered pointing out that it wasn't until the sequel to *Romancing the Stone - Jewell in the Nile* - that Joan and Jack went cruising around in a yacht. And they got mighty bored being stuck together on a boat doing nothing much.

Joe had suggested she might write a book. "People retire and try their hand at novel-writing all the time." She then asked him to name one person out of their friends who had attempted to write a novel when they retired.

"Well, I'm sure someone has."

Not the type to sit around all day – even if she were on a boat surrounded by beautiful scenery, it would not inspire her to write – or paint; that was Joe's other suggestion.

"There has to be something you want to do with your life besides shopping," he'd said matter-of-factly. That was the end of the conversation. She only shopped because she was unhappy. She'd said as much. Joe's answer was, once again, to go travelling on his yacht which so far hadn't materialised.

Conversations about retirement always came back to sailing around the med. It didn't help that every time he'd asked her what she wanted to do instead, Clara didn't have a clue. However, as time passed, the likelihood of Joe's dream coming true diminished with each failed investment opportunity. What Clara wanted to do with her life became a moot point as it became clear their lives weren't about to change any time soon.

Now she wished she hadn't been negative. She'd tell him she would love to go sailing around the med with him. The alternative didn't bear thinking about. What would she do without him?

18

Clara opened the door to Joe's home office and walked straight over to the desk to find his will. She recalled what had precipitated Joe's sudden urge to make a will a few years ago. A friend who worked as a cab driver had died suddenly of a heart attack. It had rocked Joe to the core. One day his friend was there, making jokes over the radio, and the next he wasn't.

He had given it to her to read before he'd placed it in the envelope and sealed it. There were no surprises. She knew what was inside. She picked up the envelope and closed the drawer. On top of the filing cabinet was a black concertina file containing details about the mortgage, along with bank accounts, loans and credit cards he'd had over the years. The bulging file was fit to burst. Joe chucked nothing away.

Debs had mentioned something about giving Gerald any financial paperwork she could find. She might as well take the file with her too.

Perhaps if Joe took longer to recover, it was a good idea for Gerald to examine their finances. Bills had to be paid. She was never involved with the financial side of things. Joe brought in the money and paid all the household bills. The rest went on surprise gifts and breaks away for his wife. Then there was the cash he gave her so she could indulge in her favourite pastime – shopping.

Joe must have taken on loans to pay for his man cave not to mention those bad investment decisions which led to a black financial hole. Looking at the bulging concertina file, she didn't want to open a Pandora's Box and find out what was inside. She lifted it down from the filing cabinet disturbing the large pin board above. A piece of notepaper floated down, landing on the work surface. She put the folder down on the floor and looked at his desk covered in paperwork.

She sat in the comfortable leather chair and picked up a scrap of notepaper at random. Written on it were the directions to the hotel in Southwold. She sat there for a few minutes fashioning the papers into a neat pile and glanced out of the window. Clara was stalling. She didn't fancy walking back to the house and entering the fray of two argumentative grandchildren and a demanding mother-in-law. For now, Kevin was keeping the peace.

Under the last scrap of paper, she discovered a notepad hidden from view. In the past, whenever Joe bought himself a pad, it heralded the start of a new investment idea.

'Some things never change,' she said sadly as she opened the pad and flicked through the pages, wondering what the seminar had been about. She had taken little notice of the details when he'd been talking about it the night before he left. Now, she wanted to know what he was getting himself into.

Kevin knocked on the door, making her jump. He poked his head inside. 'Tamsin's back.'

'Already?' she said in surprise. 'Has Joe woken up?'

'I don't think so.'

'I need to speak to Tamsin.' She stepped outside and locked the door behind her. Through the glass doors she saw the envelope and concertina file she'd left on the desk. When she was ready, she'd pay a visit to Gerald and hand them over.

She slipped the key in her coat pocket and noticed she still had Joe's notebook in her hand. 'Oh, bother.' She was intending to put the notebook back on his desk, when Kevin said, 'Tamsin didn't get to see Joe. That's why she left. The hospital only wanted one visitor at a time in his room. Apparently, there was already somebody there.'

Clara looked at him quizzically. Unless some long-lost relative had turned up, as far as she was aware all Joe's close relations were right here in this house. 'Who was it – do you know?'

'Some woman – I think.'

'A woman? What woman?'

Kevin shrugged. 'You better ask Tamsin.'

Clara hurried up the garden towards the house feeling upset for Tamsin that she didn't get to see her dad. She imagined Tamsin could do with a hug, but she was sitting at the kitchen table texting on her phone like it was just another ordinary day.

Who on earth was she texting? She was approaching forty for goodness sake, not some love-struck fourteen-year-old with a crush on a boy she couldn't wait to tell her friends about. Thinking of those two words, *love struck,* Clara caught an expression on Tamsin's face that she hadn't seen in a long time.

Kevin walked through the back door. Tamsin wasn't texting her husband. Maybe it was just one of her friends keeping her buoyed up under these difficult circumstances, much like her own friend, Debbie. Except Debbie hadn't buoyed her up.

She remembered the white envelope and the concertina file containing financial documents she'd promised to drop off at Gerald's firm of solicitors when she had a chance. Clara would rather not think about that; it was making her anxious. However, she felt her anxiety levels rising anyway as she stared at Tamsin. She hoped it *was* just a friend she was texting. Her next thought did not help her anxiety levels – who was the woman sitting at her husband's bedside?

'Tamsin.' She stared at her daughter. 'Tamsin!'

'Oh, Sorry, I didn't see you there.'

'Well, I'm not surprised. Put that away for a moment please? I want to ask you something.'

Tamsin tore her eyes from the phone. 'What is it?'

'Kevin said you didn't get to visit Dad this morning because there was someone else already with him.'

'Uh-huh.' Tamsin didn't seem too perturbed by that. She stole a glance at her phone which did not go unnoticed.

Clara folded her arms. 'I want to know who was visiting your father?'

Tamsin shrugged. 'How should I know?'

'Didn't you notice who it was?'

'Uh-uh.' Tamsin shook her head. 'Some woman.'

'Would you mind looking at me while I'm talking to you?'

Tamsin rolled her eyes. 'What is the problem?'

'I would like you to answer my question, please.'

'I just did,' she replied sarcastically.

Clara stood her ground staring at her daughter.

Tamsin eyed her mother and realised she meant business. She put her phone down on the table. 'Look, I imagine it was a family friend – one of your friends. I don't know her. Why don't you see for yourself?'

'I might just do that.' She fetched her handbag, looked at the notebook still in her hand, slipped it inside her bag and returned to the kitchen. 'Do you want to come to the hospital with me? I'll have words with the doctor. There is no reason we cannot visit him together.'

'Ah.'

Clara turned around at the sound of Kevin's voice. He had something on his mind.

'Oh, do spit it out, Kev, for god's sake!'

Clara wished she wouldn't speak to Kevin like that. He'd move heaven and earth for her and the girls and reminded Clara of Joe. He was just the same. A family man through and through. Kevin had started his business to secure his family's financial future. From what she had seen over the years he had been a good husband and father. If guilty of any failings, it was not spending enough time with his children as he grew his business.

'I'm afraid a meeting has come up,' Kevin replied.

'So, you can't look after the girls,' Tamsin said flatly.

'I'm sorry. It's an important client.'

'Of course. All your clients are important. When are you going to put us first for a change?'

'If it had been anybody else, I would have rescheduled…'

Tamsin's face said she'd heard it all before.

Kevin edged out the door and Clara followed. 'I can give you a lift to the hospital. It's on my way.'

Clara nodded, called out to Tamsin that she was off and then grabbed her coat.

Kevin opened the passenger door for her. She eyed Kevin as she got into the car. 'He will be all right, won't he?' He gave her a smile of reassurance as he started the car. 'If anyone can pull through this, it's Joe. He's not a quitter; I'll say that for him.'

Clara managed a smile. She was thinking of the new notebook in her bag she had picked up from his desk, no doubt outlining his next scheme for The Big Payday. Joe wasn't one to give up without a fight. He'd proved that with every new venture he'd started after the last one failed. Joe just picked himself up and started again. That's who he was. He wouldn't quit. It wasn't in his nature.

'You're right, Kevin. He'd fight to his dying… breath.' Clara's face dropped. She wished she hadn't couched it in quite those terms.

19

They drove to the hospital in silence apart from Kevin's lame attempts to cheer her up. She knew was being kind, but it made her feel worse.

Kevin apologised. 'I can be an ass sometimes.'

She looked at her son-in-law. 'Nothing could be further from the truth.' Kevin was one of the nicest young men she had ever met. She could not understand Tamsin's behaviour of late. What had got into her? She forced herself not to dwell on Tamsin and Kevin's problems.

After pulling into a parking space in the hospital car park, Kevin left the car engine turning over and shifted in his seat to look at Clara. 'I feel terrible, but I can't come in and see Joe right now because I've got to meet this client.' Kevin winced as though he'd said the most awful thing imaginable.

She placed her hand on his arm. 'I understand, Kevin. Please go to your meeting. There's nothing you can do here.'

Kevin sighed in relief. 'You have my number if—' He stopped short unsure where he was going with that.

'When he wakes up, I'll let you know.'

Kevin nodded.

A moment later, she was standing at the kerb watching Kevin draw out of the parking space. He stopped the car to give her a wave before setting off for his meeting.

She turned around and stared at the depressing nineteen seventies building. Joe had to wake up thought Clara as she walked inside the hospital entrance. It couldn't all end here.

Three floors up, she stepped out of the lift and made her way toward the ward. He had a side room to himself. The door was open. She heard a voice from inside the room. Her heart quickened. Was he awake? She slowed forcing herself not to get her hopes up with the miracle she'd been praying for.

She paused near the open doorway and realised it couldn't be Joe because the voice was distinctly feminine. Maybe it was a nurse doing her rounds. She put on a brave face, about to walk in and ask the nurse how he was doing when she spotted a woman sitting at Joe's bedside. Clara stopped in surprise. The visitor Tamsin mentioned was still here.

Clara furrowed her brow. Who could she be? Apart from Debs, she'd told no one else what had happened yet.

She was about to step into the room and find out, when she overheard the woman say, 'You silly fool. Now what am I going to do? We had plans, you and me.'

Clara found herself rooted to the spot. Plans? She shifted her attention to Joe. Since when did he ever make plans besides these hare-brained schemes for The Big Payday which never amounted to a hill of beans?

The woman continued, 'Did you even tell her about us?'

Her? Us? What was this all about? Her heart raced as she listened to the brazen woman visiting Joe in the hospital when his wife or family might turn up.

She was about to walk into the room and introduce herself to the woman who had designs on her husband, when the sound of a high-pitched alarm startled her. As she lingered in the hall outside, she got caught up in a wave of nurses and doctors running down the ward with a medical emergency.

More staff followed with a crash cart. She stepped into the room next door out of the way. Relatives were sitting around another patient's bedside. Clara apologised for the intrusion. When the alarm stopped ringing, and everything went quiet in the main corridor, she returned to Joe's room. The person sitting at his bedside was no longer there. Clara retraced her steps to the nurse's station. 'Did a woman pass this way?'

'Lots of visitors come and go this time in the morning. Can you describe her?'

Clara frowned. 'Well, let me see. She had short dark hair, rather overweight, and around my age…?'

The nurse shook her head. 'I'm sorry, but with all the commotion I left my desk for several minutes to help. She may have passed by when I wasn't here.'

'The consultant said your husband is improving.'

'Is he now?' said Clara seething underneath her calm exterior. "We had plans, you and I," she repeated under her breath.

'I'm sorry – what was that?'

Clara glanced at the nurse. 'It's nothing.'

But it wasn't *nothing*. She returned to Joe's room and took a seat next to his bed where the woman had been sitting less than five minutes ago. She stared at her husband. He looked like he was sleeping, which he was – kind of. A sleep from which he couldn't wake up – not yet anyway.

'Wake up – damn you!' Clara demanded. 'Who was that woman?'

Every time she heard footsteps approaching the room she looked up, her eyes wide, her heart skipping a beat expecting the woman's return. Nurses passed back and forth outside the room, but there was no sign of the lady who had been sitting at Joe's bedside. Clara guessed she wasn't coming back – not today at any rate.

She breathed an audible sigh of relief. Although she wanted to confront the woman and ask her what she was doing talking to her husband as though… as though… Clara bit her lip. As though they were having an affair.

She shook her head no; it wasn't true. It couldn't be. She stared at Joe and asked, 'Were you having an affair?' Saying the words out loud made it sound ridiculous. Joe – having an affair? There had to be a mistake. She read too much into what might have been an innocent remark.

No matter what explanation she came up with to convince herself nothing was going on between Joe and this woman, she'd heard what she'd heard. We had plans, you and me. Whether it was innocent, her husband was keeping a secret from her.

A shrill sound snapped her back from the brink of self-pity. It took a moment for her to recognise the sound of her mobile phone. She opened her handbag to find her phone and had a thought. Perhaps she was a colleague. Clara had informed his boss about the accident. She had little choice. He was meant to return to work on Monday after his weekend away in Southwold.

She sighed. On top of the worry over Joe's health, was her concern over what would happen if he was unfit to return to work at all. They depended on his income.

She reached for her phone, but the caller rang off. She checked the missed calls and discovered it was Tamsin. If it were important, she'd call back. Clara put the phone back in her handbag and pulled the chair closer to Joe's bed. She put a tentative hand on his, squeezed it gently, but got no response in return; no strong fingers closing around hers. Not even a twitch.

Clara heaved a sigh. 'Come on, Joe. You've had the mother of all lie-ins. Now it's time to wake up.' She looked him over. 'I refuse to believe anything is going on between you and that woman.'

She changed tack. 'I've got an idea. We will get a few brochures and save-up to go on a Mediterranean cruise? I know you wanted to sail away on your own private yacht, but let's try it out before The Big Payday arrives?' It was a splendid idea.

She suddenly came over tearful at the thought Joe would never see The Big Payday. He might not even see the

Mediterranean. Don't go there she berated herself. He's not dead. She stared at the bandage around his forehead. He's just sleeping to enable his body to heal.

'Come back Joe? I'm not meant to be on my own. You're the only one who understands why that is.'

She delved into her handbag for a tissue to wipe her eyes. Her hand closed around Joe's notebook instead. She took it out, placed it on the bed and found a small packet of travel-sized tissues. She dried her eyes then picked up the notebook. She was about to put it back in her bag when it occurred to her she had brought nothing to read. She wasn't interested in Joe's next scheme to make a quick buck, but it would occupy her while she sat with Joe. Besides, it wouldn't hurt to find out what he was up to next.

Clara opened the notebook.

Ten minutes later, Clara jumped out of her seat and stood staring at Joe in disbelief. 'How could you!' she yelled, before running out of the room.

'Mrs Delaney…?' the nurse called after her as she ran past the nurse's station and out the door.

20

Clara sat in the taxi trying to calm down. On her way home from the hospital, she had time to reflect on what she'd read in the notebook and wondered if she was overreacting. Joe's next outlandish plan for The Big Payday was so fantastical that it was a stupid idea even for him. She slipped the notebook out of her bag and sat there leafing through the pages. There had to be an explanation. If it were true, and this was Joe's plan, then she couldn't believe he would do that to her.

As the taxi turned down their street, she thought of the office at the bottom of the garden – Joe's man-cave. He knew she never ventured down there. Why would she? That was his centre of operations for the stupid schemes he got himself involved in that Clara wanted no part of. He always had something in the pipeline.

She remembered the paperwork strewn on his desk which she had taken no notice of when tidying it into neat piles. She stared at the notebook. There was a way of finding out if what he had written in these pages was true.

'Er… Miss?'

Preoccupied, it hadn't registered she had arrived home. She handed over her fare and watched the taxi disappear down the street and wondered if the driver was one of Joe's work colleagues.

She glanced at the notebook in her hand and thought of the lady sitting at Joe's bedside. She had convinced herself the woman had been talking nonsense. Now she wasn't so sure.

She turned on her heel and headed for the front door. Was it only a few days ago she had returned home in a taxi from her lunch date with Debs? Apart from a twinge of guilt at the money spent, she did not have a care in the world. Dependable Joe would work another shift to pay for all her new purchases.

Clara frowned. Dependable, reliable Joe. She looked at the notebook. Not dependable *or* reliable if what he wrote in these pages was true. Quite the reverse.

It crossed her mind as she put the key in the lock that perhaps Joe was sick of working all hours to cover everything – including her hefty shopping bills. But he'd never complained about it. It made this discovery if true, even more shocking.

She let herself into the house and made her way to the kitchen. She wanted to get to Joe's man cave and look through his paperwork before Tamsin, the girls or, heaven forbid, Dorothy nabbed her for something.

She paused before stepping out into the back garden. The house was quiet. Too quiet. Clara backtracked and popped her head in the lounge. She then called up the stairs. Nobody was home. She returned to the sitting room and looked out the front window. Joe's car wasn't there.

Then she remembered her mobile phone and the call from Tamsin and guessed she had taken Dorothy and the girls to visit Joe. She'd just missed them and debated whether to phone Tamsin and let her know she had left the hospital. Everyone would expect dinner when they arrived home. Clara decided not to make the call. There was something else more important to do first. Find out if Joe intended to go through with the plan she'd discovered.

She returned to the kitchen, opened the back door and stalked down the garden path. Inside Joe's man cave she stood staring at his desk, eyeing the paperwork she collated into a neat pile earlier. She didn't know what she was looking for. Evidence? But evidence of what? That he'd put the plan in motion he wrote in his notebook?

Clara sat in the office chair and picked up a piece of paper from the pile. It was the electricity bill. She put that to one side. There were odds and ends like the window-cleaner's bill and quotes for a conservatory on the back of the house. She recalled asking him where the money was coming from.

Sifting through the paperwork she found nothing to worry about. That's when she saw it at the bottom of the pile. It was a newspaper cutting from an article about a missing person. They went out canoeing in the sea and drowned but were found months later alive and well. It turned out he faked his own death.

Her attention shifted from the newspaper article to the notebook. She narrowed her eyes and reached across Joe's desk wondering what research on his computer might unearth. Clara switched it on. She could find her way around the computer to locate Joe's files, and his most recent online search history.

There was a password. She knew what it was; there were no secrets between them – or so she thought. She logged on with Joe's password, which was her name and age: Clara59. She would be sixty this year. They both were.

'Hell of a way to celebrate turning sixty,' she said out loud, wondering if the contents of the notebook were true: he was planning to leave her. She tried not to feel guilty about going through his personal files. She'd never done this before, having no reason to think Joe might leave her for someone else.

She brought up Joe's search history and scanned the websites he'd been looking at over the last few weeks. Someone more savvy might have deleted their search history. But then he had no idea he would end up comatose in a hospital bed with his life, his plans, unravelling in his absence.

A short time later, Clara logged off and sat there staring out the glass doors into the garden beyond. A question kept running through her mind, *why now? After all these years, why was he leaving her now?* Was it something to do with that woman? Did she help him come up with this stupid plan?

Clara picked up Joe's notebook, unsure what to do with it. She couldn't leave it lying around in case Tamsin or the girls found it. She looked around Joe's man cave, wondering where she could hide it. The sound of her mobile phone made her jump. Was it the hospital calling? Oh, how she wanted him to wake up so she could confront him over *this!* Clara threw the notebook across the room and reached for her phone.

'Clara, it's Debs. I wanted to see how you are?' Before she could answer, Deb's said, 'You will see Gerald and drop off the paperwork?'

She narrowed her eyes and replied, 'You bet I am,' as she walked over to retrieve the notebook on the floor by the door.

'Good, because I made you an appointment to see Gerald. You don't want to hear it, but as your friend I think you should consider the worst-case scenario and get his affairs in order in case—'

On hearing the words, *worst-case scenario* and *affairs*, she burst into tears.

'Oh Clara, has something happened? Is it Joe? Has he…?'

Clara realised what she was trying to say. Had Joe taken a turn for the worse or died? She looked at the notebook and wished he *had* perished in that car accident.

'Clara, honey, what's happened?'

The words spilled out in a jumble, 'It's Joe. He was planning to leave me. There was a woman at his hospital bed talking about their plans. He was intending to fake his own death and—'

'Clara, you're not making any sense.'

It sounded ridiculous. Debs was right: it made little sense. But she had the notebook, the newspaper clipping, and his search history on the computer. Then there was the hotel in

Southwold where they held the seminar. Why didn't he go to the conference in London? He knew she wouldn't want to come with him to Southwold. Was he planning to go with someone else? Why was he there two nights when the seminar was one day?

Clara was thinking aloud, still on the phone to Debs.

'This woman you said you saw at his bedside,' said Debs, 'perhaps he met her there, in Southwold, like a secret liaison?'

Clara was about to answer when Debs cut in, 'Why was Joe so sure you wouldn't have gone to Southwold with him?'

Not prepared for that question. She stalled.

Debs must have sensed she'd touched on a delicate subject. 'Sorry, it's none of my business.'

Clara sighed. 'It's… it's just something that happened a long time ago. It's nothing.'

'Well, it can't be *nothing* if you still cannot bring yourself to revisit a place from your past.'

Clara swallowed hard. She couldn't recall that time in her life without feeling overwhelmed with sadness. 'I don't want to talk about it.'

Debs fell silent.

Clara worried she'd offended her friend. 'Debbie? Are you still there?'

'I'm still here. Is there anything I can do? Anything at all?'

'Will you look in on Joe?'

'I meant what can I do for *you* – not Joe.'

'I know. The thing is I can't guarantee Tamsin will call into the hospital every day as the girls are on their summer break from school. I need someone to be there if…' Clara trailed off.

'If…?'

'If something happens.'

Debs sighed. 'After everything you've told me, you're still worried about Joe. A word of advice, Clara. You need to put yourself first.'

Put myself first? Clara almost laughed. Debs didn't realise, that's what she'd been doing her whole life, and maybe things had come home to roost. She thought about Joe and his reasons for leaving her.

Not wanting to get into that with Debs, she said, 'Will you do it – will you look in on Joe?'

There was a pause. 'Why – are you going somewhere?'

She looked around Joe's home office. 'I need to get away for a few days.'

'Good girl. You could do with a break. I'll pop in to see Joe, I promise.'

'Thank you, Debbie.'

'Are you going anywhere in particular?'

Clara stared at the notebook in her hand. 'Southwold.'

'But you said—'

Clara told herself she couldn't go back there. Now she must.

'I'd better go.'

'Don't forget you're meeting Gerald with the paperwork.'

'Oh. Right.' She'd almost forgotten. 'I'll pop into his office on the way to the train station.'

She got off the phone before Debbie asked her any more searching questions. Her friend wasn't a busybody, trying to pry into her personal life. They had known Debbie and her husband, Gerald, for years and were lifelong friends. What Clara heard in her friend's voice was a genuine concern. If Debs asked any more questions, she might bottle out of the trip. She wanted to do it now; pack a bag, gather the paperwork for her detour to Gerald's office and head for the train station before she changed her mind.

After forty years, Clara was returning to the place she once called home.

21

'Take a seat. He will be with you shortly.' The receptionist informed Gerald his next client had arrived.

She was just saying, 'I'm not a client,' when Gerald popped his head around the door and smiled at her. 'Come on in, Clara.' He closed the door behind her and perched on the edge of his desk, offering her a seat in one of the leather chairs. She declined and put her suitcase down on a chair. 'I won't be long. I stopped by to drop this off.' She placed the concertina file alongside the envelope containing Joe's will on his desk.

Gerald eyed the large bulging file before turning his attention to Clara. 'I was sorry to hear about Joe's car accident. Debs told me to expect you.'

'I promised Debs I'd bring along the paperwork so you can make sure everything is in order.' 'It's not necessary,' she added. 'Joe will pull through.'

Gerald nodded. 'All the same, it doesn't hurt to be…' He searched for the right word, 'pragmatic.'

It wasn't the word he was looking for. He'd rather not upset Clara by expressing his concern over the possibility Joe might not walk out of this with all his faculties intact. In which case, Clara needed to know where she stood financially if left on her own.

They both fell silent. Gerald studied his friend. The strain was showing on her face. She seemed tired. He spotted the suitcase. Was she going on a trip? Perhaps getting away from it all was just the ticket.

Clara caught Gerald eyeing her suitcase. 'I'll be away for a few days.' She reached over and picked it up, avoiding his gaze. 'Well, best be off.'

'Let me see you out.' Gerald walked over and opened the door. 'Can I get in touch with you if I have any questions?' He threw a glance at his desk where she had left the concertina file and Joe's will.

'Ah.' She hadn't thought of that. She couldn't imagine why he would need to get in touch with her, but she gave Gerald her mobile phone number in case something cropped up.

Gerald whipped over to his desk and wrote the number down on a jotter. He looked at Clara, she was about to close the door. 'Are you going anywhere in particular…?'

He let the sentence hang; it was none of his business. He didn't mean to pry. They'd been friends for years and he was worried about how she was coping. She looked in need of a break. It was odd she was leaving now with things so up in the air with Joe. Perhaps now was not the best time to go on a trip.

Clara paused in the doorway. 'I'm visiting my brother.' And with that, she shut the door.

'Remarkable!' said Gerald to the empty room. In all years he'd known her, he never knew she had a brother.

She stepped outside and hailed a taxi to take her to the train station. She could have left her luggage in the cab that brought her here, but she didn't know how long she'd have to wait to see Gerald. The prospect of shelling out money to let a taxi sit at the kerb waiting for her return seemed an extravagance. She wouldn't have thought twice about doing that in the past.

She climbed into the taxi and was gearing up to wallow in another bout of self-pity, when her phone rang. Clara thought it was Gerald phoning with a query about the paperwork. A quick glance at her phone confirmed it wasn't Gerald but Tamsin.

Clara answered the call wondering what Tamsin's reaction would be when she found out her mum was skipping town.

'You're *what*?'

'I'm going away for a few days.'

'But… but you can't!'

'Why not?'

'Because… because…. well there's Dad – for one thing. Don't you want to be here when he wakes up?'

'Oh, you have no idea.' Clara tried to curb the sarcasm in her voice.

'And what about the girls and me?'

Clara frowned. 'What do you mean?'

''We *are* staying at yours…' Tamsin let the sentence hang.

'Meaning…?' She knew what Tamsin was getting at. Since they were staying at her house, she should be at home, cooking, shopping and entertaining her grandchildren.

Despite her best efforts, Clara could feel the guilt trip creeping in. She racked her brain trying to remember what food was in the fridge and worrying that there was nothing for dinner. *Perhaps I should have done a grocery shop before I set off?* Then she remembered Tamsin had already been shopping.

'Mum, did you hear what I said?'

Clara noted the inflection in her voice, reminiscent of when she was a teenager and about to throw a strop because she wasn't getting her way.

She imagined Tamsin was enjoying slipping back into her teenage self and letting her mum cope with everything on the domestic front. Tamsin did nothing at her own house. She had a cook, a cleaner, and a provider all rolled into one – her husband, Kevin. He worked hard so Tamsin didn't have to lift a finger.

Kevin reminded Clara of Joe until he'd come up with some outlandish scheme to leave her. Tamsin leading the life of Riley, thanks to Kevin, made her cringe. She thought of Joe working long hours while she swanned off meeting her friends and spending outrageous sums of his hard-earned money.

'Well?'

Tamsin's voice snapped her back to the here and now. 'Are you coming home? You can't leave us here on our own. And there's Dorothy and Marley, and Winston, the dog. You cannot expect me to look after them too.'

'I'll be home in a few days.'

'But where are you going? What's so urgent that you've got to leave right now? Dad *is* lying unconscious in a hospital bed,' Tamsin said sarcastically.

'Yes, I'm aware of that thank you.' Clara was also aware of something she could not share with Tamsin right now. Joe had kept things from her. She was determined to get to the bottom of it by visiting the hotel where Joe had stayed. She wanted to find out if he had a secret liaison with *that* woman.

'I don't believe this,' Tamsin was saying over the phone when she realised she couldn't change her mind. 'Can't you at least tell me where you're going?'

Clara didn't answer.

'Dad's in a coma. You're off god-knows-where.' There was a pause. 'Everything will be all right, won't it?' she said in a small voice.

Clara swallowed hard and remembered the woman sitting at Joe's bedside talking about the plans they had together. Tamsin wasn't talking about that and knew nothing about it. Clara wanted to keep it that way – for now. Tamsin was referring to her Dad's condition.

'Everything will be fine,' Clara promised. 'The nurse said he was improving.'

'She did? That's great news.'

'It certainly is.' Clara wanted to confront him about the notebook she had in her possession. She glanced out the taxi window. 'The taxi has arrived at the station. I have to catch my train.'

'A train? You're not flying off anywhere then?'

'No, of course not. I'm going to—' Clara caught herself before she said any more. 'I must go. Call me if there's any change. Don't worry if you can't make it into the hospital every day, Debbie said she'd drop in on him.'

'But that's just it,' said Tamsin. 'Now is not a good time for you to go on a trip—'

Clara had a feeling Gerald thought so too, but she was not about to sit around and wait for Joe to wake up. 'Look after yourself and the girls, oh and Dorothy. Don't forget to feed the cat and dog.' And with that Clara ended the call.

22

Clara looked at the train station and did an about turn, intending to climb back in the taxi and bottle out of her trip. One thing stopped her in her tracks; the woman sitting at Joe's bedside.

Standing in the queue at the ticket office, Clara wondered whether she should have hung around to see if the stranger returned. Then she wouldn't have to wait for Joe to wake up to find out if it were true. Did he intend to leave her?

That's why she was making this trip; a fact-finding mission to learn as much as possible about Joe's weekend jaunt to Southwold. Did he attend the seminar or was he with another woman – with *her*?

'Mummy, who is that lady talking to?'

'Come on, sweetheart, let's move down the platform.'

Clara watched as the mother and child walked past, giving her a wide berth. She looked about her wondering who the youngster was talking about until she realised, *she* was the lady standing on Platform Three chatting to herself.

'Pull yourself together,' Clara hissed under her breath. She wouldn't be surprised if she were losing her marbles. It had been quite a shock; the police arriving at her door in the dead of night to tell her Joe was in surgery after a car accident. Then the discovery of *that* woman. She frowned at Joe's notebook and put it away in her handbag.

As the train pulled into the station, she looked at her ticket and wondered if she could go through with it; she once vowed never to return to Southwold. Despite those feelings of trepidation, something compelled her to board the train.

She chose a seat in economy class. A nice, pleasant gentleman insisted on lifting Clara's suitcase up into the overhead storage. 'Thank you. That's very kind.'

'Oh, no trouble at all,' he said, surprising her by taking a seat opposite. She glanced around the empty carriage and wondered why he'd decided to sit there. She caught him glancing at her hands. Clara moved her hand over her ring finger. For a split second, she thought she'd lost her ring until she remembered taking it off in a fit of anger and throwing it at Joe's computer. It had pinged off the screen and fallen on the floor. Clara found it and put it on Joe's desk. She'd left it as a statement. If he woke up, went home and visited the shed at the bottom of the garden she hoped she'd sent a clear message.

'So, are you going on holiday?'

Clara looked at the gentleman in surprise. He seemed to think the little exchange over her suitcase was an invitation to join her on the journey and have a chat. But to what end? Clara gave him the once over. Her generation, dressed in a business suit, suggesting he might still be working he had no wedding ring either. Clara blushed. Was he chatting her up?

She was astonished. Not that she didn't think she was still attractive. She had aged well and tried with her appearance. The designer clothes helped. She knew how to make the most of her complexion by applying makeup which accentuated her large brown eyes, full lips, and high cheekbones.

Debs always said she looked more like an ageing movie star than a taxi-driver's wife. Clara joked *you could drop the ageing bit if you don't mind.* She spent a small fortune on hair products along with having her hair cut and coloured each month at a London salon.

Clara didn't think at her age someone would take notice of her – not in *that* way. She felt self-conscious as she replied to the gentleman sitting opposite, 'It's not really a holiday. I fancied a break away – that's all.'

It was a fib, but she wasn't about to tell him the real reason for her trip. Although she added, 'I might visit my brother.'

'That's nice. Where are you headed?'

'The coast – Southwold.'

'Oh.' He looked disappointed. 'I live in Woodbridge. My stop is a good hour before yours.'

'I've heard of Woodbridge. It has a river walk.'

'Yes.' He paused as if searching for what to say next. 'You know Southwold was my first choice to live when I semi-retired and moved out of London. It's a really nice place, too far away for a commute though.'

Clara nodded.

'Do you get down there often?'

'It's been a while,' said Clara. She turned her head towards the window, closed her eyes and hoped the gentleman opposite got the message. She wasn't in the mood to chat. Or get chatted up. Flattered by the attention, right now she had too much on her mind to make small talk.

Despite brushing him off she couldn't help a wisp of a smile. Who would have thought at her age it was still possible to meet somebody, purely by chance, that might lead to something more if she was open to the possibility? Suddenly Joe came to mind and the woman sitting at his bedside. That wiped the smile off her face.

Is that how it happened to them? A chance encounter? Perhaps Joe picked her up in his taxi one day. After all, that's how she and Joe first met all those years ago. She remembered the purpose of her journey. This wasn't a break away as the kindly gentleman had put it. She stole a glance at him. He was reading a newspaper spread out on the table.

She turned back to the window and closed her eyes once more wondering what she hoped to gain by this trip. Was she really looking for answers as to why Joe decided, after all these years, to walk out and disappear from her life?

She recalled the conversation she'd had with Tamsin on the phone. How could she tell her only child what she was doing on this train – travelling to the hotel where her father stayed while he hatched plans to leave? But that wasn't the worst of it. Now she was on the train, Clara felt like shedding her old life and starting over too.

What had Debbie said about worst-case scenarios and the importance of thinking about her future? After she'd discovered he was planning to leave her, she realised the worst-case scenario had already happened. If Joe woke up with his faculties intact or did not wake up at all, she had to prepare herself for a future without him.

Perhaps this trip wasn't about Joe at all. She didn't know anymore. She wasn't sure what she was doing on this train. After all these years, something was drawing her home.

23

Jolted awake by the train pulling out of a station Clara stared out the window at the passing scenery as the train gathered speed. It was etched in her memory; small villages nestled in rolling meadows, parish church spires in the distance, and farms with fields full of bright yellow rapeseed. She hadn't visited Suffolk for decades, but the scene was familiar.

She turned her head intending to say something to the gentleman sitting opposite, but he was no longer in his seat. The newspaper spread over the table was gone. Clara realised she must have fallen asleep and missed his stop and was disappointed he departed before she said goodbye.

The carriage had emptied, which begged the question: just how many stops had she slept through? She glanced out of the window as the train slowed on its approach to the next station.

'Oh crumbs!' This was her stop. She wrestled her suitcase from the overhead compartment and alighted from the train. She watched it leave the station and wondered what she would have done if she *had* missed her stop. Chickened out of this silly expedition and just caught the next back to London no doubt.

She walked through the small ticket office. Southwold didn't have a train station; the line didn't go that far, which meant catching a bus to complete her journey.

Outside the station she saw the bus that connected with her

train waiting across the road. Clara sighed. The last time she'd sat on that bus contemplating her future was over forty years ago when running away to London. She wondered what her life would have been like if she hadn't caught the London train and just stayed on the bus and returned home.

'But I didn't,' she whispered, feeling a sudden pang of regret at the life she'd left behind.

She glanced at her watch. It wasn't that late in the evening but she had been the sole passenger standing on the platform when the train departed. There were no commuters. It was quite a journey from here to London.

Clara knew Southwold's reputation; mostly second homes and practically a ghost town out of season. Except this wasn't out of season. There would be families holidaying at the English seaside resort, making the most of the sunshine during the long summer holidays.

'You're the only passenger, Luv,' said the bus driver.

They left the station and set off down the country back roads. Clara settled in for the thirty-minute journey hoping there weren't many holiday-makers when she arrived because she hadn't thought to phone ahead and book a hotel room.

Silly woman, she berated herself, but she *had* spent most of her adult life married to a man who did everything for her including booking accommodation if ever they went away.

The whole point of her trip was to spend the night in the same hotel where Joe stayed. What if they had no vacancies when she arrived? She opened her handbag and found the pamphlet Joe left in the kitchen with the details of the seminar and the hotel in Southwold.

Thirty-five minutes later, after a short walk from the bus stop, Clara stood outside the hotel with her suitcase. She remembered this hotel. Not because she'd stayed here before – she was barely out of her teens when she ran away to London – but everyone knew the poshest hotel in town; a white Georgian building with black leaded windows and a large cast-iron lamp beside the sign – *The Crown Inn.*

Positioned towards the end of the main thoroughfare, it was surrounded by old-fashioned shop fronts. There were many little cafés and eateries selling traditional English cream teas, buns and finger sandwiches. Modern, fashionable barista-style coffee houses catering to the younger set. All this within a five-minute walk of the seafront and the pier.

Clara hesitated. What did she hope to find? Proof that her husband had been unfaithful? She felt uneasy about what might be unearthed if she stayed. Was she thinking about Joe or the past life she'd left behind?

Glancing down the street in the fading light she saw the street lamps flick on one by one. It was too late to turn back. She was only intending to stay one night and then head home.

She stepped into the cosy foyer and walked up to the small reception desk near the grand staircase. She handed over their joint checking-account card to the friendly receptionist and secured a room for the night. Clara smiled. It wasn't just a room – it was a suite. She cast her eye around the foyer and thought if she was staying in the most expensive hotel in town she might as well push the boat out and pay for a suite; not that she had a choice, the standard rooms were sold out.

A member of staff started up the stairs with her suitcase. Clara turned to the young lady on reception with a question. 'My husband came here last weekend to attend a seminar, and I wanted to find out—'

She stopped short staring at the receptionist. How could she couch the question without it sounding as though she was spying on her husband; checking if he had attended the seminar and whether he'd been alone or with another woman?

'We have no information regarding the seminars. They're run by a company not affiliated with the hotel.'

'Oh.' Clara's face dropped.

'The desk over there might be able to help.'

'Ah, you're here!' exclaimed the seminar rep as she approached.

Clara glanced about her wondering who he was talking to, but she was the only guest in the hotel foyer.

The young man thrust a pamphlet in her hand and directed her to the information desk where another rep was handing out name badges. There was one left on the table. The woman leaned across the desk and stuck a name badge on the lapel of Clara's coat.

Before she knew it, she was standing the other side of the double doors in a large conference room. As they closed them behind her, she overheard the young man say, 'Phew, she left it tight.'

Clara tried to open the door when the lights dimmed. There was a hushed silence. The seminar was about to start.

24

Clara was mortified when people turned in their seats to see who was last through the door. She spotted an empty seat and sat down. It was an aisle seat at the end of a row.

She looked down at the name badge; it said Ellen. Good grief, what if Ellen turned up? She might walk through those doors at any moment, flanked by the reps from the foyer, demanding to know why she had stolen her place. There was only one spare seat; the one she was now occupying.

She sat there waiting for the seminar to start. Her thoughts turned to Joe. Was it aimed at people past middle-age, disillusioned with their lives, and looking for a way out – like Joe. When he first started down the road of searching for The Big Payday, he believed attending something like this would solve all their problems.

She shook her head. Look where that led. What was that saying? If it was too good to be true, it probably was. Clara felt sorry for all the people who were here today to change their lives. Instead, it would cost them a lot of money and cause them heartache when they discovered there were no get-rich-quick schemes.

Besides, when did money ever solve your problems? Joe lying in hospital in a coma came to mind. What good would The Big Payday do him now – or her, come to that?

She didn't want to sit through a single minute of this nonsense. Turning in her seat, she looked for another exit when her attention was drawn to the audience. They were mostly retired or soon to be. There wasn't a pre-menopausal woman in sight. The entire crowd, both men and women, appeared to be over fifty. Clara knitted her brow. How strange.

When Joe showed her the leaflet with facts about the seminar, she took no notice of what he said. It was too dark to read the pamphlet thrust in her hands. Propelled into the conference room; she didn't have time to read the details on the large notice board outside the double doors. Growing old gracefully or retiring with dignity, or how to get your Mother-in-Law out of your house and into a home before you can say, she's driving me up the wall?

Joking aside, Clara wasn't interested. She wanted to know when there was a break so she could leave without drawing attention to herself.

Clara heard someone at the podium introduce themselves. She closed her eyes. Here we go…

'Today we are here to reinvent ourselves. My mantra is it's never too late. And I'm guessing that's your mantra too, after all that's why you're sitting here today in a seminar called, *Reinventing Yourself.*'

Clara opened her eyes. What did he say?

'Maybe you had a dream career that never materialised,' continued the speaker, 'or a relationship you want to start, end or even rekindle.'

Clara narrowed her eyes thinking about her husband and that woman at his bedside. Had they met up here and attended this seminar together? Is this where they planned how Joe could end his marriage?

'I'm here to help you realise that dream.'

'It's never too late!' the audience chanted, taking Clara by surprise and making her jump.

The speaker smiled at the audience. 'I see we have a fair few of you that have attended my seminars before.'

A murmur arose in the audience.

'Is this your first time?' asked the woman sitting in the seat next to her.

Clara looked at the woman awaiting a reply who was around her own age.

'First time?' repeated Clara.

The woman nodded toward the speaker, sipping a glass of water during the interval. Consumed with thoughts of Joe, the first half of the seminar was over before she knew it.

'Oh er yes. I've never been to one of these before.'

She smiled at Clara. 'If you want to change your life, you've come to the right place. It gave me the courage to leave my husband at fifty-nine.'

Clara frowned. Is that what this seminar did for Joe – gave him the courage to leave her?

Despite her scepticism, she didn't escape at the interval as she'd planned. There was still no sign of the woman whose name badge she was wearing. Clara didn't expect her to turn up now. But that wasn't what had encouraged her to stay. She was interested to find out more about this so-called reinventing yourself seminar.

Thinking it was another means of parting gullible baby boomers from their cash, she stayed to the end. She gave the friendly woman sitting next to her a sideways glance as they waited for the second half to begin. She felt a pang of guilt the woman had told her life story during the interval. Clara hadn't divulged her real name or the circumstances which led her here today. The second half was over too soon. Clara realised she was so enthralled by all the real-life stories and exploits of her generation who had renewed old passions, found old flames, or rediscovered their true selves, that an hour and a half had flown by.

'Ellen, are you coming for day two?'

The lady sitting next to Clara gently nudged her arm when she got no response. 'Ellen?'

It took a minute for Clara to remember her alias. 'Oh sorry, pardon?'

'The fun begins tomorrow when we explore our inner selves, what makes us tick, and how we can plan our future. Today was just an introduction. You're coming, aren't you?'

Clara peeled off the name from her lapel. The question wasn't whether she was coming, but whether the real Ellen whoever she was, would make it for the second day. That aside, Clara knew she couldn't stay on another day.

'I'd like to,' she said. 'But I have to go home tomorrow.'

Do I? said a little voice in her head. What was there to go home for? Nobody was waiting for her return. She knew that wasn't true. Tamsin was expecting her to come home and take Dorothy and the girls off her hands while she sorted things out with Kevin. But that wasn't what was on Clara's mind. Joe leaving her was occupying her thoughts. All that was waiting for her was an empty house – an empty life.

She stared at the leaflet and resolved to stay another night. She turned to the friendly woman. 'Perhaps I might see you tomorrow evening, after all.' That assumed Ellen didn't turn up.

'Wonderful. Well, have a lovely evening. I'd invite you back to mine for dinner but….'

Clara shook her head. 'I understand.' She had already filled Clara in on her domestic situation. She was still living under the same roof with her husband while they went through selling the house along with an acrimonious divorce. Even if she had invited Clara back for a cuppa, Clara would have politely declined. She had enough on her plate right now without a front-seat to another woman's marital problems too.

They were just parting ways when she turned to Clara. 'I'm guessing something's happened in your life to bring you here…'

Clara looked at her. She'd opened up about her life, but Clara couldn't bring herself to talk about Joe.

'It's all right. I understand if you don't want to talk about it. I felt the same way in the beginning.' She smiled. 'Have you thought about what you might like to do? How you could reinvent yourself?'

'Reinvent myself?' Clara shook her head. 'I have no idea what I want to do now.' For years, her life, her dreams were all bound up with Joe's.

She could pinpoint the exact moment she buried her hopes and dreams for her future. She died a little that day. All she wanted after that was a safe harbour. That's what she found when she came to London all those years ago and met a man who adored her – or so she thought. She had been content in the life she had with Joe. As for dreams, she'd left those behind a long time ago.

The friendly woman was still smiling. 'Don't look so worried. You're in good company.' She cast a hand around the packed foyer of people their age spilling out of the seminar. 'They probably haven't got a clue either. But there is one thing that unites us all.'

Clara stopped, eager to hear what she had to say.

She said, 'We want to change our lives, have adventures and discover new horizons before it's too late.'

But that's it, thought Clara, I'm not sure I do.

She nudged Clara's arm as though she had read her mind, and said, 'Just remember, "You cannot discover new oceans until you have the courage to lose sight of the shore."'

25

The receptionist looked up from her computer. 'The suite is taken, but we can accommodate you in a different room if you want to stay another night.'

Clara handed over her key, resigned to the fact she would have to change rooms.

'You can pay when you leave.'

'Oh, it's no trouble.' Clara handed over the card to their joint checking account. The receptionist took her card once more and swiped it through the machine.

Clara put her suitcase on the floor and glanced over her shoulder at the table where she was given Ellen's name tag. She hoped the lady didn't make an appearance the next day.

'Excuse me, madam?'

Clara turned her attention back to the receptionist.

'Your card has been declined.'

She looked at her blankly. 'Declined?'

The receptionist handed back the card.

'There must be a mistake.' Clara frowned. 'It worked fine yesterday when I paid for the suite. Try again.'

'I've tried three times. You will have to speak to your bank. It could be a glitch in their system or…' she lowered her voice, '…insufficient funds. We can secure the room with another means of payment,' she added.

Clara looked at the card. She didn't have another means of payment. 'I think there's a problem *your* end,' she said haughtily. 'Do you accept cash?'

The front desk clerk nodded.

'Well, in that case, I will go and withdraw some money and pay for the room in cash, if that's all right with you.'

'Of course, madam.'

'Can you give me directions to the nearest cash machine?'

Certainly, madam. The bank is on the other side of the street.

'Will you reserve the room while I nip across the road—?'

'I'm sorry, I can only secure a room with a debit or credit card, but as yours was declined…' she trailed off giving Clara an apologetic look.

'Fine. I'll be back in two ticks.' Clara turned around and nearly fell over her suitcase. 'Do you mind keeping an eye on my suitcase while I'm gone?'

'Of course, madam.'

As she headed out the door, she glanced over her shoulder and noted the couple behind her collecting their room key. She wondered why their card had worked and hers hadn't. *Perhaps they prepaid,* thought Clara dismissing any notion that there was a problem with her card.

A short walk down the high road brought her to the only bank in the town. It was Saturday and the bank was closed, but there was a cash machine outside.

Clara put her card in the machine and punched in an amount that would cover the room and an evening meal. She stood there listening to the whirring sound of the machine. She wasn't about to feel guilty about the cost of staying in the most expensive hotel in town. Since when did she feel guilty about spending Joe's money? In truth, she worried every time she went out on a shopping expedition with her friends while Joe was busy working. She frowned. That was assuming he *was* busy working and not picking up his lady friend in the taxi.

She forced herself not to dwell on that as she waited for the cash machine to spew out the money. The cash didn't materialise, what she got instead was a flashing screen saying *insufficient funds – would you like to check your balance?*

'This is ridiculous,' she hissed as she hit the *yes* button. It was the only bank account they had. Together with Joe's salary, all their savings were in that account. She didn't know the exact amount, but it was way beyond the cost of a two-night stay in a hotel.

When the figure flashed up on screen, she blinked in surprise. 'That can't be right.' She hit the *yes* button again, this time for a printed balance. She stepped away from the cash machine and found her reading glasses. Clara stood there studying the slip of paper. According to the number in black and white, not only was there *no* money in the account, but it was overdrawn by a thousand pounds. Joe had withdrawn all their savings – and some.

Clara was having a hard time believing what she was seeing. 'It's all gone,' she said in disbelief to the hole in the wall. She reached out to take her card.

'Nooo!' The bloody machine not only refused to give it up but swallowed up the card whole.

And the bank was closed.

She stood there staring at the little slip of paper thinking there *had* to be some mistake. She looked up at the bank. Even if it were open, it wouldn't do any good inquiring within. They didn't bank with them. Now she had no card either. Clara bit her bottom lip wondering what to do. She couldn't stay another night in the hotel. Unless…

Clara fished in her purse for some loose change and walked along the high street looking for a payphone. She gave up and returned to the hotel, explaining to the receptionist she needed to make a call to clear something up. 'And then I will check in.'

'Of course, madam.' The receptionist moved the phone on her desk to one side for her.

Clara picked up the receiver wishing she'd remembered to recharge her mobile last night. It was a stupid oversight under the circumstances; she was waiting for that call from the hospital — good or bad. She soon heard Gerald's familiar voice on the end of the line. 'Ah, Clara, just the person. I've been trying to get in touch with you.'

She raised her eyebrows. It sounded as though something had cropped up since she popped in to see him yesterday with the paperwork. Whatever it was, it would have to wait.

She cut to the chase, but not before she'd cupped her hand to the phone and lowered her voice. 'Gerald, there's a problem with the joint checking account. The card was declined by the hotel, and when I tried to withdraw some cash, the machine swallowed my card. And we're overdrawn which I can't understand. Someone must have got hold of our account details and stolen our money. Do you think we've been a victim of fraud?' The words came tumbling out so fast that Clara barely paused to draw breath.

'That's why I've been trying to get hold of you,' Gerald said.

'What do you mean?'

Five minutes later, she replaced the handset and handed the phone back to the receptionist.

'Is everything all right, madam?' she asked.

'Yes,' Clara lied.

'Would you like to check in now?'

She shook her head. 'I have to go home.' Another lie.

'You came by train, didn't you?'

Clara nodded.

'I can phone for a taxi to take you to the station?'

She would have liked that very much. The trouble was she didn't have the taxi fare. All that remained in her purse was the bus fare to the station. And the last bus had gone. Clara shook her head. 'No, that's all right. Change of plan. I will visit my brother before I go home.'

'Here in town?'

'Yes. It's not that far to walk.'

'Then your brother can give you a lift to the station.'

Clara smiled at the receptionist. Her smile faded as soon as she picked up her case and turned toward the door. She stared at the opulent foyer before turning on her heel and stepping outside. She *was* intending to go and see Tommy, although she had been putting it off. Clara sighed. At least she had somewhere to go.

She trudged along the street frowning at her own stupidity for not checking the balance on their account. If she'd known that was all there was available before the card maxed out, she would not have spent it on one night in the best hotel in town.

Clara wished she hadn't missed the last bus to the train station. She could have returned home and spent a few more hours in blissful ignorance until Gerald contacted her. Now she knew the truth. The money was gone. And it wasn't fraudsters — it was Joe.

But where did the money go, she had asked Gerald? He didn't have a clue. So, her bright idea of having Gerald wire her money, or whatever one does these days to get hold of ready cash when the banks are closed and you are away from home, went up in smoke. But that wasn't the worst of it. It turned out there were a few things she didn't know about their financial circumstances.

She trudged along the street going over the conversation she'd just had with Gerald. It turned out that Joe had cashed in his small pension and taken a lump sum instead of an annuity.

'But what does that mean?' she'd asked Gerald.

'It means he took the money to invest himself and it looks like those investments went south.'

'But at least we've still got equity in the house.'

It wasn't a question. They still had a mortgage because every time they came close to paying it off another 'great' investment opportunity presented itself. He'd never re-mortgaged up to the hilt. She knew that for a fact or thought she did before Gerald told her he'd found another mortgage document. 'Don't you remember signing it?'

'Signing what?'

'You and Joe re-mortgaged the house five years ago.'

She shook her head. 'That's not possible. I wasn't in work. How could I get a mortgage?'

Gerald sighed down the phone. 'You'd be surprised. Before the recession they were giving them away like hot cakes. The house is mortgaged up to the hilt.'

She could only guess at where the money had gone. After all, how did he get hold of the cash for all those schemes he'd invested in, hoping to realise The Big Payday?

Clara recalled what she had asked Gerald next. 'But isn't there a life insurance policy for eventualities like this?' She was referring to Joe in a coma after his car accident. In those circumstances the debt would get paid off.

'Unless you can take over the mortgage, or you have some other savings vehicle to pay it off, then I'm afraid—'

'You're afraid *what*?'

'You stand to lose the house.'

'But then I'll be left with nothing. Homeless,' Clara had said in a hushed voice with her hand still cupped around the phone, hoping the receptionist didn't overhear the conversation.

'Oh, I'm sure things aren't as bad as that. Besides, you have Tamsin,' Gerald had said.

She'd felt like snapping, *what's that got to do with it?* But she knew what he was getting at. Yes, she had Tamsin, but she couldn't go and live with them. They've got their own lives. She didn't want to turn into Dorothy – a burden on her family.

At the end of the conversation with Gerald, she was confused. Until recently they'd had more money in their joint account than the cost of this seminar. Where had it all gone?

Gerald couldn't say. All he knew was what was in front of

him. And things didn't get any better. Clara found out he'd never paid for life insurance which meant if something happened to him – if he didn't wake up or if he couldn't return to work – there was nothing to fall back on.

What am I going to do? How am I going to pay the mortgage and the bills? She didn't voice her concerns to Gerald even though he was a good friend. Aware he would help her out, Clara was too embarrassed to let him know what desperate straits she was in. Perhaps Gerald assumed she had money of her own, some savings, maybe an inheritance, at least a brother to confide in.

Gerald added, 'Until Joe comes out of the coma, you're in financial limbo and stuck if you decide you want to sell the house.'

'What if he doesn't regain consciousness?' she asked.

'Unless you have some money set aside or come into a windfall or find a well-paid job . . .' He'd paused at that point when he recalled Clara mentioning she had a brother. 'Perhaps another family member could help you out?'

And that was the last thing Gerald said before Clara made her excuses and hung up. Savings? A windfall? She barely had the bus fare to the station. And where did Gerald think she would come up with a well-paid job at her age?

Before she stepped outside the hotel, she looked in her purse and discovered she had less change than she first thought. She doubted she even had the bus fare to the station.

Clara realised she was stuck unless she phoned her daughter and asked her to deposit money into her account. She imagined Tamsin did online banking. It was Saturday evening, and the banks were closed, but if Tamsin transferred the money into her account straightaway, it would be there first thing in the morning ready for her to withdraw.

Clara sighed. There was just one fly in the ointment. She wouldn't dream of asking Tamsin for money. She was the parent, not the other way around. Clara was back to thinking *where did all the money go?* She thought of the woman sitting at Joe's bedside. What was it she overhead her saying? "We had plans together – you and me." Did those plans involve withdrawing all the cash from their joint account?

She picked up her suitcase and walked out of the hotel convinced that's what had happened. So it was true, he *was* planning to leave her. At that moment, Clara knew her life would never be the same again.

26

Clara continued walking, taking in her surroundings as she made her way down the street carrying her suitcase. As she was here in Southwold, she might as well visit Tommy.

When they were growing up, he was the first person she turned to if she was in trouble. He was her brother – her twin. They had been inseparable. Clara frowned. She hadn't been back in so long. She slowed as she neared the gate. The wooden gate was still the same as she remembered – if a little weather-beaten. Rusty metal hinges creaked as she swung it open.

Clara closed the gate behind her and walked along the familiar narrow path bordered by grass either side. Eventually, she arrived. She put her suitcase down on the soft grass and sat down, perching on the top. It wasn't very comfortable, but her old leather case was reliable. She knew it wouldn't give way or crumple under her weight if she sat down for a few minutes.

She sat and reflected on all the places she had intended to travel once upon a time. She'd got as far as London, met Joe and the rest was history; a history that did not include foreign travel. There was no Paris, or New York, or Amsterdam, or the Greek Islands — or anything. Those colourful labels stuck on her suitcase years ago were still discernible, the vibrant colours had faded with age.

'Like me,' Clara said out loud.

She looked at the gravestone. 'Hello, Tommy.' Her eyes shifted to the inscription below his name. The years had gone by in a blink of an eye. 'I've still got the suitcase you bought me.'

Clara remembered that day like it was yesterday; a day that was etched in her memory. It was their birthday. They were eighteen. It was the day that would change her life forever; the day she lost Tommy.

She brushed away a dead leaf from his headstone. 'I never told you that my present from you wasn't what I expected to get for my eighteenth birthday – a leather suitcase.' She smiled. Was it meant as a joke? It wasn't something pretty. And it wasn't practical either. Clara was a homebody. Unlike her twin brother, she never wanted to travel. He knew that. So why did he buy her something she would never use? Was it his way of saying she should spread her wings?

She never got the chance to ask. That night she lost him forever.

'I set off for London, Tommy, intending to visit all those places on the stickers you'd put on my new suitcase.' She heaved a sigh. 'The trouble is that was as far as I got. I bet if it had been you, you would have travelled to all of them. You were always the adventurous one.'

Clara fell silent. Glancing about her at the other gravestones and small village church she felt self-conscious talking to Tommy out loud. But she needn't have. The graveyard in front of the church was empty.

She turned back to Tommy's headstone. 'Remember the travelling circus that used to come to town every summer?' She smiled at the memory. 'How you teased me when I told you that each year, I'd try to pluck up the courage to see the fortune teller. I wanted to know what the future had in store. Was that so idiotic?'

Clara pursed her lips. In hindsight, it didn't seem stupid; who wouldn't want to know that life would turn out okay? Besides, didn't every young woman want to find out she would meet the man of her dreams, fall in love, and live happily ever after? She lowered her voice. 'I never told you this,' she whispered, 'but I did it, Tommy, I saw the medium when the circus came to town.'

Every summer the circus came to town, and it didn't disappoint. They brought with them live animals and trapeze artists, a huge circus tent, thrill rides, stalls and sideshow amusement arcades. Back then it was quite an event in the small Suffolk coastal town. People came from miles around.

She glanced behind her toward the large green on the cliffs overlooking the sea and wondered if the circus still came each year. She closed her eyes. So many places and people had faded in her memory, but when she closed her eyes, she could still see the woman's face as clear as day.

She remembered when she first set eyes on her. Clara expected to meet a woman of advanced years shrouded in black with a serious deadpan expression. Instead in the dim light sat a young senorita in a low-cut red dress with silky long black hair and bright red lips. She smiled at Clara. Had she had stepped into the wrong tent? The only distinguishing feature that stopped her from turning on her heel and walking out was the tarot cards on the table in front of her.

The beautiful young senorita turned one over and said, 'Clara, something in your future haunts you.' It shocked Clara. She imagined the medium would talk about all the wonderful things the future had in store. Not facing someone who was about to tell her that the bad feeling she'd harboured for years was not in her imagination.

It was one of Clara's friends that persuaded her to face her fears. Her friend had seen the medium several years in a row with the same outcome: she would marry a local lad, have three beautiful children, and lead a happy life. Clara bet she told the same story to each of the local lasses who darkened her tent because it was what any girl wanted for their future.

'So why didn't she tell me that too?' she had asked after she'd found out, unlike everybody else, her future would not follow a conventional path. At least that's how she took it when the medium turned over a card and announced, 'I see azure waters, clear and green, and a villa nestled in a valley full of orange and lemon trees.'

Azure waters? Clara didn't think the sea off the Suffolk coast was azure. And there weren't any villas. It sounded like the Mediterranean. And what was all that talk of orange and lemon trees? Despite her brother buying her a suitcase for her eighteenth birthday, travelling was the furthest thing from her mind. Mind you so was settling down, getting married and having children. Clara didn't have a clue what she wanted back then. She still didn't.

Her childhood friend had said, 'Maybe what the medium told everybody else wasn't what *you* want for *your* future.'

'It is,' Clara had scoffed. Although that wasn't entirely true.

Her friend had added, 'I assumed you wanted to travel. After all, Tommy bought you the suitcase. What was that about?'

Clara stared at Tommy's headstone. How vividly she remembered that conversation. It had been years and years since she'd thought about it, stored in some dark recess of her memory. She also recalled her response…

'That's Tommy's dream – not mine.'

'Are you sure?' she had said. 'Maybe you will meet some tall, dark, handsome stranger who whisks you off to live in a white-washed villa by an azure ocean.'

Clara hadn't thought about that visit to the medium for a long time. She didn't remember the villa, the azure waters or the orange and lemon trees. All she recalled were the medium's prophetic words about losing the person she loved most in the world as though she knew what would happen to Tommy.

Clara reached out and touched his headstone. 'After you disappeared that summer, I went back to see her. I got it into my head she could help me find you. But she was gone.' Clara shook her head. 'It was the strangest thing… when I returned to the tent to speak to her again, she wasn't there. In her place was an old woman. I had a stand-up argument with her demanding to see the young woman, but she kept telling me there was no one else who read the tarot cards and I must be mistaken. I wouldn't take no for an answer, so they escorted me out of the circus.'

She managed a smile. 'Knowing you, you would have cheered me on if you'd seen me standing my ground.' She frowned when another memory resurfaced. 'My friends didn't believe me when I told them I'd seen the young senorita. They'd all seen the old woman.'

Clara sighed. 'Why am I telling you all this now? As if it makes any diff—' She stopped mid-sentence and looked about her. She heard something. Perhaps someone had entered the graveyard to pay their respects?

She stood up and took a moment to look around the cemetery. There was nobody else in the small graveyard, so she turned back to her brother's gravestone. 'I'm in trouble, Tommy.' She sat down on the suitcase and rung her hands. 'All I see in my future is divorce proceedings and financial stress and ending up alone.'

Clara wondered if she visited a medium now, would her future still look so rosy? She doubted any medium would tell her there would still be azure waters, clear and green, and a villa with orange and lemon trees.

'What did all that mean, anyway?' She thought of the old woman telling her she had imagined the young lady with the long silky black hair and the red flamenco dress. Convinced she'd been the butt end of a practical joke, she would have believed that if it wasn't for the one part of the reading that had turned out prophetic – she lost the person closest to her heart – her twin, Tommy.

Now, there was nothing in her future – nothing at all. 'I'm

almost sixty. What am I going to do without Joe?' For the first time since the police called at her door and her life turned upside down, she cried. 'Oh Tommy, I honestly don't know what to do. My life feels like it's over —' Clara stopped. This time she definitely heard a sound. And it was coming from behind her.

She wiped the tears from her eyes and glanced over her shoulder. She gasped in surprise as a large dog came bounding towards her out of nowhere.

'Oh!' Her eyes went wide as she lost her balance and the case toppled over taking her with it. She landed squat on her rump in the damp grass. Instead of getting up and running away, she sat there staring at the animal, rooted to the spot in fright. This wasn't how she thought she'd go – mauled to death by a dog.

The dog skidded to a halt a few paces in front of her.

She watched, her heart pounding, as it crouched down until his belly was on the damp grass. Slowly, he inched towards her as though he sensed she was afraid. He whined a little as he approached then nuzzled her hand as if to say, *I'm harmless. You can stroke me – I won't bite.*

Clara tentatively reached out and patted the dog on the head. On closer inspection, he wasn't as big as she first thought – or at all scary. She wasn't an expert on dogs. She wasn't even sure she liked them. But she recognised the breed. It was a golden retriever.

Clara got up and brushed the grass from her clothes feeling rather foolish. She looked down at the dog. It was almost dusk and there was nobody else in the graveyard. Nobody was calling for their pet. 'You must be lost.'

The golden retriever cocked his head to one side listening to the sound of her voice and barked.

'I'm lost too, you know. I'm sure there's a cosy hearth waiting for you, and people who care and are eager to find you.'

The tears welled up in her eyes. There was no cosy hearth or people waiting for her to come home. That wasn't strictly true;

there was Dorothy and Tamsin and the girls. But she wasn't thinking about her extended family, but Joe.

Clara reached down and picked up her suitcase. Lights were on in the cottages backing on to the church grounds and she guessed that the golden retriever had sneaked out of someone's back garden. She looked down at the dog. He was sitting looking at the gravestone, panting softly. He appeared well cared for.

'You go on home now, there's a good dog,' she said before turning her attention to the gravestone. 'Well, I guess this is goodbye, Tommy. I will not be coming back.' She paused. 'I wish I knew what happened to you that night.'

Clara never stopped believing that there was more to it that night. Tommy getting drunk at their eighteenth birthday party and taking a sailboat out in the dead of night intoxicated, only to fall overboard and drown. They said his body would eventually wash up on shore, but it never did.

She felt a little foolish talking to an empty grave. She knew if they had found Tommy, her parents would have flown him home and buried him here in the town he was born. But that never happened. To their dying day, they always believed they would find him. Despite hiring countless private detectives to search for him, the irony was her parents never returned to the place they once loved, and the place they used to take their twins to every summer – Mallorca.

It was a tragic end to a love affair her parents had with an Island they had discovered on their honeymoon and where their twins were conceived. How painful that they would lose one of their children there. Like her parents, Clara wondered if she too would go to her grave never knowing what happened to Tommy on that beautiful Mallorcan summer's night.

Although she had never been back – she hadn't set foot abroad since that fateful summer holiday when they turned eighteen – Clara had visited Mallorca many times growing up. Every year they returned to the small fishing village near Pollensa in the shadow of the Serra de Tramuntana mountain range. Even now, if she closed her eyes, she could conjure up those long, hot summer days and the small sailboat her father used to hire. They'd take the boat out in the cool calm waters and sail around the bay to find uninhabited coves in which to go swimming.

Everything seemed more vivid in Mallorca; the sun was hotter, the landscape greener. The colours, tastes, and sounds were more vivid, vibrant, alive. It was a world away from the grey, dull overcast Suffolk seaside resort she had grown up in. When she was a child, Clara always came home from those holidays promising herself that one day she would return to Mallorca and live there forever.

27

Clara was making her way toward the gate to leave the churchyard when she thought she heard something. She stopped and did an about turn only to find the dog was no longer sitting at the graveside. He was standing there, a few paces behind, looking at her expectantly.

'Go home. Go on!' Clara waved her hand in a shooing motion and turned on her heel. If he had escaped from a garden overlooking the churchyard, it wouldn't be the first time. He knows his way home, thought Clara trying to convince herself she was doing the right thing leaving the dog behind.

She paused a few moments later. Something told her he was still following. She glanced over her shoulder and spied the dog a few paces away. Every time she moved forward, so did he. When she looked behind her once more, the dog was sitting on his rump as though he hadn't moved an inch. Clara knew better. She backed up. The dog stood up and followed.

She sighed. 'Go on – *get!*'

She had no experience with dogs. She made the mistake of picking up a stick and throwing it, thinking that might spook him and he'd run off.

A moment later, something brushed her thigh making her jump. There at her side was the dog. In his jaws was the stick. He dropped it at her feet. Clara rolled her eyes. 'Oh, no. You've got it all wrong, you silly dog. This isn't a game. Come on now, you must go home. It's getting dark. Go on – *shoo!*'

He nudged the stick with his nose then looked up at her as if to say, *throw it again*. She picked it up, glanced at the dog, and threw it as high as she could. It lodged in a branch in the tree. She watched the dog chase after the stick. He came to a skidding halt under the tree and barked.

Clara saw her chance. She made a quick getaway out the gate and hurried along toward the beach. It wasn't far. All she had to do was make it to end of the street, past the village green with the quaint pub and the row of white-washed cottages overlooking the sea, then she could take the sloping path down to the seafront.

By the time she arrived at the beach, the dog was nowhere in sight. She was breathing heavily and had no idea why she'd lugged her suitcase all this way. Where she was going, she wouldn't need it. 'I should have left it with Tommy, silly woman,' she said. There was no point in lugging it any further. She dropped the suitcase in the sand and kept walking. Discarding her shoes, she threw her scarf to the wind and took off her jacket, leaving it behind where it fell. She was already feeling better, lighter – free.

'Free,' Clara breathed.

Then suddenly the gentle whoosh of the ocean beckoning her to come closer, to be free of it all, was shattered by the sound of a dog barking. She turned around and saw the golden retriever bounding towards her. 'Not you again!' She ignored him and continued walking toward the ocean, feeling the soft sand between her toes. Street lamps on the promenade illuminated the beach just as far as the water's edge. The ocean beyond was as black as night.

The dog didn't get the message. He ran full circle around her several times, making her dizzy, but she kept on walking towards the water's edge. 'This isn't a game, you know.'

She was almost there when the dog stopped running in circles and came to a standstill in front of her. He stood there with the water lapping around his paws as the gentle surf broke on the beach. Every time she moved to the left or the right, trying to get past him, he shifted with her keeping himself between her and the sea. She realised what the clever dog was attempting to do — stop her.

'It's for the best, you know. I've got nowhere to go. I've got no one. If I go home, how will I manage until Joe wakes up — *if* he wakes up? And even if he is okay, things will not go back to the way they were. He was planning to leave me. And he's taken all the money.' She stared at the dog and thought she heard Tommy's voice on the gentle breeze, *Cheer up old gal, things can only get better.*

'But how, Tommy? Tell me.'

The dog came towards her. He nudged her hand and licked it.

She saw her chance and sidestepped the dog. Her forward momentum was stopped by something tugging on her skirt. She glanced around to find the dog had clamped his jaws on the hem. He pulled her back so hard Clara let out a surprised yelp falling backward on her rump.

She sat there on the sand for some time with her head in her hands sobbing until she felt a weight on her lap. Wiping the tears from her face, she looked down to find the dog resting his head on her lap.

Her first instinct was to push him away. Instead she stroked the top of his head. 'Where on earth have you come from, eh?' Stroking his soft fur, she discovered a dog collar beneath his thick coat. Under the collar she came across a small coin-shaped metal object. It was a name tag with engraved lettering. She looked closer. In large lettering was one word, 'Bailey.'

The dog barked.

'I know why you want me to stay, Bailey. You don't want to be alone. Are you lost too?'

Perhaps he hadn't got out of a back garden. 'If you want me to take care of you, you're barking up the wrong tree. I can barely take care of myself.' She laughed. 'Did I just say that? Barking up the wrong tree?'

Bailey nuzzled her hand.

She shivered. The sea breeze had picked up, and it was now pitch dark. All she could see beyond the shoreline where they were sitting was a dark, forbidding blackness. She glanced at the dog. The impulse to join Tommy had dissipated. She picked herself up and brushed the sand from her skirt.

The dog got up as soon as Clara moved and stood once again, as if on guard, between her and the sea.

She stood for a moment staring into the blackness before glancing at the golden retriever. 'Don't worry, because of you I've come to my senses.' Clara decided today was not the day she would meet her maker.

'Come on.' She turned away from the shoreline and headed up the beach toward the promenade. The street lamps were illuminating the way. She slipped on her shoes and picked up her scarf and jacket as she went; wrapping the scarf about her even though it wasn't cold.

Clara followed her own footprints in the sand until she came upon her suitcase. She picked it up and continued toward the promenade, followed by a bouncy, exuberant dog named Bailey. She glanced at the dog and wondered what she would do with him.

When she looked up, she stopped in surprise. She hadn't walked in a straight line; the dog had diverted her attention. The gentle sloping pathway up to the town was further over to her right. In front of her was a row of beach huts.

She looked up and down the row, her eyes growing wide. 'Oh, my goodness, how could I have forgotten?'

28

Would it still be here? That's the question Clara was asking herself as she inspected the row of beach huts. She hadn't set foot in Southwold for almost four decades, having left the past behind and moved on with her life. She'd forgotten about the beach hut she'd inherited when her parents passed away — until now.

It wasn't a house, but it might be a roof over her head, shelter from the wind and elements – if only for a night. God knows what the state of it would be after all these years, but at least it was something. Now all she had to do was remember which one. She had an idea what she was looking for – the most rundown of the lot.

She glanced at Bailey. 'Come on, let's go find my beach hut. You can stay the night, but in the morning, I've got a train to catch, so we better find out who you belong to, hadn't we.'

The trouble was from where she was standing Clara couldn't see a rundown beach hut in sight. 'Oh, bother!' Her plan was going south. In the fading light she walked along the row to take a closer look.

Bailey barked and followed Clara as she walked along the beach scrutinizing each hut; she was looking for a blue beach hut with a name above the door. She stopped in front of one that looked as though it had seen better days, it didn't seem familiar.

Giving a cursory glance at the well-maintained huts something caught her eye.

It was a hut she had dismissed in an instant because it appeared new. However, there was something incongruous about it that at first, she could not put her finger on. Then she saw it; an old, hand-painted sign. Tatty and weather-beaten it looked out of place above the door of the well maintained pale blue hut. She read the sign twice just to be sure. It didn't seem possible, but it was *her* beach hut.

There was a door and one window, just how she remembered it. She stepped on to the small wooden veranda and took a coin from her purse. There was only one way to find out for sure if this was her parents' beach hut. Kneeling on the wooden veranda she scratched off some new paint from under the window. It didn't take long to reveal two tiny sets of initials scrawled in childish handwriting. *CM and TM forever.*

Clara recalled with a grin they'd both got into a heap of trouble that summer for writing on the front of the hut. But despite their parents' disapproval, each time they added fresh paint, they always left the initials that their children, Clara and Tommy May – two mischievous eight-year-olds – had etched into the wood all those summers ago. It was only covered up by one coat of paint which meant this overhaul was recent.

She vaguely recalled getting the key and the legal paperwork from the solicitor when her parents passed away ten years ago. At the time she had no intention of returning. In all these years, she had never once visited. The key must be somewhere, stored for safekeeping, but she couldn't remember where. Not that it would have mattered. The padlock looked new. She stood there taking it in. Even when her parents were alive, the beach hut never looked this good.

She narrowed her eyes. Someone had noticed a hut, empty and unused, in a prime position at the end of the beach, and decided it was there for the taking. Clara frowned thinking they couldn't do that – could they? She had the legal paperwork which proved it belonged to her. Trouble was she didn't have the paperwork on her person.

She looked up at the night sky. She had no money for a hotel room or a night's stay at a local bed-and-breakfast and didn't fancy sleeping on a park bench like a homeless person.

There was another option; return to the nice hotel in town and phone Tamsin to pay for a room for the night. If she didn't want an earful from Tamsin about when she was coming home and sending her on a guilt trip about leaving Dad's bedside, there was always Debs or Gerald who would help her out.

'Oh Bailey, what shall I do?' She did not want to return to the hotel and ring Tamsin, Debs or Gerald. Even Kevin would stump up the money for the hotel room. She could come up with some excuse, passing her lack of funds off to forgetfulness; she'd brought the wrong bank card, or the bank was closed, and she hadn't drawn off enough cash.

What she didn't want to come up with, however, were her reasons for being here. They were bound to ask. That's why she didn't want to trouble anybody for money. Besides, she didn't trust herself not to spill the beans and tell them about Joe. She wasn't ready to go down that road just yet.

'We're staying the night in *my* beach hut.' Clara decided. She looked about her and picked up a large pebble. It was as big as her hand. She held it up. 'This will do.' Clara took a swing.

Behind her, she heard a dog barking.

'Oh do be quiet, Bailey.'

He didn't.

When she looked around, it wasn't the golden retriever barking but another large dog, and it was hurtling along the beach in her direction. Clara froze, her hand suspended in mid-air. She was still holding the very large pebble. In the corner of her eye she caught sight of Bailey backing away as the large dog raced across the beach towards them.

The dog skidded to a halt in front of her and continued to bark at the frightened woman standing rigid with her hand raised.

Clara expected Bailey to bark or at least growl, but contrary to expectations he hid up the side of the beach hut.

'Some friend you are,' she said through gritted teeth. Then to her relief a man appeared out of the shadows. He must have been walking along the beach when his dog ran off. He raced towards them, calling frantically to his dog.

Clara still didn't move a muscle.

The young man grasped the dog's collar and pulled him away but not before he saw her standing there, hand raised, holding a large pebble. His eyes flickered to the beach hut door and the lock which was dented.

'Oh, thank god!' Clara lowered her hand. 'You should keep an animal like that on a lead. He's dangerous.'

'He's not dangerous.'

'I beg to differ. He gave me quite a fright. You must learn to keep your dog under control.'

'He's normally putty in my hands.' The young man knelt and gave him a fuss. The dog rolled over to have his tummy tickled. 'See. He only ever behaves like that when he's alerting me to a crime in progress.'

'A crime in progress? What on earth are you talking about?'

29

Clara was sitting in the back of the young off-duty policeman's car. Bailey was lying next to her. The dog who had got her into this mess, stowed safely away in a cage in the rear. She noticed the words, Suffolk Dog Unit, in large black lettering along the side of the police car as he frogmarched her towards it.

'I told you, I've done nothing wrong,' she protested. 'Are these necessary?' She held up her hands; clasped together in handcuffs.

'Just a precaution.' The young police officer eyed her in the rear-view mirror as he started the car. He didn't make a habit of arresting innocent passers-by out with their dog. But she had been walking along the beach after dark carrying a suitcase and aroused his suspicions. Then he'd caught her trying to break into a beach hut which she said belonged to her. If that were true, why didn't she have a key? She didn't look like a vandal or some homeless down-and-out looking for a warm place to sleep. However, as a police officer he knew all too well appearances can be deceptive.

He made small talk on the way to the station trying to glean information about his passenger. He'd rather not have to sit her in an interrogation room this late at night. The young officer heard all about the night she discovered her husband had been in a car accident returning from a business trip. He was still in a coma, but she needed to visit Southwold – something about seeing her brother before she returned home.

He didn't push her on the matter. When they arrived at the station, a quick phone call established she was telling the truth: her husband was in a coma in a hospital in London. The poor woman was clearly going through a rough patch.

'If you don't mind sitting in the waiting room while I fill out my paperwork.' He took off her handcuffs, deciding he could trust her to stay put. There was something bothering him; she hadn't been forthcoming regarding where she was intending to stay the night before travelling back to London in the morning. If she had nowhere to go, then the only option was for her to remain at the station in a police cell. He hoped it wouldn't come to that. That's why he would drop her off at a hotel or bed-and-breakfast once he'd finished the paperwork.

Although telling the truth, she *had* visited her brother, she'd omitted an important detail: he'd died on his eighteenth birthday, almost forty years ago. It was his graveside she'd visited. That ruled out driving her over to her brothers' house to stay the night.

He turned his attention from the report and looked through the glass door into the reception area where the woman was seated. His eyes flickered to the old-fashioned brown case decorated with stickers that had seen better days.

The officer tapped his pen on the paperwork. What was she doing walking along the beach at dusk carrying a suitcase? With her husband lying in a coma in hospital in London surely, she'd want to be him? He would. In those circumstances, there would be nothing and no-one that could keep him from his loved one's bedside.

Not that long ago he'd been in a similar position, and hoped for her sake, the nightmare ended soon, and her husband woke up. He knew the toll it took when it didn't and wouldn't wish that on anybody.

'Paul? Everything all right?' asked the desk sergeant as he

placed a mug of tea in front of him, throwing him one of those concerned looks Paul was all too familiar with. A few months ago, he wished everyone would stop asking. Now, he'd almost got used to it. Almost. Paul looked up at the overweight middle-aged sergeant. 'Thanks for the tea, but I'm off home in a minute.'

'Are you pulling another all-nighter?'

Paul shook his head aware that his colleague was no stranger to his tendency to stay behind and pull all-nighters. They had very little crime to investigate in the small Suffolk market town and were not exactly snowed under with work. And with the sweeping budget cuts after the last recession, it was debatable how long their police station would remain operational. But that didn't stop Paul from finding any and every excuse to stay behind at work. Everyone who worked with him knew that Paul was just avoiding going home to an empty house.

The sergeant picked up the mug of tea. 'I'll have this then.'

'You go ahead,' said Paul.

He walked out of the room with the mug, paused in the doorway and glanced back at the young police officer wondering when, if ever, he would get over his loss. He shook his head thinking, how sad that our lives, our happiness, can turn on a dime. Paul was a case in point. One minute they were newlyweds, the next moment she was—

'Excuse me!'

The sergeant had just set the mug of tea down. He looked up from his desk to find the woman with the golden retriever standing there. She didn't look happy.

'Can I go yet?' she snapped.

'If you would just take a seat, Ma'am, my colleague will be with you shortly.' The desk sergeant looked at the mug of tea and said, 'Would you like a cuppa?'

Clara took a seat. The tea was a small consolation but a welcome one. Staring off into space, bored, she sipped her drink and then absently dunked the digestive biscuit the desk sergeant had offered her – she'd taken two – in her tea. That's when she noticed Bailey wasn't sitting by her chair. She looked around the room and spotted him. She furtively glanced at the sergeant, who was busy on the phone, and called the dog in a hushed voice, 'Bailey, come back here.'

The dog had his nose in a wastepaper basket in the corner of the room. She rolled her eyes. What did he think he was doing?

Bailey rifled through the bin with his muzzle and then trotted back to Clara with something in his jaws.

She rolled her eyes when she saw what it was. 'Good grief, I do not want a newspaper.'

The dog was insistent. Clara sighed as she took the paper. Although she wasn't in the mood to read the news headlines, it beat staring at four walls or the overweight, balding desk sergeant. She finished her digestive biscuit and offered Bailey the other one. He wolfed it down. She sat there skimming the pages while she downed the last of the sweet tea. She turned the final page, about to discard the newspaper, when something caught her eye.

There was an advertisement in the classifieds section for the position of a house sitter right here in town. Clara eyed her suitcase. The young officer was bound to ask her where she was staying tonight.

She had mentioned in the police car visiting her brother. Perhaps he assumed she was residing with him. But what if he asked outright? What if he offered to drive her there? She didn't have the money for a taxi. What choice would she have? But she could hardly say she was staying with a relative; her dead brother, Tommy.

She stared at the ad in the paper. It was too late to ring the agency and say she wanted the job. Although she couldn't imagine it would be easy to waltz into an employment agency with no references and be handed the keys to someone's house. Still, house sitting. She liked the idea of that; somewhere nice to stay for a few days *and* get paid for it.

She studied the advert. They hadn't included the address. That didn't surprise her. An empty property with the owners away was an open invitation for squatters. Clara sighed. It was a nice thought while it lasted.

Clara glanced at the photo of the large Georgian detached property included in the job advert. She was about to discard the paper when she did a double take. The house looked familiar.

There was a caption below the photo in small print she found hard to decipher and she slipped on her glasses. The agency advertising the position hadn't provided the address, but they might as well have. Below the photograph of the property was a small caption; it was the name of the house. Clara slowly took off her glasses.

'You're free to go.'

Lost in thought, she barely registered the young officer standing in front of her. 'I'm sorry — what?'

'Look, I could call you a taxi but it's late. Come on.'

Clara looked up. 'Where are we going?'

He frowned. 'I'm giving you a lift to your hotel or bed and breakfast. Unless you want to spend the night in a prison cell.' He wasn't joking. 'I presume you've got someplace to stay the night. We can't have you wandering the streets—'

'Of course, I've got somewhere to stay the night,' she blurted. The last thing she could imagine was spending the night in a prison cell. She'd rather sleep on a park bench.

'Well, let's go.'

Clara slowly rose from her seat, picked up her suitcase and accompanied him out the door.

The golden retriever followed close behind.

Clara dragged her heels. Where was she going to ask him to drop her? The hotel in town was one option. She could walk into the foyer and then as soon as he left, walk straight out again. The problem was what if he insisted on accompanying her inside? He might even offer to carry her suitcase right up to her room?

Something told her that the young officer was thorough. Clara felt her options fading to zilch.

He opened the car door for her, and said, 'So where are you staying tonight?'

Anywhere but in a police cell. She couldn't imagine phoning Tamsin from the police station to ask for money and having to explain the predicament she'd now found herself in.

The young officer eyed the dog. 'You know, you ought to put him on a lead.'

'He's not my—' Clara began and stopped. She'd got herself in enough trouble as it was for one evening without appearing to have stolen someone's dog to boot.

She looked at Bailey and in a hushed voice said, 'Behave yourself, won't you? Play along and everything will be fine.' Clara groaned. What on earth was she thinking? Lying to a police officer was bad enough. But getting away with what she was about to do next was another.

30

'The address?' Clara swallowed.

The police officer started the car engine and turned in his seat to look at his passenger in the back. 'Yes, where am I taking you?'

She mumbled '*The Gables*.' She was about to give him the address when he said, 'Ah, *The Gables*. I know it well.'

'You do?' she said in surprise. She didn't ask how he came to be familiar with the property considering his line of work.

The police officer nodded. 'It's where a famous photojournalist bought a home. I expect he's off again to some far-flung place. He's quite the celebrity around here. The photography club is popular…'

Clara wasn't listening. Consumed with the realisation that just when she thought she'd solved one problem, another problem presented itself. She rolled her eyes. Any minute now the police officer would ask her—'

'So how come you're staying at *The Gables* while his away? Are you a friend of his….?' He let the question hang, waiting for her to enlighten him.

'Oh, er no, I'm not a friend,' she replied. She *was* intending to tell him she was looking after a friend's house while they were away, but now that was out of the question. He might ask her something about him. She was at a disadvantage not knowing who the famous photojournalist was. Besides, what if the officer had seen the advertisement for a house sitter? After all, she *had* found the newspaper – or rather the dog had – in the waiting room at the police station.

'I'm a house sitter,' announced Clara, trying to sound as confident as possible and hoping he didn't detect an anxious tremor in her voice.

"Interesting line of work,' replied the officer.

She nodded her head unsure what he meant by that comment.

Almost immediately, she saw another flaw in her plan. It wasn't much of an idea. All she had in mind was to be dropped off at the house, hang around outside until she was sure the police officer's car was out of sight, and then return to the beach hut – this time undisturbed. She couldn't spend the night in an empty house unless she had the house keys. There was one thing breaking a lock on a beach hut which she owned, but another thing to break into someone else's property.

Clara wondered whether she should have just been honest and told the officer she'd got stuck out with no money. A night in a prison cell and a lift to the train station in the morning was now looking a much better prospect. A little deception might get more complicated.

What if the police officer dropped her off and hung around? He'd soon find out she didn't have the house keys. How was she going to explain that? She could dally with her own house keys and make a show of pretending to put them in the lock. If she took her time, he'd just leave. She frowned at Bailey. 'It's all your fault if this goes wrong.'

The police officer glanced in the rear-view mirror. 'What was that?'

'I said I hope we haven't taken a wrong turn.' She winced at yet another bare-faced lie.

'Don't you worry, we're almost there.'

They arrived at the house a few minutes later. It was down a side street off the town's main square. Pretty terraced period cottages lined the narrow street either side. It was a cul d sac. They stopped at the end of the road in front of a pair of tall wrought-iron gates. She'd forgotten about the double gates which opened on to the driveway leading up to the house. Now what?

The police officer wound the window down and pressed the button on the small metal box next to the gates. He said, 'I was up at the house recently because a neighbour thought they saw somebody in the grounds. With the owner away they called us to check it out. When I arrived, the neighbour told me to drive on up to the house. What's the point of these gates if they're not locked?'

As Clara sat watching the wrought-iron gates open, she thanked her lucky stars they weren't locked. When she was last here many years ago, the gates were always wide open.

She leaned forward in her seat as they approached the ivy-clad detached property and stared at the familiar façade. It hadn't changed much since she was here last; floor-to-ceiling Georgian bay windows on the ground floor and small leaded windows upstairs, with the little turrets on the slate roof above, were just the same as she remembered.

The house was well maintained, with gleaming white exterior paintwork. The exterior paintwork was a gleaming white. Shutters at the windows were no longer weather-beaten with peeling paint. They'd been restored and painted a vibrant shade of vintage green.

Her first impression was a city-type from London had bought the property and done it up as a second home. The well-dressed gentleman chatting her up on the train came to mind. It wasn't him. He'd alighted way before her stop. She didn't care who owned the property as long as they weren't home.

This was a bad idea. If it had been any other house… why

did it have to be here? She wished Bailey had never found the newspaper and couldn't wait to get the charade over with and leave. It wasn't the dog's fault she'd got it into her head to pretend to be the house sitter. There was one thing looking at the house in a photo, but another arriving here to discover it had hardly changed in the intervening years since she was here last. Clara sat there staring at her childhood home.

'Are you all right?'

Lost in thought, it hadn't even registered that the car engine was no longer turning over.

The police officer turned in his seat. He stared at his passenger in the back, his face a picture of concern. 'Are you all right?' he asked again.

She glanced at him and was about to tell him to take her back – she'd much rather spend a night in a prison cell –when Bailey barked and pawed at the passenger door eager to get out of the car.

He eyed the dog. 'Right, let's go.'

Before she could say *turn the car around I want to go back,* the young man was already out of the car and opening the back door for her. She hadn't stepped out of the vehicle when Bailey clambered over her lap in his eagerness to get going.

'Well, I never!' she exclaimed as Bailey's tail flicked her in the nose as he jumped out of the car.

'Here.' The young man's hand appeared.

'I don't need any help.'

'Suit yourself.'

Clara got out of the car heaving her suitcase out behind her.

'Let me take that for you.' Before she could object the young officer had the suitcase in his hand. 'Shall we?' He motioned towards the front door.

Clara reached for her case. 'I can manage, thank you.'

'No, no. I insist.' He kept hold of the suitcase. 'After you…'

This was what she was afraid of; that he would insist on

walking her to the door. It would never surprise her if he carried her suitcase inside. *Damn and blast.* What was she going to do?

Clara ambled towards the front door and made a show of looking in her handbag for the keys. She stopped on the front porch. 'I'm sure the keys are here somewhere…' She turned to the police officer. 'It's all right. You can put my case down. I'll find my keys in a minute. Why don't you head off? I don't want to keep you.'

'It's no bother.'

She kept a smile plastered on her face until she turned to the front door. This was getting beyond a joke. Why wouldn't he just leave?

His presence right behind her wasn't the only thing bothering her. When she discovered the ad for a house sitter, she had not checked the date. The newspaper could be weeks old, and the position already filled.

She glanced up at the house. There were no lights on. The house exuded an air of emptiness.

Behind her the police officer commented, 'I guess you're glad you brought your dog. The place seems kind of creepy, if you ask me.'

Clara nodded in agreement and then saw an opportunity to get rid of the police officer. 'Well, I suppose in that case you'll want to skedaddle,' she said hopefully.

'Not at all. I've always wanted to have a look inside *The Gables.*'

Clara was still fumbling in her purse wondering what on earth she would do now. Bailey wasn't helping matters. He was barking and getting excited. His tail was swishing back and forth. He backed into a plant pot by the front door and knocked it over.

The police officer knelt to put it upright. 'What do we have here?' He tutted. 'The times I tell people not to leave a house key under a plant pot.' He held up the key.

Clara stared wide-eyed at the key not quite believing her

good fortune. She whipped it out of his hand. 'At least that will save you waiting on the doorstep while I empty my bag for the door key.' She was losing count of how many *Hail Mary's* she'd have to say for all these fibs she was telling.

'Just promise me you won't leave it there in future.'

'It wasn't me,' she countered. 'I didn't leave it there.'

'I'm not saying you did. I expect that was the owner in case he returned from overseas and couldn't find his door key.'

'Oh, I see. Yes, that explains it.'

He looked up at the grand old house. 'A house like this standing unoccupied…' he mused. 'If someone found the key under the plant pot, the owner might find himself with an unwanted house guest.' He shifted his attention to Clara.

She could feel her cheeks growing bright crimson. 'An unwanted house guest?'

'I'm talking about squatters,' clarified the young police officer.

She put the key in the lock praying nobody was home. She opened the front door and walked inside followed by the young man carrying her suitcase.

They'd just stepped over the threshold when the golden retriever barged past and dived into the first room on the left.

'You need to teach your dog some manners.'

Clara frowned. Once again it was on the tip of her tongue to say it wasn't her dog. She kept her mouth shut and followed the dog into the room where, to her astonishment, she found him curled up making himself comfortable in a dog basket.

'Well, he certainly knows his way around,' said the police officer in surprise. 'Did you say you arrived today?'

She nodded staring at the dog basket, thinking about Bailey getting excited when they arrived at the house. At this rate, the police officer would suspect something wasn't quite right here. It was as though Bailey knew the house. As though this dog basket belonged to him.

She wasn't the only one staring at the dog. 'You know, it

seems like the dog has been here be—' He stopped dead. 'I thought I recognised that dog!'

Clara nervously chewed a fingernail; the game was up. Despite his faded jeans and polo shirt he was an off-duty police officer. How long would it take him to put two and two together?

He turned to her. 'Why didn't you tell me you were looking after the owner's dog too?'

'The owner's dog?'

'I used to see him walking the golden retriever along the beach. Rumour has it that before he went abroad on his latest trip, he'd found the dog a new home.'

She looked at Bailey settled in his dog basket.

The young man followed her gaze. 'I'm glad that wasn't the case. If it was *my* wife's dog—' He stopped.

She looked over at the young man and saw a pained expression cross his features before he composed himself. 'He lost his wife, you see – the photojournalist. They bought the house intending to retire here, but within weeks of moving in she was gone.'

'Oh. That's so sad.'

'Yes. Best laid plans and all that. We make all these plans for the future and then…' he shook his head and sighed, 'shit happens.'

She knew all about that. Joe was never far from her thoughts. She glanced at the young man. Had someone left him like her Joe? Or worse, had he suffered a bereavement?

'I better get going and leave you to settle in. Where would you like me to put your case?'

'Oh. Right. Um…' She looked about her. 'I'll er take it up to my room.'

He handed over the suitcase and walked to the door.

Clara followed. 'Thank you for the lift.'

He stepped outside. 'When I saw you on the beach at dusk I jumped to conclusions.'

Clara raised an eyebrow.

'It's not unheard of for homeless people to break into a beach huts.'

'I quite understand,' she said thinking what rotten luck to get caught by an off-duty policeman, of all people, doing just that – attempting to break into a beach hut to spend the night. Although, it was *her* beach hut, but until she had the paperwork, there was nothing she could do to prove it.

After she told him about Joe – the part about the car accident and the coma, not the bit about Joe planning a disappearing act with all their savings – he hadn't questioned her any further about the beach hut incident.

He'd filed the paperwork and sent her on her way – almost. Clara was thankful there was a key under the plant pot and now the police officer was standing the other side of the front door about to leave.

He said, 'They advertised the position for a house sitter in the local paper.'

'Is that so,' she said feigning ignorance. She hoped he didn't ask her how she came by the position. 'I'm surprised the position was still vacant.' Which she was. You couldn't ask for a cushier number; living in someone's rather beautiful residence and being paid for the privilege.

'I shouldn't say this…' He leaned in close and said it, anyway. 'They were having trouble filling the position because rumour has it the house is haunted.'

'Haunted?' She swallowed. Although she was pleased to hear there wasn't a stream of people beating a path to the door to take up the position, after hearing the word *haunted* she didn't relish the thought of staying the night.

'Ever since I heard the rumours, I meant to check out *The Gables* to satisfy my curiosity that nothing untoward was going on.' He cast a glance about him. 'I can't discern anything out of the ordinary. Makes me wonder how the rumours started.'

'Would you like to stay for a cup of tea?' Suddenly, she didn't want to be alone in this big old house.

'That's kind of you to offer, but I must go.'

'Of course.' She was relieved he couldn't stop for tea. What was she thinking? She only had to get through one night and then she intended to make a quick phone call to Gerald first thing in the morning, asking him to find the paperwork that proved she owned the beach hut.

Clara closed the front door picked up her suitcase and paused at the foot of the stairs. She decided not to venture up there and walked into the lounge.

She sat down on the couch and prodded the soft cushions with her finger. 'This will do.' She looked at Bailey. At least she had company – of sorts. He was asleep in his dog bed, his muzzle resting on the lip of the basket.

She looked around the familiar room until her eyes settled on the dog. 'I guess I'm not the only one who has my reasons for coming home – what's yours?'

31

Clara placed her case on the sofa next to her and opened it. The first thing she saw was the newspaper with the ad. There was one thing staying a night in her own beach hut, but this was different. She was trespassing – pure and simple.

The police officer had no clue he had just taken a squatter and deposited her, and her suitcase, in some absent owner's home without their permission. She was worrying that if found out, she would get him into trouble too. That's the last thing she wanted to do. Clara groaned and woke the dog.

Bailey stepped out of his basket and walked over to her.

She eyed the dog. 'This is all your fault, you know.'

He sat down on the carpet beside the sofa and put his muzzle on her lap, sad brown eyes looking up at her.

She patted his head. 'Well, I guess we're in this together.'

Bailey barked an affirmative. At least that's what she thought it was. 'Shush, Bailey.'

Suddenly he shot out of the room.

'Where are you going?' Clara got to her feet concerned that Bailey had heard a car approaching the house. What if the police officer had returned? She walked over to the bay window and glanced into the back garden but couldn't see much; it was pitch dark outside. The newspaper was still in her hand. Clara tossed it onto the window seat and made her way across the room into the hallway just in time to see Bailey's tail disappear into the kitchen at the end of the hall. She followed him.

Although the lounge had modern furnishings, a wall-hung flat screen television, and new oak flooring, there were still things that remained, like the huge fireplace with the wooden mantle that dominated the room. She remembered those chilly evenings, even in the height of summer, when her parents used to light the fire. They would all sit on a rug in front of a roaring fire playing board games. Sometimes her and Tommy would dress up and entertain their parents with a little play they'd made up. She smiled at those happy childhood memories.

The kitchen was different. There was nothing here she recognised apart from the back door into the garden. The old green painted kitchen units, butler sink, free-standing appliances and pantry had been replaced by an ultra-modern kitchen with cream shaker-style kitchen units, granite worktops and a tiled floor. The old Aga changed for a shiny modern version in cream with black oven doors. They had spared no expense. She thought it had a woman's touch.

Standing in the doorway admiring the spotless kitchen she looked down and saw the mess all over the floor. 'Bailey!' she exclaimed thinking of the police officer's comment about teaching the dog manners. Bailey's tail wagged as he chomped his way through the dry doggy food spilling out over the kitchen floor from a large bag of dog food. He was standing by an open kitchen cupboard. Clara rolled her eyes. The dog knew where to find his dinner.

She walked into the kitchen looking for a dustpan and brush and discovered two brown ceramic dog bowls with the name Bailey running around the rim. 'After your owner found you a new home, I guess he forgot to dispose of these. Come on, let's do this properly.' She grabbed Bailey by the collar and prised him away from his meal.

The dog stood watching Clara as she picked up several

scoops of dried dog food in her hands and put it in the ceramic bowl. She picked up the bowl and walked over to the back door followed by an eager dog hungry for his dinner and placed the bowl on the doormat. The other one she filled with tap water, setting it on the mat beside the food bowl. She stood up. 'There, that's better.'

Watching Bailey wolf down his dinner reminded her she hadn't eaten since breakfast. She glanced in the cupboard at the rows of tinned fish, vegetables, beans and a lot more besides. She placed a carton of long-life milk by the kettle and found a small dustpan and brush under the sink unit. Clara set to work clearing up the mess Bailey had made on the floor. When she looked up, he was licking his bowl clean.

From the cupboards and drawers, she found a mug, teabags and a sugar bowl, and put the kettle on. An hour passed in a flash during which time she had found some frozen ready meals in the freezer, heated one up in the oven and sat down to eat a lasagne. After washing up her plate and making herself a cup of tea, she retired to the lounge once more. This time Bailey joined her on the sofa. She looked at the dog. 'Are you sure you're allowed on the sofa?'

To her surprise, Bailey jumped off, walked over to his dog basket and with a resigned whimper sat down.

Clara's shoulders sagged. 'Oh, all right.' She patted the seat next to her. 'One good deed deserves another. I suppose letting you sit on the sofa is the least I can do.' She was thinking of Bailey knocking over the flower pot and revealing the door key.

Bailey came charging over and jumped up beside her. He sat down and put a paw on her lap.

'Are you sure your owner won't be arriving home today?'

Bailey barked.

Clara put a finger to her lips in a shushing motion, afraid the neighbours might hear. She kicked off her shoes and prayed the owner didn't choose tonight to return from his travels.

32

Woken by the sound of a dog barking he sat bolt upright. The blankets piled on top of him to keep warm through the cool summer nights fell in a heap on the floor.

'Oh, damn and blast it.' The camp bed creaked under his weight as he threw his legs over the side and stood up. He shivered, picked up one of the old blankets and wrapped it around his shoulders as he trudged the few paces to the small window of the outhouse. It was his lookout. From this vantage point he had a clear view straight down the garden to the back of the house. That's why he chose this one out of the three.

He'd hit the jackpot and found a stove to cook on and heat the small stone outhouse. Wool blankets that despite being itchy and eons old served as bed covers. He'd been lucky. Almost three months had gone by in perfect solitude.

Holding the makeshift curtain to one side – a blanket hung at the window, so he could light an oil lantern in the evenings without drawing attention – his stomach lurched. There was a light on in the house. He pulled the curtain shut, afraid whoever was in the house would see him at the window. That wasn't possible; he hadn't lit the oil lamp. The outhouse was pitch dark.

He stood nervously fingering his beard. Had he imagined it? His face crumpled into a frown at the prospect he would have to pack up his stuff and move on? He was tired. Sleeping on a camp bed at his age, night after night was taking its toll. In the ordinary course of a day he didn't feel almost sixty. What was sixty meant to feel like anyway? It was the mornings when he staggered out of bed stiff and sore that he knew the years had caught up with him.

The property was empty – or at least it was. He had, in a moment of madness, walked up to the house one night having a particularly rough time on the camp bed, and considered moving in. A proper bed in a centrally heated room was tempting. He didn't even have to look for an open window or smash a pane of glass in the kitchen to gain entry. All he had to do was use the key under the plant pot by the front door.

He had walked around the grounds of the property, gathering up debris and sweeping the garden path after a storm one night. That's when he discovered some plant pots at the front of the house had blown over. And there it was – a key. He'd stood turning it over in his hand before putting it back where he found it.

Two weeks after moving into the outhouse, he'd ventured down to the beach early one morning for a refreshing dip in the sea, and found a local newspaper discarded on the promenade. He cast a glance at the paper on his makeshift bedside table – an old stool he'd found – and thought of the advertisement for a house-sitter. If he couldn't live in the property, then he would make it his business that nobody else could.

There had been visits from the estate agents with prospective house sitters. A few branches brushing a window pane, the odd shutter outside banging loudly, reverberating around the house, the front door slamming shut behind them, a creak on the stair. It was surprising how a rumour spread.

He'd heard it in the local library when he was strolled out the door with a library book tucked under his coat. He had clamped a hand over his mouth in surprise when he discovered the local estate agent having problems filling the position. "They say the house is haunted." Those were someone's exact words. He had no idea his little ruse would be so effective.

He frowned when it occurred to him that if there was a house sitter, how had he missed their first visit? The only vehicle he'd spied was a police car earlier this evening.

When he heard a car coming up the gravel driveway at the front of the house, he thought it was the estate agent again. He'd got the shock of his life when he went to investigate and saw a police car. And it wasn't just any ordinary police car. It was the Suffolk Dog Unit. His little ruse to make the property appear haunted had backfired. The rumours had attracted the local police who had come to investigate strange goings-on at the empty property.

He'd raced down the garden path to gather up his belongings, afraid a growling police dog would appear any moment and give the game away. But that didn't happen. When he stepped out of the outhouse, listening for the sound of a dog crashing through the undergrowth towards him, all he heard was a car moving off down the driveway followed by the sound of the iron gates clanging shut. He was all alone again – or so he thought.

Holding the edge of the makeshift curtain he stole another look, hoping in the haze of semi-wakefulness he'd imagined a light on up at the house. He closed the curtain and breathed a huge sigh. 'I *did* imagine it.' There was no light on in the lounge at the back of the house.

He stood for a moment at the window checking there were no lights on upstairs either. At this time of night that would be a tell-tale sign someone was home. Nothing. The house was dark.

He withdrew to his camp bed, lit the oil lamp and opened the novel he had borrowed from the library. As with the others, as soon as he'd read it, he would return it. 'I didn't steal it, just borrowed it.' Drowsy and too tired to read, he snapped the book shut and blew out the lamp.

As he drifted off to sleep, he tried to ignore the thought that it was time to face his demons and move back into his house. He couldn't go on like this forever. His G.P. would skin him alive if he saw him now, three months on from leaving the hotel, living like a vagrant in his own backyard. It was the stuff of mental breakdowns. Perhaps that's what they call it when you cannot make sense of life anymore once there was nobody to share it with.

Ralph felt a backache coming on already. The camp bed seemed to get more uncomfortable with each passing day. He turned over with difficulty, the narrow bed creaking as he moved. One day he wouldn't be surprised if he got into bed and the thing collapsed. Ralph's thoughts turned to his house. All he had to do was get up, walk down the garden, collect the key from under the flower pot, and open the door. A comfortable bed, a bath and a hot meal courtesy of the frozen ready meals sitting in his freezer beckoned.

So why don't you?

He had this silent conversation with himself every night as he tried to get comfortable. 'Because I'm not ready,' he said out loud. 'Perhaps in the morning I'll feel different,' he mumbled, his eyes growing heavy as he stared at the painting of Mallorca propped up in the corner.

He closed his eyes and drifted back to another place in time; a place he couldn't wait to return to every night. He was walking barefoot on a Mediterranean beach holding her hand. She was holding on to his arm and he could feel her soft cheek against his shoulder…

In his recurring dream, Clara was forever by his side.

❖

'There, that's better.' Clara pulled the thick velvet curtains to block out the draught from the floor-to-ceiling bay window. That wasn't the only reason she suddenly got up from the sofa and pulled the curtains. It was just in case someone spotted a light on in the house. She didn't think that would be the case; the house was in extensive grounds and set well back from the road. Although not overlooked, it didn't hurt to err on the side of caution.

She was about to return to the sofa when she remembered she'd left the newspaper on the window seat. She fancied having another look at the ad for the house-sitter position. She pulled the curtain aside, reached for the newspaper and closed them behind her. That's when she came to an abrupt halt. She opened the curtains a chink, but all was dark in the garden.

For a moment there she thought she'd seen a hazy yellow light at the far end of the garden. She shook her head. It was just tiredness, or perhaps it was still on her mind the thought the owner would show up.

She glanced at the curtains thinking she ought to phone Tamsin and ask her to pay for a hotel room. It wouldn't take long to walk back to the hotel. There was a twenty-four-hour reception. She'd still get a room for the night.

She reached in her handbag to get her phone and disturbed Bailey lying sprawled on the sofa. He looked up at her with those brown soulful eyes. Clara sighed. She couldn't take him with her to the hotel. But leaving him all alone in this big old house worried her. There was also the question of what to do with Bailey tomorrow when she intended to return home. But for now, she decided tomorrow would just have to take care of itself.

She sat down on the sofa beside Bailey and found the pamphlets in her handbag she had collected from the seminar. She put her bag to one side and stared at the brochures. Was it only this morning that she was railroaded into attending under the guise of some woman called Ellen?

She unbuttoned her coat and looked down at the label stuck on her blouse. It was still there. Clara rolled her eyes. Thank goodness she was not asked to take her coat off at the police station. She'd forgotten all about the name tag from the seminar.

Carefully peeling it off, cast she gazed around the room looking for a wastepaper bin. She'd better not leave behind evidence of her stay; she put the sticky label in her handbag instead. Turning to the pamphlets spread out on the coffee table, she picked one up and leafed through it to take her mind off the fact that she was doing something unthinkable; squatting in a stranger's property.

She focused on the leaflet. It was all about reinventing yourself. There were lots of examples in the booklet of people from all walks of life who had changed their lives. All their paths were different, all their stories unique. But the one thing they had in common was that they'd been through or were going through a life-changing event.

Clara fell asleep on the sofa surrounded by the pamphlets from the reinventing yourself weekend, with those personal stories of people who were facing many challenges and turned their lives around.

She dreamed strange dreams of circus tents and a young woman in a red dress with long silky black hair. She was leading her by the hand around a villa in a valley full of orange and lemon trees. Then the cold, smooth tiled floors gave way to sand and the hand holding hers was no longer that of a woman but a man, a young man. He was walking barefoot on the beach holding her hand. She was holding on to his arm, her cheek resting on his shoulder, wishing this perfect moment could last forever…

33

Clara roused. For a moment, she imagined the last few days had been a bad dream. She opened her eyes to find it wasn't Joe kissing her good morning, but a golden retriever sitting on the floor beside the sofa licking her face.

'Ewww!' She pushed his muzzle away and sat up. 'Oh. My. Goodness.' It wasn't a dream; she *was* squatting in a stranger's house, sleeping on their sofa.

She reached for her handbag and grabbed her mobile phone. In the cold light of day, she was still angry at Joe for going along to the seminar on false pretences. She glanced at the pamphlets scattered on the floor. This wasn't about The Big Payday. He'd decided to change his life and leave her high and dry. Despite all that, he was still her husband; the man she had met and married almost forty years ago – in sickness and in health. And now he was in hospital. What sort of person does that make me thought Clara, on a guilt trip for taking off?

She switched on her mobile phone expecting messages from Tamsin or the hospital with bad news. The worst news. She held her breath and counted one… two… three… *nothing*. It didn't make a sound. There were no text messages. No voice messages.

Clara remembered to exhale. *No news was good news – right?* Then her phone rang. *Oh, crumbs.* She answered it with a trembling voice. 'Hello?'

'Mum? Where are you? You need to get back home ASAP!'

'Oh my God. What's happened?'

'What's happened? I'll tell you what's happened. You left me with Dorothy – that's what's happened. She's doing my head in.'

'Wait. What about your father? Has he… is he…?'

'Oh, Dad?' Tamsin said almost as an afterthought. 'No change. I tried to persuade her to go home, but she said she was living in our house now. Is that right?'

'*Our* house?'

'Our house, your house – what's the difference?'

Clara sighed. Tamsin didn't realise that *our house,* the house her parents lived in which had been her childhood home, would have to be sold whether or not Joe recovered. There would not be a right time to tell Tamsin that Joe was planning to leave. And where Dorothy got the idea she would move in with them was anyone's guess.

If Joe was in the process of planning his exit route from their marriage, who would care for Dorothy while he started a new life with that woman? Clara's train of thought came to an abrupt halt. She couldn't believe he would disappear and leave her to deal with his mother. *Nice one, Joe.*

'When are you coming home?' demanded Tamsin.

'Did you say there was no change? Your father is still…'

'He hasn't woken up yet – if that's what you're asking.'

Clara noticed she wasn't the only one clinging to comforting euphemisms. It made it sound more reassuring, like he was just taking a nap rather than in a coma with a head injury from which he might never recover.

'Tamsin, there's something I need to do here before I leave. I'll catch the train later today.'

'You do realise it's Sunday. Isn't there a reduced service at the weekend?'

'Oh.' Clara hadn't anticipated that. She didn't relish another night squatting in this house on a stranger's sofa, even if the sofa was comfortable. But it felt good to get away and think about herself for a change.

'Mum?'

'Oh er…' Clara's mind had wandered. 'Don't worry. I'll find out what time I need to be at the station. I won't miss the train home today, I promise.'

'Good. Just make sure you don't because I must say you're being quite selfish, you know. I've got to deal with the girls *and* Dorothy all by myself. And visit Dad. It isn't on, you know.'

'Pardon me?' *Did she call me selfish?* Clara didn't get a response. Tamsin had already signed off. Satisfied that her mum had told her what she wanted to hear; a promise she was on her way home to be at everyone's beck and call – look after Dorothy, keep an eye on the grandchildren, visit Dad.

Clara put her phone away in her handbag and turned to find Bailey sitting beside her on the sofa. He had something in his jaws. He dropped it on her lap. She picked up the pamphlet from the seminar which now had four teeth marks and looked at the dog. 'Are you trying to tell me something?'

Bailey barked, jumped off the sofa and disappeared out of the room. She could hear him running down the hall, his paws tapping on the wooden flooring. Then all was quiet. She wondered what he was up to. A moment later he reappeared at the door.

Clara looked at him. 'What?'

He turned full circle as though chasing his tail and then ran down the hallway again.

'Ah.' She realised this was his way of telling her he had a call of nature. Unlike her cat at home who could use the cat flap, she had to let Bailey out into the back garden.

She followed him down the hall to the kitchen and unlocked the back door. 'Now be quiet. No barking when we go outside,' she was saying as she unlocked the door. When she turned around Bailey was no longer in the kitchen.

Clara sighed. 'Does the dog want to go out or what?' Hands on her hips, she yelled 'Bailey!' forgetting to keep her voice down.

The dog reappeared with something in his jaws.

'What's this?'

Bailey dropped it at her feet. He barked and spun around full circle before disappearing down the hall once more. Clara bent down and picked up the lead. When she looked up, he was back again, this time with a ball in his jaws. She looked at the dog standing in front of her, wagging his tail. 'Are you telling me you want me to take you for a walk *and* play ball?'

Bailey barked. 'You don't want much do you?' Clara glanced at her watch conscious of the fact she had a train to catch today, which reminded her – what was she going to do with Bailey? She couldn't take him home with her. It was bad enough that her cat, Marley, had to put up with Dorothy's dog. At least Winston was a small dog, and afraid of Marley. He hid every time the cat appeared.

She didn't want to think about what to do with Bailey when she left. First, she would take him for a walk. Perhaps the answer might come to her.

Brushing her blonde bob, she tried not to feel self-conscious about the fact that she'd slept in her clothes. Clara knelt and attached the lead to his collar. She stepped outside the house, closed the back door behind her and said, 'Okay, where to?'

Bailey barked and pulled on his lead.

Clara followed.

❖

He was frying bacon on the camping stove in the corner of the outhouse when he heard it again – that same guttural bark from last night. Except this time, he wasn't half asleep. It was most definitely a dog.

Ralph hesitated as he looked at his breakfast in the pan. 'Oh, damn and blast it!' He put the spatula down, switched off the stove and walked to the outhouse door. He glanced over his shoulder at his crispy fried bacon before heading out.

He could have left the grounds of his property through the gap in the hedgerow at the bottom of the garden. It brought him out into the street where a path led down to the beachfront. Instead, he aimed towards the house. Nobody was there.

He'd got over last night's jitters when he was tired, and his imagination was running away with him. In the cold light of day, he thought it was a neighbour's dog. But instinct told him he was no longer the only one living here.

He slowed as he neared the back of the house, his eyes darting this way and that, looking out for any sign of life. If someone spotted him, he knew he could pretend to be selling door-to-door. It was a sure-fire way of getting a door slammed in his face without too many questions asked.

Ralph frowned. What is wrong with you? You own this house. All you have to do is come clean, tell them who you are, and then tell them to bugger off. Simple as that.

Ralph wiped his greasy fingers down his dirty jumper as he approached the back of the house. He looked about him before peering through the lounge window. Then the kitchen window. There was no sign of life. He scratched his chin and felt the beard where he hadn't shaved in weeks. He nervously run his fingers through his hair and unwound a strand of grey hair from his index finger. That's when he caught his reflection in the kitchen window and stopped dead.

'I look like a vagrant,' he whispered to his reflection, surprised how his life had changed in just a few weeks. He was taken aback what sleeping rough does to a person after only a short time. And therein was the flaw in his plan if he caught someone on his property; who would believe him looking this – a down-and-out tramp – if he told them he owned this grand old house?

He was more likely to find himself bundled into the back of

a police car if he wasn't too careful. He didn't even have his wallet on him with any identification.

After his first night in the outhouse when he didn't return to the hotel, the receptionist had rung him on his mobile phone concerned that he hadn't shown up. His suitcase, travel bag, passport, and even his wallet were in his hotel room. Ralph had come up with some bull about bumping into an old friend and staying over at their house. But there was still the problem of what to do about his possessions.

Ralph didn't want to return to the hotel, so he'd asked the receptionist to check him out and send someone over with his belongings, with strict instructions to leave them in the wardrobe in the apartment above the triple garage. He'd told them where to find the spare key; it was on the ledge above the door. They'd just have to send someone tall enough who could reach up and retrieve the key.

He had arranged a day and time, and lo and behold a young man arrived by car with his belongings. Ralph had watched from the gardens as they did as he asked. Now all he had to do was walk up those wooden steps to the apartment and retrieve his wallet, then he wouldn't have to worry about being caught in the grounds of his own property.

The trouble was Ralph wasn't ready to walk up open the door on all his photographic equipment reminding him of a past life, and a few things he'd rather forget; that his wife died on his last assignment abroad. He wished he'd known the key was still under the flowerpot where his wife had left it. Perhaps it wouldn't have bothered him half as much if they'd put his stuff in there.

Ralph sighed and backed away from the house, afraid if someone *was* inside, they might call the police if they saw his face peering in at them. He stopped after a few paces, his tense shoulders relaxing. The house appeared just as devoid of life as it had been on every other day he'd checked. A quick nip around to the front of the house confirmed the key was still under the flower pot. There was no house sitter inside. The coast was clear. He stood there for a moment staring at the flower pot. There it was again, the inclination to take the key, unlock the front door and sleep in a proper bed.

Ralph turned around and headed back toward the outhouse. If it wasn't for his breakfast of streaky bacon and scrambled eggs, he might well have given into temptation and thought *to hell with it.* Besides, he hadn't been gone long, and although he'd turned off the small stove, he reckoned his bacon and eggs would still be warm.

His mouth watered. It was surprising what you could find rummaging through the bin at the rear of the local supermarket. It was quite shocking what good food they tossed out just because it was past its sell-by date.

Ralph walked back into the outhouse and reached for the saucepan. 'What the hell?!' He held up the pan. It was empty.

❖

'Where have you been?' Clara eyed the dog. 'And what are you eating?' Whatever Bailey had found in the garden, he had enjoyed it. He licked his lips. Clara thought she smelled… 'Bacon?' She raised an eyebrow and shook her head. Feeling hungry, she hadn't had breakfast or even made a cup of tea before walking out of the house.

'Don't run off like that again, Bailey,' she admonished him as she reached for his lead. 'We've got to stick together. We can't hang around in the garden, even though it is quite lovely, in case a neighbour—'

Bailey shot off.

'Oh, for goodness sake!' She was about to run after him when her attention was drawn to her surroundings. She'd only glimpsed the garden last night in the dark; the car headlights had fleetingly illuminated those parts bordering the driveway. Beyond that all had been pitch dark. She had forgotten how beautiful it was. Not your typical English country garden. The flowers and plants reminded her of somewhere different – Mediterranean almost.

She didn't know how long she had been standing there staring at the garden. Bailey interrupted her peaceful solitude, along with thoughts of a faraway place by appearing from a corner of the yard and racing toward her. He stopped in the middle of the lawn and looked back from whence he'd come.

Clara got the message. She walked towards him. 'Come on, then. You know where you're going.'

Bailey turned full circle in an excited spin and raced across the garden. Clara picked up her pace and followed, thankful that for once he hadn't barked. She was worried someone might have heard the dog.

34

Clara threw the ball. Bailey raced toward it, kicking up sand in his wake. They did not allow dogs on the beach from May to September, but it was early in the morning and the beach deserted. Bailey had done his business before they reached the promenade. Dogs weren't allowed down here in the summer; in case inconsiderate dog owners didn't clear up the dog poop. It was a health hazard for children playing in the sand.

It did cross her mind after what happened last night – getting caught by an off-duty police officer – that perhaps returning to the scene of the crime wasn't such a good idea. She checked there were no other dogs in the vicinity. Clara wasn't just looking for *any* dog, only the police dog that caught her red-handed trying to break the lock on the beach hut. She wouldn't make the same mistake twice; next time she would bring bolt cutters.

She hadn't thought to search in the brick-built outhouses at the bottom of the garden before taking Bailey for a walk. That might be the place to find them among the garden tools she assumed were inside and made a mental note to look when they returned from the beach. The garden was so beautiful, she would search for a garden chair too, and find a nice spot to sit on the patio at the back of the house.

She glanced at her watch. She was meant to catch a train

back to reality not plan to sit and admire some stranger's back garden that reminded her of a far-away place. The Mediterranean.

Clara looked up and saw Bailey racing back along the beach towards her with the ball. 'One more time and then we've got to head back.' She had no idea why she was talking to Bailey. Clara smiled as she watched him cock his head to one side listening to her voice. He knew she was about to throw the ball again and spun around in excitement.

She tried to throw it as far as she could to expend the dog's energy. She watched him race down the beach before turning her attention to the sea and the surf lapping on the shore. It was a calm summer's morning. The sea breeze fresh, if not a little chilly. Clara didn't mind. It felt good to be alive. Staring at the ocean she shuddered at what she did last night. Would she have gone through with it if Bailey hadn't been there, like a guardian angel, saving her from herself?

Last night, with the prospect of Joe leaving her alone and penniless, she didn't know how to face the future. Tamsin wouldn't see her own mother out on the street even if they weren't that close. Kevin would help his mother-in-law in any way he could. And there was always Debs and Gerald to rely on. But the financial situation did not bother her. It was Joe, her dependable Joe, who knew how much her brother's disappearance had affected her. He'd made a promise that if they were wed, he would always care for her and never leave.

How could he do this to me? That's the question that had her emotions spinning out of control as she walked down the beach last night. How was she to cope with the devastating realisation he too would leave her, and in the worst way imaginable; like Tommy all those years ago.

Clara wasn't excusing Joe's behaviour, but with time on her own to mull things over she knew she was partly to blame for the predicament she found herself in; *didn't I get what I deserved?* She'd treated Joe like a doormat. He'd slaved to provide everything in his means possible to give her the life he thought she wanted; a life of leisure, swanning around with her friends, spending Joe's money without a care to the hours he worked just to indulge her. It got Clara thinking: what did I ever do for Joe?

'It was all me, me, me.' Clara choked back a sob. She wasn't wallowing in self-pity. It was the thought of those left behind if she'd *had* walked into the sea last night. Thank god for Bailey. Consumed by the situation she found herself in, she hadn't stopped to consider how one last selfish act would have robbed Tamsin and the girls of a mother and grandmother. Whether or not Joe made it, he intended to walk out of their lives. They couldn't afford to lose her too.

Clara turned away from the sea. It was time she went home. Bailey hadn't returned with the ball, she furrowed her brow and called out his name. She walked along the beach with visions of Bailey under citizen's arrest by a disgruntled passer-by who had caught the dog on the beach. Clara didn't want another run-in with the law.

35

Clara followed Bailey's fresh paw prints in the sand. It didn't take long to find him. She could see the dog in the distance, further up the shore toward the beach huts. She picked up the ball as she made her way towards her four-legged friend. She already knew what had caught his attention and the reason he had suddenly lost interest in the ball game. Bailey must have a fondness for bacon, thought Clara with a smile. Her mouth watered at the smell wafting up the beach.

She knitted her brow wondering where the smell was coming from. It wasn't from the little wooden tea hut on the promenade which was closed. They would doubtless be open later to catch the passing trade.

Clara kept walking. She passed the ball from one hand to another as she made her way along the beach. 'Bailey!' she called out. She could see the dog up ahead, but it was only when drawing closer she realised he wasn't alone. The dog was sitting beside a young woman kneeling on the sand. He watched her as she flipped over a piece of bacon in a pan set on a small barbecue grill over a campfire.

Clara slowed, debating whether to turn tail and walk away in case she got into trouble for letting him on the beach. The last thing she wanted was any aggravation. She was about to leave, knowing he would find his own way home, when the young woman waved. Clara looked about her. There was no one else around. Clara raised her hand and waved back as she continued walking in their direction, hoping the young women wasn't about to have words with her about Bailey. Dressed in a long baggy tee-shirt over a bikini, she looked as though she'd been for an early morning dip in the sea.

'Is he your dog?' she asked.

Clara nodded warily.

'He's sooo cute.' She stroked his silky coat. 'I love dogs. What's his name?'

'Bailey.'

'What a nice name.' She turned to look at the dog sitting beside her. 'I know what you're after. You smelt my bacon.'

Clara relaxed. 'He hasn't eaten yet. Come to think of it, neither have I.'

The young woman's face lit up. 'Why don't you join us?' She turned her head and said in a good-humoured voice, 'There you are. It's about time!'

Clara followed her gaze to see a young man standing on the porch of *her* beach hut. He stretched his arms high over his head and said, 'What a glorious morning. Why didn't you wake me?'

Wake me? Clara looked from the young woman busy cooking breakfast to the young man standing yawning. Had they slept the night in *her* beach hut?

'I thought I'd let you sleep,' she answered. 'Will you bring out more bacon and eggs? We have a guest joining us.'

'A guest?' His ready smiled faded when he spotted Clara. He eyed her warily. 'What's going on?'

'I told you. She's joining us for breakfast.'

Clara, noting the tension in the air, would have declined to join them if it wasn't for one grating fact: they were using *her* beach hut. She had a good mind to tell them she was the owner, and they had to pack up their things and leave otherwise she would call the police.

Contacting the police would have been a bluff. Until she got the legal paperwork from Gerald proving ownership, she didn't have a leg to stand on.

Her thoughts drifted to the episode yesterday when she was carted off to the police station. She was already well-acquainted with the law in this town and didn't fancy renewing that acquaintance. All the same, if she only had to ask the young woman to leave, Clara would not have hesitated. However, the fact she had a boyfriend, or husband, was a whole other ball game.

The young man had gone back inside, to fetch more bacon and eggs – and to put on a shirt. He'd only been wearing boxer shorts. Clara's first impression was that he wasn't pleased she was joining them for breakfast.

Clara chose not to give the game away, although she did ask, 'Are you sleeping in the beach hut?'

'Why?' she replied defensively.

Clara noticed her friendly demeanour slip.

She was hiding something, Clara could tell.

'Just making conversation.' Clara shrugged as if it was of no consequence. Hoping they weren't homeless people who had found an empty beach hut and moved in. Surely, they couldn't get away with that? Clara cringed, her face flushing at the thought she had done just that – found something empty and moved right in. Except it was far worse; she was squatting in someone's home.

She noticed two back-packs on the beach spilling out with clothes. Their luggage looked new, not the sort of thing she'd expect homeless people to own. The couple reminded Clara of young backpackers. She knitted her brow trying to fathom what they were doing on a beach in a sleepy Suffolk town instead of backpacking somewhere exotic like Thailand or Australia?

The young woman turned to Clara and followed her gaze to the two back-packs. She flipped over a slice of bacon in the saucepan under Bailey's watchful eye and said, 'Why pay for a hotel room when we can stay here for—'

Clara raised her eyebrows when the woman stopped short. 'Stay here for…?' she prompted despite already guessing the next word; *free*. When the young woman clammed up Clara changed tack. 'So how did you come by *this* beach hut…?'

'We're renting it for the summer. That's er what I meant about not paying for a hotel room.' She looked away, avoiding Clara's gaze and added, 'it's *so* expensive, holidaying in this country – don't you think?'

Clara nodded. It was on the tip of her tongue to reply, *so why didn't you go abroad somewhere cheaper?*

Clara kept that thought to herself. Besides, she wasn't convinced they were renting the beach hut. Although it *was* possible that at some point over the last two decades somebody had discovered the abandoned hut, done it up, and let it out in the summer months.

Clara was in no doubt it would be a nice little earner and could only blame herself if that were the case. She hadn't been back to Suffolk to check on her property since inheriting it. If it was rented, she doubted you could bunk down there for the night – not legally, anyway.

But not that that interested her. The titbit of information she did hone in on was the mention of a *holiday*. That meant they were leaving – soon. Clara needed to get her hands on the beach hut. If it was true, and they were only here on vacation, perhaps by the time she gained the paperwork from Gerald, had the hut valued and put it on the market, her unwanted guests would be gone. Fingers crossed. She could well do without this little complication.

'Did you say you were here on holiday?'

The young woman nodded. 'We're here for the summer. I'm in my last year of a nursing degree, so I need to return after the summer break. I'm hoping it's long enough for Elliot to—'

'For Elliot to *what* . . .?' The young man asked harshly.

Clara turned to see the young man standing outside the beach hut holding a packet of bacon and a carton of eggs. He'd overheard the last snippet of their conversation. He stared at the young woman with cold blue eyes.

'Oh um, I was just saying you always wanted to learn to surf. I was hoping we were here long enough for you to do that.'

Clara's head swivelled in her direction. She'd said no such thing.

'Oh, I see.' He seemed to relax. He handed over the bacon and eggs. 'Don't cook a lot on my account, will you? You know I won't eat it.'

'Elliot, you must eat *something*.'

'I wish you'd stop fussing!'

Clara felt uncomfortable. She was about to make her excuses and leave when the young woman said, 'Have a seat. It's ready to dish up.'

Bailey barked and wagged his tail.

Clara sat down on the sand the other side of the campfire. Despite her inclination to leave, the cooked breakfast was far too tempting to resist. The young woman passed her a paper plate piled with a full English breakfast worthy of a good hotel in town; bacon, eggs, a sausage, some hash browns and beans.

'This looks delicious,' commented Clara in surprise.

Bailey agreed with the sentiment as he licked his chops and followed the plate being passed across to Clara.

'May I?' asked Clara as she picked up a piece of streaky bacon and motioned at Bailey.

'Sure. There's plenty more where that came from.'

Bailey wolfed down the bacon and sat watching Clara, waiting for his next treat.

Clara picked up the plastic knife and fork and paused, still taken aback that the young woman had offered a perfect stranger to join them for breakfast on the beach. She would have thought, considering the romantic setting, the young couple would have preferred to be alone.

Clara said, 'Thank you, this is so nice.' She wasn't just referring to the breakfast. Even though she wasn't happy they were using her beach hut, she appreciated the kindness of strangers. She felt so alone, the like of which she hadn't felt since losing Tommy, it was nice to have company – she glanced at Bailey – *human* company.

36

'I enjoy cooking.'

Clara glanced at the young woman sitting on the sand.

She continued, 'It's surprising what you can whip up with next to nothing. I'm a dab hand after being a student for three years. Hope you like it.'

'I do. It's the nicest English Breakfast I've ever tasted.' Clara wasn't exaggerating. Was it the company of strangers, or the setting, or the possibility of shedding her old life and starting anew; a thing she would never have contemplated if she hadn't discovered Joe was planning to leave?

'I'm Evie, by the way?'

Clara looked up from her plate, smiled at the young woman and introduced herself.

'It's lovely to meet you, Clara. This is my brother, Elliot.'

'Your brother?' 'Oh, I thought you two were…'

'A couple?' Evie laughed good-naturedly as she shook her head. 'Can't you see the family resemblance?'

'Now you mention it…' Clara glanced over at Elliot. He had his sister's piercing blue eyes, long slender nose and high cheekbones, but not her brown hair or svelte appearance. He was tall, slim and blonde and seemed younger than his sister, although it was hard to tell his age.

Clara recalled what Evie was saying to her about their

holiday while she was cooking the breakfast. *I'm just hoping it's long enough for Elliot to—'* Clara wondered what she was about to add before her brother appeared and Evie clammed up.

'You do look alike.' Clara could see the family resemblance.

'I should think so.' Evie said good-humouredly. 'We're twins.'

'Twins?' Clara said in astonishment.

'We looked more alike when we were little.' Evie turned to her brother. 'Don't you think?'

'Dunno.' He shrugged his shoulders and changed the subject. I want two rashers of bacon and an egg then I will put the finishing touches to the beach hut.'

Clara was just biting into a plump fried sausage, enjoying the novelty of eating a cooked breakfast at dawn on a deserted beach, when she realised what he'd just said. She turned to Elliot. 'Did you say you were putting the finishing touches to the beach hut?'

'Yes, you wouldn't believe what a wreck it was when we discovered it. I was astonished it hadn't fallen down, but the wood was sound. It just needed a good repaint. The lock was knackered, so we replaced that.'

'Replaced what?' asked Evie. She had returned from the hut with a bottle of tomato ketchup.

'The lock. I was telling Clara how rundown the beach hut was. Perhaps the owners abandoned it or maybe they passed away, so we thought what's the harm in doing it up?'

'Elliot.' There was a warning note in Evie's voice. 'I'm sure Clara does not want to hear all about your DIY skills.'

Clara suspected there was more to it than that. Evie wasn't being entirely honest when she said they'd rented the beach hut for the summer. It wasn't true. They'd looked for a rundown semi-derelict one and set about making it their own rather than checking into a hotel. Did this mean they had a claim on her beach hut? Is that what they were after?

Clara narrowed her eyes. 'So, this is *your* beach hut now, is it?' she asked, expecting Elliot to say yes.

He looked over at the wooden hut sitting on the beach. 'I wish it was. We're just borrowing it for the summer.'

Borrowing it. That was an interesting choice of words. Clara glanced at Evie who was noticeably quiet. Little wonder. Elliot had just contradicted her story and confirmed Clara's suspicions; they weren't renting it for the summer. Clara wouldn't be surprised if this had been their plan all along, so they didn't have to pay for accommodation. They'd hit the jackpot when they saw her beach hut forlorn and forgotten.

'I took some before and after photos on my phone. Do you want to see?'

'Elliot!'

He ignored his sister. So did Clara. She put her empty plate down on the sand, wiped her mouth with the paper napkin Evie had provided and stood up to walk around the campfire. She joined Elliot who was sitting next to his sister. Clara was very interested to see what had become of her hut over the years.

'Oh my!' Clara was shocked at the state of it. It was much worse than she imagined.

'If you think that's bad you should have seen the inside!' exclaimed Elliot when he caught Clara's expression. 'It's taken a good month of hard work to restore it to its former glory.'

'And don't forget the expense,' Evie reminded him. 'It wasn't cheap getting all the bits and pieces we needed from the local DIY store in town. I swear it was more expensive than going to one of the large superstores out of town, especially the paint. I don't know why you insisted on having that superior duck-egg blue paint.'

Elliot smiled at his sister. 'You know what I'm like: if you're going to do a job, you might as well do it properly. Besides, it looks bloody nice.'

They all turned to look at the beach hut. No one disagreed with that sentiment. Elliot had done such a fantastic job restoring it and coupled with his decision to use expensive materials, and install brand new shutters, it looked brand new. From what Clara remembered, her parents never spent a lot of money on maintenance; a quick dab of paint to cover any bare wood and replacing the odd patch of roofing – that was about it. In all the years they owned the beach hut, it never looked like this.

Evie sighed. She muttered, 'I wonder if it would have been cheaper to hire a local handyman to do the job. Or stay in a hotel.'

'There was that strange man who helped us re-do the roof, remember, when I needed a hand re-felting it.'

'Strange man?' said Clara looking from Elliot to Evie.

'Yes. There's this man who comes every morning at the crack of dawn for a swim in the sea. We always wave, but he never acknowledges us, does he Elliot.'

He nodded in agreement.

It was only when he saw Elliot lose his balance on the step ladder, and fall off the roof one morning, that he came running up the beach. Elliot was all right, thank God, but he told us re-felting the roof is a two-person job. He insisted on helping. Didn't talk much. Never knew his name. He stayed for breakfast, though.'

Who could resist thought Clara glancing at her empty plate? She wouldn't normally have seconds, but the cooked breakfast was so delicious she might well have found room if they had offered her another helping.

'He didn't ask for any money either, although we offered to pay for his time,' added Elliot.

'That's right. He wouldn't take a penny. He just said that it took him back – sitting on the beach around a campfire.'

Clara looked from one twin to the other. 'Took him back?'

Elliot and Evie exchanged glances before Evie said, 'We reminded him of some people he once knew a long time ago. Anyway, I was kind of pleased he wouldn't take any money because I couldn't afford to fork out any more on the repairs.'

'Where do you think he came from?' asked Clara, intrigued.

'I don't mean to sound unkind, but he looked like a homeless person.'

Elliot tutted. 'Just because he was unshaven—'

Evie rolled her eyes. 'It wasn't just one night's worth of stubble. He had a *beard*.' Evie said the word *beard* in such a way that made it sound as though he had something quite horrid like a third eye.

Elliot's face creased in a broad smile at his twin sister. 'Just because he has a beard doesn't mean he is homeless.'

'He was kind of old too.'

Evie suddenly turned to Clara and said, 'No disrespect intended.'

Clara looked at her. Are you saying I'm old?

'Not that I'm saying you're old or anything,' Evie added. 'It's just he was around your age.'

Elliot rolled his eyes at his sister. 'I think what Evie is trying to say—'

'What I'm trying to say, Elliot – and I'd rather speak for myself if you don't mind – is that he's more like Clara's generation.'

A smile played on Clara's lips as she listened to this banter. It brought back fond memories of her and Tommy and the way they used to finish each other's sentences; they knew what the other was thinking before they'd even opened their mouths. It was maddening sometimes.

Clara glanced at Elliot. He reminded her of Tommy. Although he seemed younger, more fragile than his twin sister, she bet he was the firstborn, the eldest, the voice of reason; the one who stepped into the breach when his sister committed a faux pas and needed helping out of a tight spot. Tommy always felt less her equal, her twin, and more like a big brother who looked after her, who was there for her until—

'We haven't seen him this morning.' said Elliot.

Clara looked his way, thankful her thoughts were interrupted before they moved on to the question that plagued her: what had happened to Tommy all those years ago? Clara groaned when her mother-in-law's words of wisdom came to mind: *Nothing good ever came from raking up the past.*

Dorothy loved her sayings, but that was one piece of wisdom she reserved for Clara's benefit. Despite their mutual dislike, Dorothy seemed to have a sixth sense when it came to Clara and her twin brother. Perhaps it was that faraway look in her eyes when sometimes, out of the blue, her mind wandered back to that age-old question – *what happened the night of their eighteenth birthday party?*

Evie glanced toward the sea. 'I didn't see him go for his early morning dip. Perhaps he's moved on.'

'Moved on?' Elliot shook his head. 'Honestly, you're too quick to pass judgement. I bet he's not a homeless person at all but lives in one of those nice houses up there overlooking the sea.'

Clara glanced up above the promenade to the cliff top where she was squatting in the house behind the high hedgerows.

'If that's the case,' said Evie, 'then why doesn't he own a beach hut too?'

'Dunno. Maybe he doesn't need one if he lives just up there.'

Evie sighed. 'It was such an expense doing it up that sometimes I wished we'd never laid eyes on it.' She looked at her brother. 'I could have spent that money staying in a nice hotel.'

'You don't mean that,' chided Elliot.

Clara guessed which hotel Evie was talking about: the five-star hotel where she was intending to stay another night until she discovered she'd run out of money.

'I do mean it, Elliot.'

'No, you don't, and you know why…'

Clara waited for Evie to respond before she realised it wasn't a question. Whatever their reasons for wanting the beach hut for the summer was staying between the twins – for now.

'I don't regret it,' continued Elliot. 'I've been enjoying myself. Besides, it was a great idea paying the owners in kind by doing it up for them while we were borrowing it for the summer. I would have loved to see their faces when they find out what we did with the place.'

Evie grimaced. 'I'd be careful what you wish for, Elliot.'

'What are you saying? That they'd rather it fell down?'

'What I'm saying, Elliot, is that it *is* someone else's property. They might not take kindly to the makeover – even if it was with the best intentions. '

Clara couldn't resist offering her opinion. 'Oh, I'm sure it will delight the owner.' She *was* delighted and rubbing her hands at how much value had been added, not to mention the money and time saved having someone else do it up.

'There, you see. Someone agrees with me.'

Evie frowned at her brother. Determined to get the last word in, she said, 'And let us not forget that there is always the possibility they might just turn up out of the blue.'

'Turn up?' Elliot cast a worried frown in his sister's direction. 'Do you think so?'

Clara looked from Evie to Elliot. Perhaps now would be a good time to tell them the truth.

'Maybe they've got wind of how much these things are worth nowadays.' Evie glanced at the hut. 'I imagine they'd be rubbing their hands if they saw what you've done to the place.'

Clara felt her face glow in embarrassment; that's just what she'd been thinking.

Evie looked worried. 'If you want to spend the rest of summer here, you better hope the owners don't turn up and turf us out. Apart from the train fare back to London, we've pretty much run out of money.'

'We're broke? You're kidding!'

It was Clara's turn to frown. Now they were on the subject of the owner turning up, why didn't she tell them? If they found out she'd returned to claim her beach hut, they'd pack their bags and move on. She couldn't imagine they would kick up a fuss. They didn't seem the types who would want any aggravation. However, Clara couldn't bring herself to ask them to leave. And the reason? Because she knew what it felt like to be down on your luck and have nowhere to go. Unbeknown to the twins she was in the same boat: right now, she didn't want to return to London either.

If she was here with Joe, she knew what he'd do. With thoughts of The Big Payday – Joe would demand the keys; except her husband wasn't here to decide. For the first time in decades, Clara was free to make her own choices. As fabulous as that sounded on paper, all she felt was vulnerable, frightened – and alone.

The last time she'd felt this way was in the aftermath of losing Tommy. Except back then she was a young eighteen-year-old privately educated madam with a plummy accent and the optimism of youth. That optimism, the belief she had the world at her feet and things would get better, had led her to abandon her life here after Tommy's funeral, up sticks and move to London. Back then, she had taken what seemed in hindsight a huge step to leave behind everything familiar for the big unknown.

Clara was worried she had reached that juncture in her life once more. However, this time she didn't have that naïve optimism of youth that comes from not having experienced the disappointments and regrets that life throws at you.

Regrets. Clara didn't want to think about her reasons for leaving; running away from everyone that reminded her of Tommy – including his best friend.

Clara shook her head. She didn't want to rehash the past and that time in her life. Her greatest fear after losing Tommy had always been ending her days alone. But she wasn't that young girl anymore looking for someone to take care of her. She wanted something more. *Something more?* Clara knitted her brow trying to fathom where such an unexpected idea had come from. She'd been thinking about falling in love. *What a ridiculous idea. At her age?* Besides, she'd done that with Joe – hadn't she?

Joe did all the romantic things that Clara knew used to take her friends by surprise. After years of marriage, her friends never woke up with a rose on their pillow or got breakfast in bed, or fresh flowers brought home after work for no reason. They were envious of all the attention her husband still lavished on her. Was she ungrateful? Not a bit of it. Did she take him for granted? Possibly. Did she ever love Joe the way he loved her?

That stopped her in her tracks. *Did I ever really love Joe?*

Clara frowned. Of course she loved him. She'd married him – hadn't she? But was she ever really *in love* with Joe? She knew what distinguished the two because Clara had been *in love* once before.

'Well, they're not here now so they won't object if I do one last job.'

Clara was miles away. She looked over at Elliot and barely registered what he'd just said.

'Then the beach hut will be finished.' He handed Evie his plate.

'Can't I tempt you with seconds? Perhaps a hash brown or more scrambled eggs? And there's plenty of bacon.'

He shook his head.

'In that case, I'll give it to the dog.'

Bailey woofed.

Elliot got to his feet. 'Go right ahead.'

Clara glanced at the beach hut. It sounded as though Elliot still had one more thing to do before his work was complete. There were no odd patches which he'd missed when painting. 'I don't see what else there is to do,' commented Clara.

'Oh, there's an old decrepit sign.' Evie pointed. 'See.'

Clara didn't need to look. She was familiar with that old sign above the door. Tommy made it in the woodwork class at school the year their parents bought the beach hut. They had been over the moon when Tommy presented it to them on his last day of the summer term.

They had stood on the sand watching as their father nailed it above the door. He was especially chuffed with the sign even though there was no name on it, just a picture Tommy had painted of their father's sailboat.

Clara smiled when she recalled how talented her brother was. Tommy had always been good at drawing. She'd often wondered if he might have become an artist. But their father pressured him to get a *real* job and join his firm of solicitors. But that was all water under the bridge now. He never became an artist or a solicitor. All Clara had left to remember him by was an empty grave, an old, worn suitcase and a decrepit sign above the door of a beach hut that one day soon, she would have to sell.

Elliot brought out a pair of step ladders from behind the hut.

Clara turned to Evie. 'What if that sign has sentimental value? It looks handmade.' She knew for a fact it *was* handmade. 'Perhaps the owners wouldn't want it taken down.'

Evie studied Clara for a moment.

Clara hoped she hadn't given the game away. She sat there worried Evie had guessed the truth.

Evie called out, 'Elliot!'

Elliot had just put his foot on the first rung of the step ladder. He turned around.

'Clara suggested the sign may be of sentimental value. Perhaps we should leave it.'

'You think so?' Elliot stepped off the ladder. He walked over. 'But the beach hut must have stood abandoned for years.' He cast a glance back. 'Why would the owner return now?'

Clara tried to keep her emotions in check. She shouldn't be here. Her place was at home, asleep in her own bed until Joe brought her up a morning cup of tea. Then she would hear him preparing the breakfast before he went to work while having her customary lie in. Instead, she was here sitting on the beach eating breakfast with strangers – and a stranger's dog. Clara glanced at Bailey wolfing down the last of the bacon from the frying pan. Did dogs eat bacon? Was he going to be sick all over the kitchen floor when they arrived home?

Home. It wasn't *her* home –not since childhood. She didn't feel as though she had a home anymore. Not what made a home; someone with whom she shared her life.

'I've been thinking…' said Elliot cutting straight across Clara's wallow in self-pity. 'We might have a claim on it.'

'On the beach hut, do you mean?'

He nodded. 'I know you kept all the receipts proving the amount of money we spent on it.'

Evie considered it for a moment. 'Now, I'm not a solicitor… but I suppose if you're talking about squatters' rights, I guess there has to be statute of limitations regarding abandoned property. If we've been using it and we spent money on it…' she trailed off.

But it's not abandoned. At least, not anymore. Clara tried to maintain a neutral expression which wasn't easy when she knew how much time and expense *had* gone into doing up the hut. But that could change. She'd seen the before and after photos. It *was* virtually derelict. They'd done it up while the owner had left it to go to wrack and ruin. In those circumstances, was Elliot right: could they have a claim on it?

Would it have even been saleable if the twins hadn't come along and fixed it up? They hadn't just fixed it up – they'd transformed it. Now, because of them, it would most likely sell quickly and at a decent price. But how willing would the twins be to vacate the beach hut if they thought they had some claim on it? Could she make it worth their while? She wasn't sure by how much; hopefully, enough to put them up in a nice hotel for the rest of their holiday.

There was an alternative.

Clara raised an eyebrow, shocked that the idea would even enter her head. She shook her head *no.*

'What's the matter?' asked Evie. She'd noticed Clara shaking her head.

'Oh, nothing. Nothing at all,' said Clara, most definitely not entertaining the possibility of inviting them back to The Gables for a hot shower and a comfy bedroom – each. The large house on the clifftop was much nicer than one cramped room in a hut with no facilities save for breakfast on the beach at dawn. And staying at The Gables wasn't like a hotel – it wouldn't cost them a bean. Clara couldn't believe she was still considering it as she handed Evie her empty plate.

37

Evie got up and brushed the sand from her bare legs. 'I'll make a cup of tea.'

Clara watched her walk over to the beach hut and pour some bottled water into a kettle before placing it on a small stove. Maybe they ate breakfast this early so no one would catch them sleeping in there. She eyed their backpacks and caught Elliot staring at her out of the corner of her eye. She turned to him and said, 'Evie tells me she's training to be a nurse. What line of work are you in?'

The sound of a dog barking interrupted them.

Clara looked over at Bailey and had a sudden sensation of déjà vu. It wasn't Bailey. She turned her head and groaned at the familiar sight of a large German shepherd dog bounding across the beach towards her. 'Not again!'

'Do you know that dog?' Elliot had spotted the dog too.

Clara froze where she was. At least this time she didn't have a large pebble in her hand, in the throes of trying to break open the lock on the beach hut door.

The German shepherd came bounding right up to her.

Bailey made no move to come to her aid. He shuffled along on his belly towards Elliot instead. Clara shook her head at the golden retriever. What a wuss.

She wasn't sure it was the same dog because this time he

stopped in front of her and licked her hand. Clara gave him a tentative pat on the head. The dog turned his attention to the empty plate where Bailey had just polished off the last of the bacon. The German shepherd whined.

'It looks like your dog isn't the only one with a fondness for bacon,' commented Elliot.

'Murphy – come back here!'

Clara turned around when she heard someone call their dog and recognised the off-duty police officer – Paul. Her face coloured with embarrassment. She cast a glance at the beach hut and got up from the sand as fast as she could. It would be very awkward if he mentioned what he caught her doing last night. 'Well, it's been lovely having breakfast with you, but I must dash.'

'What about your cup of tea?' Evie had just emerged from the beach hut carrying a tea tray. She noticed the other dog. 'Where did he come from?'

'He's mine.' The young officer arrived at the small gathering on the beach and grabbed hold of Murphy.

'What's his name?' asked Evie.

'Murphy.'

Clara noticed an awkward silence during which Evie and Paul's eyes locked. Evie looked away shyly.

'Sorry, police dogs are usually well-behaved.'

'Police?' Elliot looked at the dog in surprise. 'It's not illegal to light a campfire on the beach, is it?'

Paul shook his head. 'No. You've picked the right morning for it. Weather's good.'

Clara caught Evie and Elliot exchange a nervous glance.

Paul's eyes shifted to the two back-packs on the sand as he commented, 'Get down here early – did you?' He looked from Evie to Elliot.

Clara stepped in and said, 'That's right, we came down to the beach early this morning. Evie cooked, and you're great at fixing things up, aren't you Elliot?'

'Oh, um yes.'

'The house…' Clara pointed toward The Gables, 'needs a bit of work.' So far, Clara hadn't told an outright lie. She inferred that the young couple were staying with her at The Gables.

'I see.' Paul stared at Clara making her feel uncomfortable. 'I don't recall seeing anyone else up at the house when *you* arrived.'

Clara willed her face not to turn crimson at the thought of telling the officer another fib. 'Oh, they arrived this morning.'

'Is that so?'

Clara, avoiding eye-contact, continued, 'we thought what a marvellous idea to come down here and have breakfast on the beach before it gets busy.' Clara cringed. She could feel all three sets of eyes staring at her. Even the dogs seemed to have her attention.

'So, how is the house-sitting going?'

'Fine,' said Clara sheepishly. She didn't know the twins. What if they knew the owner? Clara doubted that. Besides, they weren't from around here. Clara didn't want too many people finding out she was living at the house; if word spread in the local community, they were bound to discover she was squatting. 'We're settling in,' Clara added, meaning her and the dog but implying the twins too. 'Still no ghosts – if that's what you're wondering.'

'Ghosts!' said Evie in surprise.

Paul turned to Clara. 'She doesn't know about the things that go bump in the night?'

Clara shook her head. 'I haven't heard a thing.' Although Clara thought she had *seen* something. There was that light in the garden. It was still bothering her. She'd been pulling the curtains in the lounge, but then when she double-checked all was pitch dark. She must have been mistaken.

Clara eyed Paul. He was looking at the beach hut. The door was ajar where Evie had stepped outside with the tea tray a moment ago. Clara hoped he would not bring *that* up. The twins must have been out having an evening meal and weren't around when she tried to break in.

'Would you like tea?' asked Evie, passing out mugs of hot tea and stopping in front of Paul. Evie looked at her empty tray. 'Here, have mine. I'll go and make another.'

'I'm fine.' said Paul. 'Besides, I'd better go.' He checked his watch. 'I'm on duty in an hour. Come on, Murphy. Get your nose away from that saucepan.'

Murphy let out a disgruntled whine and backed away from the open fire.

Put the fire out when you're done.'

Evie said, 'Of course, officer.'

'It's Paul.'

'I'm Evie.'

Once again, their eyes locked.

Elliot coughed into the empty silence. 'I'm Elliot.'

Paul nodded in Elliot's direction but was quickly drawn back to the young woman. There was another awkward silence. 'Perhaps I will have that mug of tea, after all.'

'Great – here.' Evie was quick to pass the mug to Paul. 'I'll make another.' As Evie turned towards the beach hut, Clara caught Elliot giving his sister a look. Evie saw it too and mouthed, *what?* before stepping inside the hut and emerging with another mug of hastily poured tea.

Clara looked at Elliot and suspected he was not in favour of his sister having a holiday romance. Although from what she'd overheard at the station when arrested, it appeared Paul had lost someone dear to him in the recent past. A holiday fling might be the last thing he wanted.

A holiday fling. If I was her age… Clara stared wistfully in Evie's direction. Who was she kidding? If she was her age, with the world at her youthful feet, she still couldn't bring herself to have a fling even if it was a holiday romance. She'd want more than that. Clara would want someone special to spend the rest of her life with. *But I'm too old for that.* She bet her newly single friend Debs would have something to say.

Clara sipped her tea and glanced around the campfire at Evie, Elliot, and Paul. They were all now sitting in silence waiting for the sunrise. Bailey and Murphy were quiet, sensing something was about to happen.

Clara looked towards the sea waiting for the sun to appear on the horizon. Clara knew why she couldn't sleep, why she was up at dawn taking the dog down to the beach in the twilight hours – that eerie in-between time when it was just getting light and everyone was tucked up in their beds, sleeping soundly. It was the thought of having the beach to herself.

Clara wondered why the twins were up at daybreak and what Paul was doing walking his dog on a deserted beach in the grey half-light before sunrise. She looked at the small group of strangers gathered around the campfire and thought, whatever our reasons, we're insomniacs – all four of us. Perhaps we all rose early with the promise that today will be a better day. Clara didn't feel that way at first. But now, seated around a campfire on a deserted beach watching the sunrise changed her mind – today life was worth living.

Something brushed her hand. She looked down to find Bailey had joined her. He flopped down on the sand and put his head on her lap. He looked up at her with those brown soulful eyes. Clara gently stroked his head, the warmth of the sun's first rays on her face.

She closed her eyes and imagined the clock had turned back; she was a teenager again sitting with Tommy on the porch of their parents' beach hut with a cocker spaniel, their parents' dog, sitting between them.

How could forty decades go by – a lifetime – and yet she still felt that loss as painful and raw as if it was only yesterday? She knew the answer to that conundrum; Tommy was her twin, a part of her since birth, and she would always suffer the loss like an irreparable tear in the fabric of her life that would never heal. But he wasn't the only one she grieved for. What had become of the boy she thought she was destined to marry all those years ago?

Sitting here on the beach in front of the hut where she and Tommy used to spend so much time, her thoughts returned to Mallorca where she had last seen her brother before that fateful night, he disappeared from her life forever. All she had left to remember him by was a gravestone marking an empty grave. Her parents' dying wish was to find his body and repatriate him so they could bury him in the grounds of the little church where he was christened. They never got their wish.

It wasn't what Clara wanted. Years ago, after they found the boat missing from the boathouse, they called off the search concluding that he'd got drunk at their eighteenth birthday party, fallen overboard and drowned. They assumed his body would wash up on shore; that never happened, and decided he was lost at sea. Clara didn't believe that. Not at first. She was relieved they never found a body.

She recalled that awful summer when, day-after-day, they would go down to the shore searching for Tommy. Without a body there was still hope. She refused to believe he was gone. Through the hell of it Clara remembered she'd clung to the idea it was a practical joke and one day Tommy would walk back into their lives as though he'd never left. But as the days dragged into weeks, with no sign of her brother, her parents decided to return home without him.

Clara had never known such emptiness. Tommy was the practical joker, the person in the family who seemed to be more alive than the three of them put together. He was the glue that kept them together. It was no surprise that when he was gone, they all drifted their separate ways.

Her father went through as many official channels as possible to keep the search for his son going. Her mother withdrew into herself and forgot she still had another child.

Clara had just blossomed into a young woman and needed her mother now more than ever.

Clara remembered struggling with the realisation she might never see her brother again. And, the guilt that if she'd stopped to listen to whatever Tommy was desperately trying to tell her at the party, then he wouldn't have stormed off like that.

It would always haunt her, that if it wasn't for her, he might not have disappeared that night. Clara and Tommy were inseparable growing up but that summer, the year they turned eighteen, Clara discovered there was someone she wanted to be with more than him. She'd fallen in love. He was the only person who could ever fill the void after Tommy, and he had been right under her nose the whole time – Tommy's best friend, Ralph.

So why did you leave him, never to return? Clara concentrated on the horizon, trying to push all thoughts of *what might have been* from her mind. It was pointless to dwell on the past, although she couldn't help but wonder where she might be now if she hadn't run away to London, straight into the arms of a man who she'd married on the rebound.

Clara sucked in a breath. She'd never admitted to herself that that's what it was.

Clara's gaze shifted from the horizon to Evie sitting cross-legged on the sand, her head resting on Elliot's shoulder. She saw Paul stealing furtive glances at the pretty young woman. God, it took her back. It could have been her, Tommy and Ralph sitting there on the beach around a campfire outside her parents' beach hut.

If her brother were still alive would he be living here, in the place they grew up? Perhaps he'd be retired now walking a dog on the shore at sunrise – she glanced down at Bailey and smiled. What had happened to them? The two men she had cared about most in this world.

38

Up on the cliff top, high above the promenade, a man with a grey beard, dressed in old track-suit bottoms and a threadbare jumper was sitting on a bench with a blanket wrapped around his shoulders as he watched the sunrise. Ralph poured a cup of coffee from a thermos flask into a chipped tin mug and glanced down at the shore below.

He raised an eyebrow and sat forward in his seat. Two more people had joined the young couple who were eating breakfast on the beach; that was unusual. He wished he had binoculars or a pair of glasses to see more clearly. He squinted in the early morning sunshine and saw a young man, two large dogs and a slim older woman who looked, even from this distance, quite elegant in a floral dress, blue blazer and linen scarf.

My eyesight can't be half bad he thought as his eyes lingered on the mature lady with the blonde bob. He wasn't the only one having trouble sleeping.

Watching her get up, she brushed the sand from the folds of her skirt. The twins followed suit, rising and reaching for their backpacks.

He finished what remained of his coffee, screwed the lid on the old thermos flask and decided to make a move before the young policeman with his German shepherd dog walked up from the beach on his way to work. He knew the routine. The young man always took his dog for a walk early. Perhaps he had trouble sleeping too? He guessed that was him with his police dog sitting around the campfire, and hoped the twins weren't in trouble. Ralph was pretty sure there was a law against sleeping in beach huts.

The faint smell of a cooked English breakfast wafted up on the gentle sea breeze making his mouth water. It reminded him of the bacon in his frying pan that had mysteriously disappeared. Still, he had plenty more where that came from – thanks to a good rummage in the supermarket bins yesterday.

If he'd wandered down to the shore, the youngsters would have invited him to join them for breakfast. They knew who he was. He'd helped fix up the roof of the beach hut although he had refused their kind invitation to join them on that occasion. Doubtless, they'd ask again. But it was too late now. Besides, he didn't fancy the police officer asking too many questions. He knew what he looked like. A vagrant. He'd be arrested and thrown in a prison cell.

The sound of a dog barking startled him. Down below one of the dogs had spotted him. He hastily gathered up his things. It was time he left. Soon the town would wake up and the tourists would appear, walking along the promenade below, some venturing along the clifftop walk where he was sitting. He knew he would stick out like a sore thumb. He should make himself scarce.

Risking one last glance down to the beach, he saw the fire being doused and the party getting ready to leave. Turning on his heel he retraced his steps along the clifftop walk until he reached some thick hedgerows. He slipped through an almost indiscernible gap and came out in the gardens at the back of the house.

A moment later, Bailey appeared and stood growling at the mysterious figure disappearing between the thicket. He then turned and belted back down the path to the beach.

❖

'There you are.' Clara turned around to find the dog standing behind her panting.

Bailey barked and ran toward the path.

Clara sighed guessing walkies was over. 'All right, Bailey, I'm coming.'

She turned to the twins standing holding their backpacks. When Clara decided it was time to leave, Paul asked if they were going with her. A silent exchange between the twins, followed by an almost imperceptible nod of the head by Clara confirmed the invitation to The Gables still stood. She'd already intimated the twins were staying up at the house. It would seem odd if they didn't return to the house with her. Clara realised she'd got them all in a bind.

'I'm not going anywhere. I haven't finished my breakfast,' announced Elliot, dumping his backpack on the sand and sitting back down, throwing Clara and Paul a defiant look which said, no one is making me leave.

Evie stared at her brother. 'But I thought you weren't hungry. I gave the rest to the dog, remember?'

'Well, I've changed my mind. There's plenty more in the freezer box.'

Evie narrowed her eyes realizing what her brother was up to – staging a sit-in.

Clara could tell she was torn between coming with her back to the house and staying with her brother.

Paul glanced at Elliot sitting on the sand, refusing to budge, and said to Evie, do you need a hand with the stove? It looks as though the fire's gone out.

'Oh, yes please.'

Elliot frowned. 'I can light the stove.'

'Have you had breakfast, Paul?' asked Evie, ignoring her brother.

'Well, now you ask, no I haven't.'

Clara looked at Evie's smiling face. She guessed they weren't coming back to the house after all. Perhaps it was for the best. She got the feeling Paul might have tagged along. The last thing she needed was another police escort – this time with two more potential squatters in tow.

She smiled at Paul and Evie and caught Elliot frowning at them. Clara had a feeling he wished he'd taken up her invitation to come back to the house. He hadn't factored in Paul joining them for breakfast. Well, it was too late now.

'Goodbye. Thank you for breakfast.'

Evie dragged her gaze from Paul. 'Clara, next time you're down here walking Bailey, come and join us for breakfast, won't you?'

'Thank you,' Clara replied although she didn't think they'd be a next time. It hadn't slipped her mind she was meant to be going home today.

Paul looked at Evie. 'I thought you were staying up at The Gables with Clara?'

Evie's face went bright crimson.

Elliot rolled his eyes and stepped in to cover her faux pas. 'We get down here early. I enjoy going for a swim before the holiday hoards arrive then we cook breakfast on the beach. Clara . . . um . . . doesn't always get up that early.'

'Oh, okay.' Paul lit the stove.

Clara waved goodbye and was making her way towards the promenade with Bailey by her side when he stopped and turned around, sniffing the air. Clara anticipated what he would do next. She grabbed him by the collar. 'Oh, no you don't.' He'd smelt sizzling bacon again. 'We're going *this* way.'

39

Ralph was washing up his thermos flask thinking of the person he'd seen on the beach with the twins. He'd never seen the woman and her dog before. Maybe she'd never ventured out this early or she had just arrived in Southwold. Either way, he had no intention of striking up a conversation to find out. Instead, Ralph had made himself scarce.

After rinsing out his flask in the bowl he left out to catch rainwater, Ralph walked into the outhouse and dumped his stuff on the camp bed. He glanced at the empty frying pan on the stove. After finding his bacon had vanished, he hadn't bothered to cook any more, but headed out, as he did every morning with his thermos to watch the sunrise and have an early morning dip in the sea.

Perhaps it was the sea air, but Ralph was now famished. He still had the remains of the packet of bacon he'd opened and half-a-dozen eggs. Ralph was about to light the stove when he thought he heard something. There it was again, like a dull thud as though something was hitting the ground.

Ralph walked over to the outhouse window and pulled the makeshift curtain to one side. 'What the…?' There was the woman he'd spied having breakfast on the beach with the twins standing in his garden. Her back was to him so he couldn't see her face, but he recognised her clothing. He raised an eyebrow in astonishment. She was playing a game of fetch with the dog. The ball landed way up the garden near the house and the dog raced after it.

'What the…?' said Ralph once more as he watched from the window. This was private property, not a public park. Ralph thought of the gap in the hedge that led from the clifftop walk into his back garden. Perhaps her dog had spied the gap and ran into the garden, or she'd thrown the ball from one of the neighbouring properties by accident. Either way, he reckoned it wouldn't be long, and she'd take the annoying ball, and her pesky dog, and leave.

Ralph stepped away from the window and let the makeshift curtain fall back into place. He found the box of matches and lighting the stove was just reaching for the packet of bacon when the sound of a ball landing in the ground stopped. He breathed a sigh of relief. They were leaving.

Picking up the spatula Ralph was just moving the bacon around the pan to get it nice and crispy when he heard a woman's voice. 'Now if I could find a deckchair, then I might have time to sit in the garden? What do you think?'

Ralph stood frozen to the spot holding his spatula in mid-air. She was talking to her dog. But it wasn't that that took him by surprise; his late wife used to do that all the time. Footsteps were discernible coming down the cobbled path towards the outhouses.

How did she even know about the outhouses? They were tucked away at the bottom of the garden behind the foliage of established trees. What was he going to do if she walked into this one? There were three, but his was the first door she would come to along the path.

A split second later he heard the snuffling sounds of a dog's nose the other side of the door. Ralph nearly dropped his spatula as he darted to the door. The only way to keep her out was to…

Ralph got to the doorknob just in time. Fortunately, he'd

shut the door already, but there was no lock. With his hand on the doorknob praying he had the strength to stop her from opening it, he could feel her attempts to turn the doorknob on the other side of the door. Ralph held his breath. His grip was slipping. Ralph cursed himself for picking up a rasher of bacon in his hand; it was greasy.

'That's locked,' a woman's voice said from the other side.

Oh, thank god, Ralph nearly said aloud.

He listened as she moved on to the outhouse next door. The dog was still outside. He sniffed under the door again and whined as he pawed at the door.

'What's got into you?'

Ralph rolled his eyes. She was talking to her dog again.

'There's nothing in there for you unless you think there's some bacon. I know you and your fondness for bacon, but I can assure you there's nothing of the kind in there, so come here.'

Ralph looked at his spatula. His eyes drifted to the empty saucepan he'd found this morning where he's crispy bacon had been. He thought of the dog outside and narrowed his eyes.

He made the mistake of shifting his weight from one foot to the other. One of his knees clicked. That elicited a low guttural growl from the other side of the door. Ralph's eyes went wide. *Oh god, now the dog knows I'm here.*

'Oh, stop that silliness and come here.'

One last snuffle at the bottom of the door and the dog was gone.

'Ah, what have we here?' He heard the woman's voice again, followed by the creak of a door. Ralph was still standing there holding on to the doorknob even though she was moving about in the outhouse next door. Something was being dragged across the floor. 'This will do,' said a muffled voice. 'I might have to fetch a cushion from the house, though.'

Fetch a cushion? Ralph frowned. Why didn't she go and sit in her own garden?

She closed the outhouse door and walked past, footsteps growing fainter as she made her way along the cobbled path into the garden. He listened just to make sure they weren't coming back and then released the doorknob with a huge sigh. His fingers felt stiff. He left the spatula in the pan and ran over to the window. There she was making her way up the garden carrying an old wooden garden chair. She set it down on the patio at the back of the house, outside the kitchen door.

'Unbelievable!' Ralph said. 'Just who does she think she is?'

The house-sitter, a voice in his head said.

But I cancelled that advert – didn't I?

In the aftermath of his wife's funeral he'd placed the property with the estate agents expecting he'd be abroad on assignments, but his health said otherwise. He was sure he cancelled the advert for a house sitter. Perhaps he'd forgotten.

He had an idea how to get rid of his unwanted guest, and he wouldn't even have to speak to her to get her to leave. All he had to do was jump out from behind a tree and scare the bejesus out of her. The dog wouldn't be happy, but he had a plan for that too. Ralph would make sure he had enough distance between him and them, at least a hundred yards, so he had the advantage when he made a run for it back to the outhouse if the dog gave chase.

Ralph gingerly opened the shed door. He winced when it creaked on its hinges. The coast was clear. Ralph stepped outside, walked along the cobbled path into the back garden.

He crept from one tree to another until he couldn't get any closer without stepping out in full view in the middle of the lawn. There was no movement from the woman in the deckchair – or the dog. Were they asleep? Ralph wasn't sure.

He stood there staring at her. Even from this distance she seemed familiar. *Do I know you?* Ralph stepped out from behind the Sycamore tree. He felt drawn to her. Ralph wasn't aware of how far he had walked across the lawn, entranced by the lady sleeping in the chair. Without his glasses he couldn't see her face.

He edged closer. *Who was she?* Three more steps and Ralph froze. *Clara?* His idea of jumping out from behind the tree and scaring her, to make her leave, had taken flight. Was she real or was his mind playing tricks on him? He was just settling on the latter when the dog growled; that was real enough for him. Ralph held up two hands as if to say, *just calm down, I'm not a threat* and retreated to the tree out of sight before the dog woke her up.

He hid behind the tree, fighting to catch his breath, his heart beating fast. Ralph gulped down breaths of fresh air. He stood there in a state of shock with one question running through his mind, *why now, after all these years, had Clara returned?*

He stole a glance around the tree trunk just in case he *had* imagined it. She was still there, asleep in the deckchair. Ralph was stunned.

❖

The sound of Bailey growling woke Clara. 'What is the matter with you today?' For a dog that so far had shown no predisposition to be a guard dog – he was more likely to turn tail and scarper at the first sign of trouble – his behaviour was most peculiar. All the same, Clara looked about her wondering if he'd spotted someone in the garden. To her relief there was nobody there. 'Shush, Bailey.'

Bailey quietened down and got a pat on the head for being a good dog.

Clara yawned and stretched in her chair. Surprised she had fallen asleep she was disturbed by her dream.

Clara wiped a tear from her cheek. 'Fancy getting all emotional over a silly dream.' Except it wasn't just a silly dream. She hadn't thought about that night with Ralph in years. It was the happiest day of her life. But it was also the saddest. When she left her eighteenth birthday party with Ralph, she found out afterwards her brother had been looking for her. Then he disappeared – never to be seen again.

Bailey stood up and put a consoling paw on Clara's lap as if to say, *don't be sad.*

Clara couldn't help it. She did an awful thing blaming Ralph for Tommy's disappearance. A silly, immature eighteen-year-old girl who dealt with her grief in the only way she knew how – by blaming someone else. She wished she could turn back the clock and right that wrong. It wasn't his fault she'd fallen in love with him.

40

Ralph glanced at the fresh flowers arranged in the vase on the base of the headstone. 'You've had another visitor' he said in surprise. In all the years he'd been coming here, to his knowledge nobody else visited – until today. Ralph stared at the wild flowers. The only person who would visit Tommy was . . .

Ralph swallowed hard. It *was* her. After seeing the woman in the garden, he'd retreated to the outhouse licking his emotional wounds. It can't be her, he thought. After all these years, what were the chances she would return at the same time? No chance.

It would be too much of a coincidence that fate brought them both back to Suffolk. Besides, he didn't believe in destiny or serendipity. Shit happens. And not in a nice way either as he could testify with his wife. When he retreated to the outhouse a question was still running through his mind – was it her? Was it *really* her? He looked at the flowers. Now he had his answer.

'I didn't think, in a million years, I'd ever see her again in my lifetime. What shall I do?' He stared at Tommy's grave and whispered, 'Should I tell her about you?' Despite the intervening years he still felt she had a right to know.

But then you must tell her everything, and she'd never forgive you.

'But what does that matter now, Tommy? She left me years ago.'

But what if you had a second chance?

'Love at my age?' Ralph shook his head. 'Besides, she might have a husband and a family.' Even if she was, by some miracle, the girl he'd known all those years ago, she must have moved on with her life. 'She wouldn't remember me.'

You're wrong. How could she forget you? You were my best friend. She was in love with you. She ran away to London and disappeared because she couldn't deal with losing me. It had nothing to do with not loving you.

That was just wishful thinking. If it *was* her, she wouldn't even recognise him.

But it's been years, Ralph, and you haven't been well. Perhaps when your health improves, and you put on some weight . . . the beard doesn't help – you never had one before.

Ralph tugged on his beard. 'But if she did love me the way I loved her, why didn't she come back?'

The voice in his head masquerading as Tommy was silent.

Ralph stared at his gravestone. After so many years, what did he imagine would happen if he walked up to her and introduced himself? Was it possible to pick up where they left off decades ago? They would have to get to know one another all over again.

If she *was* Tommy's sister, it would be tough not to at least try to reconnect with her. He shook his head sadly. As much as he would love that to happen, he knew it wasn't possible.

When he saw her in the garden and retreated to the outhouse, Ralph sat down on his camp bed in front of the painting of Mallorca, reminiscing about the love of his life. He was shocked to discover that the intervening years had not diminished that love – not at all.

Staring at Tommy's gravestone, it made him wonder about going through that all over again. Rejected a second time by the woman he'd always loved. Although that was a good reason enough to steer clear of her, there was another reason he needed to avoid Clara.

Ralph closed his eyes. He had few regrets in life. There was no time to ruminate over all the things one should or shouldn't have done in the past. There was nothing you could do about it. But there was one thing in his life he would regret to his dying day.

He opened his eyes and stared at the gravestone. Ralph had kept a secret from Clara all these years – about Tommy. 'Why did you do it, Tommy?' Ralph felt the anger welling up inside him. 'Why did you make me promise not to tell her?'

What haunted Ralph over the years was the real possibility that if he'd broken that promise, Tommy might still be here today.

But what if you put things right?

Ralph shook his head. 'What does that even mean?' His subconscious goading him that seeing her again might give him the opportunity. But that wasn't possible. Nothing he said or did would bring Tommy back – not now, anyway. Back then it might have been different; that's why if Clara ever found out she'd never forgive him. He'd never forgiven himself.

'Tommy, wherever you are – I hope it was worth it.' Ralph turned from the gravestone and headed down the path and out the churchyard gate knowing what he had to do; avoid Clara at all costs.

41

Clara stepped out from under the hanging branches of a large Elm tree and stood on a cobbled pathway heading towards the outhouses. She'd been here before when looking for a garden chair earlier in the day and had returned to see if there was a parasol to go with it. She wanted to continue sitting on the patio, but there was no shade from the midday sun.

Thinking back to this morning, she made her way down the path. After falling asleep in the chair – she blamed it on the hearty English breakfast she'd eaten with the twins on the beach – Clara woke from a dream about the boy she once loved and realised it had been a huge mistake coming back here.

She'd gone inside the house to collect her suitcase, intending to catch the bus to the train station and return home, when she remembered she no longer had her bus fare. That was no excuse. Paul, the young police officer, would give her a lift to the station. She still had her open return train ticket. Clara got out her mobile phone to ring Paul but there was no reception. Once again, that was no excuse to stay. She could walk into town and use her phone there.

Clara collected her suitcase, opened the front door and found Bailey sitting on the doormat.

'Oh, you startled me,' she'd said to the dog.

Bailey had sniffed Clara's case and whined. His sad eyes

making her feel guilty that she'd forgotten about him. 'I can't stay here forever – you know,' she'd told Bailey, leaving her suitcase by the door.

❖

Clara sighed when she thought back to this morning and her decision to stay a little longer. She'd left her case and gone to find a book from the library instead. Satisfied she wasn't going anywhere Bailey fell asleep on the patio beside her chair again.

She had found several books on photography, but it hard to concentrate. Still feeling the after-effects of that vivid dream; thinking about him and wondering where he was now. *'I should be thinking of my husband lying unconscious in a hospital bed, not a man I haven't seen in forty years.'*

She knew why she couldn't get him out of her mind; he was her first love. On that beach in Mallorca she'd told him there would be nobody else.

Clara thought of Joe. She'd married him and grown to love him. But could she honestly say she was ever *in* love with him? There was a difference. Ralph taught her that. But what did it matter now? That was a long time ago. If she met him today, would she still feel the same way about him as she did back then? Clara shook her head. Why was she even asking herself that question; the chances of running into him now, after all these years, were practically zilch.

Clara looked about her as she made her way down the cobbled path. This time, without Bailey in tow being a nuisance, she took more notice of her surroundings. To the left and right of the garden path she discovered she was walking through a vegetable garden.

'How lovely,' Clara said wistfully. She'd always liked the idea of a kitchen garden; there was something very English about growing your own vegetables. She wondered why she'd never considered doing it back home in their semi in North London.

There was a large enough patch of ground to use. *Probably because I was too busy shopping to escape my boring existence.*

On a makeshift wooden trestle table part way along the path was a basket. Clara stopped to look. Inside were carrots, swedes, some potatoes and a cabbage. They looked as though they'd just been dug up. Clara stood there staring at the basket thinking *that's odd.* She picked up a carrot and looked about her. Someone had been in the garden.

Putting the carrot back where she found it, she continued down the path which stopped at the row of single-story vine-covered outhouses. Something caught her eye. The first door which had been locked this morning, was now ajar and there was a peculiar odour coming from inside.

Clara sniffed the air. It smelt like…

She pushed the door open and got a strong whiff of fried bacon. Clara gingerly stepped into the outhouse and spotted the two-ring hob powered by a portable gas cylinder. There was a dirty frying pan on top that appeared to have the remnants of an English breakfast.

She gasped in surprise once her eyes adjusted to the gloom as she saw what else was in the outhouse; there was a camp bed at the far end of the room with what appeared to be old army blankets. The blankets were in a heap as though someone got out of bed and tossed them to one side.

Clara stood there staring at the camp bed, her eyes shifting from the bed to the stove and back again. 'We've got a squatter!' exclaimed Clara, suddenly realising the absurdity of what she'd just said. She had the impulse to laugh – *two* squatters. But this was no laughing matter. The last thing Clara expected to find was that she had company.

She shifted her gaze and spotted a small window to one side of the room with a makeshift curtain and some paperback books on the low windowsill. Clara pulled back the makeshift curtain and looked across the gardens to the back of the house.

Something occurred to her. Her eyes drifted to the oil lamp on the overturned crate. She could have sworn she'd seen a light at the bottom of the garden when pulling the curtains last night. She hadn't imagined it. Someone was living here.

Stepping outside she closed the door, leaving it just the way she found it. Clara breathed a sigh of relief when she saw nobody was making their way down the path towards the outhouse. But the smell of cooking, the freshly picked vegetables in the basket, even the fact that there was a vegetable garden smacked of someone making this their home, at least for the last few weeks – if not longer. That meant she wasn't here first. She couldn't imagine they would take kindly to someone moving in on their turf – so to speak.

Clara quickened her pace. She didn't want to have a run-in with whoever was living in the outhouse, now wishing she'd left this morning and caught the train home. How long did she really think she could live in someone else's property and not get found out?

She hurried along the path toward the house, her eyes darting about her hoping she didn't see him. Clara knew it was a man living in that outhouse. There wasn't anything of a personal nature, but some old clothes were hanging up on a makeshift clothesline suspended from the rafters. Men's clothing. Whoever he was – some vagrant who got lucky and discovered an empty property – even he hadn't had the cheek to squat in the house.

Clara slowed when something occurred to her. She had the keys to the property. Not on her person; always leaving them under the flowerpot when popping out just in case someone turned up, like the letting agent, and checked that they were still there. But she had access to the keys to the house, nonetheless. Who's saying she wasn't the house sitter? How would some vagrant, a squatter, know the truth? All she had to do was act as though she was meant to be here. What could he do about it? Not a lot unless he knew the owner of the house.

Clara stopped in her tracks. She shook her head and managed a smile. Well, that's just ridiculous. If he knew the owner, what would he be doing sleeping rough in the outhouse? Clara relaxed. There was nothing to worry about. In fact, it was possible the squatter had already gone. He may have seen the light on in the house last night, perhaps even spotted her in the garden today and fled before someone caught him.

Clara arrived at the patio. Bailey opened his eyes for a moment, registered it was only Clara, and flopped his head back on his paws to resume his forty winks. She noticed Bailey had moved under her chair for some shade which reminded her she'd forgotten to look for a parasol. 'Oh, bother. Perhaps there's one in the house.' Clara walked up to the kitchen door and discovered she'd locked herself out. The kitchen door had blown shut in the breeze. 'Blast!' Now she had to go around to the front of the house and get the key.

Clara rounded the corner on the gravel drive in front of the house and walked straight into a stranger.

42

She stepped back in shock. So did he. Clara caught his expression. The stranger looked as surprised as Clara, suddenly running into someone else in the grounds of the house. Trying to keep her voice level, she said, 'Who are you?' She knew who he was; he was the stranger living in the outhouse. He looked how Clara pictured him; shaggy grey hair that needed a good cut. He hadn't shaved in months. The beard looked matted.

Her eyes were drawn to the scar down his cheek on the left side of his face. If he'd thought a beard would hide the wound it hadn't worked. She stared at the disfigurement. Someone should have told him facial hair won't grow over scars. He smelled of bacon and sea salt. Had he been bathing in the sea?

Clara stood her ground. Although she took several steps backwards, uncomfortable under his intense gaze. It's as though he was scrutinising her as a person would a museum exhibit.

She looked away, embarrassed. 'I said, what do you think you're doing here?' She noticed he was holding a plastic carrier bag from the local supermarket bulging with provisions. He must have been making his way back to the outhouse.

She was waiting for him to come up with some excuse, trying to wheedle his way out of the fact he was squatting here, but what she got was something she hadn't expected. 'I live here' he replied.

So much for any thoughts that the squatter might have taken flight at the first sign that someone had moved into the house. Clara narrowed her eyes. 'I'm the house sitter,' she said, trying to keep her voice even as she told an outright lie.

'Of course you are. And I'm a monkey's uncle.'

'What does that mean?'

When he didn't answer, she stood her ground and said, 'This is private property. You need to leave.'

'Why? I was here first.'

Clara looked at him in surprise wondering what made him think she was squatting too. 'Well, I don't care. I'm the house sitter.'

'Okay. I'm the gardener. I think we have an understanding.' He held out his hand.

Clara chewed her bottom lip, extended her hand and took his giving it a shake. She suddenly felt self-conscious when she realised, he was holding her hand for longer than necessary, green eyes studying her intently.

Bailey suddenly appeared and growled at the stranger.

Clara looked at Bailey in surprise. He was at it again, acting out of character.

'Ahem.'

During their little exchange, neither Clara nor Ralph had noticed someone walk up the driveway towards them.

Clara turned her head and for a split second, she didn't recognise the young man who had interrupted them. It was the first time she'd seen him in uniform. 'Oh, er Paul. What are you doing here?'

'Am I interrupting something?' Paul looked from Clara to the stranger. They were holding hands.

Clara quickly extricated her hand from his and glanced at Paul sheepishly. 'Not at all.'

There was a moment's awkward silence. Paul said, 'I er came to call on Evie.'

'Who?' the stranger butted in.

'The young woman I met on the beach this morning.' He directed his question to Clara, 'My early shift finished, so I thought I'd call on her – if she's in?'

Clara stared at him. Why on earth would she be here? Then she realised. It was hard keeping up with all the little white lies she kept spinning. At this rate, something was bound to catch her out – or someone. Clara stole a glance at the other squatter. He was making her feel uncomfortable.

'Oh, yes er Evie is down at the beach with Elliot,' Clara said, trying her best to sound nonchalant, hoping Paul asked no more awkward questions in front of the other squatter like *when do you expect her back?*

'Okay. I'll walk down to the beach then.'

'Good idea,' said Clara relieved.

He turned to go, then turned back to them with a question. 'Are you two…?' he left the question hanging, but Clara knew what he was getting at.

'God no!' Clara blushed bright crimson in front of the strange man with the dirty, threadbare clothes, straggly beard and a plastic carrier bag. 'Don't be ridiculous. It's not like that.'

'Yes, it is,' the stranger interrupted.

Clara glared at him. 'Will you stay out of this!'

'Suit yourself.'

During this little exchange, Paul had smiled a knowing smile and left them to it. He'd caught the couple in the middle of having words. It looked as though they'd had fallen out over something. He hoped he would be fortunate enough to meet someone and they would still be together bickering into old age.

Clara waited until Paul was out of earshot then she rounded on the stranger. 'Now look what you've done!' Worried the off-duty police officer might have left with more on his mind than Evie. Like, for instance, the suspicion that Clara wasn't really a house sitter and that she and this man might be in cahoots squatting in an empty property. She turned her nose up at him. He looked like a squatter whereas Clara imagined she was making a passable impression of a house-sitter.

'What do you mean – look what I've done? I have done nothing.'

Clara could do without being seen associating with the likes of him. 'Why did you say that?'

'Say what?'

'You gave him the impression we know each other.'

The rude, smelly man barged passed her without having the decency to answer.

'Well, ex-cuse me!' Clara turned around and followed him. 'I'm talking to you.'

He still didn't answer. Just kept on walking. Clara knew where he was headed. She followed him down the back garden to the cobbled path that led through the vegetable garden. He walked straight into the outhouse at the end of the track and slammed the door shut behind him.

'How rude!' exclaimed Clara. She was about to march down the path and give him a piece of her mind when she paused mid-stride, her annoyance at this insolent man giving way to caution. She didn't know who he was and wasn't about to follow him into that outhouse.

Clara gave up, turned on her heel, and stalked back up the garden. Now she had two problems: there was another squatter and, to make matters worse, Paul called on Evie all because she'd given him the impression the twins were living here at The Gables. H*ow am I going to get around that one?*

Clara was considering inviting the twins up to the house again, not just for Paul's benefit, but to get them out of her beach hut. She still had the added complication of that very annoying man living in the outhouse; his presence put a whole new perspective on her squatting in the property. It made her shudder to recall that last night she was in the house all alone save for Bailey and there was a stranger in the hut at the bottom of the garden. *Who was he?*

Many scenarios were running through Clara's mind. Was he an escaped convict? Clara had the urge to laugh. That sounded like something straight out of a novel. Even so her imagination was running away with her at the possibility of an axe-wielding psycho at the bottom of the garden. Clara tried to recall if she saw an axe in the outhouse amongst the dog-eared paperback books, oil lamps and the little possessions he seemed to have.

She walked up the garden berating herself for being so silly and tried to put her practical cap on; there was a simple solution – *go home.*

The sound of her mobile phone ringing interrupted Clara's train of thought. She breathed a sigh of relief at the welcome distraction. Finally, she had reception again. Clara stopped where she was to answer her phone. However, relief quickly gave way to anxiety. Her hand shook at the prospect it might be the hospital ringing with news; good or bad she knew her life would never be the same. Perhaps it *was* time to return home to face reality.

She bit her lower lip and glanced around the garden wishing she could stay here in this peaceful haven forever. She frowned when she caught sight of the shed at the bottom of the garden. That horrible man she'd run into earlier had shattered her illusion of peace and tranquillity.

Clara was standing there, her phone still ringing, when she thought she saw the makeshift curtain in the outhouse twitch. Had he been watching her this whole time? Clara glared in his direction before she turned her back on him to answer her phone.

43

Ralph dropped the curtain back into place. Had she caught him spying on her? *Dammit.* He wished she wasn't still so darned attractive. Why couldn't she have put on a lot of weight and sprouted facial hair and gone grey? Not that there was anything wrong with oversized women or people who chose not to colour their hair. If that were the case then Clara wouldn't be Clara; she would have been unrecognisable, and Ralph would not be standing there alternating between wanting to take her in his arms and declare his undying love for her and running her off his property.

He slumped down on his camp bed and discovered the hurt, angry Ralph from forty-years ago had won out. When he came face-to-face with her, he realised time was not a great healer and was surprised how quickly he had reacquainted himself with his broken-hearted nineteen-year-old self. He had no intention of going through that rejection all over again.

She wasn't aware he had returned, let alone that he owned this house. There was no flicker of recognition when she came face-to-face with him. That was no surprise. These past few weeks Ralph hardly recognised himself. *You could clean yourself up, shave, get a haircut, dress in some of your smart casual clothes; show her a whole new you.*

'Don't do that!' Ralph admonished himself, 'Don't imagine

you might be in for a chance. She will only break your heart all over again.'

Don't you want to find out why she really left all those years ago? There had to be more to it than the fact she felt guilty over being with you when Tommy disappeared.

'She blamed me because she was with me that night, that's all there is to it,' Ralph told the empty room, trying to convince himself.

But what if there was something more? Don't you want to know once and for all?

He lay down on the camp bed and stared at the painting of Mallorca.

Ralph's eyes grew heavy. He drifted off to sleep, exhausted.

He was back again on that beach in Mallorca, walking barefoot on the sand holding her hand, except this time they weren't teenagers anymore…

Ralph woke hours later in the pitch dark and remembered his dream; a vision conjured up from his subconscious, taunting him with a future that would never be. Ralph turned his back on the painting. He wished she'd never returned. There was a solution – *go home.* All he had to do was walk up the garden and open his front door. Then she'd have to leave, and that would be the end.

He couldn't turf her out in the dead of night. He might act like a vagrant living in an outhouse, and he might not want her around, but he hadn't lost all sense of propriety. Not convinced she was the house sitter, he couldn't give her, her marching orders at this time of night. Where would she go?

Ralph thought of the nice hotel only a five-minute walk up the road. *Why not stay in a hotel? Why come here?* Surely, this house would be the last place she'd want to return to. Perhaps she needed the money. *But I withdrew the house-sitting job, didn't I?* Ralph wished he could remember.

Ralph struggled with the dilemma of wanting her to be gone while desperately wishing to know what had brought her home after all these years. As Ralph drifted back off to sleep, he recalled her phone call. He'd heard a mobile phone; that's what had drawn him to the window. Despite his feelings of hostility towards her, he hoped she was all right. Her reticence at answering the phone made him think there was something – or someone – she was avoiding.

❖

Ralph woke and imagined it had all been a dream – seeing Clara down at the beach and then discovering she had moved into his house. Then he remembered his visit to the cemetery and the fresh flowers left at Tommy's grave. It wasn't a dream. She was back.

Throwing off the blankets he got out of bed and stretched. Normally he was awake before dawn, heating hot water for the flask and walking to the clifftop to drink his coffee and watch the sunrise. For the first time he'd missed it this morning and slept through.

'What time is it?' Since moving into the outhouse Ralph hadn't bothered with a watch or a clock. With no formal routine simply getting up when he awoke sleeping when tired and eating when hungry. Disorientated and with no idea what the time was he wondered how long he had slept. Ralph didn't bother trying to find his watch. He'd taken it off three months ago and put it down somewhere.

Clara was on his mind. He walked over to the window and pulled the makeshift curtain aside to see if she was sitting in the garden or throwing the ball for her dog.

She wasn't in the garden. Ralph stepped outside. He guessed from the position of the sun in the sky and the wet morning dew on the grass it was still early. Perhaps she was having breakfast. He walked along the cobbled path and appeared by the willow tree at the bottom of the garden. From here he could see the entire lawn and the patio at the back of the house. The garden was empty. All he could hear was the sound of chirping birds interspersed with the odd seagull's cry.

He walked up the lawn towards the house. It seemed eerily quiet and still. Ralph stopped in his tracks. He'd assumed she was still here, but what if she'd gone? Had she left last night because of that phone call? *That's what you wanted – wasn't it? To see the back of her.*

Ralph frowned as he walked up to the back of the house and peeked through the glass door into the kitchen. There was no sign of her and no sign of her dog. He didn't see her through the lounge window either. He made a detour to the front of the house, his footsteps crunching on the gravel driveway, half-expecting to run into her again like yesterday. He tried the front door. It was locked. A quick glance under the flower pot revealed the key.

He stood there staring down the drive. *She's gone.* Although that's what he wanted, a lump rose in his throat at the thought he would never see her again. He might not get another opportunity to ask her the question: *why did you leave me?*

'You stupid fool,' he berated himself when it occurred to him there might be a simple explanation for why she left him all those years ago; maybe she didn't feel the same way about him that he felt for her. Ralph trudged back to the outhouse. The bottom had just fallen out of his world; he thought that when he woke, she would still be here.

For the first time in three months he broke with routine. He couldn't face going to the beach for his morning swim or sitting on a bench on the cliff top and seeing that beach hut. He opened the door and walked into the outhouse his mind made up. Today was the day he would move back into his house.

He lit the stove, deciding to have one last cooked breakfast before returning to the house. It was time to go home, put his affairs in order, get the house on the market and leave this place forever. Ralph had no idea where he would go.

He looked at the painting of Mallorca and frowned. 'Don't even go there…' he said to himself, quashing the thought of returning to Mallorca. In fact, the next thing he would do was burn the bloody painting. It was half burnt anyway; he might as well finish the job. 'Then perhaps I'll stop having those blasted dreams!'

44

Paul stood up. 'I better get going. My shift starts soon.' He looked at his watch. It was gone eight. His shift started five minutes ago. That didn't stop him looking at Evie and asking, 'Are you going my way?'

Evie glanced at Clara. She didn't have a clue where The Gables was.

Clara nodded in answer to Paul's question. 'Yes, if you're aiming back up to the clifftop walk.' She pointed toward the promenade. The pathway rose in a gentle slope up to the cliff top and the town beyond. 'We turn left at the top,' she added, for Evie's benefit as the young woman picked up her rucksack.

Talk about déjà vu, thought Clara. Here they all were again, down on the beach eating breakfast. Except this time Paul was there even earlier on the off chance the twins would be there so he could join them.

It wasn't Clara's intention to avail herself of the twin's hospitality for the second morning in a row, but she'd been up at the crack of dawn, unable to sleep after that phone call yesterday.

Clara had money on her mind. She needed her beach hut now more than ever.

She'd had a message from Gerald to call him, but it was Debs who'd phoned when Clara had mobile reception yesterday. Deb's was doing her ex-husband a favour. Clara guessed Gerald didn't want to break the news. He'd looked at more of their paperwork; it turned out they were worse than broke.

Considering the strange, rude man she'd discovered in the outhouse, Clara had been ready to pack up and leave. She had little option but to return home. Before she left, there was some business to take care of – making sure she got her hands on the beach hut. She prayed the man in the outhouse would not make life difficult when he realised she was inviting yet more freeloaders to the house. But then again what could he do about it? He didn't own the place.

Bailey barked and ran back and forth between Evie and Elliot as though he understood the twins were coming home too.

Out of the corner of her eye, Clara spied Elliot's disgruntled expression as he gathered up his rucksack. This time there was no getting away from the fact that he had to come too. Paul had already told them of his visit to the house yesterday hoping to see Evie. Now he was heading to work, he assumed the twins were returning to The Gables with Clara.

Elliot closed the beach hut door and locked the padlock.

Clara saw Evie hanging back and falling in step with Paul. She glanced at Elliot coming up behind them. The look on his face said he'd noticed it too. He barged in between them, almost knocking his sister out of the way.

'Watch it,' exclaimed Paul as Elliot's rucksack bumped him.

'Don't mind him,' said Evie.

Clara heard that exchange as she stepped on to the promenade.

Elliot caught up with Clara. Out of earshot of Paul, he said, 'It's great that you covered for us. I mean you made it sound as though we were staying at… what was it now?'

'The Gables,' replied Clara.

'The thing is I know we shouldn't be sleeping in the beach hut…'

My beach hut thought Clara.

'I didn't expect the police officer to hang around. He didn't leave us much choice. We have to come with you.' Elliot cast a black look behind him. 'God, why does he have to walk with us?'

Clara turned to Elliot as they made their way up the path heading for the cliff top. 'The police station is in the town and this is the only way up from the beach.'

Elliot frowned. 'I know.' His frown continued when he cast another glance over his shoulder. 'God, now he's carrying Evie's rucksack!'

At the top of the path Clara turned left. Paul was still carrying Evie's rucksack. This development pleased neither Eliot nor Clara; it looked as though Paul would walk Evie all the way back to The Gables.

Clara rolled her eyes at the thought of another police escort back to the house. However, if it wasn't for him, she reckoned Elliot would have persuaded his sister to decline Clara's invitation to The Gables. Clara was undecided whether that was a good thing. She wanted to get them out of her beach hut, but she had no business inviting them back to the house. No business at all.

Clara walked up the street feeling self-conscious. It was first thing in the morning and unlike when she arrived in the dead of night, with curtains pulled and neighbours sleeping, people were up and about. Curtains were open. A couple emerged from their home and said good morning. She could feel their eyes lingering as they passed by. Although holidaymakers coming and going weren't unusual in the Suffolk coastal town, she prayed no nosy neighbour confronted them when they arrived.

Clara pressed the button on the little metal box beside the double gates. The gates opened immediately. Clara turned to Paul. 'Didn't you say your shift started soon?'

Elliot stepped forward and grabbed Evie's rucksack out his hand. 'I can take it from here.'

Paul said, 'Yes, I better get going.' He was looking at Evie the whole time.

Evie stepped inside the gates and was almost knocked over by Murphy darting forward. Paul had him on the lead, but that didn't stop the dog pulling frantically toward the gardens. He barked.

Clara winced. That's all she needed. Curious neighbours coming to their front doors at the sound of a dog barking. But no sooner had he started, a quick tap on the nose from Paul shut him up. Clara sighed in relief and glanced into the garden wondering if he had seen something – or someone. The annoying man in the outhouse came to mind.

Paul sighed. 'Murphy's got a thing about squirrels, 'I reckon in a garden this size he spotted one darting up a tree.'

Clara nodded, her eyes shifting to the terraced period cottages in the street outside hoping nobody opened their front door to see what that racket was. The road remained deserted. Clara sighed in relief as she pressed the button once more. The three of them watched the gates close with Paul and Murphy on the other side.

Bailey barked.

'Oh, for goodness sake!' exclaimed Clara, grabbing him by the dog collar. 'Not you as well.' She tapped his nose, copying Paul's tactic with Murphy, and it seemed to do the trick. She waved at Paul and turned up the drive towards the house dragging Bailey by the collar.

Elliot followed Clara until he realised his sister wasn't beside him. He turned around, leaned back and grabbed his sister by the arm. 'Come on.'

Evie was still waving at Paul.

Paul stood by the gate holding Murphy in check, smiling at the young woman with the pretty name and gentle nature. He was already thinking about his shift patterns and when he might be free to call on her at The Gables.

Murphy interrupted his thoughts still pulling on the lead and pawing at the gate. Paul looked down at the dog. 'What has got into you?' He stood for a moment at the gates staring into the gardens beyond and had half a mind to open them and check the grounds of the property.

He was about to do just that when he saw a grey squirrel scamper out from behind a tree. It paused in the middle of the driveway and looked right at them.

'Ah ha!' Paul stared at the squirrel and braced himself. 'I thought so.'

True to form, Murphy went ballistic and got a tap on the nose. 'Quiet!'

The squirrel sat in the garden watching the dog being yanked away from the double gates.

Paul lingered a moment longer in front of the gates. Evie glanced over her shoulder. She waved one last time before the driveway curved to the left and they all disappeared out of sight.

He turned away with a smile on his face and the faint smell of bacon, coming from the garden, wafting past his nostrils. Paul knitted his eyebrows for a split second then thought nothing more of it as his thoughts turned to Evie. He wanted to know everything about her. He was looking forward to calling at the house again when he wasn't on a shift to ask her out on a date.

45

'This is The Gables,' announced Clara. They'd arrived at the front door. She found the key where she'd left it under the flowerpot. Anxiously looking around, she put the key in the lock. Clara hoped her partner-in-crime didn't choose this moment to appear. It would be very awkward trying to explain to the other squatter what she was doing inviting people to stay.

'Is he gone? Did you see him leave?' Elliot was asking his sister.

'I guess so,' Evie said in a dream-like voice. 'He stayed at the gate until I was out of sight.'

Elliot frowned at his sister. 'Do you mean he was still standing there while we were walking up the drive?' Which meant they couldn't risk going back the way they'd come carrying their rucksacks in case the police officer was lingering by the gate. 'Damn.' He turned to Clara. 'Is there another way out, like a back gate or something?'

Clara had just opened the front door. She turned and looked at Elliot. Perhaps it was for the best they didn't stay. It would be just her luck for the owner to choose today to return. 'If you come through the house and out the back door, there's a path through the garden that takes you out on to the cliff path above the promenade.'

'Great. Lead the way.'

Clara hesitated. She'd replied without thinking. She didn't fancy Elliot bumping into the other squatter at the bottom of the garden.

Elliot heaved a sigh. 'Are we going in – or what?'

'Oh yes, of course.' Clara opened the front door.

Elliot stepped inside the house and followed Clara. When they got to the kitchen door, Evie wasn't with them. 'Oh, for pities sake!' exclaimed Elliot when he realised his sister wasn't there. He retraced his steps and stared at his sister. 'What are you doing?'

Evie was standing outside admiring the gothic-style lodge with its floor-to-ceiling bay windows, romantic turrets and creeping ivy-clad walls. She turned to her brother. 'It's like something out of a Daphne du Maurier novel.'

'We're not in Cornwall,' remarked Elliot sounding exasperated.

'I know.'

'Well, let's get a move on.'

Evie stepped inside the house and followed her brother through the entrance hallway to the kitchen at the far end of the hall. Clara was busy putting the kettle on. Evie deposited her rucksack on the floor.

Elliot opened the back door. When he glanced behind him, he discovered Evie pulling out a kitchen chair. Elliot marched over to her. 'Now what are you doing?'

'Having a cup of tea,' responded Evie cocking her head in Clara's direction. 'Why – what are *you* doing?'

'*We* are leaving.'

Evie sat down. 'You know what, Elliot? I'm tired of trying to sleep in sleeping bags in the beach hut. I want a shower or a piping hot bath and a comfortable bed—' Evie stopped and turned to Clara. 'Oh, I didn't mean to presume.'

Clara looked at her dry, windswept hair and the dark circles under her green eyes and thought she could do with a shower and a good night's sleep. 'You can stay as long as you like.' Clara cringed. She didn't know how she had the audacity and had no idea how long she would get away with being here before someone found out the house had squatters.

Evie took off her coat. 'You did a lovely thing making out that we were staying here and not sleeping in the beach hut. It saved us a lot of bother trying to explain ourselves to Paul. Now I'm here I would rather stay. Just for the night,' she added not wanting Clara to get the impression she would take advantage. 'I want to wash my hair and not smell all sea salty. It would be nice to sleep in a proper bed and not worry about getting up at the crack of dawn to make sure no one knows we're camping in the beach hut. Someone else's beach hut – I might add.' Evie directed that last comment at her brother.

Elliot shot her sister a filthy look. 'It was your idea, as I recall.'

'Yes, I know,' she replied in a small voice. Evie twirled a strand of her long blonde hair between her fingers and stared at the table.

'Well, I'm going back.' Elliot stepped out the door.

'Elliot, why don't you stay just for one night? I'm sure there's room in a big old house like this.' Evie looked at Clara with an expression that said *help me persuade him to stay.*

Clara put the teapot down. 'There are plenty of bedrooms – and hot water.' She hoped there was because she also fancied a bath and a decent night's sleep in a proper bed tonight. Clara was still camping out on the sofa. It was as though by not sleeping upstairs she could kid herself that she hadn't moved in.

Elliot shook his head. 'No thanks.' And with that, he walked out and slammed the door.

Evie rose from the table half-heartedly and looked towards the door.

Clara poured hot water into the teapot and turned around to find Evie staring at the door, no doubt hoping Elliot would come back. Evie wasn't the only one disappointed Elliot was not staying. Clara had the beach hut on her mind, wondering what it was worth. She walked over to the table and poured Evie a cup of tea.

Evie sat down. 'Have you got anything stronger?'

'Stronger? Like coffee?'

'No, Clara, like alcohol.'

'Oh. I see.' Five minutes later Clara returned from the larder with a bottle of wine and a corkscrew from one of the kitchen drawers. So far, she had used nothing that she couldn't afford to replace. Clara thought about the change left in her purse as she opened a bottle of wine and ear-marked two frozen lasagnes for their meal tonight – assuming Elliot stuck to his word and didn't return to the house. She might be a squatter, but she didn't want to add thieving to her repertoire of criminal activities.

Clara poured two glasses of wine. There went her bus fare to the station. At this rate she would have to get a job. If only she could house sit for real, then she could stay here bona fide *and* earn money.

Clara's eyes flickered to the clock on the kitchen wall. She turned to Evie. 'Are you sure you want a glass of wine at this hour?'

'Why not? I'm on holiday. I can do what I fancy.'

Clara shrugged and handed her a glass.

'To new beginnings!' announced Evie.

46

Clara raised her glass of wine and looked at the young lady seated opposite her at the table. What had motivated Evie to suspend her nursing degree and travel down here with her brother, she wondered?

They clinked glasses. Clara watched her gulp down the wine.

'Drink up.' Evie held out her empty glass for a refill.

Clara followed suit and downed her glass in three large gulps, burning the back of her throat. She patted her chest and wheezed. 'Goodness. I can't remember the last time I drank a glass of wine that fast.'

Clara poured them both another glass, feeling guilty about helping herself to a bottle of wine while debating whether to fetch a second. Evie was downing them almost as fast as Clara could pour, but then Clara was no better.

A short time later the bottle was empty.

'I'll just be two ticks,' said Clara hoping she wasn't slurring her words; she was feeling tipsy.

'You go right ahead,' said Evie. 'I fancy another bottle. The owner of this house has a good taste in wine. I bet these bottles are costly.'

'Oh.' Clara stopped in her tracks. 'What makes you say that?' She'd assumed she could replace it with a cheap bottle of plonk from the supermarket. Not that she had the money for a bottle of plonk. It made her feel better if the wine wasn't expensive. Picking up the empty bottle she studied the label looking for a price tag but couldn't find one. She turned to Evie wondering how she knew the different between an expensive bottle of wine or a cheap one.

Evie guessed what she was thinking. 'An ex-boyfriend fancied himself quite the wine connoisseur – among other things. It rubbed off.'

'I see.' Clara got the impression it wasn't quality Evie was fussed about.

Evie pointed at the empty bottle. 'Are you sure it's okay helping ourselves?'

Clara was thinking she'd helped herself to his house wine. What's the difference a bottle or – or two?

'Who owns this house by the way?'

'I have no idea,' replied Clara before she stopped to consider what came out of her mouth.

'Oh. Sorry, I forgot. You're just the house sitter. I expect the agency didn't tell you much.'

'Hmm,' was all Clara said in response.

'Are you sure they're okay with us – I mean me staying here?'

'Of course,' Clara lied, managing a reassuring smile for Evie's benefit.

'Well, in that case, let's have more wine.'

Clara returned with another bottle.

Evie said to her glass, 'My twin brother can be a bit of an ass.'

Clara smiled. There was many a time she thought the same about Tommy. Sometimes she told him so too, right to his face. 'What brought you here?' asked Clara as she replenished their glasses.

'A lovely lady we met on the beach one morning.'

Clara smiled. 'Oh, I didn't mean what brought you to The Gables. I meant here to Southwold.'

'I know what you meant.' Evie held up her glass. 'New beginnings.'

'New beginnings,' mused Clara. 'I thought you were returning to London to finish your nursing degree?'

'Maybe. It's Elliot. That's why we came. It messed with his head when he admitted he was in love with my best friend. I wasn't surprised myself.'

'Does your friend know?'

'She's already in a relationship with someone else.'

Clara put her glass down. 'Oh.'

'Precisely.' Evie finished her wine and looked up at Clara with glazed eyes.

Clara hesitated before pouring another.

Evie held up her glass.

'Last one,' said Clara, hoping Evie didn't take offence.

'Yeah. You're probably right. It's not like me to drink in the morning. God, I'm turning into Elliot.'

Clara put the bottle down. 'Your brother…?'

Evie breathed a sigh. 'Elliot ended up crashing on my couch. I don't mind myself, but I'm not single, at least I wasn't until my boyfriend issued me with an ultimatum – "It's him or me." Evie stared at her empty glass. 'So here we are, having a little holiday away from my boyfriend, who's now my *ex*-boyfriend.'

'I'm sorry.'

'Don't be. He was a dick – pardon the expression. I hope this trip was worth it and Elliot sorts himself out.'

'Couldn't you go to your parents?'

Evie smiled. 'Dad wouldn't understand. He'd just say, "Stop all this nonsense, Lad, and pull yourself together." As you can imagine that wouldn't be very helpful. Besides, out of the two of us I always felt they pinned all their hopes, dreams and expectations on his shoulders. It's as though what he was doing with his life, what he would achieve, was more important to them somehow – especially Dad.'

Sounds just like Tommy and my father, thought Clara.

'Anyway, my parents live in London. That's not the best place for Elliot right now.'

Clara was getting the picture. Evie and Elliot had come here to get away from it all. 'You're on your summer holidays. You can go back in the Autumn and finish your nursing degree, surely.'

Evie shook her head. 'I'm on a placement working in a hospital. We don't get the long summer breaks like other university students. If I don't do my placement, I don't know if I can go back and complete the degree.'

Evie downed another glass of wine. 'Elliot doesn't know. He'd kill me if he found out. Well, not exactly. What I mean to say is the last thing he'd want is to drag me down with him. He's said as much. He thinks I'm just on vacation from college.' She paused, staring into her glass. 'But I had to do it. He was sinking into the depths of depression over this girl and I had to do something even if I risk losing my place on the course. You understand – don't you?' Evie looked at Clara with pleading eyes.

She understood all right; the lengths Evie would go to looking after her twin. Clara wished that whatever had been troubling Tommy the night of their birthday, all those years ago, she had been there for him the way Evie was for Elliot. At least Evie wouldn't have to carry that guilt around with her for the rest of her life if, heaven forbid, something happened to Elliot.

'You do understand, don't you?' Evie said again.

Clara looked into her pleading eyes and got up from the table to take a seat next to Evie. She put a tentative hand around her shoulders. 'You have no idea.'

Evie cried.

Bailey appeared at the kitchen door; his head cocked to one side listening to the sound of Evie crying. He scooted over and disappeared under the table. Suddenly his head popped up from under the table and rested on her lap. Then a paw appeared on her knee.

Evie looked down at Bailey and laughed. 'You silly dog. If you're trying to cheer me up, it's working.' She wiped her nose with the sleeve of her blouse and stroked the top of his head. 'I'm not surprised Elliot wanted to return to the beach hut. It's been a godsend finding that place. We were close to our grandparents. They used to own a beach hut here. We spent our summers with them when we were children. Elliot especially loved it here. When they passed away the beach hut got sold.'

'That's a shame,' remarked Clara staring around the kitchen. She wished her parents hadn't sold the house. It would have been nice if they'd left her this too, so there was a place to call her own. Then perhaps she could keep the beach hut for her own grandchildren to spend time here in the summer. Clara shook her head. Tamsin and Kevin wouldn't have been interested in bringing their children to Southwold in the summer. They spent the holidays jetting off first class to exciting foreign destinations.

'It was when we first arrived off the bus and were strolling along the shore that we came across the old wreck of a hut. When we saw the state of it we knew nobody would be using it, so I thought what harm could it do to borrow it for the summer?'

When she put it like that, Clara was inclined to agree.

'Then Elliot got it into his head to fix it up. He's not the type to sit around and do nothing. Me – I'm fond of just lazing around on the beach with a novel. But despite my reservations, it turned out the perfect project for Elliot to keep him busy and his mind off… other things.'

Clara nodded. Perhaps that's what *she* needed; a project to keep her busy and her mind off Joe and what was coming next. Whether he pulled through, Clara had no idea what to do with her life without him.

Before the accident she'd never stopped to consider how dependant she was on Joe. *But he promised he would never leave me*, the voice of that childish eighteen-year-old reminded her. But I'm not that heart-broken teenager anymore looking for someone to take care of me. I'm a mature woman, thought Clara. Isn't it about time I took responsibility for my own life?

What she needed was a job. She wasn't a lady of leisure who didn't have to consider the roof over her head and the food on the table.

'… cost more to do it up, and bang went the money for our holiday accommodation. That's why we ended up giving up our room in the bed and breakfast and staying in the beach hut.'

Clara caught the tail end of Evie's monologue. 'I'm sorry…?' She wasn't paying attention, consumed with her own situation.

'Don't be sorry,' Evie replied not catching her meaning. 'It isn't your fault I spent all our holiday money on doing up the hut. *I'm* not sorry. It turned out to be the making of Elliot. He's got his health back. My only worry is what will happen now the beach hut is finished?'

Evie sighed. 'This summer isn't going to last forever, is it? It's already the end of August. In fact, we were going to pack up and leave last week, but the sunny weather came back and we thought what the heck. What harm could it do to stay on as long as the weather holds?'

Clara frowned. It could do plenty of harm; she needed to take back ownership of the beach hut as soon as possible.

'Perhaps it will be an Indian Summer? Wouldn't that be great? It's not unheard of for the whole month of September to be warm and sunny too.'

A month. Clara couldn't hang on at The Gables for an entire month. Technically she could. There was enough food in the freezer and none of the utilities were disconnected – there was power, light and hot water on tap. But the longer she was here, the greater the likelihood she'd be discovered. And if the twins were planning on extending their stay in Southwold, she could hardly invite them to stay on with her.

Clara took a breath and decided it was time to come clean and tell Evie the truth. She wanted her beach hut back.

47

'Look, Evie, there's something I meant to—'

'I know I'm dragging it out, but I'm worried what will happen when we return to London. He's in a good place right now. I want nothing bad to happen to my brother.'

Clara stared at Evie. 'What do you mean?'

'Before we left London, Elliot attempted…' Evie shook her head. 'He didn't think life was worth living.'

There was a long pause during which Clara got the picture.

Evie looked at Clara. 'I'm sorry for cutting across you like that. What were you going to say? It sounded as though you had something to tell me.'

Clara pursed her lips. 'It's nothing.'

'Are you sure?'

Clara didn't have time to change her mind as the kitchen door flew open taking them both by surprise.

'You're back!' exclaimed Evie when she saw her brother standing in the doorway.

'I'm not staying.' He stepped into the kitchen. 'The batteries in our torch have died, so I want to borrow a torch.' He looked across the room at Clara. 'If you have one.'

'Oh, Elliot.' Evie rolled her eyes. 'Why don't you stay the night in a nice warm bed? Then you won't need a torch. And wouldn't you like to take a shower or soak in a hot bath?'

Clara remained seated at the kitchen table wondering if Evie could change his mind. Elliot's rucksack was still slung over his shoulder. He made no move to put it down.

'I told you I'm not staying.' He shifted his gaze to Clara. 'Have you got a torch or not?'

Clara felt like saying, *don't take that tone with me, young man.* But it wasn't her place. Besides, she was the one who had practically railroaded them into stopping. Poor Elliot would probably feel lonely down on the beach without his sister tonight. Clara could sympathise with Evie though; she craved creature comforts as any sane woman would.

Clara got up from the table. She had no idea where to find a torch. A quick rummage through cupboards and drawers unearthed a large, almost industrial-sized flashlight. It looked like something a workman would use. She put it on the table in front of Elliot. 'I'm afraid it's quite large.'

Elliot shrugged. 'It'll do.'

Evie appealed to her brother. 'Please stay. We could sit in the garden or…' Evie seemed to struggle with what they could do all day around the house.

'There are plenty of books,' ventured Clara. Yesterday, she had poked her head around another door downstairs, which used to be the library in her parents' day, and discovered to her surprise that it hadn't changed; the oak bookshelves were lined with books except they weren't the legal volumes that she remembered from her childhood – her father was a solicitor.

Instead there were novels, mostly by H Rider Haggard which led Clara to conclude that the owner of the house rather liked adventure yarns set in far-flung places. That made sense considering what she knew about the man; he was a photojournalist who travelled the world. That also explained the interesting books on photography.

The little room was cosy. She rather fancied spending more time looking through those books on photography.

'Well, I guess now I've got a torch for this evening I'll take you up on that.'

'I'm sorry – what?' said Clara, not following.

'Elliot wouldn't mind taking a book with him.'

'All right.' Clara rose from her seat. 'I'll show you the library.'

'Library?' repeated Elliot casting a look over his shoulder at Evie and rolling his eyes in disdain. She knew what he was thinking: who has a *library* in this day and age?

As they walked down the hall, Elliot said to Clara, 'Why don't you call it a study?'

Clara stopped outside the door and pointed at the nameplate.

'Ah. I see.'

Clara smiled at Elliot. The bronze nameplate on the door said *Library*. 'Personally, I think it's pompous if you ask me. I mean who has a *library* in their house, anyway?'

Elliot nodded in agreement and returned Clara's smile. 'I couldn't agree more. Although there are an awful lot of books in here,' he said as Clara opened the door.

They both stepped into the small room with floor-to-ceiling bookshelves and a large bay window overlooking the garden. 'Nice view,' commented Elliot. He looked at the desk in front of the window and sat down in the green leather chair behind the desk, trying it out for size. 'This is comfortable.' He leaned back in the chair and eyed the bookshelves. 'So, who owns this house?'

Clara picked up a book on photography and held it up. 'He's a photojournalist.'

'What's he like?'

'How do I know?' blurted Clara without thinking. She could feel her face flushing bright crimson.

Elliot leaned forward in his chair. 'What did you say you're doing here?'

'I told you already. I'm the house sitter. Now, what about that novel you were after?' Clara turned her back on those intense blue eyes and gazed up at the bookshelves. She picked a book off the bookshelf at random, doing her best to change the subject. 'What have we here? It's a novel by H Rider Haggard. Or how about Edgar Rice Burroughs? Maybe Rudyard Kipling is more your thing?' Clara glanced at Elliot. 'Do you like adventure stories?'

Elliot got up from behind the desk and joined Clara in front of the bookshelves. 'Hmm, if this were a proper library, they'd be more choice.'

'Nothing takes your fancy?'

Elliot picked a book off the bookshelf. 'I've seen the movie, but never read the book.' He held it up.

Clara read the title on the spine. '*King Solomon's Mines.*'

'How did you come by the position of house sitter?' Elliot asked as he thumbed through the pages.

'In all honesty, it sort of fell in my lap.' Clara glanced at Bailey, who had followed them into the library, and recalled the events back at the police station when Bailey had found that old newspaper in the wastepaper bin and brought it over, depositing it on her lap.

'Sounds kind of like Evie and I coming across the beach hut.'

'I don't know what you mean.' said Clara defensively, hoping he hadn't guessed the truth: that she too was squatting in someone else's property.

'What I meant, Clara, was that like you, an opportunity presented itself when we needed it – that's all.'

'Oh, I see. Well, in that case, yes that's exactly what happened.'

Bailey barked.

Elliot glanced in his direction. 'I see your dog agrees.'

'He's not my—' Clara stopped short before she got herself in a bind and had to explain how she found herself with someone else's dog. She knew she ought to find out where he'd been re-homed and return him, but it was obvious this was Bailey's proper home. He belonged here. Right now, she wasn't going to concern herself with the problem of what to do with Bailey when she had to leave.

While she'd been standing there staring at Bailey, Elliot returned to the desk, sat back down in the leather chair and opened the book.

Bailey followed him and settled down on the floor by his feet. He gazed out of the window.

Clara walked over to the door with a large book about photography tucked under her arm. She paused at the door. Elliot had put his feet up on the desk and was leaning back in the leather chair, engrossed in the adventure novel. He licked a finger and turned the page without even noticing Clara was heading out of the room. She glanced at Bailey. She got the impression that the dog was accustomed to spending many an hour sitting at his owner's feet gazing out of that window or having a doze as was the case now.

Standing there looking into the room, Clara had a strange thought: *I'd like to meet him, the famous photojournalist.* She shook her head not knowing where that crazy idea came from. Things were complicated enough, the last thing she needed was Bailey's owner turning up out of the blue.

Clara stepped out of the library. As she closed the door, she didn't notice a face in the window. Ralph was standing outside, peering in at a young man – he could only see the back of his blonde head. What Ralph noticed, however, was that he had his feet up on the desk, reading a book from his library.

Ralph saw Clara closing the library door. What the heck was going on? Was she inviting people to stay at his house now? He had a good mind to walk in and confront her. In fact, that's what he would do. Ralph took a deep breath and decided it was time to come clean and tell Clara the truth. He wanted his house back.

48

Clara walked into the kitchen expecting to find Evie sitting at the kitchen table, but she wasn't there. Clara knitted her brow and went over to the kitchen door. She poked her head outside but couldn't see any sign of Evie in the back garden.

'That's odd.' She left the book on the kitchen table and walked into the hallway, glancing up the stairs. She didn't hear the creak of floorboards upstairs or the sound of running water. Evie wasn't having a bath and the house was quiet.

Clara wandered into the lounge and found her on the sofa curled up in a ball fast asleep. She wasn't surprised. An entire bottle of wine would do that. Perhaps sleeping in that beach hut had also taken its toll. Not to mention the worry over her brother. Little wonder it had all caught up with her. She walked over and pulled the thick curtains at the windows to block out the light and didn't see the face peering in.

Keen to find out if the young man wasn't the only new house guest, Ralph had made his way to the lounge window. He had just cupped his hands to the windowpane when Clara drew the curtains closed.

'What the...!' Ralph stepped back from the window and frowned. He was sure he'd spotted someone else in the room, sleeping on his sofa.

Clara looked about her and reached for a throw on the

armchair. She draped it over the young woman. Although it was summer, it was cool in the large airy house.

She stood for a moment staring at Evie sleeping, and had the sudden urge to phone Tamsin and check she was all right, which reminded Clara that she hadn't checked her phone this morning. What if something had happened while she was at the beach?

Clara walked back to the kitchen to find her handbag. When she switched on her phone, she discovered she had four missed calls. Her stomach lurched at what might have happened in her absence. Clara was thinking about Joe.

She scrolled through the missed calls, relieved to discover none of them were from the hospital. They were all from Tamsin. She could hazard a guess the calls were related to Dorothy, and when Clara was coming home. She was not inclined to return right now – if at all. It was almost as though she had already left that life behind.

Even though she was already light-headed and tipsy, Clara discovered the half-empty bottle of wine on the kitchen table and against her better judgement decided to re-fill her glass – several times.

She had just poured the last of the wine into her glass when the kitchen door flew open. Clara turned her head. 'Oh, hello.' Clara raised the glass to her lips. 'Fancy meeting you here.' Clara giggled at her own joke. *Fancy meeting you here. Of course he'd be here; he only lived at the bottom of the garden.*

Ralph stood there staring at her, his eyes shifting to the three expensive and now empty bottles of wine on the kitchen table. 'What do you think you're doing?'

Clara looked at her glass. 'Having a little tipple is all. Why, what do you think *you're* doing?'

Ralph stared at her. 'Are you drunk?'

Clara shook her head up and down making herself queasy. 'Possibly.'

Ralph stared at Clara. Her behaviour was outrageous. He

didn't know her at all. Whether or not she was house sitting he had yet to find out. What was plain to see was that she was helping herself to whatever took her fancy and inviting friends over to stay. This was just what he was afraid of when he left the property empty. The whole reason he'd given the keys to the estate agent was to keep an eye on the house while he was away; they clearly weren't doing their job.

Ralph glared at her. 'You need to leave. Right now!'

'Who says?' Clara managed, her words slurring.

'Me – that's who. I own this house.'

Clara looked him up and down and burst out laughing. 'What do you take me for? I may be drunk, but I'm not stupid. I know your game. You want it all to yourself.' Clara downed another glass of wine. 'Besides, I can't leave just yet even if I wanted to.'

'Why not?'

Clara stared at her empty glass. 'It's my husband, Joe…'

'Your problems are not my concern,' announced Ralph haughtily, trying to keep his composure at the mention of her husband, the man she'd married instead of him.

Clara turned to look at him, and to Ralph's utter dismay, she burst into tears. 'Oh, crap.' He didn't know what to do.

Ralph's eyes darted about the room searching for something to say. When he looked back at Clara, she had her head in her arms sobbing. Ralph walked over wondering what he should do. He put a tentative hand on her shoulder. He thought she'd shrug him off, but she didn't. 'Clara?' he said without thinking, realising too late she hadn't introduced herself; how would he explain that?

It turned out Ralph didn't have to explain anything. Clara had fallen asleep. He gave her shoulder a little shake.

'Wha…what is it?'

'Why don't you sleep it off upstairs, Clara?' Ralph whispered in her ear, his lips so close to her cheek he closed his eyes for a moment and caught the scent of her perfume. God, it took him back. He couldn't believe, after all these years, she was using the same fragrance. He remembered the sweet-smelling scent like it was yesterday, etched in his memory as vivid as their first kiss, their first everything, on that beach in Mallorca.

Clara lifted her head too fast and came over dizzy. 'Oh, my head!'

'Ow, my nose!' said Ralph as Clara head-butted him.

Ralph stood up and ran his fingers along his nose. Thankfully, nothing was broken although it was sore. 'Come on.' He helped Clara out of her seat. 'Where are we going?' Clara asked. She was finding it challenging just putting one foot in front of the other. She looked at the man helping her out of the kitchen. 'Who are you again?'

I'm the man you left broken-hearted – don't you remember? Ralph heaved a sigh at her blank expression. *Obviously not.* 'You'll feel better after a lie-down.' He steered her into the lounge, intending to settle her down on the sofa, but he'd forgotten it was already taken. He glanced at the young woman asleep on the couch and recognised her instantly. She was one of the twins. He raised an eyebrow. 'Evie?' She stirred but didn't wake.

He'd helped them do up the beach hut. Ever since meeting them he'd kept his distance, but he felt compelled to keep an eye on them; that was the reason he made it to the bench on the clifftop promenade early each morning, to check they were okay. Now he guessed he didn't have to.

Although Ralph was not pleased when he discovered Clara had invited other people back to the house, with the twins that was different. She must have taken pity on them, sleeping rough in the beach hut.

Ralph steered Clara out of the room and put a finger to her lips when she was about to say something. 'Shush, let's not wake Evie.'

Clara nodded which made her head spin.

Ralph wasn't just thinking about Evie. He now knew who was sitting in the library at his desk reading one of his books –

Elliot. If it had been anybody else, he would have been in there like a shot to turf them out of his house.

He'd got talking to Elliot as he helped him fix the roof on Tommy's beach hut. Ralph discovered the twins had spent their own money fixing up the dilapidated hut expecting nothing in return but the use of it over the summer. Whoever owned it was in for a pleasant surprise when they turned up to claim it. For that reason, Ralph couldn't imagine the twins would take advantage and so he did not begrudge Elliot the use of his study or his reading material; he would have preferred him not to have his feet up on his desk though.

Ralph crept past the library hoping Elliot didn't suddenly walk out of the room and discover him in the house. Right now, he didn't want to explain what he was doing here.

At the foot of the stairs, Ralph looked up. 'I hope you can make it up the stairs.'

'I'll try,' Clara whispered back although she had no idea why they were whispering. She felt a fit of giggles coming on. She cupped her hand to her mouth.

Ralph rolled his eyes. 'God, you really are drunk, aren't you?' He breathed a sigh when they reached the top of the stairs.

He deposited her in the first bedroom on the left, in the large double bed, took off her shoes and pulled the patchwork quilt over her. Ralph drew the blinds at the window overlooking the garden and stood for a moment staring around the room. His late wife enjoyed interior design. She'd done a grand job bringing the house into the twenty-first century while keeping many of the original features like the wooden doors, dado rails and intricate coving that were a feature of the house.

Ralph frowned when something occurred to him. Even though the bedrooms were similarly furnished, it probably wasn't the best idea to put Clara in this bedroom. *Why didn't I think of that?* Ralph paused at the door before he left wondering how Clara would feel waking up in Tommy's bedroom.

49

'What time is it?' Clara was standing in the hall feeling disorientated; she supposed waking up in Tommy's old bedroom would do that. How did she get upstairs; she didn't remember climbing into bed.

Clara walked down the stairs, the distinct smell of bacon and eggs wafting from the kitchen. Someone was cooking breakfast.

Evie passed the stairs on the way to the kitchen and spotted Clara. 'Ah, there you are. Do you want breakfast?'

'What – again?'

Evie looked at her perplexed. 'Well, yes, that's what one does every morning,' she said, 'although we are breaking from tradition by not having it on the beach.'

Clara stared at her wide-eyed. 'How long have I slept?'

'All yesterday and last night. I thought *I* slept like the dead. This place is so quiet it should come with a health warning.' Evie smiled. 'So, what about breakfast?'

Clara shook her head still feeling the after-effects of consuming all that wine. It probably explained why she couldn't get up. 'Later. I'll step outside and have some fresh air first.'

'There's plenty if you change your mind. I sent Elliot down to the beach to fetch the cooler box before he cooked breakfast.'

'Did he stay the night?'

'No. He stopped by the house this morning to see what I

wanted to do about breakfast on the beach.' Evie worked her finger through some strands of hair as she said, 'Perhaps I could work on him if that offer extended to—'

'Yes, stay as long as you like,' Clara said off-hand.

'Really? Are you sure the owner won't mind?'

'Of course not.' Providing they didn't find out, thought Clara as she walked to the front door. She recalled that strange dream last night. The owner had turned up and told her to leave, and she'd burst into tears, the result being that he'd reconsidered.

Clara rolled her eyes. As if that would happen. They were more likely to call the police. She wasn't the type to burst into tears and share her sob story to any Tom, Dick or Harry? Clara thought of all the wine she'd consumed last night and thanked her lucky stars she'd taken herself off to bed before embarrassing herself in front of anybody, not to mention revealing what she was really doing here. The twins were still none the wiser – thank goodness.

Opening the front door, she heard something and turned around to find Bailey belting down the hall towards her. 'Oh Bailey, I bet you wondered where I was.'

He acted like Clara had been gone for a month, not just a day. 'Come here, you silly dog.' She knelt and gave him a big fuss and got lots of doggy kisses in return. 'I was only upstairs.' Clara stood up and opened the front door, followed closely by Bailey. 'Don't worry, I'm not going anywhere.'

Bailey promptly disappeared. She bet he had more important things to do like begging at the kitchen table for bacon. Clara stepped outside, surprised to find Bailey was back. 'What's this – you want a game of fetch?'

He put the ball down on the gravel by her feet and barked.

'Shush. What have I told you about keeping it down?'

Bailey nudged the ball with his nose.

'Oh, all right, but it's a chilly. I must fetch my coat then we can go into the back garden to play ball.'

❖

Ralph heard a dog bark and put his spatula down to listen, worried about the policeman turning up to call on Evie. It wasn't the policemen that concerned him but his dog who might, given half a chance, sniff out the strange man living in the outhouse. Ralph wasn't in the mood to explain himself. He'd rather abandon his breakfast.

He looked out the window on to the back garden to see if it Clara was playing a game of fetch with her dog. There was no sign of them. Ralph left his breakfast and walked down the cobbled pathway aiming straight across the lawn to the driveway in front of the house. He stood by a tree and checked there was no tell-tale sign of a police car.

He stood there for a moment staring at the flower pot. Talk about déjà vu. He looked up at the house. The inclination to take the key, unlock the front door and go inside for a hot shower followed by a nap in a proper bed soon took flight at the thought of the three occupants inside. He'd tried that yesterday morning when he found Clara in his kitchen. She had dissolved into fits of laughter when he told her he owned this house. Admittedly she'd been drunk at the time, but what sort of reaction did he expect looking like this? Nobody would take him seriously.

Ralph turned around and headed back to the outhouse, his mouth watering at the prospect of streaky bacon and fried eggs still warm in the pan.

He walked back into the outhouse and reached for the saucepan. 'What the heck?!' He held up the pan. It was empty. 'Not again!'

❖

'I thought we were playing a game of fetch? Where have you been?' Clara eyed the dog. She got a distinct feeling of déjà vu. Bailey was sitting on the damp grass in the garden, his head bowed, ears twitching at the sound of Clara's cross voice. 'And what have you been eating?' She looked at Bailey licking his chops. Clara was thinking of the outhouse with the cooking stove and the smell of bacon permeating the air. The last thing she needed was a run-in with her neighbour. However, Clara had no intention of returning to the house to avoid him. If they were going to have a confrontation, she'd rather it was here in the garden out of earshot of the twins.

She started the game of fetch expecting him to come out and have words with her over his missing bacon.

Perhaps he's gone. Packed up his stuff and left? Clara continued to throw the ball. It was a possibility. He looked as though he wanted to be on his own. When he discovered the house was no longer empty, he decided it was time to move on. Clara threw the ball waiting for him to appear. She wondered if she should venture down to the bottom of the garden to see if he was there and check he was all right.

Where did that idea come from? He's not my responsibility. I don't even like the man.

Bailey returned and taking the ball Clara gave him a pointy finger instead. 'Don't think I've forgotten what you've been up to. Stop stealing that man's bacon!'

Bailey licked his lips as soon as she said the word bacon and turned his head toward the outhouse.

'Don't even think about it!' Clara warned the dog. She'd been lucky this time. Perhaps he hadn't noticed a rasher missing, or simply didn't care. Whatever the case, Clara was glad there were no consequences – this time.

After the game of fetch, Clara left Bailey basking in the morning sunshine on the patio and decided she fancied some breakfast after all. She wondered if the twins were still cooking. Clara cast a glance behind her. She was thinking about Bailey and whether she should venture down the garden to apologise.

She was just debating whether she should pay him a visit

when she opened the kitchen door and discovered there was no need to traipse to the outhouse; he was right here sitting at the kitchen table. Clara's eyes went wide. What was he doing in the house? Clara blurted, 'What are *you* doing here?'

Before he answered, Elliot stepped out from the pantry with a can of baked beans in his hand. He looked at her across the room. 'Hello, Clara. I hope you don't mind…'

She didn't know whether he was referring to helping himself to the can of baked beans or the strange man sitting at the kitchen table.

Elliot caught Clara frowning. 'Oh, um this is…' Elliot smiled at the man sitting at the table. 'I just realised I don't know your name.'

Ralph avoided Clara's gaze. This was awkward. After all this time in the outhouse agonizing over stepping foot in the house, this wasn't how he pictured returning home. Elliot had been down to the beach to fetch the cooler box and discovered the shortcut through the gap in the hedge at the back of the garden. Ralph had careered into him as he thundered down the cobbled path on his way to the shops for more bacon.

Elliot recognised the man who had helped him do up the beach hut. The outhouse door was wide open he put two and two together – and assumed he was sleeping rough in the outhouse. That's when Ralph got the invite to have breakfast up at the house.

Ralph had done his best to decline the invitation, but Elliot wouldn't hear of it which left Ralph cursing under his breath. If only he hadn't been such a good Samaritan and had minded his own business. Perhaps if it had been any other beach hut or maybe it was seeing the twins which took him back to his youth and thoughts of Clara and Tommy. Whatever the case he was regretting it now.

They were still waiting for Ralph to tell them his name. Elliot stepped into the awkward silence. 'I insisted he come and join us for breakfast. I never repaid him for helping us fix up the beach hut.'

Clara turned to look at Ralph. 'You helped them fix up the beach hut?'

'It was nothing – really.'

'Nothing?' Elliot shook his head as he opened the can of beans. 'We couldn't have done it without you. The roof especially.' Elliot glanced at Clara.

Clara knew what he was thinking: why wasn't she taking a seat at the table? She shook her head. She wasn't sitting down to have breakfast with—

Elliot saw her shaking her head. 'Clara, will you sit down already! Seriously, what is with you two? Most people would jump at having someone offer to cook them breakfast.'

Clara reluctantly took a seat at the table opposite him.

'I was cooking anyway, so it's no trouble,' said Elliot misreading the reason Clara had to be cajoled into joining them for breakfast. She glanced around the table. There were only two place settings; hers and the irritating man sitting opposite her.

Clara turned in her chair to look at Elliot. 'Aren't you having any?'

'We've already eaten. Evie is down at the beach hut.'

Clara noticed a frown cross his features. She bet Evie had gone down to the beach to meet Paul. Clara sighed and turned in her seat. She caught the annoying man staring at her across the table.

Ralph was sitting there staring at her wondering if she remembered anything from yesterday morning when she was drunk. She still looked a little worse for wear.

'What?' Clara snapped at him.

Ralph averted his gaze.

Clara breathed a sigh. She might not be pleased to see him here in the house, but that was no excuse to be rude. 'Sorry, I didn't mean to snap.' It wasn't his fault she'd drunk too much last night. And why was she getting all territorial over him coming into the house? It wasn't as though she owned the place. He was here first it should be the other way around. So far, he had said nothing about the fact that she'd invited more people to stay.

Clara looked at him. She could at least be civil. 'Is this the first time you've been in the house?'

And that answered Ralph's question. She didn't remember yesterday.

'Of course you haven't.' She rolled her eyes at the stupid question. 'You live in the outhouse.'

Elliot placed two plates in front of them on the table. 'I'll leave you guys to get acquainted.'

Re-acquainted thought Ralph.

There was an awkward silence when Elliot left the room.

Clara picked up her knife and fork. 'Look, I know what you're doing here.'

Ralph raised an eyebrow.

'The dog stole your bacon this morning, didn't he?' Clara realised she had Bailey to thank for the fact that he was sitting in the kitchen eating breakfast.

Ralph shook his head. 'Well, at least that solves the mystery of why my bacon keeps disappearing.'

'Sorry about that.' To Clara's surprise she saw him smile. She couldn't help smiling herself at the image of him returning to the outhouse to find his breakfast had vanished. In fact, the more she thought about it…Clara put her hand to her mouth to stifle a laugh.

He saw her face light up the way it used to when she smiled.

Clara apologised. 'Sorry – I didn't mean to laugh.'

'Not at all. It is kind of funny.' Ralph picked up his knife and fork and cut into the streaky bacon on his plate. 'I used to know a dog who liked bacon,' Ralph commented.

'Ah and there I was thinking he was one of a kind. I mean, I thought dogs preferred sausages. But then what do I know? I've always had cats.' *Careful, Clara. The next thing you'll be saying is that you've never owned a dog.* Clara steered the conversation away from herself. She asked, 'So, was it your dog that liked bacon?' Clara ventured.

'My wife. It was my wife's dog.'

Another awkward silence followed. Clara said, 'So how long have you been here?'

Ralph looked up. I was born here. I went to school with you. I sat behind you in class and fell in love with the six-year-old girl with blonde pigtails and the biggest brown eyes I'd ever seen. But it was ten more years before you noticed me when I became best friends with your brother – don't you remember?

'I've been living in the outhouse three months.' Ralph tucked into his breakfast disheartened that she didn't recognise him. Then again why would she? He wasn't exactly looking his best and made no effort with his appearance.

Clara looked at him a moment. Something told her he was holding back. But then it wasn't as though she would sit here and divulge to a complete stranger her life story either. *A stranger.* Clara stared at him. There was something about him…

He looked up and caught her staring. 'What is it?'

Clara looked away. 'Nothing. I was just wondering what brought you here.' She didn't really expect him to answer that question. It was none of her business. Besides, what she really meant was how did he come to be in this state – homeless?

Ralph put his knife and fork down. 'My wife died.'

'I'm so sorry.' She stared at him, taking in his beard, the unwashed grey hair falling over his eyes, the dirty clothes he was wearing. Something in his voice, his demeanour said he hadn't always been like this. Clara remembered the homeless man she'd bumped into in London when she was out with Debs. He'd said he had a job and a home only a short time ago. Then something happened and his life had fallen apart – just like that.

Was that what had happened to him when his wife died – his

life fell apart? Maybe he wasn't homeless. Was this some sort of breakdown? She imagined he might have a life somewhere with a house and people who cared about him. Perhaps it was too painful for him to face going home without her. Clara could empathise. She couldn't face being at home right now either. But at least she was holding it together – only just.

'What about you?' asked Ralph. 'What brought you back? I mean *here*,' Ralph hastily rephrased. He inwardly cringed at his gaffe; however, she didn't seem to notice. She looked miles away, preoccupied.

'My husband was in a car accident.'

'I'm sorry for your loss.'

'Oh, he's not… he's in a coma.'

'Then what are you doing here?' asked the hurt, angry Ralph who didn't want to hear that she was still with the man she'd married so soon after she dumped him and moved away to London.

Clara stared at him. She knew what he was asking: why was she here and not sitting at her husband's bedside? Clara's bottom lip quivered. 'It's complicated.'

'What do you mean – it's complicated?'

Clara took one look at the mean man sitting across the table who knew nothing about her situation, about what Joe had done, and burst into tears.

Oh crap – not again! This was yesterday morning all over again, except this time Clara was stone cold sober. Ralph stared at her and didn't know what to do. He hadn't meant to sound so accusatory as though she was in the wrong. It made him wonder – what had her husband done? Whatever it was, if Ralph could get his hands on him, he'd string him up.

Ralph's eyes darted about the room searching for something to say. When he looked back Clara was no longer sitting opposite him. He turned his head in time to see the kitchen door to the garden bang shut.

Ralph sat at the table for a long time. His impulse was to go after her. But what would he say?

'Oh, sod it!' Ralph jumped out of his seat and followed her out the door. She wasn't in the back garden. He hurried down the path and through the gap in the hedge out on to the cliff top walk.

A young couple holding hands were walking by. They crossed the street to avoid him. Ralph noticed, but he didn't care. He crossed the road too and looked down at the beach. As far as he could see, she wasn't on the beach. Ralph turned and glanced down the street towards the town. He saw the church spire and knew where she was. She'd gone to talk to Tommy.

50

Ralph retraced his steps to the outhouse. He sat down on the camp bed and stared at the painting of Mallorca. What he wouldn't give to turn back the clock.

He didn't know how long he'd been sitting there staring at that painting when he heard a dog barking. They were back!

Ralph sprung out of his seat. He had an idea and retrieved an old notebook and a pen from the shelf. In the evenings, by the glow of the oil lamp, he'd been trying to figure out what to do with his life. The notebook was still blank. He tore off a piece of paper and wrote her a note apologising for upsetting her. He made the mistake of signing it. Ralph screwed up the paper and started again, this time signing it, *the man in the outhouse.*

Ralph re-read the note. Now how was he going to give it to her? Ralph smiled as he lit the stove and opened a new packet of bacon. He slapped two rashers in the pan. While he waited for the bacon to cook, he walked outside to retrieve the basket filled with fresh vegetables he'd dug up that morning. He slipped the note in between a carrot and a swede.

Ralph sat outside on a rickety wooden chair and waited. It didn't take long for the golden retriever to appear at the top of the cobbled path. Ralph made sure he'd left the door to the outhouse wide open. 'There you are,' said Ralph.

Bailey let out a low growl and backed away.

Ralph whipped into the outhouse and came out with the pan. 'Now here's the deal. If you take this basket to Clara, I'll give you the bacon.' Ralph used a fork and held up two strips of crispy fried bacon. 'Do we have a deal?'

Bailey looked at the bacon.

Ralph placed the bacon on the path beside the basket and backed up to the chair. He sat down, hopeful the dog understood. If not he'd have to take the basket himself.

Come on, Ralph willed the dog.

Bailey edged closer, sniffed the basket, grabbed the bacon and ran back down the path.

'Hey! You forgot something.' Ralph shook his head. Did he really think the dog would—

Bailey came running back and clamped his jaws around the handle. Ralph watched in astonishment as he lifted it up and strolled down the path, the basket swinging from side-to-side with his gait. 'Well, I'll be. What a clever dog!'

As soon as the dog disappeared at the end of the path, Ralph shot into the outhouse, aiming straight for the window. He watched the dog walking up the garden. Clara was back in her spot on the patio, sitting in a garden chair with a book. She put the book down as the dog approached and took the basket. For a split second, Ralph thought the dog was in trouble. It hadn't occurred to him that after the bacon episode earlier she might think the naughty dog had stolen the vegetables.

Has she found the note? Ralph was straining his neck, wishing he had a pair of binoculars. She leaned forward in her chair. Then he saw a flicker of white. *She'd found it!* Holding his breath, he saw her look toward the outhouse.

Ralph dropped the makeshift curtain back into place wondering what she would make of his apology. He'd had no right to take such an accusatory tone. It was none of his business why she was here and not with her comatose husband.

Five minutes later Ralph was sitting outside on his rickety

chair when the dog appeared at the end of the path. He had returned with the basket. *Damn!* She'd rejected his peace offering.

Or had she? As the dog approached Ralph noticed the basket was empty apart from for a single white sheet of folded paper. The dog and the basket were just out of reach.

Ralph called to him, 'Here, boy.'

The dog growled.

Ralph sat back down in his chair. He wished he'd kept quiet. He got the distinct impression the dog didn't like him very much.

'What have I ever done to you?' Ralph said under his breath. He perked up when he had an idea. 'What if I go inside and you can leave the basket by the door – eh?' Once again Ralph rose from his seat and walked inside.

A moment later Ralph was back again, looking for his basket. There it was by the door. So was the growling mutt. When Ralph attempted to take the basket, the dog clamped his jaws around the handle. It was a stand-off.

'Oh, come on!' Ralph was getting exasperated. He could see the note in the bottom under a carrot, but he daren't put his hand inside. 'What have I got to do to get my basket back?' Ralph rolled his eyes. 'Oh, I get it – you want to trade.'

Bailey released the basket although he wouldn't budge from his spot standing guard over his bargaining chip.

'Fine. But you must wait. I can't magic crispy fried bacon out of thin air you know.' Ralph did a double-take when the dog sat down. 'Seriously? I swear you understood every word I just said.'

Ralph stepped back into the outhouse, lit the stove and peeled away two more rashers of smoky back bacon from his dwindling packet courtesy of the local supermarket bin. At this rate, he'd have none left for tomorrow morning.

A few minutes later Ralph was back at the door holding the pan of sizzling bacon. 'Trade?'

Bailey woofed.

'Thank goodness. Here.' Ralph used a fork to take the

rashers out of the pan and deposit them on the floor beside the basket. Bailey sniffed the bacon.

'Does it meet with your approval?' He watched the dog nudge the basket in his direction. 'I'll take that as a yes.'

Before the clever dog changed his mind, Ralph grabbed the basket and reached inside for the note. After all these years, he still recognised her handwriting. He raised not one but two eyebrows as he read the message. 'Dinner?'

The dog pricked up his ears. Ralph glanced at the dog. 'Not you. Finish your bacon. It's me. She's invited *me* to dinner.' Ralph smiled. 'Well, isn't that a cook up for the books – excuse the pun.'

He re-read the note at a more leisurely pace the second time around, now he knew she had accepted his basket of vegetables as an apology for being an ass up the breakfast table this morning. The note began, *Dear man in the outhouse, I'm sorry for bursting into tears like that when it got on to the subject of my husband. Joe is a… not who I thought he was.*

A smile played around Ralph's lips when he deciphered the crossed-out words *shit* and *bastard* before the words *not who I thought he was.*

Whatever her husband had done before he ended up in a coma, she'd found out. Perhaps he'd been having an affair? It wasn't good if she was not at his bedside. Ralph wondered if her reason for returning to Southwold was forge a new life for herself. Ralph had already surmised that she'd left him.

The note continued. *Cooking is not really my forte unless microwavable meals are your thing, but I'm sure I can cook a tasty stew with the fresh vegetables you have kindly given me from your garden. Such a lovely gesture. . . .*

Ralph smiled and re-read that paragraph. The note went on … *Would you like to join me for dinner this evening? RSVP.*

Ralph glanced at the dog and scribbled a reply. He'd love to join her. He popped the note in the basket and called the dog. 'Hey, boy? How about one more favour, eh?'

Bailey was standing there licking his chops. The bacon had gone down a treat. He poked his nose around the outhouse door and sniffed the air.

Ralph sighed. He didn't want to give the dog any more bacon; it couldn't be good for him. He resolved to get hold of some proper dog food. Besides, the last thing he wanted was the dog returning to Clara and then being sick all over the patio.

'What do you say – eh?' Ralph nudged the basket with his foot in the dog's direction. He watched the dog sniff the basket. 'That's it – go on. Pick it up.'

The dog didn't make a move to take the basket, in fact he didn't make a move at all, just stood there looking at Ralph.

Ralph breathed a sigh, trying not to feel silly about making a deal with a dog. 'Look, if you do this for me, I promise I'll cook double helpings tomorrow morning – how's about that?' It beat getting his breakfast stolen every morning when he wasn't looking. 'Do we have a deal?'

Bailey wagged his tail, clamped his jaws around the basket and strolled down the cobbled pathway.

Ralph stared after him in astonishment. He'd never met a dog like him. Well, he had; his wife's dog.

As soon as the dog was out of sight he rushed into the outhouse, straight up to the window. Sure enough, there was the dog walking up the garden, the basket swinging back and forth with the note in the bottom under a carrot just to make sure it didn't fly away on the summer breeze.

Ralph turned from the window. Now he had the rest of the day to debate what he should do about his appearance. Should he dress in a clean set of clothes from his luggage the hotel had delivered to his apartment above the garages? A good shave wouldn't go amiss. Ralph fingered his beard. Perhaps a trip to the barbers too. He knew he could do it: transform from homeless Ralph into a retired professional in one afternoon. *She might find me attractive. She might even recognise me.*

Ralph frowned. And there was the rub. What if she recognised him? He could imagine after all that effort, their dinner date – if it was a date – would backfire spectacularly if she found out who he was before he told her the truth.

Ralph settled on going incognito for now; he would just be the man in the outhouse. Besides, from what he'd heard about her husband, it sounded as though Clara could do without the complication of running into an old acquaintance. *Don't you mean lover?* Ralph shook his head trying to get some perspective. They were teenage sweethearts – that's all. So why did it appear the bottom had fallen out of his world all these years later when he saw her again? Time hadn't changed the way he felt about her.

Ralph grabbed his towel and walked to the door deciding to go down to the beach and bathe. At least he wouldn't smell of fried bacon at his dinner date this evening. He was feeling nervous. He rolled his eyes. *Stupid man, it's only a stew up at the house, remember. And stop thinking it is a date. She's just repaying you in kind for the fresh vegetables.* He nodded, agreeing with his inner voice.

Ralph opened the door to the outhouse and almost tripped over the basket outside. He looked up in time to see the dog disappearing into the garden at the end of the path. He was about to swear at the dog when he saw something in the basket. 'It's another note! By Jove, you're a clever dog!' Ralph picked up the basket and retrieved the message. It said, *See you at the beach hut at seven.*

Ralph stared at the note. 'The beach hut!' He sighed. Perhaps he wouldn't have agreed to dinner if he'd known the venue. How was he going to keep it together, sitting with her at the beach hut? Ralph had a good mind to light the stove, get some bacon sizzling in the pan and write another note. It wouldn't take long and the dog would be back. He could then dispatch the note.

Ralph scribbled a quick message: Sorry, but something's come up so I must decline your invitation.

'Something's come up?' Ralph frowned. 'Really?' That was a

lame excuse. He lit the stove and was about to throw the last of his bacon in the pan when he stopped. He recalled yesterday morning when he awoke and thought she was gone. Ralph remembered what was going through his mind: *what if I never see her again? I might not get another opportunity to speak to her, to ask her the question: why did you leave me?*

Ralph screwed up the note and turned off the stove. He gathered his towel and picked up the basket on his way out the door, depositing it on a small wooden trestle table in the vegetable garden. A little voice in the back of his mind was saying, *don't get involved. Steer clear. She will only break your heart again.* But Ralph wasn't listening to the voice of reason. As he made his way to the beach his thoughts returned to Clara and why she was here. It didn't sound as though things were going well with her husband.

I thought you wanted to find out what happened all those years ago that made her leave you, never to return? It sounds as though you want to start a relationship. Ralph shook his head trying to clear his mind of the jumble of thoughts and conflicting emotions. He never felt confused when he was with his wife. That's because you weren't in love with her. 'Yes, I was.'

Ralph got a strange look from a passer-by. He ignored it and resumed talking to himself – silently this time.

No, you weren't. You loved her, but you were never in love with her like Clara – admit it.

Ralph sighed. Why were things so complicated when it came to Clara? Something he once read came to mind: *the course of true love never ran smooth.* Forty years later, it appeared with his true love nothing had changed.

51

A woman was walking a dog along the beach. He saw her stop at the shoreline. She stood there staring out to sea. Ralph came to a halt. He had come down to the beach to swim, but he wasn't about to undress in front of a stranger even though he was wearing swimming trunks.

He forgot about the swim in an instant when he realised it was Clara. His immediate impulse was to tell her that he was declining her invitation to dinner this evening. On the other hand…

Don't a voice in his head warned him as he glanced up the beach at the brightly coloured huts in the distance. What did he think he would do? Walk up to her and say, *Hello, Clara, it's me – Ralph. I need to know why you left me all those years ago. Why didn't you spare a thought for me when you disappeared from my life? You weren't the only one who was grieving over the loss of Tommy, and yet you had to put me through losing you too.*

He came to the conclusion that she couldn't have felt the same about him. It was the only way he could come to terms with what had happened that summer.

Rooted to the spot a few paces behind her, all she had to do was turn around and she would see him. *Don't!* The voice in his head warned him again. Nothing good ever came from dragging up the past. Besides, it wasn't as though they could pick up where they left off. She'd disappeared from his life. She must have had her reasons. He imagined if she knew who he was she wouldn't want to tell him why she left.

Ralph lingered for a moment longer, staring at her back, taking in her blonde, wavy, shoulder-length hair – clearly coloured because she wouldn't still be a natural blonde at her age. He sighed. Why, after all these years, did she have to choose this moment in time to return so their paths crossed once again?

He went to take a step forward but the voice in his head reminded him that she wasn't the only one with secrets. If she knew who you are. If she found out what you'd kept from her about Tommy. *You must let sleeping dogs lie.*

He was just turning away, when the dog standing by her side sniffed the air. Before he had taken another step, the dog whirled around and barked at Ralph.

Ralph held his hands up as if to say, *be quiet you stupid dog,* but it was too late. Clara was already turning around. His impulse was to run and put some distance between them before she realised it was the man from the outhouse. However, he wasn't in the best of health to be attempting to make a run for it on the sand. The bigger problem was he hadn't factored in the hound.

The dog raced towards him, kicking up sand in his wake. Ralph didn't fancy being chased along the beach. He stood stock still hoping the animal realised he wasn't a threat and didn't get antsy and bite when he discovered there was no bacon in the offing.

Ralph held his breath as the dog jumped up, launching himself at him, front paws landing on Ralph's chest knocking him backwards. The sand softened his fall, but he was winded and struggling to catch his breath. It didn't help that the stupid dog was furiously licking his face.

'Oh, my god!' Clara had turned from the shore in time to see Bailey knocking over a man on the beach. She ran up the beach in their direction as fast as she could, but the shifting sand slowed her progress, making her feel as though she was running in slow motion.

In the distance, she spotted Elliot emerge from the beach hut. He must have seen Bailey jump up and knock the gentleman over too for he was also running along the shore towards them.

Clara reached him first. It was the man from the outhouse. 'I'm so sorry,' Clara began as she came upon the man lying on the sand. 'He doesn't normally jump up at people.' It was true. In Clara's experience, Bailey had never jumped up at anybody. Quite the contrary, Bailey was a big scaredy-cat who'd much rather run a mile and hide. It was weird though; one minute he was growling at the man in the outhouse, the next minute he was acting as though—

'What happened?' asked Elliot, running up to Clara and kneeling on the sand beside Ralph.

'Bailey knocked him over,' replied Clara.

Ralph was trying to sit up, but the dog was all over him, licking his face, whining, and furiously wagging his tail.

'Anyone would think he knows you,' observed Elliot as he dragged the dog off.

That'll be the bacon, thought Ralph.

Elliot frowned. 'For god's sake, Bailey, give the man some breathing space.'

Bailey? Ralph sat up and looked at the yellow retriever. Now the dog didn't have his snout right up against his face Ralph thought he looked familiar. The bronze doggy tag attached to his collar that he hadn't noticed before confirmed his suspicions. Ralph looked at Clara and thought *where the hell did she find my dog?* He stared at Bailey furiously wagging his tail. *Why are you so pleased to see me? I kicked you out – didn't I?* That probably explained why Bailey wasn't happy to see him at first. It took a few rashers of crispy fried bacon to bring him round.

Ralph hadn't exactly kicked him out; he'd found a new home for the dog in the next village. Bailey wasn't a problem dog – not at all. The issue was all his; Bailey reminded him of his dead wife. Every time he saw the dog, he expected to see her following him into the house or into the next room. Oh how she loved that dog. She'd always said Bailey chose them, not the other way around.

When they first bought The Gables, his wife wanted a puppy to round off their retirement dream. For Ralph, a dog, like the house, was just another nail in the coffin, tying him down to a retirement he didn't want. So, he found every excuse to sidestep the issue and avoid going to look at puppies. Then along came Bailey.

One day a yellow puppy turned up on their doorstep, yapping to be let inside. They'd opened the door and somehow, he'd dodged their feet before either of them could stop him. They'd found him in the lounge where he promptly settled himself down by the fireplace, curled himself into a ball and fell asleep on the rug. His wife wouldn't hear of sending him to the RSPCA, so they'd come to a mutual agreement: he could stay until they located the owners. Ralph reckoned he'd escaped from someone's back garden.

Ralph had flyers put up in the local library and community hall and even contacted the local radio station. He did everything he could to get rid of the puppy, but not a soul came forward to claim him apart from a few crank calls. Ralph had not specified the dog breed or colour. And so the puppy that Ralph called Bailey, after the famous photographer, had stayed.

Despite his misgivings about keeping the dog, Bailey became a permanent fixture in their household and a surrogate child for his wife. They were inseparable. Wherever she was, he wasn't far behind – and vice versa. To Ralph's surprise, his wife's fondness for the dog rubbed off on him; he missed Bailey when he was away on assignments abroad. When he returned from overseas without his wife, Bailey was a constant reminder of her absence. Far from making him less lonely, Bailey made him feel worse.

Bailey broke free of Elliot's grasp and launched himself at

Ralph once more, licking his face and licking his hand, angling for a kind word and an affectionate pat on the head. 'Get off me!' Ralph pushed his dog away.

'God, I am *so* sorry.' Clara threw Bailey a black look. 'Are you all right?'

'I think so.' Ralph hoisted himself up on one elbow to a sitting position.

Clara sighed in relief and turned to Elliot. 'Can you take Bailey back to the house?'

Elliot had hold of the dog by his collar. He shrugged. 'Sure.'

Ralph watched the reluctant dog being led away by the collar.

Clara stepped forward and reached for Ralph, giving him a hand as he stood up.

Ralph got to his feet, brushed the sand from his trousers and picked up his rolled-up beach towel.

Clara looked at the towel. 'Were you going for a swim?'

Ralph shook his head. 'Maybe later.'

'Would you like a cup of tea?'

Before Ralph responded, Clara added, 'It's the least I can do.'

He glanced around the beach. There weren't any beachfront café's this far along the promenade which was just as well; he couldn't imagine any coffee bar would want the likes of him, looking like your common variety local tramp, in their establishment. It's not that he smelt; he washed every morning, taking a chilly dip in the sea, but he wasn't dressed appropriately for a trip out. Ralph looked up and down the beach. 'Where shall we go for a cup of tea?'

'I know a lovely little place not far from here,' said Clara, smiling. They strolled along the beach together. Clara glanced at the man from the outhouse checking he was all right. She had taken several more steps before she noticed he wasn't there. When she turned around, he was standing holding his sides, taking deep breaths. Clara rushed over. 'Are you sure you're all right?'

'I'm fine.'

He didn't look fine, thought Clara. He looked pale, pallid even, and fragile as though he was ill. 'Do you need a doctor?' Clara hoped not. She vaguely recalled where the local G.P. surgery used to be, but whether it was still there, she had no idea.

He stood up straight. 'I'll be all right.' He offered a reassuring smile. He didn't add this is what happens when you go abroad and forget to take your malaria tablets. But it really was no joking matter. Along with the bout of pneumonia that had left him gravely ill he was, at one point, at death's door.

'I'll go ahead while you catch your breath' said Clara.

He knitted his brow. 'How will I find you?'

'Easy. It's not that far.' She pointed toward the beach huts. 'I'm heading over there to the blue and white one. I'll wave.'

Ralph had a sneaking suspicion she would say that. He stood on the beach, catching his breath, and watched her walk in a straight line towards the small row of huts placed on the beach in front of sand dunes. As he neared, she emerged from one of them and waved then disappeared inside and reappeared carrying two plain white mugs.

Ralph stood on the sand outside the hut staring at her.

Clara paused on the small veranda and caught Ralph's expression. She looked at the two plain white mugs and said, 'I know what you're thinking…'

Ralph very much doubted that.

'It's probably not what you had in mind for afternoon tea, but there's no café along here so we will just have to make do.' She smiled at him and beckoned him to come over as she placed the empty white mugs down on a small folding table. The folding table belonged to her parents. She guessed that Elliot and Evie must have discovered it stored in the hut.

'Here, take a seat.' There were two old-fashioned deckchairs on the small wooden veranda. The wooden frame and legs had been painted white, but she recognised the red, white and blue striped canvas that made up the seat of the deckchair. Elliot had done a grand job of breathing new life into her parents' old deckchairs.

Clara had inspected both chairs before offering him a seat. The last thing she wanted was another accident. When the twins came across the rundown beach hut, the deckchairs must have been rusted and almost beyond repair. She hadn't realised how much trouble they'd gone to, to restore it to its former glory – both inside and out.

'I'll fetch the milk.' Clara stepped back into the beach hut. She was surprised when she first stepped foot inside and discovered Elliot and Evie hadn't just restored the exterior. They'd painted it white inside from floor to ceiling. There was a multi-coloured rug on the floor and colourful cushions on the seat boxes that ran its length either side. In the corner were two sleeping bags rolled up and stored. She imagined they must have been sleeping on the seat boxes which didn't look very comfortable. But they were young and probably looked at it as a big adventure.

From Clara's perspective at her age, with no job and just some loose change in her pocket, she'd find living in a beach hut far from a big adventure. Although getting her hands on the proceeds from the sale would make up for a few uncomfortable nights if that's what it came to. She'd reimburse the twins for all their hard work and the money they'd spent, but it was still her beach hut. Glancing around the inside, she was confident an estate agent could find a buyer quickly.

Standing there she suddenly had a pang of guilt at the prospect of selling Tommy's beach hut. It wasn't really her brother's she told herself, but it always felt like Tommy's when they were teenagers. Perhaps it was because he spent so much time down here after he'd had another falling out with father.

For reasons Clara never understood he didn't seem to have the same close relationship with their parents that she had.

Although she never had the chance to find out why, she often wondered if it was because they placed such high expectations on his shoulders. She knew for a fact he didn't want to follow father into the legal profession and become a solicitor. Tommy, like his best friend Ralph, wanted to travel and have adventures. The library in The Gables came to mind. Those adventure yarns by H. Rider Haggard would have been right up his street.

Tommy wasn't the only reason she felt reluctant to part with the beach hut. She had fond memories of the time spent here with her brother and his best friend, Ralph. They used to call themselves the three musketeers. Although there were no women musketeers, Clara fancied herself a female version of Porthos; loud, brash, and a little vain as teenage girls often were, but loyal to a fault. Ralph was Aramis through and through; handsome, quiet, ambitious and a romantic at heart. Tommy was Athos; brave, intellectual, melancholy and the glue that held them together.

For a moment she stood there thinking back to the three of them and those endless summer days spent on the beach until sunset. If anything could keep her from selling her beach hut, it was pure nostalgia for those simpler, happier times before their lives unravelled in a way neither of them expected.

52

Clara turned around to find the man she had left sitting in the deckchair, standing in the doorway. He asked if she needed a hand. She didn't know how long she'd been lingering there in front of the small kitchenette, staring off into space, lost in the past. 'I was just fetching the milk.' She paused. 'Do you have milk in your tea?'

Ralph smiled. 'Of course.' There were many things he missed about the British way of life when he was away, even the weather, and especially a good cup of black tea with a splash of cold milk.

Ralph took a seat once more in the deckchair and looked down the beach towards the sea. He was reflecting on another time and place when the three of them had been together. It was the first summer he had gone with Tommy, Clara and their parents on holiday to Mallorca.

Every year Tommy and Clara wanted him to come with them to Mallorca, but Ralphs' parents said they couldn't afford the airfare. Years later Ralph suspected it was less about the money and more to do with the fact they'd miss their only child. When he turned eighteen, Ralph had saved up enough cash from his Saturday job to go with them, only to discover his parents had already booked and paid for his flight.

Ralph breathed a sigh. He didn't want to think about the

other reason he would never forget that summer in Mallorca. It was to be the last time they were all together. Ralph stared out to sea. He closed his eyes for a moment. He could hear the surf in the distance washing up on the shore and a seagull's cry overhead. A gentle breeze brushed his face.

Clara opened another cupboard door in the small kitchenette at the back of the hut. She was looking for a spoon. The gas cylinder, positioned out of sight in a cupboard, was attached to a small two-ring hob on the worktop. On the hob was an old-fashioned whistle kettle she imagined the twins had found in one of the charity shops in the town. It was just coming to the boil.

Clara poured the boiling water into a brown chipped teapot and took the pint of milk out of the cooler box. She carried the teapot and carton of milk outside, setting them down on the table. She sat in the deckchair and was about to apologise for the chipped teapot when she noticed his eyes were closed. Had he fallen asleep? It was very peaceful at this end of the beach. The warm summer sunshine was enough to send anybody off to the land of Nod. Suddenly her eyes grew heavy.

Clara shook herself. That wouldn't do at all. What if her guest stirred and discovered she had dozed off? The pot of tea would get cold if she didn't wake him. She was sitting there staring at him, wondering what to do, when she had the strangest sensation they'd met before. But where? Clara racked her brain trying to figure out where their paths might have crossed. Perhaps they'd passed each other in London, and that's why his face seemed familiar.

Clara studied his features. If he had a haircut and shaved off his beard, then she might remember. Was it the hair and the beard and the old clothes? Clara recalled the homeless man her and Debs had passed on the street corner in London. He was younger than this man, but perhaps that's why he seemed so familiar; he may well have been another homeless man begging in London whom she passed without a second glance.

She wanted to ask him if he'd come from London. Clara's brow furrowed. She couldn't just come out with it and say; *did I pass you begging on a street corner in the capital?* Try as she might, she could not figure out where she had seen him.

'Oh goodness, did I nod off?' He sat up with a start.

'Yes, you did,' Clara replied lowering her gaze, hoping he didn't catch her staring at him. She picked up the teapot. 'Some tea?'

'Yes, thank you.'

'I must apologise for the chipped teapot and the mugs' said Clara.

Ralph shook his head. 'There's no need to apologise.' He rather liked the large white nondescript mugs and the little sachets of sugar.

He picked up the carton of milk and poured some into his tea. It reminded him of a simpler, happier time when they were young and life seemed full of endless possibilities, like spending time with the woman he loved. He gave her a sideways glance.

Clara looked his way and realised she didn't even know his name. 'I'm sorry, but I don't know your name. I can't keep calling you *The Man in the Outhouse*.'

'My name is—' *Just tell her your name.* Ralph hesitated. If he told her who he was, would she tell him what happened all those years ago; why she disappeared to London never to be heard from again?

He wondered what to say, afraid what her reaction would be. It crossed his mind that perhaps he was an episode in her life she wouldn't even remember. 'I'm Henry,' said Ralph, avoiding eye contact as he lied to her.

Ralph frowned. He should have given her his middle name although he knew he wasn't likely to forget the name *Henry* in a hurry. Henry was the Christian name of his favourite author whose stories set in far-flung places he loved as a boy, and whose books lined the bookshelves of the library in his house. That writer and his adventure yarns inspired him to take his photojournalism career abroad. Most people were familiar with H. Rider Haggard, although he imagined only a few would be familiar with his first name.

'Henry,' repeated Clara, staring at him.

He noticed her staring and blurted, 'What is it?' For a split second, Ralph thought she'd seen right through him and guessed that wasn't his real name.

Clara shook her head. 'It's nothing – really.'

Something told him it wasn't *nothing*. For a moment he imagined he saw a flicker of recognition, or disappointment he wasn't who she thought. *Well, why don't you tell her?*

Ralph didn't want to spoil the moment. Despite his initial reservations over joining her for dinner at the beach hut, he was enjoying himself. Although he was still quite stunned that he should just run into her after all these years.

'Henry,' repeated Clara. She lifted the mug of tea to her lips and commented, 'You remind me of someone – that's all.'

Ralph almost dropped his mug. 'Who?'

'Someone I knew a long time ago.'

'Was this *someone* a friend?' he ventured, itching to know if she was talking about him, although he couldn't come out with it and ask, *are you talking about Ralph*?

Clara sighed and turned in her seat to look at the beach hut. 'We were more than friends,' she said wistfully.

More than friends. Ralph raised his eyebrows. Was she talking about a teenage boy from her past? All he wanted now was for her to say his name. 'Did this friend have a name?'

Clara smiled. 'How about another mug of tea?'

Ralph tried not to let his disappointment show. 'Sure, why not?' If it meant he could sit here a while longer in her company.

His late wife came to mind. He'd been lucky, after Clara, to find someone else. Although compatible, there weren't any special moments they'd shared. By *special moments* he was thinking of something out of the ordinary and spontaneous. You could never find those sipping coffee out of a china cup in a posh restaurant or boutique café. It was the sort of thing money couldn't buy. It was the unexpected, like finding oneself sitting in an old deckchair on the veranda of a beach hut with a mug of tea from a chipped teapot.

'This is nice,' he said.

Clara looked at him and smiled. She thought so too. Not that long ago her regular haunt was lunch in Fortnum and Mason or afternoon tea at Claridge's in London followed by designer shopping. And yet, for reasons she couldn't quite fathom, she was enjoying this more; tea out of an old mug and the company of a stranger. Clara gave Henry a sideways glance. The peculiar thing was he didn't look like a Henry. Clara dismissed that odd thought. Why would he lie?

She glanced down the beach at the ocean. There was something appealing about a simple life; walking the dog on the beach, having a vegetable garden, and sitting outside a beach hut with a mug of tea watching the world go by. It beat afternoon tea in Claridge's or designer shopping any day. Except this wasn't real. It wasn't her house up on the clifftop with the vegetable garden, and this wouldn't be her beach hut forever. She would have to sell it if she wanted any chance of finding the money to make a life for herself. And along with the beach hut she would have to say goodbye to her new friends – Evie, Elliot and Henry.

53

'Penny for your thoughts?'

Clara turned to him in surprise. Lost in thought, she'd forgotten she had company. 'I'm sorry. I've just got a few things on my mind.'

Ralph waited a moment or two, but she didn't elaborate. He guessed perhaps she was reflecting upon her husband. Ralph hoped she would not give him another chance. Whatever he'd done, whatever she may have discovered, the last thing Ralph wanted was the possibility she was having second thoughts about leaving him.

Ralph looked at Clara. 'Is this your beach hut?' he asked, knowing full well it was but asking anyway to strike up a conversation.

'I inherited it from my parents.' Clara didn't see the point in hiding the truth this time. She still wished she'd told the twins straightaway that the beach hut belonged to her. Hiding the truth from people never ended well. Clara thought of Joe.

Ralph looked about him. 'It's very nice. You took care of it over the years.'

'Over the years?' Clara repeated feeling guilty that *no* she hadn't taken care of it at all. She'd left it to deteriorate and was surprised to find it still standing – let alone in such a lovely condition.

Over the years? Ralph regretted that remark. *How would a stranger know she'd owned it for years?* He knew how long her parents had been gone – decades.

'I assumed you inherited the beach hut some time ago. I didn't mean to cause offence,' he replied.

Clara smiled. 'None taken. You're right though. It has been a long time.'

Ralph was about to put his foot in it again and tell her how much nicer the beach hut was now to how he remembered it. 'It's nice though,' he mumbled.

'Yes, it is,' replied Clara, hoping he didn't ask her any questions such as what colour paint she had used to paint the outside or where she got the old deckchairs repaired? Or worse still, why the twins had been doing up her beach hut? She remembered they'd told her he'd helped them out. Thankful he hadn't brought that up otherwise the conversation could get awkward.

Ralph put his mug down on the makeshift table. It wobbled on the uneven decking and almost toppled over. He caught it just in time.

'Well saved!'

Ralph smiled and said, 'Backatcha!' when Clara placed her mug on the folding table and caught it before it slid off.

Clara's smile dropped instantly.

'Did I say something wrong?'

'It's all right. It's just I haven't heard that phrase in years.'

'What – *backatcha?'* Slipping into the easy familiarity with Clara they once shared years ago, it was something he used to say to her when she told him how much she loved him. *Backatcha* he'd reply.

He tried to hide his surprise she remembered. It was a turn of phrase he hadn't used in years, and something he never recalled saying to his wife.

Clara stood up.

Ralph took that as his cue to leave. He rose from his seat. 'It was nice chatting.'

Clara grinned. 'Yes, much nicer than the to-ing and fro-ing with the notes in the basket, although Bailey enjoyed the bacon rewards each time.'

'It worried me he was would end up being sick on the patio.'

'Retrievers will eat anything. They're always hungry.'

Ralph nodded. 'Especially Bailey, he'd eat you out of house and home – given half a chance.' Ralph cringed. He'd done it again, given the game away, remembering all too well their greedy dog. Ralph gave her a sideways glance.

Clara eyed Bailey lying on the wooden decking, his muzzle resting on two front paws, eyes closed, snoozing. Although Elliot had taken him back to the house, he must have escaped from the garden, making his way to the beach hut where the clever dog knew he'd find her.

Ralph glanced at Clara. She didn't appear to have noticed anything amiss. He still couldn't quite believe, after all these years, she'd come home. He thought he'd never see her again. Tears filled his eyes. He hadn't cried since the day he found out Clara had married, and he'd lost her forever.

He wiped his eyes on the sleeve of his jumper, walked over to the balustrade and leaned on the rail to compose himself.

Clara stepped towards him and placed a hand on his arm. 'It's the worst thing isn't it – losing the ones we love.'

Ralph looked at her hand on his arm and lifted his gaze to those beautiful brown eyes. He guessed she was referring to his dead wife, clearly under the impression that was who he was thinking about. Ralph placed a hand on her arm. She couldn't have been more wrong. For the first time he noticed there was no wedding ring on her finger. His heart leapt. Whatever her husband had done, she'd left him for good. It was all falling into place now, why she was here. She was looking for a way to move forward with her life. As was he.

Clara caught him glancing at her hand probably wondering where her wedding ring was. She wasn't about to tell a perfect stranger that her husband was planning to leave her, even if every time she looked at the man from the outhouse, he reminded her of someone else.

Clara withdrew her hand.

After she had returned from Mallorca that summer and then left Southwold suddenly, he used to come down to the beach hut on his own. Her parents said she'd gone to London. He should have followed her, and at least tried to find her, but to his lasting regret he didn't. And now here they were forty years later – strangers. Perhaps that was about to change. He brightened. 'Are we still on for this evening?' Ralph asked eagerly.

Clara nodded her head. 'I will set up the camping stove and cook the stew on the beach so we can have dinner under the stars.'

'Sounds romantic.' Ralph regretted his choice of words.

There was an uncomfortable silence during which Ralph wondered if he'd blown it. What must she be thinking? That I was entertaining romantic notions about her – which was true. But looking like this? She must be repulsed.

Clara smiled at the man from the outhouse. Behind that unkempt appearance was an unhappy man struggling to come to terms with his changed circumstances. She could empathise. She knew how it felt to have the rug pulled from under you leaving your life in complete disarray.

'You don't mind coming back to the beach hut then?'

Ralph looked at her in surprise. Either his off-hand comment had gone right over her head or she was entertaining the idea of getting to know him. Ralph hoped it was the latter and not just a kind gesture, inviting the homeless man to share her meal out of pity.

She was waiting for an answer. 'I would love to have dinner at the beach hut,' he said. 'It reminds me of—' Ralph stopped.

'Reminds you of…?' Clara prompted.

Ralph looked into those large brown eyes of hers. By god it took him back. All they needed was Tommy to reappear … Ralph shook his head. If he were still alive, surely he wouldn't have left it all these years to get in touch.

Clara saw him shaking his head. 'Are you all right?'

Ralph stared at her; could they recapture what they had all those years ago? Although he had no family to complicate things, he bet Clara did. She'd always wanted children. Should that make a difference? They'd be grown up with lives of their own now. Even so, it wouldn't just be the two of them. He'd have her extended family to contend with.

Ralph put that little complication to the back of his mind and answered Clara's question. 'Ah, yes, it reminds me of a time in my youth.'

'Me too,' said Clara surprising him.

He gave her a sideways glance wondering if she was thinking about a young man she once dated by the name of Ralph.

They stood there together in silence, both wishing they could turn back the clock. The spell was broken by Bailey waking up and chasing a seagull that had landed on the beach. It soon took flight again. When Bailey tired of chasing seagulls, he came lolloping over, straight up to Ralph.

Clara smiled. 'Oh look, you've made a friend,' observed Clara. 'I must admit, his behaviour was odd the way he kept growling at you. That isn't like him at all.'

Ralph didn't find it odd. Bailey was one clever dog. He bet Bailey thought he might send him away again, and the dog was having none of that.

After Ralph gave him a reassuring pat on the head, Bailey switched his attentions to Clara.

Ralph watched Clara give Bailey a big fuss. He wanted to ask Clara how she came by the dog, but then again he supposed he already knew. They'd all found their way home, one way or another, the question was, were they here to stay? Ralph just had to ask, 'So, do you live in the area or are you considering moving here?'

'Truthfully, I don't know where home is anymore.'

They exchanged a smile, their eyes lingering on one another, both surprised how comfortable they felt in each other's company.

54

'You're at the station – what station?' Clara said in surprise.

'I phoned you like several times. Don't you listen to your voicemail, Mum?'

'I've been busy.' Clara glanced his way. They were sitting on the veranda outside the beach hut enjoying the morning sunshine. He was reading yesterday's newspaper that he'd salvaged from a litter bin on the promenade. That wasn't the only thing he brought back with him every morning when Clara and the twins came down for breakfast. He also returned with a bag full of shopping from the local supermarket.

For someone living in an outhouse with not much more than the clothes on his back, he was resourceful. Clara didn't question where the groceries came from. She was just thankful he shared his bounty otherwise she really didn't know how she would have remained here in limbo these past four weeks.

Joe's condition hadn't changed, so Clara saw little point returning to London. Besides, she knew what would be waiting for her – Dorothy, Tamsin and the grandchildren still living in her house. As much as she loved her family, and despite the constant guilt trip, Clara needed this time on her own. Except she hadn't really been on her own these past few weeks – far from it. Clara wasn't thinking about the twins who had practically moved into the house. She gave him a sideways glance. They'd spent more time together than she'd care to admit. In fact, she'd probably spent more time with him over the last four weeks than she'd spent with her husband in the previous four years.

Despite Joe surprising her with flowers and remembering their anniversaries, they did little together. He worked. She shopped. That was the extent of it for some time. She hadn't realised what she was missing until that morning when she first sat with the man from the outhouse on the veranda outside her beach hut. There followed a lovely meal al fresco on the beach later that evening. Homemade stew cooked with the fresh garden vegetables he'd given her as a peace offering.

Clara smiled at the memory of a beautiful evening under the stars with a simple but delicious meal and the man she'd grown fond of. She couldn't believe almost a month had gone by in a flash since that day.

He was the reason she hadn't got around to putting the beach hut up for sale. This was where they met up every morning after breakfast. They talked, went for walks along the shore, and often spent time just sitting together watching the world go by – those contemplative but not uncomfortable silences only interrupted by Bailey chasing seagulls or wanting a game of fetch.

It was a world away from her relationship with Joe. Although she wasn't having a physical relationship with this man, Clara felt more connected to him than she ever did with Joe. Why was that?

Clara glanced his way as she recalled a recent phone call from Debs. Worried why she still hadn't returned home, Debs only expected Clara to be away a few days at the most – not an entire month. That's when Clara mentioned the beach hut she was intending to sell.

So, put it on the market and come home Debs told her. That's when Debs realised there must be something more keeping her in Southwold – or someone.

❖

'Busy doing what?' Tamsin cut across Clara's thoughts with a curt reply snapping Clara back to her unexpected phone call.

Clara was still looking his way. *Busy getting to know someone.* She wouldn't dream of voicing that thought to Tamsin.

'Oh, never mind,' Tamsin said dismissively. 'Look, I need you to come and pick me up.'

'Pick you up?' Clara frowned. 'Where are you? You do realise I'm still in Suffolk.'

Ralph lowered his newspaper and threw Clara a questioning look; something was up – he could tell.

'Yes, Mum, Debs told me.'

Clara rolled her eyes. Debs was hopeless at keeping things to herself. 'I came here by train, Tamsin, so I haven't got a car.' Which reminded Clara to ask again, 'Where are you?'

'I told you, at the train station.'

'You mean…' Clara took a second to cotton on what she meant. 'You've travelled down here too?' When she didn't get a response, she said, 'Tamsin, are you still there?' Clara looked at her phone. 'Oh blast!' she'd lost the signal.

Ralph folded his newspaper in two. 'Is something wrong?' Wondering who Tamsin was and whether it had something to do with her husband. He hoped not. Things were going so well between them. It had been unexpected, spending so much time together this past month. After all these years, it thrilled Ralph to discover a spark, a connection, a desire to get to know each other – and not just from his side. As far as he could tell it was reciprocal.

However, he wasn't complacent. These precious moments together wouldn't last. This wasn't real. One way or another – whatever she was running away from, her husband he guessed – would catch up with them.

Clara was flustered. She needed to tell Tamsin to get the next train home. Clara turned to him and said, 'I've got to make a phone call, but the reception is not great down here.'

Ralph rose from his seat.

'No, don't get up. I'll be back – I promise.'

Ralph stood there watching her walk along the beach and continue up the cliff top path until she was out of sight. He paced up and down the veranda, his expression grim. The moment he was dreading had finally arrived; their wonderful hiatus together had ended sooner than he'd expected, before he'd had a chance to summon the courage tell Clara who he really was.

55

Clara spent a good ten minutes walking around the house, first on the lower floor, then venturing upstairs, holding her phone up high trying to get a signal.

'Now what?' She hadn't told Tamsin where she was staying in Southwold. Clara sighed. She couldn't wait to get a signal and tell her to get straight back on the train and return to London. What was she doing here, anyway? Had she come to tell her some bad news about Joe she didn't want to disclose over the phone? Clara's stomach churned. That must be it. She'd left the girls with Kevin and travelled down to collect her and accompany her home – to what? A person in a permanent vegetative state or a funeral to arrange?

'Is something the matter?'

Clara turned around at the sound of Elliot's voice.

'I can't get a signal on my blasted phone. I need to call my daughter back.'

Elliot shrugged. 'I haven't got a mobile reception either. I'd suggest asking Evie, but she's gone out to meet Paul – yet again.' He looked at Clara. 'Isn't there a landline?'

'Ah.' Clara stared at him wide-eyed. 'I hadn't thought of that.' They went in search of a phone.

'The library!' exclaimed Elliot after they'd scoured the kitchen, lounge and hallway. 'Here we are.' Elliot found the phone on the desk in the library. 'It's surprising what you don't see right under your nose.'

'Isn't that the truth,' said Clara thinking of Joe and the probability that he was having an affair with that woman she'd seen at his bedside.

'Oh.' Elliot's face dropped. 'The line's dead.' He turned to Clara holding the receiver in his hand. 'That's ridiculous! Who doesn't have a phone?'

'Someone who isn't home much?' Clara wasn't all that surprised. *Or someone who doesn't want the outside world intruding on their privacy.* That was possible. She imagined the famous photographer wanted a bolt hole in Suffolk to get away from it all when not on assignments. That still left the problem of arranging a taxi. 'Now, what am I going to do?'

'You could walk into town and get a taxi. It's not far.'

'That's true.'

'Or I have a better idea.' Elliot grinned. 'Wait here.'

'Where are you going?'

'Just give me a minute.'

It was longer than a minute, but Clara waited in the hallway by the front door wondering what Elliot had in mind. Bailey stood next to Clara looking up at her. She glanced at the dog and shrugged. 'Don't ask me. I have no idea what he's up to.'

The words were barely out of her mouth when she heard a car engine outside. Clara rushed to the door. Someone had turned up at the house. She had visions of the owner turning up in a taxi, unloading his suitcases and approaching his front door only to find no door key under the plant pot.

Clara took a deep breath and opened the door; deciding that honesty was most definitely *not* the best policy. She would pretend to be the housekeeper hired by the agency. It would be an outright lie, but it beat telling him she was squatting in his property. Then all she would need to do was grab her things – and her new friends – and leave.

Clara imagined coming face-to-face with a gentleman around her own age wearing a Panama hat and smoking a cigar. She had no idea why she pictured him that way. It was just her idea of an Englishman abroad; apparently, he travelled a lot with his job.

Clara couldn't even google to find out what he looked like. She didn't have a laptop, and as Elliot had pointed out, there was no internet service here. In fact, she didn't even know his name and would have quite liked to satisfy her curiosity whether he was good-looking. Clara paused at the front door, before she opened it, wondering where that thought had come from. What did it matter what he looked like or whether he was good-looking?

A suave, well-travelled baby boomer was not standing on the doorstep; it was Elliot smiling from ear-to-ear and leaning out of a car window.

'What on earth—?' Clara stared at Elliot behind the wheel of what looked like an old Aston Martin. It was in such impeccable condition it looked brand new, even though she guessed the car must be at least forty years old.

She wouldn't normally recognise a make of a car, but she'd seen enough James Bond movies in her day, courtesy of her husband who always loved Ian Fleming and the settings of the films in the South of France. Clara could spot an Aston Martin from that era anywhere. And it was green.

She stared at Elliot. 'Where in heaven's name—?'

Elliot pre-empted the question. 'I found it in the garage around the side of the house.'

'There's a garage?' If she had ventured a little further along to the right of the front door, she would have discovered the driveway led to a detached triple garage which looked much newer than the original structure of the house; it wasn't there when her parents owned the house. It must have been a recent addition. She walked round to have a look.

It was not a single storey structure; above the garage there were windows in the apex roof space and a wooden flight of stairs that led up from the ground floor to a stable door. There appeared to be a guest apartment or perhaps a home office in the roof.

Joe's man cave came to mind. Clara had no idea why their shed at the bottom of the garden had popped into her head. This was nothing like it. The building was of proper brick construction with decorative dark wood cladding and small gable windows in the roof. The owner had gone to considerable expense to have the separate garage constructed in keeping with the property.

Clara stared up at the two-storey building and wondered why, with all the rooms in the house, the owner felt the need to have yet more accommodation added to the property. Perhaps that's what wealthy people did; built unnecessary extensions just because they could.

Clara jumped at the sound of the Aston Martin's powerful engine revving. She even knew the name of the engine because of Joe's obsession with the car many years ago when they first met. Once upon a time, he used to daydream of owning such a car and travelling around the South of France.

She thought she'd never hear the end of it until his obsession moved on to owning a yacht. Better to sail around the med, he used to say, it would be much more relaxing than driving especially with the state of the roads nowadays. How would *he* know the state of the streets in the Mediterranean? He barely ventured the other side of the North Circular.

Clara guessed that after so many years driving a taxi for a living, when Joe hung up his car keys and retired, he wouldn't fancy driving at all. That probably explained why he wanted a yacht. God knows, Joe had always dreamed of travelling, but he always wanted to do it in style.

Clara turned around and stared at the Aston Martin with the very excited young man behind the wheel. Joe would probably never drive an Aston Martin down to the South of France, let alone sail a yacht around the med. Even if, by some miracle, he snapped out of his coma and walked out of the hospital with no lasting damage, there would be no yacht waiting for him.

All that would be on the horizon was his old life driving around a London taxi. The only difference was Clara would not be there every evening heating his favourite TV dinner and asking him for money.

She cringed. Was that why Joe wanted to leave? Perhaps she wasn't the only one bored with their dull, monotonous existence doing the same thing day in and day out. Maybe he'd got sick and tired of working overtime to cover her excessive spending habit.

The sound of the car engine roaring snapped Clara out of her reverie. She ran back to the house and shouted, 'For God's sake turn it off!' She glanced about her, worried about attracting the neighbours.

Elliot wound his window down. 'I'm sorry – what?'

'Take your foot off the accelerator and turn the damn thing off!'

Elliot eased his foot off the accelerator until the engine was idly turning over.

He leaned out of the window. 'I thought you needed a ride to the station to pick someone up?'

'Yes, but I didn't expect you to help yourself to someone else's car. And where did you find the car keys?' Clara couldn't imagine Elliot found the keys in the ignition.

When Elliot didn't respond she walked up to the car. If he didn't switch it off, she would reach in and take the keys out of the ignition herself. Clara knew where he had most likely found them – in the library in the desk drawer.

'I want you to put the keys back where you found them,' Clara said over the purr of the engine. 'Put the car back in the garage first.'

'But—'

'I mean it, Elliot,'

'But you said you needed a taxi.'

'Yes. That's true. But this is *not* a taxi. Besides, you're not even insured to drive this car. Have you thought about that?' Clara eyed him. She hadn't realised the consequences herself until now. She was in enough trouble as it was, squatting in someone else's house, without stealing a car. What if something happened?

As if reading her mind, Elliot said, 'We're only going to the train station. What could happen?'

Suddenly, Joe and the car accident came to mind. Collecting her daughter in a stolen car with an uninsured driver… well, it wasn't happening. Clara gritted her teeth. 'I said *no*!'

Bailey, who had been following her around despite the roar of the Aston Martin, whined at the sound of Clara's angry voice and scooted back in the house to hide.

Elliot sighed. 'All right. I'll put it back.' He wound the window up, changed gear and reversed the car into the garage.

She watched from the driveway as the automated garage door closed.

Elliot appeared a moment later from a side door. He frowned at her for spoiling his fun and headed back to the house.

Clara stood there staring at the garage. She'd just told Elliot to put the car back where he found it, and here she was dying to have a nose around the rooms above. She had no business going up there but, like Elliot and finding those car keys, it had piqued her curiosity.

A moment later, Clara was standing at the top of the wooden flight of stairs feeling out of breath. She was about to peek through the dormer window on one side of the door when her phone rang. She'd got a signal.

56

Clara turned around, leaned against the wooden balustrade and answered her phone. She already knew it was Tamsin. Staring off in the distance, taking in the view of the grounds, she put the phone to her ear.

'Look, Tamsin, I can't come and pick you up right now. Do you think you can get a taxi from the station to the hotel in town?' Clara felt guilty for thinking of sending her straight home. The least she could do was tell her where the hotel was in town so she could spend the night. 'The address is—'

'I got a taxi from the station and am already at the hotel.'

'That's great. In that case I'll meet you—'

'No, it's *not* great. There are no rooms left because of a blasted seminar that's going on.'

'Oh – that.' Clara had forgotten all about it. The seminar was so popular they were running it for a third consecutive weekend.

'Wasn't it the one Dad was attending?' asked Tamsin. 'The *Reinventing Yourself Weekend*? Isn't he a bit old for something like that?'

Clara felt angry that Tamsin should think at sixty years of age her father was too old to change his life, even if he was reinventing himself by leaving her and starting over with someone else.

'Why don't you go home, Tamsin? I'll be coming soon.' Clara

didn't know why she said that. She had no clue when she was returning home. Clara had no clue about anything in her life at this moment. She was just taking it day by day.

'I can't turn around and travel all the way home tonight. Do you know how long it took to get here by public transport?'

Clara rolled her eyes. Tamsin said the word, *public transport,* as though it was a dirty word. She was well knew that Tamsin travelled around in her BMW most places or by taxi. Which reminded Clara, 'Why didn't you drive here? It would have been quicker.'

Tamsin ignored the question. Instead, she asked, 'Are there vacancies where you are?'

Clara thought of her two houseguests; that was already two too many. She didn't want to invite Tamsin over, but what choice did she have? Clara reasoned what harm could one night do? As long as the owner didn't choose tonight to appear. Clara put that thought to the back of her mind and gave Tamsin the address.

'Okay, Mum, I'll see you soon.'

Clara could have walked to the hotel to meet her but knowing Tamsin she hadn't travelled light. Clara sighed at the prospect of her daughter's arrival along with far too much luggage; things she wouldn't need on her *very* short break. The first thing Clara would do when Tamsin arrived was to tell her she could only stay one night.

This wasn't a hotel. That was going to be obvious when Tamsin arrived. Clara couldn't even tell a little white lie and say it was a holiday let, and she had booked a short break. How would she explain the twins? And that was the other thing. She'd implied that she was house-sitting, or Paul the off-duty policeman had told them that.

Clara decided it was best not to complicate matters and just stick to the same story – she was the house sitter. However, the one thing Clara would not tell Tamsin were her reasons for needing a job. If she asked, Clara would say she didn't want to dip into their savings because she had no idea when or if Joe would return to work. At least that sounded plausible.

She was too embarrassed to tell Tamsin the truth: Joe had cleaned out their bank account and left her penniless. Clara still wasn't ready to go home and face reality. If that's what Tamsin was up to, turning up unexpectedly to persuade her to return, then she was in for a big disappointment. Clara wasn't going anywhere until she had secured the keys to her beach hut and figured out what to do with the rest of her life. She was also enjoying her newfound independence, choosing where she lived, making new friends; the man from the outhouse came to mind.

Clara took a deep breath and walked back down the stairs. She didn't bother to try the door to the apartment above the garage. She didn't have time to nose around. Tamsin would be arriving soon. Clara meant to have a word with the taxi driver to make sure he returned to pick her up the following day.

Clara stood at the front door waiting for the taxi. She wasn't looking forward to Tamsin sending her on a guilt trip over not being at Joe's bedside. The clang of the iron gates opening at the bottom of the drive interrupted her thoughts. She heard the car before it came into view.

She gaped at the size of the taxi heading towards the house. *What in heavens name had she brought with her?* Clara imagined all her posh Louis Vuitton suitcases in the back. Just how long did she think she was staying? The car drew up outside the house. Clara waved as soon as she spotted Tamsin sitting in the front passenger seat next to the taxi driver. She walked over to greet her daughter. As she approached the car, Clara was surprised when the passenger door opened and out jumped a small dog. She was just thinking, *that dog looks familiar,* when Bailey appeared to say *hello.* The little dog bared his teeth and growled. That's when Clara recognised the dog. She frowned. *It can't be! Why on earth would Tamsin have brought along . . .*

'Winston!' A voice shouted out from inside the car, startling

Clara, not because the voice was loud but because the voice belonged to…

'Dorothy?' Clara said in astonishment poking her head around the car door. Dorothy was staring back at her with that familiar look of disdain she seemed to reserve for her daughter-in-law. It was the same expression Clara imagined one would use if you found poo on the bottom of your shoe.

Clara blurted, 'What are *you* doing here?'

'How do I know?' she barked back. 'Ask Tamsin.'

Clara was about to do just that when another voice piped up, 'I've lost my phone signal.' Clara glanced in the back of the car and saw her two granddaughters sitting there. Sophie was holding up her mobile phone, trying to get a signal, and Mia was reading a paperback book. She looked up. 'We're here! Hello, Grandma. I can't wait to see where we're spending the summer.'

Her mouth dropped open. She stepped back in shock at that innocent remark from Mia and fell over Bailey who was standing right behind her. Clara caught herself in time with a little help from Tamsin who had got out of the car and was standing next to her mother.

'I am *not* spending the summer holidays here if I can't get a phone signal,' whined Sophie. 'How am I going to stay in touch with my friends?'

Clara turned to Tamsin. 'You said nothing on the phone about all of you coming to stay.'

'Oh, didn't I?' commented Tamsin innocently.

'No, you didn't. And what's this about staying for the summer?'

'I need some help here!' A disgruntled voice interrupted Clara. Dorothy held an arm out of the car and waved at them.

Tamsin stepped in front of Clara and grasped Dorothy's hand, helping her large frame out of the back of the taxi.

As soon as Dorothy was out of the car, Clara rounded on Tamsin. 'What are you doing here?'

'This is sooo cool!' Mia shouted out as soon as she caught sight of the large old vine-covered detached property. 'We're staying in an old mansion! Is it haunted?' Mia shouted out as she ran towards the front door.

'Mia! Come back,' shouted Clara.

'I don't think it's cool!' complained Sophie as she got out the back of the taxi and wandered around the gravel drive holding her phone in the air. 'I want to go home.' Too busy concentrating on her phone, Sophie wasn't watching what she was doing and careered into Elliot. He had heard voices from the library window and stepped outside to investigate. Sophie almost dropped her phone.

She was about to have a go at the stranger, even though it was her fault, when she looked up into the eyes of the cutest boy she'd ever seen with his tousled blonde hair, tanned face and a cheeky grin.

'Hi,' he said.

Sophie forgot about her phone along with how to form words into a coherent sentence.

Her sister ran over and said, 'Hello, my name's Mia. What's your name? Do you live here?'

Clara stood there watching all this and didn't know what to do first. She needed to get them all back in the taxi and send them home. 'Mia,' Clara called out, 'will you come over here, please? You too, Sophie.'

'Why?' Sophie answered back.

'Yes, why Grandma?' asked Mia copying her big sister.

'There's been a mistake. You all need to get back in the taxi and go home.'

'I don't want to go home.'

Clara looked at Sophie in surprise. A moment ago, she'd said the complete opposite. Clara caught her staring at Elliot doe-eyed.

Tamsin looked at her mother as though she was barmy. 'Why do you want us to leave? We've just got here?'

'Well, I—'

'Where's Winston?'

Clara turned around at the sound of Dorothy's cross voice right behind her.

'Well?' said Dorothy, eyeing Clara. 'What have you done with my dog?'

'I have done nothing with your—'

Bailey chose that moment to appear, chasing Winston around the gravel drive in front of the car.

'Oh Winston, there you are.'

Winston raced over towards them and jumped up at Clara.

'Well, pick him up!' said Dorothy. 'Can't you see he's afraid of that dog?'

Clara looked at the little mutt jumping up her leg. 'Bailey is harmless.'

'Who's Bailey?' Dorothy and Tamsin said in unison.

Clara pointed at the golden retriever.

Dorothy still insisted she pick up her dog. Clara did as Dorothy asked and cradled the little dog in her arms, only because she intended to put him straight back in the car.

'What's going on?' a voice called out.

'Who's that?' asked Tamsin.

Clara looked over at Evie standing in the open doorway of the house. She was about to introduce Elliot's sister when the taxi driver slammed the boot shut. He walked over to Tamsin and said, 'Do you need a hand with your cases?'

Clara caught sight of a small mountain of suitcases on the gravel drive. 'Oh no, no, no.'

'Don't worry, Clara. I think I can manage,' said Elliot.

Clara was standing there, her face a picture, shaking her head and muttering to herself. It wasn't the mountain of suitcases that was bothering her – although they didn't help. She turned to Tamsin to ask her what on earth she was thinking, bringing everyone along with her, but Tamsin was no longer standing beside her. Clara frantically looked about. Mia was busy introducing Evie to her big sister, Sophie, and pointing out her grandmother, Clara, and great-grandmother, Dorothy. 'Don't know where Mum is,' Clara heard her say before she shrugged her shoulders.

'Isn't it the greatest,' continued Mia, 'we're spending the summer at the seaside in England. Do you know that we've always had to get on a plane and go somewhere boiling hot? It's so boring just sitting by the pool. I have to take lots of books to read, and I have to share a hotel room with my sister because I'm too little to have a room all on my own.' Which reminded Mia. 'Grandma!' she shouted out, 'can I have a bedroom all to myself?'

Clara was about to make it crystal clear they weren't staying for more than one night when Elliot walked past Clara carrying an armload of posh Louis Vuitton suitcases.

Dorothy commented, 'What a nice young man. At least someone has offered to help me inside *and* make me a cup of tea.'

Clara knew that comment was aimed at her. She sighed. The unsubtle digs had started already.

On Elliot's next trip he managed two more suitcases and Dorothy on one arm.

Dorothy paused in front of Clara as they walked past. 'I'll take Winston – if you don't mind.' She relieved Clara of the little dog.

The taxi-driver carried the remaining suitcases, leaving Clara standing there open-mouthed, still shocked by this turn of events.

'Can we go inside the house now?' Mia asked her sister.

'No, wait!' exclaimed Clara. But it fell on deaf ears.

When the taxi driver returned, Clara asked him to hang on. 'Look, there has been a misunderstanding. They can't stay here. I'm just going to find my daughter and then—'

Clara had a card thrust in her hand. 'That's the name of the taxi company and their number if you need me to come back. In the meantime, I have another fare to pick up.' He got in the car, started the engine and sped off back down the drive. Clara stood there staring after the car. When she turned around, everyone had disappeared inside the house. She looked down at Bailey sitting by her feet. 'God, this is turning into a zoo.'

Bailey woofed in agreement then something caught his attention. Clara saw it too. 'What on earth…?' The taxi driver had left a package behind on the drive. It wasn't a suitcase although it was a medium-sized boxy shape. Clara couldn't tell what it was because it was hidden under a muslin cloth that someone had draped over it.

Bailey went over to investigate, poking his nose under the muslin cloth. He jumped back in surprise and scooted over to hide behind Clara's legs.

Clara turned around and stared at Bailey cowering behind her with his tail between his legs and his ears drawn back in fright. 'What on earth has got into you?' She tutted at the silly dog and walked over to the box sitting in the middle of the driveway. She glanced at Bailey backing further away.

Clara took hold of the muslin cloth and paused. 'I can't imagine what could be in this box that has scared you so.' The box wasn't all that big. It was the size of a standard packing box.

When Clara lifted the piece of muslin, she discovered it was a metal cage, *not* a cardboard box. She said, 'Oh goodness,' when she saw what was inside. Clara took a step back in surprise and another when Marley hissed at her. She stood there staring at Marley. She couldn't believe Tamsin had brought everybody with her – including her cat.

Although relieved to see Marley – it had been playing on her mind whether Tamsin had remembered to feed the cat and let him out – Clara still wanted to get hold of Tamsin and ring her neck. What did she think she was doing, bringing Marley all this way? He was a cat, for goodness sake. He would not take kindly to being uprooted from his home and taken on a two-hour journey from London on a train.

Clara stared at her cat. He was standing there rigid, tail in the air hissing at her. She threw the muslin cloth back over the box and turned around. She could see Bailey hiding behind a tree.

'You can come out now.' Clara had no idea why she said that. It's not as though he understood a word she said – apart from *bacon.* But talking to the dog had become a habit.

To her surprise, Bailey appeared. He padded over and stood beside Clara just as Elliot walked out of the house.

His eyes settled on the last item of luggage on the driveway. 'Do you want me to…?'

Clara sighed. 'If you don't mind. Although I must warn you, he's not happy.'

Elliot's face creased into a frown. 'Who's not happy?'

'My cat.' Clara caught Elliot's expression. She thought she saw a wisp of a smile.

He said, 'You didn't mention your family were coming here for a holiday. Do they normally bring all the family pets too?'

Clara ignored the comment. 'I've got to find Tamsin,'

There was nothing *normal* about all this. Since when did Tamsin holiday in this country? *Since never.* Whatever Tamsin was doing here, Clara suspected there was more to it than bringing her daughters here for a holiday and then fetching Grandma home to be at Joe's bedside.

57

Lost in thought, Clara recalled how much Tamsin abhorred their family holidays. Their annual break was spent in Bournemouth while friends in her private school went abroad. But it was all they could afford. As soon as Tamsin earned her own money, she headed overseas. Even when she had the girls, their vacations were spent in the Caribbean or America; anywhere exciting or exotic if it was on foreign soil.

Maybe if they'd had the money, she would have taken Tamsin to Mallorca. Perhaps she would have enjoyed it as much as Clara and Tommy. There might be happy childhood memories of holidays spent there.

Clara stared up at the house. Something else occurred to her. Perhaps if things had been different, Tamsin would have spent her summers here at The Gables, doted on by the grandparents she never knew. Clara remembered those stunted phone conversations with her parents after she'd married Joe. She thought they would come around and accept who she'd chosen to marry. Then along came their first and only grandchild.

Under different circumstances, a baby should change everything – for the better. It did not. It made things worse. Her motivations for marrying quickly were confirmed when Tamsin was born eight months later. If her parents' didn't have a low enough opinion of her already, getting pregnant out of wedlock, they only ought to have known that Joe was not the father. Clara turned away from the house, recalling the handful of times her mother travelled down to London on her own – father refused to come – to see her granddaughter when she was little. Not that Tamsin remembered those visits. She was too young.

Clara didn't encourage them either. Tamsin looked nothing like Joe – how could she if she wasn't his child? She took after her father. However, back then Clara needn't have worried about her parents turning up out of the blue, seeing their grandchild and guessing the truth. Consumed with finding Tommy, they never gave up hope that somehow he was still alive.

Thinking of Tommy, Clara's mind drifted back to Mallorca. She wondered, not for the first time, whether the beautiful Balearic Islands off the coast of Spain had changed in the four decades since she was there last. Would she even recognise the enchanting little town called Pollensa? The freedom they experienced on those holidays was a world away from their stuffy private schools back in cold, grey England. It was the one place Clara felt alive.

Her parents rented a villa at the foot of the Serra de Tramuntana Mountains and Clara remembered toasting their eighteenth birthday with wine from the nearby Bodega. Then their lives changed forever. After Tommy's disappearance, Clara and her parents left Mallorca never to return.

Clara was staring off into space and for a moment imagined she was back in Mallorca. Over the years, she often daydreamed about returning to that magical island. But what she wanted, more than anything, was to know what happened to her brother. What she wouldn't give to turn back the clock to that fateful night.

'Clara? Would you like me to take the cat in?'

Clara looked at Elliot. For a split second, she'd forgotten all about the cat along with the arrival of Tamsin who had no clue she was about to become a squatter for the duration of her stay.

'Oh, the cat! Yes, take him inside,' Clara said resigned to the fact she had a house full. She shrugged. Might as well add the cat. She stood there watching him carry Marley into the house. She could hear his hissing growing fainter as Elliot took him inside.

Clara looked down at Bailey. 'Come on, let's find Tamsin.' In the house, voices were coming from the kitchen. She popped her head around the door and saw Evie putting the kettle on. Dorothy was sitting at the table with Winston cradled on her lap. Mia crossed legged on the floor was trying to console a hissing Marley. Her sister, Sophie, didn't even notice the cat; her eyes followed Elliot as he helped Evie find some mugs for tea. There was no sign of Tamsin. Clara frowned. 'Has anyone seen Tamsin?'

Everyone shook their heads. She walked back down the hall, glanced in the lounge and the library, and then headed upstairs. 'Tamsin?' Clara called out when she reached the top. There wasn't a sound, save for her own heavy breathing and the muted harmony of voices coming from the kitchen below.

Clara stepped off the top stair and looked to her left and right where the landing continued in both directions. She turned to her left and walked down the spacious hallway, feeling the deep soft-piled beige carpet beneath her feet.

She stopped at one of the bedroom doors. The last time she had been in this house was on her return from Mallorca with her parents. Tommy was gone, and the house in a perpetual state of mourning; the atmosphere heavy with loss and regret.

Clara turned her attention to the door in front of her. The bedrooms were just as cosy as she remembered with leaded windows overlooking the gardens, sloping ceilings, and beds topped with throws or quilts. Walking up and down the landing, Clara counted five bedrooms and two bathrooms. There used to be six bedrooms, but one had been turned into a second bathroom.

It was a large house for two children to grow up in, but her mother had problems conceiving, as did Clara, so the house never saw that large family her mother and father planned for.

That thought brought to mind her own problems conceiving after Tamsin. For a self-pronounced family man, Clara was surprised Joe stuck by her when it became clear Tamsin would be her only child, and he would not have any biological children of his own.

Clara opened the door to another bedroom; a twin room. The other four bedrooms were doubles. Her grandchildren could share this room for one night which would leave a bedroom each for the adults - herself, Elliot, Evie and Tamsin. Clara closed the door on the last bedroom and then remembered Dorothy. Where was she going to sleep? *Talk about Déjà Vu* thought Clara standing at the top of the stairs recalling that instance a month ago when Joe came home with Dorothy in toe.

Clara sighed. It looked as though she'd be sleeping on the couch again tonight. It would only be for one night. She turned from the foot of the stairs and glanced in the bedrooms once more, deciding which she fancied when they all left the next day. Clara settled on the one at the far end of the hall. It was cosy with sloping ceilings and a dormer window that overlooked the garden.

Her old bedroom was now a second bathroom. Clara wasn't bothered. There were too many childhood memories of Tommy. She recalled the times they stayed up late reading or making up stories by torchlight until Ma or Pa sent him packing, back to his own bedroom. Clara smiled at the memory. Her childhood wouldn't have been the same without him. It made her wonder how different her life might have turned out if she hadn't lost him. She would never have run away to London and met Joe for a start.

Joe. He was the reason she had returned here. She was trying to find a way out of the precarious financial situation he'd left her in after withdrawing all the money from their bank account.

Clara sighed. It wasn't all Joe. It was time she took some responsibility? He treated her like a princess. She treated him like a doormat. What goes around comes around, thought Clara accepting that she'd got what she deserved. It was little wonder he hadn't walked out years ago. What did she ever put into their relationship? Nothing. And yet she expected the world in return.

58

Clara glanced out of the dormer window and spotted Tamsin walking through the grounds. She attempted to open the window and call out but couldn't undo the security catch. 'Oh, bother.'

Clara rushed down the stairs and headed straight out the front door and around the side of the house. She didn't want to go through the kitchen even though it would have been quicker. She could still hear them gathered around the table chatting and didn't want to get waylaid.

'Tamsin!' Clara called out. She stood for a moment looking into the garden beyond. It was not easy to spot someone amongst the tall trees, weeping willows and hedges. The fact that the gardens were extensive and an irregular shape didn't help.

Clara turned from the house and walked in the direction in which she thought she had spotted Tamsin five minutes ago. Clara called out her name several times.

'I heard you the first time.'

'Oh, Tamsin,' Clara said in surprise when she heard her voice.

Tamsin stepped out from behind a large oak tree.

'Why didn't you answer me when I was calling you?' she said in exasperation.

'What are you doing out here, anyway? Everyone is in the house.'

'I wanted to—'

'Look, you can stay here one night, but tomorrow you have to go home.'

Tamsin eyed her mother. 'This isn't a hotel – is it.'

Clara shook her head. 'No, you're right. The thing is—'

'I recognise this place.'

That stopped Clara in her tracks. 'What place?'

'The house.' Tamsin turned around and looked back at The Gables. 'That's why I'm out here. Just to be sure.'

'Be sure of what?'

'That I recognise it.'

Clara shook her head. 'I don't understand… how can you? You've never been here before.'

'I know, but I've seen photos.'

'What do you mean – you've seen photos? Of the house?'

Tamsin nodded. 'When I was about eight, that Christmas I discovered Santa didn't exist, you and Daddy were busy doing something – I can't remember what. Anyway, I searched for my presents and found a family photo album instead. Curious, having never seen pictures of my other grandparents, I looked inside. There were photos of you with your mother – my grandmother – and a boy.'

Clara stared at Tamsin dumbfounded. She had no idea Tamsin had found the album, her only personal possession besides her clothes she had brought with her when she ran away to London. 'What I remembered most about the photographs,' continued Tamsin, 'was the setting. You were on a lawn with a house in the background – *this* house.'

Clara sucked in a breath.

Tamsin stared at the house. 'You never talk about your past before you married Dad. It was like this wall you put up. I always got the impression you were keeping something from me. Was this where you grew up? Did my grandparents live here? Was this their house?' The questions came flooding out. 'Why did we never visit them? Why did they never visit us?'

'Your grandmother visited once or twice,' Clara replied.

'Why don't I remember those visits?'

'You were too young.' Clara searched for what to say next. She never wanted to venture down this path with Tamsin in case the truth came out. 'Look, your grandparents didn't give me their blessing to marry your father. It was a class thing.'

'How petty and small-minded of them,' said Tamsin staring up at the large detached period property where her mother grew up, so different to the little terraced house in North London where she spent her childhood. She turned around and eyed her mother for a moment. 'Was that all there is to it? Why I never saw them?'

'Of course.' Clara hated lying to her daughter. Not a day went by when she didn't regret their decision not to tell her the truth, but Joe insisted. As far as he was concerned, Tamsin was *his* child and there was no reason for her to think any different.

At first, Clara was all for keeping things simple. It was easy to leave things be. In the early years, she was just thankful she had a supportive husband who wanted to bring Tamsin up as his own. Things were different back then; society less tolerant. Joe discouraged Clara from seeing her parents, afraid if Tamsin discovered the truth, she might want to track down her real father, and he would lose his little girl as a result. But as time passed, Clara questioned whether they were selfish keeping her in the dark and not giving her the choice to find her father.

Now, after all these years, how could she tell her daughter what they had kept from her? And what good would it do now? Clara didn't know the whereabouts of her biological father or if he was still alive, and that assumed Tamsin would be interested in finding him.

Clara looked at her daughter staring up at the house. Now was not the right time with Joe comatose in hospital for Tamsin to find out they had lied to her all these years. There would be a time and a place to drop that bombshell. Whatever Tamsin wanted to do with that knowledge, she deserved the truth – it was the right thing to do. Everyone deserved the truth – no matter how painful. Wouldn't she want to be told if someone knew what had happened to Tommy?

Clara studied her daughter's profile. She looked tired, strained. Tamsin had issues to sort out that may or may not have something to do with her husband, Kevin. Clara had yet to find out. It made Clara wonder how Tamsin would take it when she found out she couldn't stay for more than one night, let alone the entire summer. Clara remembered Mia mentioning spending the summer here. Was that Tamsin's intention? What about Kevin? Had they split up?

'So, if you're house-sitting, this property is no longer in your family.'

Although Clara was thankful for the change of subject, away from her grandparents and the reasons for their absence from her life, she hated lying again to Tamsin about house-sitting. But she could not tell her she was squatting.

'My parents sold it years ago, so they had the money to—' *continue the search for Tommy.* Clara stopped short. She didn't want to get into that right now; discussing the twin Tamsin never knew she had, the uncle she'd never known.

Tamsin eyed her warily. 'So… more secrets.'

'Tamsin I—'

'And what's with the house-sitting?' Tamsin butted in. 'I thought I was turning up at a hotel. Are they friends of yours, the people who now own this house?'

'No.'

Tamsin looked at her in astonishment. 'Do you mean you've got a job?'

'Well… yes.' While that wasn't strictly true, she did need a job.

'Why?'

Clara bit her bottom lip. About to tell her the explanation she'd already thought up about not wanting to dip into their savings, when Tamsin jumped to the conclusion that left Clara reeling. 'Oh. My. God. You've left him – haven't you? I don't believe this. I kept thinking why aren't you at his bedside, holding his hand and talking to him, willing him to wake up. But I didn't expect *this*.'

'Now hang on one minute, that's not—'

'If you tell me you've got a job because you're worried about money, since when did you ever worry about money? I know Dad's in hospital and not working, but you've got savings.'

Clara looked at her. *Had savings.*

'I'm not a child. There must be more to it than that for you to stay here and not come home. And get a job.'

Tell her, the voice in her head said. Tell her she's got it wrong; it was Joe who was leaving her not the other way around.

Clara stared into her daughter's beautiful brown eyes and couldn't bring herself to tell Tamsin that Joe, her Dad, was planning to leave Clara and, from what she'd discovered in his shed, to disappear from all their lives. Instead, she turned the tables and instantly regretted it. 'What I'd like to know is what are *you* doing here, young lady? What's going on with you and Kevin?'

Tamsin gave her mother a cold, hard stare then burst into tears.

Clara took a step back in surprise. Tamsin hadn't cried since a child. She was the type to get angry, fly into a rage, have a good rant. Bursting into tears – that wasn't like Tamsin at all.

Clara tried to put a comforting arm around her shoulders.

Tamsin shrugged her off. She composed herself and said, 'I'm going indoors to have a lie-down.'

She stood there watching her daughter in stunned silence as she flounced back to the house, berating herself for not telling her the truth – telling her everything. Maybe she'd got it wrong and now was the perfect time; right here in this place – her childhood home – to divulge to her only child about the past and the man she once loved.

Clara shook her head. It made her realise why they didn't have that close relationship she'd had with her own mother. Tamsin sensed she'd been keeping things from her – secrets. Over the years, Clara didn't realise how much those secrets had cost her until now.

59

Clara got the card with the taxi driver's number out of her pocket along with her mobile. She expected Tamsin would want to go home now. The only problem was finding somewhere with reception so she could phone for a taxi.

Walking down the garden towards the house, Clara thought to hell with it; she'd ask Elliot to get the car out of the garage and take them all to the station. It would involve several trips, but he wouldn't mind.

Then her mobile phone rang.

'Clara. Thank God. I realise this is a strange question, but have you any idea where Tamsin and the girls are?'

Clara raised an eyebrow. It was Kevin and, by the sound of things, Tamsin had not told him about her trip.

Kevin continued, 'She didn't come home last night. I assumed she was still staying over at yours, keeping an eye on things while you're away. But when I called round this morning, they weren't there. A neighbour said she saw them getting in a taxi but they didn't turn up at my house. Now I'm worried because I can't get hold of Tamsin or Sophie on their mobile phones.'

Clara listened. Although his anxious voice kept breaking up with the bad reception, she heard enough to get the gist of what was going on; Clara realised she wasn't the only one running away.

It made her wonder what was going on with Tamsin. Kevin was the nicest man one would hope to meet and worshipped the ground Tamsin walked on. Clara raised her eyebrows. That sounded just like her and Joe and look how that turned out.

'Do you have any idea where they are?' Kevin continued.

Clara sighed. Whatever Tamsin's reasons for not telling Kevin about their trip he had a right to know they were all okay. 'They're all fine, Kevin.'

'So, you know where they are?'

Clara looked up at the house. 'Yes, Kevin.' If Tamsin hadn't told her husband where they were going, she must have had her reasons. 'Let me speak to Tamsin and ask her to call you.'

'Can you tell me where she is—'

'Kevin, she's fine. The girls are fine. They're staying with me for a while.'

'But you're not at home. Tamsin said you skipped town.'

'I wouldn't put it quite like that. I didn't just *skip town*.' Clara's face reddened. 'I had some business to take care of.'

'Can't you at least tell me where you all are?'

Clara could hear the concern in his voice. He continued, 'I'm worried because Tamsin and Sophie's phones keep going to voicemail. Their phones are *never* switched off. After what happened to Joe my imagination was running wild at the thought they had been in an accident or something.' There was a pause. 'God, I'm sorry. How thoughtless of me. I shouldn't have brought up—'

Joe

'It's all right, Kevin. I understand.' Clara remembered that knock at the door in the early hours with the terrible news. She shivered at the thought.

The line was breaking up. 'Kevin, they're in Suffolk. We're staying at—' Clara frowned and looked at her phone. She'd lost the signal. She rolled her eyes and was about to do a circuit around the drive to try to recapture her signal when she came to an abrupt halt. Tamsin was standing on the doorstep with her arms folded. She was throwing Clara a dirty look.

'I overheard you on the phone to Kevin. Did you tell him where we are?'

Clara stared at her daughter.

'Did you?'

'No. But you shouldn't have just upped and left without telling someone where you were going.'

'Oh, you're a fine one to talk.'

Clara ignored that sarcastic remark. 'I thought you were having a lie-down?'

Tamsin didn't answer.

'What are you doing here, Tamsin? It's not just a holiday with the girls.' Clara knew there was more to it. 'What's going on?'

Tamsin shook her head. 'Talk about the pot calling the kettle black.'

'What's that supposed to mean?'

'What are *you* doing here?'

Clara didn't want to get on to that subject again even if it was on the tip of her tongue to tell Tamsin that Joe was leaving her. But the question remained; why was she drawn back here? Even she couldn't answer that.

They stood staring at each other in silence until Tamsin threw her arms in the air in frustration. She walked back into the house and slammed the door. Clara raced in behind her. 'Tamsin, I'm calling the taxi. You can't stay here.'

Tamsin ignored her mother, picked up two suitcases and started up the stairs.

Clara sighed. Their relationship had always been difficult. Tamsin was stubborn, opinionated, and argumentative. So unlike easy-going Joe. *She takes after her father.* That thought crept in unbidden in her mind. Clara stared after her. Perhaps it *was* time she told her the truth.

'Tamsin.' Clara had just stepped on to the bottom stair when the kitchen door flew open and everyone piled out of the kitchen. Mia and Sophie spotted their mum walking up the stairs carrying her suitcases.

'Hooray!' squealed Mia. 'I want to choose which bedroom I'm having.'

'Me first!' Sophie barged past her little sister as they both raced up the stairs after their mother. 'I'm the oldest.'

Dorothy gave Clara the evil eye as she passed by. Clara wasn't the least bit surprised.

Evie was holding Dorothy's arm, guiding her up the stairs. As she passed Clara, Evie said, 'I expect you'll want me and Elliot to move on now your family has arrived.'

'Nonsense,' Dorothy bellowed overhearing Evie's passing remark to Clara. 'You're not leaving on my account. I'm sure there are plenty of bedrooms in this big old house.'

Clara shrugged. 'Why not – the more, the merrier.'

Evie smiled not catching that sarcastic inflection in Clara's strained voice. She had half a mind to storm up the stairs and demand that Tamsin order a taxi and take everyone home but knew she'd get a door slammed in her face and another dose of déjà vu. She sighed, resigning herself to the fact they would have to stay the one night. Clara decided to phone Kevin to ask him to come and pick them up. In the morning they *had* to go.

Elliot brought up the rear carrying suitcases and the girls' backpacks slung over his shoulder. 'Be careful,' said Clara when she saw him loaded with all those bags on the stairs. The last thing she needed was someone having an accident. Clara couldn't afford any more complications for one day.

'I'm fine, Clara, honestly.'

All the same, Clara stood there watching him walk up the stairs. She wasn't the only one. Sophie appeared at the top of the stairs checking out Elliot too.

Thinking of complications, Clara groaned when she caught Sophie blushing. Sophie was like her mother, extroverted, loud and outspoken. Since when did she ever come over all shy and embarrassed? Clara frowned at Elliot. He was twenty, she was fifteen. Her eyes drifted to her impressionable young granddaughter. Now her mind was made up. Whether Tamsin liked it or not, they were leaving tomorrow.

Clara was still standing at the bottom of the stairs when Elliot reappeared. He walked down the stairs with Sophie hot on his heels. Elliot was carrying his backpack.

'Are you leaving?' Sophie and Clara said in unison.

'There's no room at the inn,' he motioned up the stairs. 'The bedrooms are all taken.'

'I'll share with my sister.'

'I am *not* sharing!' Mia called out.

Sophie cast a glance up the stairs and caught her little sister sitting on the top step. Sophie glared at her. 'Stop spying on me!'

Mia poked her tongue out and disappeared into her bedroom.

Sophie turned to Elliot. 'Can't you share with Evie in the twin room?'

Clara realised what had happened; the girls had chosen separate bedrooms. It's what they were used to in their big home back in London. The only time they ever had to share was when they stayed at their grandparents' and when they went abroad to fancy hotels on holiday. But with the girls in separate rooms, that left Dorothy in one double bedroom, Tamsin in the other and Evie in the twin room. And Clara on the couch again.

By the looks of things, Evie didn't want to share. After staying in that cramped beach hut, it was little wonder Evie wanted some space. That meant Elliot would return to the beach hut. She knew she should have put it up for sale the moment the twins moved into the house, but then along came the man from the outhouse.

Clara was standing there staring into space, a smile playing on her lips when she thought about him. She didn't notice Sophie following Elliot outside.

60

Elliot dropped his backpack outside the front door and looked at Sophie. 'I suppose I could hang around for a bit.'

Sophie swept her long dark hair over her shoulder and smiled up at the handsome boy with the green eyes, sun-kissed complexion and tousled blonde hair. She wanted to ask him how old he was and where he came from. She hoped he was only here on vacation, like her and was about to ask when the mobile phone in the pocket of her jeans suddenly started to ring.

'Hey, you've got reception!' exclaimed Elliot. 'You better answer that before you lose the signal. It might be important.'

For the first time ever Sophie had absolutely no inclination to answer her phone. She didn't care if it was her friends or her dad. If Justin Bieber himself was at the end of that phone she wouldn't answer it.

Sophie didn't reach into her back pocket. Instead, she took a couple of paces to the left. It had the desired effect; her phone died in mid ring. Sophie shrugged. 'Oh dear, no signal. What a shame.' She smiled. 'Let's do something.'

'What did you have in mind?'

Sophie's eyes dropped to his lips. She wanted to kiss him. She turned away. 'I've seen the house, but I haven't seen the gardens. Why don't we go and explore?' She cringed hoping she didn't sound like a little girl, like her little sister. She *was* nearly sixteen. Although hard to gauge Elliot's age, she guessed he must be at least a year older than her, perhaps two years, in his last year of Sixth Form.

Elliot shook his head. 'I've got something to show you that's *way* cooler.' He tentatively took her hand. 'Follow me?'

Sophie curled her fingers around his and beamed at him. 'Let's go.'

Together they ran from the house in the direction of the detached garage. Elliot opened the garage door. 'What do you think?'

'It's a car,' said Sophie flatly.

'I know, but it's not just *any* car.' He opened the passenger car door. 'It's an Aston Martin like the one used in the old Bond films.'

Sophie shrugged and got in the car. Elliot got in next to her. 'Wait till you hear the engine. Now *this* is really cool.'

Sophie gasped when she saw what he was up to. She'd seen enough action movies with her dad to realise what he was doing. 'Are you hot-wiring the car? This is *so* cool.'

Elliot paused with his arms under the dash and two wires between his fingers. 'You're parents aren't er police or anything?'

'Of course not. My dad runs a business. Why do you ask?'

'Isn't it obvious?'

'Yeah.' Oh my god, she was so excited she thought she'd scream. 'Where did you learn to do that?'

'I fell in with the wrong crowd.' Elliot tapped the wires together and the engine roared into life. He put his hands on the steering wheel and turned to Sophie. 'Do you fancy a spin?'

'You drive?'

'Of course. I passed my test two years ago as soon as I turned eighteen.'

'You're *twenty*?'

'Uh-huh. Why – how old did you think I was?'

'Um twenty,' said Sophie telling a fib. He didn't look twenty.

Elliot neglected to say that although he had a license, he wasn't insured to drive this car. Details thought Elliot. What did it matter? He was only intending to take her down to the beach two streets away to show her the beach hut. He put the car into gear. Sophie blurted, 'Are you like my boyfriend now?' Her friends would not believe this. She was going out with a boy who was *twenty*. In a car. How cool was that?

Elliot stared into the eyes of the young dark-haired beauty. Her sister was only nine-years-old. She'd told him that. So how old *was* Sophie? He saw a young woman sitting beside him, but at equal turns he saw an excited little schoolgirl who, he imagined, couldn't wait to tell her school friends what she was getting up to this summer.

Elliot liked Sophie. He liked her a lot. He hadn't felt this way since Evie's best friend had led him on and then rejected him. She'd told him she was going to leave her boyfriend, but it turned out she was just playing with him, hurting him. She enjoyed the attention. But when it became evident Elliot was serious, she dumped him. Elliot didn't tell his sister the half of it. He didn't want to upset her.

Elliot stole a glance at Sophie. There was an instant attraction he hadn't felt with another girl since. Not that he'd been with many girls – or any as it happened. That's why she scared him. It wasn't the fact that she was young. For the first time, he didn't have his head up his ass and considered someone else for a change.

He couldn't even do that for his twin sister; stop making a mess of his life. But for Sophie? He didn't want to make another mistake like taking a girl he cared for out in an uninsured car and getting her into trouble. She might think it was okay, but he didn't. The last thing he wanted was for Sophie to look at him the way everyone else did – like he was one big disappointment.

Sophie caught him hesitating and frowned. 'What's the matter?'

Elliot turned. 'You know what? Maybe this isn't such a good idea.'

Sophie wasn't that naive. 'I'm sixteen if you're wondering how old I am.'

'You should get out of the—'

'What are you doing?' Clara shouted out over the rumble of the engine. Clara had been standing at the bottom of the stairs when she heard the unmistakable sound of the car engine. Having already told him he couldn't take out someone else's car without being insured. To make matters worse, when she stepped out of the house, she discovered Sophie, who had followed Elliot out of the door like a besotted puppy, was nowhere to be found.

Breathless after racing to the garage, her worst fears were confirmed. Sophie was sitting in the passenger seat next to Elliot. *Oh no no no.* She would never forgive herself if Sophie went out with Elliot in that car and something happened.

'Get out of the car this instant!' Clara yelled at them.

Sophie was the first person out of the car. 'I wasn't going anywhere if you must know,' she said sarcastically. She peered in the car and said to Elliot, 'I didn't want to go out in your stupid car anyway.'

Sophie ran from the garage around the side of the building. Out of earshot of Elliot and Clara, she burst into tears. Would Elliot suddenly see her for what she really was – a silly little school girl and not the cool young lady she wanted to be in his eyes.

He was *so* grown up – he *was* twenty. Sophie wished with all her heart she wasn't fifteen. But in three months she would be sixteen. Would that make a difference? She doubted it.

Sophie wiped the tears from her eyes. The car engine was still turning over. Would Elliot collect his backpack and walk out of her life forever. Sophie knew she was being melodramatic.

Sophie stole a glance around the side of the garage and saw

Elliot get out of the car. He stalked towards Clara. She saw him lean in and say something before grabbing his backpack off the front step and heading off down the drive. Sophie wished she could have heard what he'd said above the sound of the car engine.

61

Clara stood in front of the car watching Elliot walk down the driveway until he was out of sight. She was thinking about what he'd just said. He had no idea how his words resonated with her.

"She looks at me like no one had ever looked at me before – apart from my sister who used to adore me before I drank too much and messed up my life. Do you imagine I want her to look at me with pity? I've met no one like her before. I know she's just a sixteen-year-old kid. But she's special. She makes me feel special. No one has ever done that before apart from my twin – until now."

Clara understood. Being a twin stops defining you when you find that special person who sees you as the individual you are. It brought back memories of that summer in Mallorca when they turned eighteen and she discovered her life didn't begin and end with Tommy. That summer she'd fallen in love.

Clara squeezed her eyes shut trying to erase that memory. It wasn't working. No sooner had her life begun, it had ended. All because Tommy disappeared. She'd carried such emptiness inside her all these years. But was losing Tommy the cause of her unhappiness or losing the man she loved? Because those two events were so linked, it was impossible to be sure.

Perhaps if she hadn't been so hard on herself. If they hadn't been together that night, they might have prevented Tommy taking that boat out alone. So, she punished him and punished herself by leaving. In hindsight, what did she hope to gain by doing that? It wouldn't bring Tommy back. But she was only eighteen, not that much older than Sophie and lacking the maturity to make a rational decision. It was all in the heat of the moment, walking out of his life forever and taking his unborn child with her.

If she hadn't been with the man she loved, would that have made a difference? Clara would never know. Whenever she let those memories resurface, and the possibility of what might have been, those thoughts threatened to open this gaping black hole, this utter emptiness that nothing, not Joe or her friends or shopping could fill. Without the man she truly loved, her life had been devoid of purpose, of meaning – of happiness.

Clara had no clue at the time, that one decision when she was eighteen would irrevocably alter the trajectory of her life. Joe had been a good husband, a good father, but they were not destined to be together. If it wasn't for Tommy's disappearance she would never have moved to London and met Joe.

For the first time, Clara considered Joe in all this. What if he was destined to be with someone else and then she came along? What of the woman he had been seeing at the time they met? Joe had a sweetheart. What became of her?

Clara stood there watching Elliot walking down the drive. He wasn't the only one who had made a mess of his life. But Elliot was only twenty and the mistakes he'd made didn't have such far-reaching consequences that Clara's had.

Elliot had the one important commodity that was all you needed to put things right: he had time on his side. If Sophie was important to him, he could clean up his act and prove to her that in time, when she was no longer a schoolgirl and he acted like a mature, responsible adult, they might have a future together. If that's what Sophie wanted too.

Clara imagined what Tamsin and Kevin would say. They'd

only just met and were kids. Would it lead to a lifetime together? But Tamsin and Kevin were teenagers when they first met. In Clara's experience there was a lot to be said for first love. An awful lot. A lifetime's worth if you were lucky enough to find the right person and stick by each other.

Clara was thinking about *him*. He was the biggest regret of her life. If only I could go back to the night of that party and take back those words: *it was all your fault. I hate you. I never want to speak to you again;* the spiteful words of a scared, grieving teenager who had just lost her brother, her twin. In hindsight, she realised things might have played out the same regardless of where she was and who she was with that night.

Clara turned around and looked at the car. She had the impulse to get in the car and drive. Just drive. Run away from her past and her life right now which, with the arrival of Tamsin, seemed to be getting ever more complicated.

Clara stared at the car. 'Oh, to hell with it.' She wanted to be anywhere but here. The door on the driver's side was wide open. It was like an open invitation. Clara got in behind the wheel and placed two hands on the steering wheel to see how it felt. She hadn't driven in years. Joe insisted on driving if they went anywhere together which wasn't that often because he seemed to spend every waking hour at work.

Clara was worried about the neighbours if they heard the engine. It wasn't quiet. A car like this would not have gone unnoticed in the local community. She imagined there would be plenty of people who would recognise this car if she drove it outside the gates.

She sat there thinking about the neighbours, the police, Elliot, and the fact that she wasn't insured. Clara shouted out over the roar of the engine, 'Oh, to hell with it!' She reached over and slammed the car door shut.

There was something exhilarating about putting her foot down and speeding off. If she went for a walk instead, she would get to the double gates and turn back. This way she would be gone before she changed her mind. A part of her wanted to leave and not come back. She didn't know where she'd go. Somewhere far away. Somewhere no one could jump on a train and find her. Clara was about to release the handbrake and put her foot down on the accelerator when she looked up and spotted Bailey standing slap bang in the middle of the driveway looking her way. 'Oh, for goodness sake!' Clara wound the window down and waved an irritated hand at the dog. 'Get out of my way. Go on – shoo!'

Bailey barked at the car and sat down on his rump.

Clara frowned at Bailey. 'You silly dog.' She opened the car door, got out and stalked over to where he was sitting. She'd almost reached him – intending to grab his collar and drag him out of the way – when he got up and ran straight past her. Clara turned around and saw Bailey jumping into the car. He disappeared for a split second then his head popped up. Bailey was sitting in the front passenger seat looking back at Clara. He barked.

Clara threw her hands up in the air. 'I get it. You don't want me to leave without you.' She shook her head and returned to the car settling herself back in the driver's seat; her resolve slipping. Clara put the car into gear before she changed her mind. She gripped the steering wheel and slowly edged the vehicle out of the garage.

So much for putting the pedal to metal thought Clara trying not to laugh. She didn't want to scuff the wing mirrors on the garage doors as she drove the car out of the garage. She drifted past the front door of the house in first gear driving slowly. Clara glanced at the speedometer and tapped her foot on the accelerator a little too hard. The car shot forward down the drive.

Bailey barked.

Clara turned her head to look at the dog. In the split second her eyes left the road something crossed her path. She yanked the steering wheel, the car swerved to the left, but it was too late; she felt the car bumper connect with something. Clara saw a shopping bag fly in the air.

'Oh my god!' yelled Clara. The car left the drive and almost ploughed headlong into a Sycamore tree. Clara slammed on the brakes just in time, stopping the car inches from the tree trunk. Then she stalled the car.

Trembling, Clara looked in her rear-view mirror. Her breath caught in her throat when she saw a man lying on the drive. He wasn't moving. 'Oh my god. Elliot!'

Clara opened the car door, her heart pounding. 'Oh, thank goodness!' exclaimed Clara when she saw the man standing there brushing himself down. It wasn't Elliot. It was the man from the outhouse, and he looked fine – but shaken.

'What were you doing walking up the driveway?'

He stopped to look at Clara. 'I got bored waiting for you at the beach hut. You've been gone an age. I thought if I returned to the house, I might run into you.' A smile played on his lips.

Run into you… 'This isn't funny. I could have run you over.'

'Are you apologizing for your terrible driving?'

'I'll have you know, I'm quite a good driver,' Clara lied. How would she know if she was any good; she hadn't driven in years.

She knelt and joined him picking up what they could salvage from the grocery bag that she'd struck as she sped by. Thank God she hadn't hit him.

Clara didn't fancy another trip up the hospital after a car accident and explaining to the emergency services just what she was doing driving someone else's car uninsured.

But added difficulties aside, although she hadn't known the man in the outhouse long, she realized she didn't know what she'd do if something happened to him.

He reached for an apple rolling down the drive and commented, 'I don't think it helped that you were driving someone else's car.'

'How do you know it isn't my car?'

'Well…' he paused. 'That car was in the garage before you arrived.'

'Oh, I see.' For a minute there, Clara was wondering how he knew it wasn't her car.

He motioned at the car. 'Any damage done?'

'No. I just stalled it. Fortunately, I missed the tree,' Clara said off-hand. She didn't care about the car, she cared about him. Where did that come from? She stole a furtive glance in his direction.

'Where were you going?'

'Anywhere but here,' she blurted. 'Sorry, I'm having a bad day.'

He looked down at his carrier bag. 'I was going to make a picnic.'

'A picnic?'

He nodded. 'Nothing fancy. Just some sandwiches and a flask of tea. I was hoping you would join me. It might cheer you up.'

Clara stood up and handed him a box of strawberries. She glanced toward the house worried that Tamsin might see her with him. Not that she had anything to worry about. Meeting up with him these past few weeks had been innocent enough. So why was she feeling guilty as though she'd been carrying on behind Joe's back?

'How about it? Will you join me for a picnic?'

Clara looked at him. He had no idea that her family had descended on The Gables – yet. Clara wished they hadn't. She wanted things to stay the way they were, just the two of them, and Bailey, and the twins, and Paul visiting most days to call on Evie. Clara shook her head. But it *was* just the two of them when they met at the beach hut.

She turned to him. 'I'd love to join you for a picnic.'

'Great. I was thinking of a picnic on the lawn.'

Clara gaped at him. 'The lawn?'

'Yes. We could spread a blanket out over there under the Sycamore—'

'Oh, that won't do at all.' Clara shook her head and linked her arm in his. She steered him away from the garden, back down the drive.

He turned to look over his shoulder. 'But I thought you enjoyed sitting in the—'

'Not anymore.'

'Pardon?'

'I meant, not right now.' Clara was walking at such a pace that he was getting out of breath.

'Where shall we have our picnic then?'

Clara didn't give it a second thought. She knew where they could be alone together with no possibility of bumping into her family. None of them knew she had a beach hut.

Clara glanced in the gardens as they walked down the drive, surprised to see Dorothy. What on earth was she doing? Dorothy was wearing a large straw sun hat and kneeling on the grass. Was that a trowel in her hand? Was she gardening? From what Clara could remember, Dorothy had never shown the slightest interest in gardening in the past. Although that wasn't surprising. Dorothy had lived for years and years in a flat in a tower block. All she had, in terms of outside space, was a small balcony and some potted plants.

Clara sighed in relief when she realised Dorothy was too busy to notice her walking down the drive arm-in-arm with another man. Thinking about Dorothy in the garden, it made Clara wonder what she would do with her time now she didn't have Joe bringing in the money that funded her shopping habit.

Clara used to enjoy photography. However, it wasn't a long-lost passion that came to mind but something else. What she wanted to do more than anything was to find out what happened to Tommy.

There was nothing for her now but ghosts from the past. The only thing keeping her here was that beach hut and getting her hands on some money. And the man from the outhouse. Clara glanced at him, walking beside her, his arm still linked in hers. At first, she didn't want him there. In the beginning he was an added problem she could have done without, but now if he upped and left, she would miss him.

'You want to have lunch at the beach hut, don't you?' he said, reading her mind.

Clara smiled at him.

He returned her smile. 'I thought so.'

'You don't mind – do you?'

'Of course I don't mind. It's become our little meeting place.'

Clara slowed down as they reached the end of the driveway out of sight of the house. She realised this wouldn't last – just the two of them meeting like this – but right now she wanted to savour their time together before he found out there was a house-full.

Although it wasn't her fault they had turned up out of the blue, she imagined he would not be happy by this turn of events. Clara was hoping she could send them all home in the taxi tomorrow morning before he found out.

However, it wasn't that, that was bothering her as they walked along arm-in-arm out of the double gates. Tamsin could be persuasive when she wanted to be. What was on Clara's mind was the possibility she might find herself in that taxi with them heading to the train station, heading home. She didn't want to go, but they were her family. Clara wanted to spend as much time as she could in his company. When tomorrow came, she might never see him again.

With the prospect of returning to London, there was something she needed to do before joining him on the beach for that picnic. She stopped at the end of the street. The beach was in one direction, the town in the other. She withdrew her hand from his arm. 'I need to pop into town. Can I meet you down on the beach?'

'All right.' He looked at her quizzically but didn't ask any questions.

Clara didn't want to tell him she was going into town to make inquiries about selling the beach hut. He was right: it had become *their* place. Was she betraying their friendship by selling it? But, with the arrival of Tamsin and her family, it reminded her that this wasn't real and eventually she would have to return home. Unlike The Gables where everything was provided – from the food on the table, to the roof over her head – back in the real world, Clara needed money and that brought her back to the original decision of letting go of her beach hut.

62

When Sophie saw Elliot walking off down the driveway with his backpack slung over his shoulder, she stopped herself from chasing after him. She had her pride. Sophie didn't want to return to the house either. In the few seconds Clara had her back to Sophie, when striding over to Bailey who was sitting in the middle of the drive, Sophie slipped out from her hiding place, ran past the open garage doors and up the wooden steps to the lodge above.

She wanted to find somewhere to get away from everybody – especially her mother. It was all her fault she was here and had met a boy who'd broken her heart. *You're being melodramatic again.* But it wasn't just Elliot treating her like a little child that had upset her. That instance with the car had opened the floodgates for what was really bothering her – what was going on at home.

Mum refused to say why they had come here for a holiday. She guessed her parents had split up – from what she'd seen her mum had left her dad – but they always holidayed abroad. Always. She'd gone with her mum and sister, just the three of them, when Dad was busy working. Even if they'd split up, why should things be any different? But something had changed.

She'd asked her mother if this meant they were poor but didn't get an answer. Worryingly, her mum just burst into tears. Sophie didn't know how to deal with that so she'd gone to mope in her room before packing her things, all the while thinking how could she face her friends in September and tell them she'd gone on holiday to Southwold – for goodness sake? It was embarrassing. The only people she imagined who came here on holiday were old people – like Grandma.

Sophie felt as though her world was about to end – until she arrived and discovered her grandmother had invited some cool friends to stay with her. They'd mentioned something about Grandma looking after the house for the summer. She hadn't really taken much notice. However, what Sophie had taken an interest in was Elliot. Now he'd left, she wasn't interested in being here. Until she got a phone signal again, she couldn't get in touch with Dad to come and collect her and take her back to London.

She stopped at the top of the stairs and peered over the rail just in time to catch Bailey dodging Grandma and running into the garage. Grandma turned around and followed him. She wished she'd turn that car engine off. The racket was getting on her nerves. Why did people like old cars anyway? They were noisy and probably took a lot of time and effort to look after.

Sophie shook her head, got out her phone, plugged in a pair of earphones which she kept in her jacket pocket and scrolled through the menu. She still couldn't get a signal, but at least it was good for something; the music app still worked. She'd downloaded a couple of her favourite albums for the train journey here.

Sophie plugged the earphones into her phone and turned it up loud to drown out the noise of the car. She bobbed her head up and down to the music and spotted Grandma slowly driving the car out of the garage. Sophie frowned. *Where was she off to?* She never realised her Grandma could drive.

Sophie shrugged and turned around to peer into one of the windows above the garage. There were net curtains up at the windows so she couldn't see in. Sophie tried the door. It was locked. She stared angrily at the locked door thinking this would have been the perfect place to chill out on her own. In a fit of temper, she kicked the door and was rewarded with a key bouncing off the ledge of the doorframe above her head and landing on her foot. Sophie stared at the silver key and couldn't quite believe her luck.

She picked it up, turned it over in her hand and then tried the key in the lock. One turn and the door unlocked. Sophie gingerly turned the door handle. Before she opened the door, she glanced over her shoulder and caught sight of the car slowly being driven past the front door of the house. Sophie quickly stepped inside, turned around and shut the door before anyone spotted her.

The last thing she wanted was anyone, especially her little sister, discovering her hiding place. Not that she imagined there was anything special up here apart from an empty roof space. So why was it locked. It was probably used for storage like the area above her parents' double garage at home.

When Sophie turned around the last thing she expected to find was a fully-furnished apartment. The walls and beamed sloping ceilings were white-washed. The warm honey-coloured wooden flooring had a variety of rugs which looked familiar; they were similar in design to the mats and throws in the souk in Marrakesh when they made that trip to Morocco the other year.

The king-sized bed that was so low it almost sat on the floor was made just like the bedrooms in the house. But rather than a sensible throw from a high-street store, there was a quilt and cushions with an Aztec theme. She recognised the pattern from that trip they did to Machu Picchu in Peru last year after which the guide had taken them shopping to a local market where her parents picked up a throw just like it. Sophie bought a necklace and matching ankle bracelet to show off to her friends.

Sophie walked up to the lamp sitting on an oak bedside table and switched it on. The light was in the shape of a globe of the world. She stared at it for a long moment. When she turned eighteen, she'd already decided she was doing a gap year before starting university. She hadn't informed her parents yet. Sophie wasn't even sure she wanted to go to college. She hadn't told them that either. The fact was she didn't know what she wanted to do at university and beyond. Nothing really interested her outside of her friends and holidays abroad – and now a gorgeous boy called Elliot.

She turned from the globe and cast another gaze around the room. She liked it. She liked it a lot. It was a world away from the very English house across the drive called The Gables. She felt transported to some hotel room in a foreign country – if she ignored the view of the cottage garden and the vegetable patch and outhouses through the dormer window.

Sophie turned from the window and slowly walked around the room looking at the framed photographs on the wall. She got out a packet of bubble gum from her pocket, unwrapped one and stuck it in her mouth as she studied each picture in turn. The mounted photos had the signature of the photographer on the bottom left-hand corner. All the images were taken in foreign climes, some of which Sophie recognised from all those trips abroad with her parents. 'I'm guessing that's South Africa,' said Sophie out loud identifying Cape Town.

Sophie stopped in front of another one hanging on the wall and stood there examining the photograph as she blew a big pink bubble of gum. Sophie burst the bubble. She sucked it back into her mouth and continued to chew as she walked around the room. There was a small kitchenette behind a partition wall and an en-suite shower room that on first appearance looked like a walk-in wardrobe.

Sophie said out loud, 'I bagsy this room!' trying to ignore the feeling that she really shouldn't be here. All the other bedrooms in the house were nondescript and seemed to have been decorated and furnished straight out of a John Lewis or M&S catalogue. She knew this for a fact because it looked an awful lot like the inside of her parents' house back in London. However, the studio above the garage was different. It was personal.

A small framed photograph sat on the desk next to a plain paper jotter and an old-fashioned phone. Sophie picked up the picture frame and stared at the faces of three young people in an old black and white photo. They were on a beach, two young men either side of a young woman. Arms around each other's shoulders in a relaxed pose as though someone had captured them walking along the beach together and asked them to pause for a moment while they took the photo.

Sophie stared at the young woman. 'That's weird.' It kind of looked a lot like her mum except she knew it couldn't be because this photo was old. 'Is that Grandma?'

Sophie's eyes shifted to a camera sitting beside the photo on the desk. She picked it up. It was secured in an old brown leather case. The camera had a large, protruding lens and it was heavier than Sophie expected. She was used to her small digital camera that weighed next to nothing.

Sophie couldn't resist holding it up. She looked at the photo on the desk through the camera lens and zoomed in on the young woman. 'Okay, that *is* weird.' She'd seen photos of Grandma when she was young. This lady in the photo looked just like her. One of the young men standing next to her might have been a relative. He had her eyes. Sophie thought she'd ask Grandma about the photo. She swiftly changed her mind when she realised then she might have to give up her hiding place. She had the key and wasn't about to tell a soul.

Sophie held the camera up. Looking around the room through the camera lens, feeling like a famous fashion photographer, she spied another door. Sophie lowered the camera and walked over. At first, she thought it was locked until she tried it again and realised it was way heavier than an ordinary door, like the fire doors at her school. Sophie yanked the door open and stepped inside the room. She made the mistake of letting go before she'd found the light switch. There were no windows in this room. She was plunged into darkness.

'Shit!' Sophie turned around, fumbling for the door to get the hell out of the creepy room, when her hand brushed a light switch. She blinked when the light came on. 'Okay, what have we here?' It wasn't a serial killer's lair or a panic room. 'It's a dark room.' Sophie relaxed. 'This is really cool!'

She still had her earphones plugged in. Her head bobbed up and down with the music as she walked around the room peering at the worktops. She recognised most of the materials and substances; that's because she had been paying attention in class. Towards the end of the summer term, when school was winding down for the summer holidays, they could choose an activity to attend, like sport or music, for one afternoon a week. For the first time photography had been offered as an option.

Her friends chose it for a lark. Taking photos around the school and developing them in a dark room was the perfect recipe for texting, chatting and generally mucking about doing nothing. Which is exactly what her friends did.

Sophie, on the other hand, was paying attention when they were shown how to use a camera lens and develop her own photographs. She even stayed behind after school to practice with the Canon camera on loan from the school and spend time in the dark room. This wasn't something she shared with her friends in case they laughed or mocked her for being a geek.

Sophie liked being the popular girl at school. Her parents had money. She always had the latest phone and trainers. You name it, she had it. And she went abroad to the sort of places her friends did. She fitted in and she wanted things to stay that way.

Developing a serious interest in photography was *not* cool. She knew that. She didn't want her friends to find out. That's why she larked about and pretended she didn't really care. But despite appearances, Sophie cared a great deal about her newfound passion, to the point where she was beginning to toy with the idea of a career in photojournalism.

Sophie looked at the camera in her hands. The one thing she wanted but hadn't dared ask her parents for was a Leica camera. Not outright at least. She remembered passing a camera shop with Mum once and remarked that she wanted the camera on display in the window. It was during a shopping trip to get some new clothes, she managed to steer them right past the shop window. When Sophie pointed it out, her mum said, "What on earth do you need that for? Have you seen the price tag?"

It was almost five thousand pounds.

As usual Mum was confusing her with her nine-year-old sister who seemed to come up with a career-of-the-week depending on which book she had her head stuck in. Last week she wanted to be a pirate because she was reading Enid Blyton. This week it was a nurse because Evie was a nurse and she liked Evie. Next week – who knows? Sophie never had a career in mind. All she wanted to do was travel the world and, since discovering photography, take pictures.

Sophie held up the camera, aimed it at some imaginary vista, and clicked the button. To her surprise the button depressed fully, and she heard the familiar whirr of the camera film as it took a photograph. Sophie didn't think there would be any film in the old camera. She smiled as she lowered the camera. She didn't know what else was on the film, but she intended to use it up taking some photos of her own.

Sophie did a quick circuit of the dark room before she headed out the door. There was all the equipment needed to develop the film when she was finished.

On her way out the door, Sophie stopped in front of a glass display cabinet. It was locked. She stared at the contents and guessed why the items inside were under lock and key. Judging by what she'd seen in that camera shop when she was trying to twist her mum's arm for her own camera, the dozen or so cameras in the case were very expensive. Just for a moment Sophie had second thoughts about whether she should be touching the camera in her hands, let alone using it. That thought passed in a blink of the eye.

Sophie turned off the light and stepped out of the darkroom. She paused to look at one of the framed photos hanging on the wall. It made her wonder if the person who owned this camera was a professional photographer. She would very much like to meet him or her and learn more about taking pictures. In the meantime, Sophie decided to head out and use up the film.

63

The first thing Sophie did when she stepped outside was put the lanyard attached to the camera case around her neck. Her eyes flickered to the house. She wasn't about to ask anyone – meaning her mum – permission to borrow the camera. And she wasn't going to mention the studio above the garage either. Not even to her little sister. Especially not to her little sister. This was *her* secret.

Sophie had it all figured out. Tonight, when everyone had gone to bed, she would creep out of the house and spend the night here. Making her way down the wooden steps, with music pounding loudly through her headphones she skirted around the garage and into the back garden. She didn't know how much of the film was left but was going to return to the darkroom and develop it as soon as it ran out. She wasn't just interested to see what photos she had taken, but what might be revealed on the rest of the film.

Sophie took some nice shots of the back of the house and then made her way down the garden, until arriving at the head of a cobbled path that led through a vegetable patch towards some brick outbuildings at the end. She took a shot of the sheds as she got closer. That's when she noticed one of the doors ajar. Sophie gingerly pushed the door open and immediately spotted the camp bed with old blankets in disarray, a cooking stove, a makeshift curtain hanging up at a window and some clothes drip drying on a clothesline.

Sophie was taking some more snaps when it occurred to her that an old tramp might be living in the shed. Quickly retracing her steps along the cobbled path in case they returned and discovered her here she spotted a basket of fresh vegetables on a small trestle table. Sophie slowly lowered her camera staring at the basket. Perhaps she should return to the house and tell her mum what she'd found; someone was living in the outhouse at the bottom of the garden.

Sophie picked up her pace. She glanced about her, afraid of whom she might run into, barely noticing where she was going until she felt gravel underfoot and realised she'd arrived on the driveway.

'What the hell…?' blurted Sophie. The little green sports car that her grandmother had driven out of the garage was sitting on the grass under a tree. There were tyre tracks on the gravel and skid marks on the grass as though it had suddenly picked up speed and veered off the drive, nearly hitting the tree.

'Grandma!' Sophie called out, yanking out her earphones. Running over to the car she discovered there was nobody inside. Sophie stood for a moment looking from the squashed oranges on the driveway to the car. She was wondering why Grandma had swerved. Was she trying to avoid something – or someone?

'Oh, no! Elliot.' The last time she had seen him, he was walking down the driveway. She thought he was leaving. What if he was just popping to the shops to get some groceries?

Sophie looked up the drive towards the house. She hadn't heard any commotion, but then she'd been listening to her music at full volume. She ran toward the house hoping she didn't see an ambulance. A police car came into view. 'Bloody hell!'

Sophie rushed past the empty vehicle into the house. She heard voices in the kitchen and burst into the room saying breathlessly, 'Where's Elliot?'

Elliot's sister, Evie, was sitting at the kitchen table twirling a finger through her hair. She barely took her eyes of the young police officer to answer Sophie's question. 'How should I know?'

Sophie shifted her attention from Evie to the police officer.

He shook his head. 'Can't say that I've seen him.'

Sophie furrowed her brow. 'What about my grandmother?'

'You mean, Clara?' replied Evie.

Paul said, 'I passed her on the way here. She was heading into town.'

'But the car…' Sophie glanced over her shoulder into the hallway. 'My grandmother was driving. I thought they'd been an accident.'

Paul offered her a reassuring smile. 'I expect she just stalled it. Perhaps she couldn't get it started again, so she manoeuvred it off the driveway for the time being.'

Some police officer you are thought Sophie as she caught his gaze reverting to Evie. So, if he wasn't here about the car… Her eyes flickered to Evie. She was staring at Paul besotted. Sophie rolled her eyes. 'So, what are you doing here?'

'Ah, yes, I came here to give Clara this.' He held out a letter.

'The envelope is addressed to your grandmother.' added Evie.

If he'd seen her grandmother on the way here, why hadn't he given it to her? Sophie glanced at Evie. He wanted an excuse to come over to the house.

Sophie stared at the crumpled envelope, yellow with age. 'It looks old. What does it say?'

Paul shrugged. 'It's unopened.'

'Where did you find it?'

'It was lost in the lining of her suitcase.'

'You found it in her luggage? What were you doing going through my grandmother's things?'

Paul looked at Evie. She threw him a questioning look.

'It's a long story.'

Sophie couldn't wait until she was older. Why did adults

imagine just because she was a teenager, they could get away with using *it's a long story* as a euphemism for *it's none of your business?* She wasn't stupid.

Paul looked at the letter in his hand. 'Would you mind giving it to your grandmother for me?'

Sophie shrugged.

He handed her the letter.

'There's no stamp on the envelope,' remarked Sophie.

'I know. At first, I thought it was something she'd forgotten to post years ago, and it's probably of no consequence.'

'But it's addressed to my grandmother.'

'Precisely, which leads me to conclude someone left the letter in her suitcase for her to find, but unfortunately it slipped through the lining of the case.

'Until you found it.' Sophie stared at him.

'Well, yes. I'd forgotten all about it, so when I found it in my desk drawer, I brought it straight over. I didn't want to post it, in case it went astray. It might be important.'

Sophie turned over the envelope in her hands. She could feel the edge of a folded letter inside. She couldn't imagine what her grandmother would want with a note that was eons old. Whatever it said was probably of no consequence after all these years. She looked at the police officer, her sceptical expression giving her away.

Paul nodded. 'I know what you're thinking. I shouldn't have bothered. It could be nothing at all,

'Then again,' chipped in Evie, 'it might be a letter from a friend, someone she knew from years ago who she lost touch with. Perhaps they left it in her suitcase for her to find.'

Paul, Evie and Sophie looked at the envelope. Evie said, 'You will remember to give it to her, won't you?'

Once again, Sophie didn't appreciate being treated like a little child, like her sister. 'Of course, I won't forget,' she snapped as she thrust the envelope into the back pocket of her jeans.

64

There were several estate agents in the town. Clara walked into the nearest one and took a vacant seat at a desk opposite an elegant young lady who could have stepped straight out of the cover of a fashion magazine.

The young lady smiled. 'Hello, how can I help?'

'I'm inquiring about the value of beach huts in the area.'

The young lady's face dropped. 'Ah, we haven't any for sale. People register an interest then when one comes to the market they're snapped up.'

'Is that a fact?' Clara said keenly.

'I'm afraid so.'

A sales assistant walked past with property details in her hand. The young lady noticed Clara taking an interest. She called her colleague over.

Clara recognised the property instantly.

'These are not sales details,' said her colleague. 'We manage the property in the owner's absence. We were looking for a suitable person to house sit while the owner was abroad.'

Clara looked at the ad in her hand that had been in the window a moment ago. 'Does that mean you've found someone?' asked Clara. Were they on their way over to The Gables right now, intending to start today? She was thinking of everyone at the house as she rose from her seat when the young woman shrugged and said offhand, 'Our client no longer wants a house sitter. He informed us some time ago, we forgot to take the ad out of the window.' She put the details in the shredder next to her colleague's desk.

With a sigh of relief, Clara resumed her seat and held out her phone with a photograph she had taken of her beach hut. 'Can you tell me how much this might be worth? I need a ball-park figure. A rough estimate would be helpful.'

The young lady took one look at the picture and asked if she owned the beach hut.

'Absolutely.' Clara hoped she didn't ask for proof.

The young lady sat forward in her seat. 'Can I get you anything – tea, coffee?'

Clara declined. 'Just a ballpark figure.'

'Are you thinking of selling?'

'Oh yes. Well, that is when I've sorted out my affairs.'

'Your affairs?'

Clara nodded. 'I'm getting a divorce.' There was no point beating about the bush. 'But I will sell it. That's why I'm here.'

'That's fantastic.' The young lady picked up a pen and wrote something on a small card. 'This is me,' she pointed to her name under the title *Sales Negotiator*. 'I have written an estimate on the back of the card. That's what the last one we had sold for. It wasn't in as good a condition as yours. It sold a few months back. Prices have risen since then, so that is a conservative figure. It's a seller's market. They go for silly money now.'

Clara turned over the card and almost fell off her chair. 'There must be some mistake. I think you've written that down wrong. There are too many noughts.'

'Oh, that's the figure all right.'

'But that could buy a house.'

The young woman laughed. 'Not round here.' She stood up and held out her hand. 'I do hope to see you again when you are ready to put it on the market. I'm sure we can find you a buyer.

We have a waiting list and the summer is the best time to sell.' Clara didn't doubt it. She got up from her chair, shook the woman's hand profusely saying, 'Thank you, thank you.' She guessed this is what it felt like if you just discovered you'd won the lottery. Clara felt as though she was floating to the door; she was on such a high at this piece of news.

Although it wouldn't buy her a house in London, or even a flat and it wouldn't buy out Joe's share of the house, Clara didn't care about that. The money from the sale of the beach hut meant a fresh start. 'A home that's all mine,' said Clara out loud as she stepped out on to the street.

❖

One of the sales negotiators closed the door behind Clara and turned to her colleague seated at the desk. 'Was she here about the house-sitting job?'

'No.'

'That's just as well. We don't need to find a house sitter.'

'Yes, you already mentioned that.'

'Ah, but I didn't mention the reason why.'

'And that is…?'

'Apparently, our enigmatic photographer is moving back in.'

'Really?'

'Uh-huh.' She stared out the window. 'Any day now.'

Her colleague was silent for a moment. 'What does enigmatic mean?'

The young woman rolled her eyes and resumed her seat behind a desk hoping that the lady who came in and inquired about selling a beach hut would return on her colleague's day off. That would be a very nice commission if she could get it. She was already calculating the figure in her head.

❖

Feeling it was her lucky day Clara kept going over the figure in her mind as she walked along the street. Not only had she found out her beach hut was worth more than she could ever have imagined, but also the position for the house sitter had been withdrawn. Now the worry over someone turning up out of the blue and the estate agent discovering them all squatting at the property had eased. All she had to think about was selling the beach hut.

'One hundred thousand pounds,' Clara chanted under her breath. 'Maybe one hundred and fifty thousand depending on how many people showed an interest.'

Clara had to say it out loud just to convince herself it was real. She'd give the twins a share; they deserved it after all their hard work doing up the beach hut. It was only right. She knew Joe wouldn't agree. His attitude most likely would be that the twins got to stay in the hut for free, so that was payment enough. Clara thought of her free sojourn in The Gables and disagreed. But then Joe wasn't here. For once in her life Clara got to make her own decisions. It was very liberating.

Clara shook her head. Who knew that property in the area would become so ridiculously expensive? Her parents' old house where she was squatting came to mind. Goodness knows what that could be worth now. It would have been lovely if they'd left her the house when they passed away, but she understood why they sold it not long after returning from Mallorca. They used the proceeds to fund countless private investigators to look into the disappearance of her brother.

The Gables must have passed through several hands until the photographer bought it to retire by the sea. So why didn't he retire? From what Clara had gleaned he was in his sixties. Surely, he should be putting his feet up, not gallivanting all around the world taking photographs.

By the sound of it he led an interesting life. Perhaps that's why he hadn't retired. Clara thought she wouldn't have minded gallivanting around the world. It beat shopping out of boredom and then returning home to find Joe slumped in front of the television. One microwavable supper later, he'd drag himself off to bed only to start the whole cycle all over again the following day. It was only now that she realised just what an empty existence they had both been leading.

65

Clara looked at her wristwatch worried how long she'd been gone. After visiting the estate agents, she had joined him on the beach as promised for the picnic. The trouble was throughout her lunch she was distracted. Clara hoped he hadn't noticed, but she couldn't help thinking of everybody back at the house. They'd be wondering where she'd got to.

There was something else on her mind. What if the owner of the house returned? After finding out they had withdrawn the house-sitting position, her initial delight at this piece of news soon dissipated when she thought about the reason a house sitter was no longer required – the owner was coming home. She didn't want the twins, or Tamsin and the girls, or even Dorothy getting into trouble all because she'd taken it upon herself to squat in someone's property.

Then there was her friend – the other squatter. She glanced at him. Should she tell him what she'd found out? Clara pursed her lips. Perhaps she should start by telling him about the new arrivals up at the house. So far, he wasn't aware. Clara was just thinking she should forewarn him now in case he bumped into Tamsin or the girls or Dorothy before she sent them home, when something caught her eye. Clara rose from her seat.

'Did you enjoy the picnic?' he ventured.

She didn't reply and appeared distracted.

Clara walked to the end of the decking, leant on the handrail and frowned. Ralph joined her. He looked along the beach wondering what had caught her attention. It wasn't the dog. Bailey was back, standing between them.

Ralph spotted a young woman walking along the shore in their direction.

Clara turned to him and said, 'I have to go.'

He looked at her and took that as *he* ought to go. But Ralph wasn't moving a muscle until he knew he could see her again. 'So, are we on for tomorrow?'

'Huh?' Clara hadn't heard a word he said; she was too busy staring at the young woman in the distance.

'Tomorrow,' repeated Ralph. 'Are we meeting up as usual for breakfast on the terrace?'

'What?' Clara had forgotten all about their routine; breakfast outside on the patio at the back of the house. That wouldn't do at all, not tomorrow morning when she had to call the taxi and make sure everyone left. Clara knew she'd been fortunate so far that he hadn't noticed more people up at the house. The outhouse was right at the bottom of the garden obscured by the trees.

Clara turned to him. 'There's something I need to do tomorrow morning. Rain check?'

She could tell by his expression he was disappointed, but what choice did she have? Who knows how long it would take for the taxi to arrive and get Tamsin, Dorothy, two pets and two reluctant grandchildren to leave.

'All right,' he said slowly, wondering if that s*omething she had to do* was related to the business she had in town before their picnic. 'We could meet up later – if you like?'

'Yes, perfect. I'll call on you when—' when they've all gone thought Clara. 'Um, when I'm free.' She turned around and gathered up the two mugs.

Ralph furrowed his brow. 'Well, I'll be off then.'

'Okay.' Clara still had his back to him.

Ralph hoped it wasn't something he said. 'Bye.'

Clara glanced over her shoulder. 'Bye.' She gave him a parting smile which set Ralph at ease. He returned her smile and resisted the urge to reply, *Backatcha* before he stepped on to the beach.

Ralph walked along the beach toward the promenade when he felt something brush his thigh. He looked down. Bailey was at his side.

Ralph came to a halt. 'I don't know how you found your way home, but you're Clara's dog now. Besides, you won't want to come back to the outhouse with me when you've got the run of the house. Bailey liked his creature comforts. His wife had spoilt him rotten since he was a pup.

'Anyway, I'm making a detour before I return to the outhouse.'

Ralph was just about to tell him to *get,* when Bailey let out a disgruntled *woof* and then took off running back to Clara at the beach hut.

Ralph breathed a sigh of relief and turned around to continue his way along the beach. The woman he'd seen from a distance when standing with Clara outside the beach hut was heading in his direction. He offered her a friendly smile as they approached one another. She was young, in her thirties, with large brown eyes and short cropped hair.

She frowned at him as they passed each other. Ralph shrugged it off, although he happened to glance over his shoulder and caught her doing the same. They both quickly looked away.

66

Clara cleared the mugs away and was folding the table, intending to stack it with the deckchairs, when she turned around to find Tamsin standing in front of the hut.

The first words out of her mouth were, 'What was that?'

Clara stopped what she was doing. She recognised her daughter walking on the beach; *all she needed now was for Tamsin to discover her sitting having tea with another man.* Although it was innocent, she would think her mum had found somebody else. Clara rolled her eyes. 'What are you talking about?'

'That?' Tamsin pointed.

He was making his way up the clifftop path heading toward the town. 'What am I meant to be looking at?' she said.

'Oh, come on! Don't play dumb with me. I saw you. *Both* of you. You were sitting together on those deckchairs.'

Clara told her what happened. 'Bailey jumped up and knocked him over. He didn't look well, so I offered him a cup of tea while he recovered.' Clara pursed her lips knowing that was four weeks ago; she'd omitted the intervening month of her developing friendship with the man from the outhouse.

'Elliot was there,' Clara added, feeling as though she had to mention someone who might back up her story. 'Is he at home?' Clara asked Tamsin, worried he had left and might not return after the car incident.

'Home?'

Clara looked at Tamsin frowning at her. Was it little wonder she slipped up and called it *home* even though in the intervening years she'd got married, had children, and grandchildren, and Tommy still hadn't returned.

'Mum?'

'Oh, sorry. Where were we?'

Tamsin wiggled her nose in annoyance. 'Evie told me he might be at the beach hut, so I walked down here and instead I find you – and that man.'

Clara was just about to reiterate there was nothing going on when she changed tack, 'Why were you searching for Elliot?'

'I wasn't. I was looking for Sophie. We can't find her anywhere.'

'What?'

'That's why I thought she might have come down here, to the beach.'

'I haven't seen her, Tamsin. She wasn't with Elliot. Once again, Clara decided not to fill in the details.

'Damn!'

'Have you had a good look around the gardens?'

'Of course I have.' Tamsin breathed a sigh of annoyance. 'Where *is* she?'

'We should head back to the house,' said Clara.

'Why?'

'I have an idea where she might be.'

For once, Tamsin didn't question her mother.

'Let's go,' said Clara eager to get back, hoping her hunch was right.

As they walked at a pace along the beach, Tamsin turned. 'Whose beach hut is that, anyway?'

'It's mine,' replied Clara.

'Yours!' Tamsin came to an abrupt halt. 'Why didn't you tell us you had a beach hut in Southwold?'

Clara kept walking. 'Let's find Sophie, then I'll explain—' Clara was about to say *everything*. She frowned. But where to begin? She'd kept so much from Tamsin about her past, about her real father.

Tamsin caught up with Clara and fell in step beside her. 'I don't understand . . . we could have come here for holidays. The girls would adore the beach hut – especially Mia.'

Clara eyed her daughter. 'Oh, really. Since when do you take vacations in this country?'

'Since Kevin's business went down the pan.'

It was Clara's turn to stop dead. 'What did you just say?'

Tamsin kept on walking. 'I don't want to talk about it.'

Clara was still standing there stunned. What about their large mortgage on the back of their business and the girls' private school fees? How much money would they need to keep themselves afloat while Kevin sorted out another venture or got a job or sold the house or found a state school for the girls?

Clara's mind was racing. They could sell their million-pound property and downsize, but that would take time. After paying off their sizeable mortgage what collateral would they have left to buy a place in London? Clara frowned. It's not as though she had any money to help them out with. Joe had seen to that. Their savings had all gone on Joe's stupid schemes in pursuit of The Big Payday. As for Tamsin and Kevin, she bet they didn't have much put by for a rainy day.

Although the company had given them a great income, she guessed that like most people they lived up to their means and spent what they earned. That's where all the expensive holidays abroad came from, and the school fees, and the massive mortgage along with their hopes and dreams of an early retirement. The trouble is they assumed the good times would never end.

Glancing back at her beach hut she sighed. It would be quicker to sell than a house. But that was *my* money, *my* future.

Clara felt a twinge of guilt at the thought of not helping her daughter. Was this why Tamsin was here? To ask her for money? Was this why she had moved out of the family home? Because Kevin's business along with their comfortable lifestyle had gone belly up? It wouldn't surprise her in the least.

As an only child with parents who doted on her, and a father who gave in to her every whim, Tamsin had never had to struggle, go without, or face difficult choices. When she moved in with Kevin and got married, she'd walked out of one secure existence straight into another.

It had crossed Clara's mind what Tamsin would do if something happened to upset her well-balanced, ordered life. Here was the result: Tamsin had run away. She couldn't blame her. Wasn't that what she did when she lost Tommy and then found out she was pregnant?

'Mum!'

Clara dragged her eyes from her precious beach hut. It was meant to be her ticket to another life; one of her own choosing.

As she set off again along the beach, all she saw ahead of her was having to stay in their North London semi until Tamsin and Kevin got back together –or not. Maybe she would have to sell the house to help them out. Frankly, Clara didn't know which was worse. She didn't want either scenario.

'Where do you think she is, then?' said Tamsin when Clara caught up with her. 'I searched everywhere. Evie and Mia helped too.'

'Just follow me.' They made their way up the gentle slope from the beach and continued along the clifftop walk, entering the grounds of the house through the back garden. Clara was on auto-pilot until she realised what she'd done; used the short-cut. She did an about-turn, stopping Tamsin in her tracks. 'Let's go around to the front.'

'Why? We're here now. Tamsin barged passed her mother.

Clara's eyes darted this way and that hoping they didn't bump into her friend. She was so consumed with the thoughts of him finding out there were more squatters.

'What's down here?'

Clara's head swivelled toward her voice. Tamsin was starting down the cobbled path that led to the outhouse. Clara reached for her arm. 'There's nothing down there.'

'What are those brick buildings then?' Tamsin said. 'I'm looking – if you don't mind.'

Clara let go of her arm, sighed and followed her down the path wondering what she would say when the man from the outhouse opened the door.

'Hi Dorothy,' said Tamsin, not giving her a second thought as she passed by.

Clara did a double-take as Dorothy raised her trowel in greeting. She was on her knees in the vegetable patch. Clara stopped mid-stride. 'What do you think you're doing?' she said.

'What does it look like?' Dorothy responded sarcastically with a trowel in one hand and a carrot in the other. She put the carrot in the basket. Clara glanced inside and saw more carrots, a turnip, a swede and some potatoes. That was his basket, the one he'd used as a peace offering of fresh vegetables, followed by their notes back and forth, courtesy of Bailey, the messenger? Clara groaned. So much for trying to keep her family's arrival under wraps.

'I'm going to make a nice homemade stew, and the best part is it won't cost a bean. I've dug them all up from the vegetable patch,' said Dorothy.

'I see,' said Clara wondering how she would explain the disappearance of his vegetables. 'Have you seen anyone pass this way?'

'We're looking for Sophie,' Tamsin butted in.

Dorothy shook her head. 'Can't say that I have. But then I've been so busy I'm not sure I would have taken much notice if someone *had* passed by.'

Clara turned her attention to the outhouse. It was possible he'd walked down the path without noticing an old lady in a straw hat kneeling in the middle of his vegetable patch. But if he was inside, things could get very awkward when she disclosed what had been going on up at the house. Clara hoped he wasn't in. But if he wasn't then where had he gone after he'd left the beach hut?

Clara raced down the path. If he *was* in, it would be better if she knocked at the door. It was possible Sophie had discovered a peaceful hideaway at the bottom of the garden where she could go undisturbed and sulk, as teenagers were wont to do. In which case, it was time Sophie left before he returned.

Clara got there first and knocked on the outhouse door. It drifted open of its own volition. She stepped inside. 'Oh.'

Elliot was sitting on the camp bed reading a book which came from the library in the house. Clara recognised the author – H Rider Haggard. Bailey was asleep next to him.

Elliot lowered his book and caught the surprised expression on Clara's face. 'Is everything all right?'

'Have you seen Sophie?' Tamsin barked, barging past Clara.

Elliot sat up. 'No – why?'

Clara was about to tell him she was missing when Tamsin motioned her to step outside and slammed the door.

'What did you do that for?' said Clara.

'I don't want him near my baby.'

Tamsin wanted to protect her daughter. The problem was Sophie is almost sixteen with a mind of her own. It wouldn't be long and she'd be off to university. She couldn't wrap her in cotton wool forever. 'He could help us find her' said Clara.

'I don't want his help.'

'Fine.' Clara set off towards the house.

'Where are you going?

'If she isn't in the house, she might have popped into town.'

'With no money?'

Clara glanced over her shoulder. 'I thought you gave them pocket money?'

Tamsin frowned. 'Not anymore. I told her to get a part-time job – a paper-round or something – like her friends.'

Clara doubted her friends at her expensive fee-paying school did part-time jobs – let alone paper rounds.

She followed Tamsin up the garden towards the house. She could see the car through the trees where she'd left it after skidding on the grass. Clara thought of Elliot. She didn't expect to find him sitting in the doghouse, *outhouse*. Perhaps he felt it was better to keep a low profile and stay out of the way rather than show his face in case he got another earful.

They stepped inside the house and called out *Sophie!*

Mia, Evie, Winston the dog, and even Marley the cat appeared – but not Sophie. Tamsin sent Mia and Evie to search for her once more, leaving Clara standing in the hall. Southwold was a sleepy, Suffolk coastal town, she couldn't have gone far.

67

Clara walked upstairs and stopped outside Tommy's bedroom. She glanced inside checking her granddaughter wasn't lounging around listening to music on her headphones.

Dorothy had chosen this room; her leather case placed on the double bed. God, I hope I don't turn into Dorothy in my old age, always complaining and being a general nuisance. Clara felt guilty at such an uncharitable thought. Dorothy's suitcase was empty. She'd left one of the wardrobe doors open and her clothes were neatly arranged on hangers.

Her nightdress was laid out on the quilt and a paperback novel placed on the table next to the bed. Clara raised her eyebrows. For someone who had dementia, she'd settled extraordinarily well in the unfamiliar surroundings. Clara felt with her condition the change of scene would be confusing. On the contrary, she was settling in so well she'd taken up a new hobby – gardening.

Clara was relieved Dorothy was out in the garden; otherwise doubtless she'd be ordering her around, demanding cups of tea and moaning at her for no good reason. It made her think of Joe, not that he expected things of her and grumbled into the bargain – quite the reverse.

He never treated her like that in all the years they were married. Clara cringed. He often brought her breakfast in bed while she sat doing her nails or reading a novel before he left for work. As much as she didn't want to think about it, he waited on her hand and foot. But it wasn't reciprocal.

Clara stood outside the bedroom door thinking about Dorothy ordering her about and realised *that was me; that's how I treated Joe.* Talk about getting a taste of my own medicine. And yet Joe had never complained. Clara frowned. He might not have groused, but was he happy? Would he have liked the same consideration and thoughtfulness he showed her every day of their married lives?

Deep down, was he fed up with their life together – with her? He worshipped the ground she walked on, but in return she treated him like a doormat. Is that why he wanted to leave and start again with someone else? Could she blame him?

Clara recalled the woman she'd seen at his hospital bedside and remembered thinking: what's she got that I haven't? Perhaps she wasn't selfish, self-absorbed and self-centred like his wife. Clara wished she'd had the gumption to have it out with her and find out who she was. She had the option to return home, but didn't want to sit by his bedside, not now she knew what he was planning.

Clara knew her behaviour was inexcusable. She should have made more of an effort in their relationship. But she never did. Why was that? Clara shook her head, trying to avoid the truth: she never loved him in the same way he loved her.

She walked along the hallway towards the head of the stairs and glanced in the other bedrooms as she passed by, trying hard not to dwell on her role in the breakdown of her marriage. There were bigger problems to resolve. How did I get myself in this predicament with all these people living in a stranger's house? Worse still there was a man who she was fond of who shouldn't be here either. Tamsin, the girls, and Dorothy would be horrified if they discovered she was squatting.

It's not as though she could come right out and tell them,

"Oh, by the by, if you wouldn't mind leaving first thing tomorrow morning because I broke into this house." Clara knew that wasn't true – she had a key. Even so, it was tantamount to breaking and entering; she hadn't committed the *breaking* part, just entering the property without the owner's permission.

Clara shook her head. How would she get them to leave? She already knew the answer to that little conundrum; order a taxi and tell Tamsin they were going home – and she was travelling with them. How could they stay if she was leaving too? The only problem was she didn't want to go back – not now.

Clara mulled that over as she walked down the stairs. Wondering what to do, she glanced out of the landing window. Clara stopped dead. Was that a light on in the apartment over the garage? Clara's breath caught in her throat. Had the owner returned? '*Bloody hell!*'

'What's wrong?' asked Evie. She was holding a mug of tea. Evie joined Clara by the window. 'Is that a light in the apartment?'

Oh god! Clara turned to Evie wide-eyed. *How was she going to explain all this?* Clara had an idea. She glanced at her watch. Thank god the estate agents would be closed until the morning. She could outright lie and say they hired her before receiving instructions not to find a house sitter. She was staying tonight and leaving the following day.

But what about the rest of them? She eyed Evie standing there with a mug of tea in her hands.

'What is it?' asked Evie, noticing Clara's worried expression.

Clara was thinking of Elliot and Bailey in the outhouse, Dorothy on her hands and knees in the vegetable patch, and Amy with Winston and Marley. Oh, let's not forget Tamsin and the teenage Sophie throwing a strop over having to share a bedroom again with her little sister. That was probably the reason she disappeared for a few hours. She was most likely hanging around the shops in town and had found a phone signal.

Clara bet she was on the blower to her Dad chewing his ear

off about her rotten holiday on the Suffolk Coast, begging him to rescue her from this hell hole.

Clara's eyebrows shot up. What an excellent idea. If she got back in touch with Kevin, he would come straightaway to pick them all up.

'Where's my tea!'

Clara and Evie exchanged a glance. They both looked down the stairs toward the cross voice. Clara threw Evie a questioning look, as her eyes drifted to the mug of tea in her hands. 'Oh, this was for Dorothy. She was feeling parched after digging up all those vegetables.'

Clara didn't need to be told. She'd recognise Dorothy's whinging voice anywhere. The last thing Clara needed was Dorothy getting on her high horse over the fact that people weren't jumping to attention.

'Sorry,' apologised Evie. 'I noticed you standing on the stairs and wondered what had caught your eye. Is it Sophie?'

Clara shook her head. She knew the door to the apartment was locked because she'd tried it herself. 'Just take Dorothy her tea, will you?' She watched Evie walk back down the stairs.

Clara glanced out the window once more and grimaced. Maybe she should tell the owner the truth – some of it at any rate. The family had landed on her. It wasn't planned. They hadn't checked with her first that it was all right if they came. It sounded plausible. Obviously, the truth didn't extend to telling the owner she was squatting. He could find that out the next morning when they had all vacated and miles away, travelling home to London on the train.

Clara nodded her head, satisfied she had a plan even though she didn't like it one bit. It wasn't the thought of lying to the owner, although that wasn't good, it was leaving The Gables, leaving *him*.

Clara took a deep breath and continued down the stairs. She glanced down the hall before she walked out of the house. The kitchen door was ajar. Dorothy and Evie were busy peeling the vegetables fresh from the garden. They were talking about making a stew for dinner.

Dorothy told Evie that Tamsin was going into town to look for Sophie and had asked her to pick up some suet in the grocery store so she could make dumplings. The mention of stew and dumplings made Clara's mouth water at the prospect of a home-cooked meal. It beat those ready meals from the freezer that she hadn't replaced.

She considered inviting him up to the house to join them for dinner, but that was impossible. She'd then have to introduce him to everybody – including her mother-in-law.

'I also asked Tamsin to pick up some milk, eggs, bread and sugar while she was at it. Clara obviously couldn't be bothered to do some shopping before we arrived.'

Clara rolled her eyes at the dig. Some things never change. What Dorothy didn't realise it was a lack of money that had prevented her from visiting the shops.

She walked out the front door and came to an abrupt halt on the gravel drive. She'd forgotten about the car. 'Oh boy!' How would she explain the absence of his motor? Clara winced.

Well, it's like this. I borrowed your car and then Bailey distracted me. It was the dog's fault, not mine that I swerved the car to avoid the squatter and skidded on the grass. I missed the tree, though.

After her rather short jaunt down the drive she should have asked Elliot to restart the vehicle and put it back in the garage. Thankfully, there was no damage, but it didn't look good sitting on the lawn under a tree, skid marks marking its route.

Clara took a deep breath and climbed the stairs to the apartment above the garage. She stood on the small wooden platform and knocked on the door. Nobody answered. Clara knocked again. Out of the corner of her eye she noticed the curtain twitching. *How odd.*

Clara narrowed her eyes. Why didn't she think of it in the first place? Clara rapped on the door, and raised her voice, 'Sophie – I know you're in there!'

68

The door opened and a chink of light spread a shadow over the balcony. Clara looked at Sophie standing in the doorway with a hand on her hip, her head cocked to one side, and a look on her face that said *don't even think about asking me to leave.*

'I am *not* sharing with my sister. She's got animals in the bedroom. They were sitting on my bed!'

'You mean Winston and Marley,' Clara said matter-of-factly. Sophie made it sound as though it was something the cat dragged in, like a dead mouse or a rabbit. 'You didn't mind Marley curling up on your bed when you were staying over at my house. And I seem to recall you are fond of Winston.'

Winston had a soft spot for the girls that did not extend to Clara or anybody else – apart from Dorothy. As with his owner, once Winston took a dislike to you – that was it.

Sophie stood her ground, not budging from the doorway which made Clara wonder: what was inside that apartment? There was more to it than not wanting to share with her sister. Clara stepped forward. 'Can I come in?'

'No.'

Clara looked at her in surprise. Not because she answered back. Sophie was a teenage girl with attitude, and Grandma was used to it. What surprised her was what she held in her hand. Sophie tried to hide it, but it was too late. 'Is that a Leica camera?'

Sophie brought it out from behind her back.

'I haven't seen one of those in years,' said Clara staring at it. 'Where did you get it?'

Sophie sighed and opened the door wide. 'There's more inside if you're interested. How did you know what type this is?'

'Oh, I used to have an interest in photography, once upon a time,' Clara replied not letting on that it was more than just a passing interest. Many years ago, she wanted to be a professional photographer. She joined the local club and begged her father to buy her a camera. He didn't see the harm as it was only a hobby. Their aspirations for their only daughter did not extend beyond her getting married to a nice fellow with prospects – meaning one of their friends' sons who went to a private school and was looking into the field of medicine or law as a career.

Her parents did not expect Clara to meet a young man at the photography club who she hadn't seen since primary school. He was everything they had in mind for a future son-in-law. His dad ran a law practice in the town with whom her father had a friendly rivalry. It was a perfect match.

The only fly in the ointment was he had no intention of following his father into law but wanted to be a photographer. Little wonder Clara and Ralph hit it off, and he became a best friend to Tommy. They had something in common; her brother didn't want to go into the family business either.

'You know about cameras and photography?' asked Sophie, snapping Clara back to the here and now. She stared at her granddaughter. Sophie's face was a picture when Clara said yes. Her expression one of incredulity that her grandmother had interests once upon a time beyond shopping.

Clara stepped inside and came to an abrupt halt. The space above the garage was not what she expected. She assumed it was a large storage room cluttered with boxes and paraphernalia. The apartment had a king-size bed decked out in Aztec bed linen and cushions. Large multi-coloured rugs covered the warm wooden floors. Ornaments that looked as though they'd come from far-flung places were scattered around. She picked up a small ivory totem pole on the desk, reflecting on its place of origin.

Unlike the house where every room was neutral white and beige, this was different. This was much more personal. Too personal. She felt as though she was invading someone's private space.

Clara stopped in the middle of the large, airy room and her eyes settled on Sophie. Little wonder she wanted it all to herself. Clara was about to burst her bubble. She took a deep breath, preparing herself for the inevitable backlash when she told her. 'You can't stay here.'

'Why not!'

'Look around you, Sophie.'

'How is this any different to the house? Your house-sitting, aren't you? You have the run of the place, looking after it while the owner is away. That's got to mean up here above the garage too.'

She had a point; if the housesitting part were true.

'Sophie, you will still have to share with your sister until you all leave.' Clara hoped that was *very* soon.

Sophie stamped her foot.

Clara suppressed a smile. She hadn't seen her do that since she was a little girl.

'But I don't want to.'

Clara looked around the apartment. 'I see.' She guessed it was less to do with sharing with her sister and more to do with this very nice room. Who wouldn't wish to stay here? But Clara didn't know if the owner might turn up. What if he arrived late in the evening and came straight up here? She turned to Sophie and shook her head. 'I'm sorry.'

Sophie stamped her foot again.

Once again, Clara resisted the urge to smile. That would not go down well at all if Sophie felt she was laughing at her. She walked over to the door. 'Come on. Let's return to the house. Your mother has been beside herself with worry over where you were.'

Sophie rolled her eyes. 'She's confusing me with my little sister. I'm not nine. I can take care of myself.'

They were Clara's sentiments, but she still couldn't stay in the apartment. Clara waited by the open door and saw Sophie trying to hide the camera behind her back as she walked out, thinking her grandmother had forgotten all about it. 'You better put that back where you found it.'

Sophie gave her grandma a cold, hard stare. 'But I was using that!'

'You were using it?' Clara raised an eyebrow. 'Do you mean to say it's got a film in it?'

Sophie gave her grandmother a look which said *do you think I'm that stupid?* 'Of course, it has a reel of film. What do you think I was doing? *Pretending* to take photographs.' Sophie tutted. 'I was going to develop it when I used it up.'

'Develop it?'

Sophie frowned. 'I thought you knew about photography. You know about developing prints – don't you?'

'I know what a darkroom is, Sophie. I'm just surprised you do.'

'For your information, Grandma, I have photography classes at school.'

'Really?' Clara had no idea Sophie was interested in anything other than boys, makeup and texting her friends.

'Yes – really.'

Clara was still holding out her hand for the camera.

When Sophie realised her grandmother would not back down, she stomped over, slapped it in her hands and stormed off down the stairs.

'Sophie,' Clara called after her. 'Where did this come from? I need to put it back.' She held up the Leica. You wouldn't find one of these in your local store. Clara couldn't believe she'd been wandering the grounds taking photos with it, oblivious to how much it was worth. If she'd dropped it… Clara shuddered.

Sophie stopped at the bottom of the stairs and shouted back, 'In the glass cabinet in the darkroom.'

'There's a darkroom?' said Clara in surprise, but Sophie was already stalking across the drive toward the house.

Clara stepped back inside the apartment and doing a quick circuit of the room discovered a walk-in wardrobe a bathroom and a darkroom. Clara opened the door and felt goosebumps. She hadn't been in a darkroom in years. It brought back a flood of memories; the excitement of developing a reel of film and watching the prints come to life. That wasn't the only exciting experience she remembered; there was a vivid memory of a stolen kiss with a teenage boy who had also joined the photography club in a place just like this.

Clara stopped in front of a glass display cabinet and stared at the cameras inside. Some she recognised; they were very rare, very expensive. Others, she wasn't too sure. One thing she knew for certain, this equipment went beyond an amateur photographer and were mostly used by professionals. She'd found what she had expected to come across in the house; things of a personal nature alluding to the owner of the property.

Clara walked out of the darkroom; she was looking at the mounted photographs on the wall, moving along studying each one when she came to the walk-in wardrobe. Perhaps she'd deposit the camera in here.

She didn't ask Sophie where she'd found the camera before she stormed out. Clara opened the door and walked into the small closet. There were two long hanging rails, one containing pressed shirts and casual jackets, the other smart chinos, jeans and chino-style shorts. There was a rack with different footwear for many types of terrain and even a flak-jacket. Clara picked it up. It was heavier than she expected.

She turned around and spotted two cases under the hanging rail. They still had airline tags attached to them. She shrugged. The owner of the apartment must have bought a new set of luggage. Maybe, like her, he was fond of his old suitcases and didn't want to chuck them out. Or perhaps he was a hoarder. At no point did it occur to her to inspect them. If she had, she would have discovered them full of clothes along with a wallet containing some foreign money and Ralph's passport.

It had been a long time since she had used a Leica. She held the camera up and looked through the lens pondering about the reel of film inside. It seemed a shame to let it go to waste.

Clara had been thinking about what she would like to do with her life. Photography was appealing but she had no camera, equipment or darkroom. Clara's shoulders sagged. Her more pressing issue was how to support herself, not taking up expensive hobbies.

Cradling the camera in her hands, Clara stepped out and closed the door to the walk-in wardrobe. What harm could it do if she used up the reel and developed it in the darkroom just for old time's sake? It's not as though she'd get another opportunity. And it wouldn't cost her a penny.

She stared at the old camera. Who knows how long it had been sitting around and the film might be decayed? Clara shrugged. That would not stop her from taking some photographs. It wasn't about developing the film, although that would be the icing on the cake. She was intrigued by what other photos might be on the roll of film.

Clara walked out of the darkroom and approached the door to the apartment. Sophie had left it wide open when she stormed out. She held the camera up and looked through the lens. If she was careful and didn't drop—

The sound of a dog howling startled her, and she almost dropped the camera, catching it in time before it slipped out of her hands on to the wooden floor. She sighed in relief. Where on earth was that awful racket coming from? She stepped outside and saw the culprit. It was Bailey. He was sitting down below on the drive outside the garages. Clara guessed he had spotted her in the open doorway. He barked.

'Shush!'

Bailey seemed to take the *shush* as an invitation. He came bounding up the stairs and dived straight into the apartment, dodging her legs and an outstretched hand trying to stop him.

Clara turned around. Bailey was already lying on the bed, making himself at home.

'Oh, no you don't.' Clara marched toward him. 'You are *not* sleeping on that bed.' She stared at Bailey as something occurred to her. She came to Southwold to get away from people not have them follow her. The thought of Dorothy barking orders as soon as she stepped back in the house made up Clara's mind.

Clara shut the door and spoke to Bailey, 'I guess you wanted some peace too.'

He barked once and laid down, placing his muzzle on his front paws. His watchful brown eyes staring up at her.

'Well, I guess we agree on something. We're stopping here for the night,' Clara replied.

69

Sound asleep, Clara heard the door open and footsteps on the wooden flooring. She sensed someone standing over her, waiting for her to rouse. Clara felt them nudging her back.

'Oh, goodness!' She woke with a start and turned her head to find Bailey lying on top of the duvet next to her. Her eyes darted around the apartment. Clara relaxed. There was no one else in the room besides the dog. His paws must have nudged her in the back while she was dreaming.

She looked at Bailey. 'You woke me up from a bad dream.' In her dream, the owner had walked in on her and wanted to know what she was doing in his apartment, sleeping in his bed.

Bailey licked her face.

'*Ew!*' Clara gently pushed him away and reached over to turn on the table lamp. A short time later, after a quick wash and a change of clothes – from her suitcase she collected last night – Clara returned to the bedroom. She glanced out of the small window. It was early, six in the morning, and the house across the drive was quiet. No lights were on, suggesting everyone was asleep.

Clara picked up the camera from the bedside table. Adjusting the focus, she checked the flash was on and took a picture of her first subject – Bailey. She snapped several pictures from different angles while he lay there watching her with interest.

Before anyone was up and about, she decided to take some shots of the gardens while she had them to herself. Opening the door, she glanced at Bailey. 'Want to come?'

She felt silly talking to the dog. Bailey sat up gazed at the open door, appeared to consider it for a moment then flopped back down on the bed.

'That answers my question,' said Clara staring at the lazy dog. 'I'll go by myself then.' She stepped outside and shivered in the fresh morning air. Fortunately, she was wearing trousers and a long cardigan over her summer top. She walked at a brisk pace to warm up and took some photos of the rear of the house and the gardens but steered clear of the outhouse.

She reached the gap in the hedgerow and glanced behind her. It was so early she could slip out unnoticed.

Clara emerged on to the street. She crossed the road and strolled along the cliff top walk. There was nobody about. She paused here and there with the camera to the ready, looking for inspiration, but there was nothing of interest she wished to snap. Then she had an idea. She started down the slope to the beach.

Clara fancied taking photographs of the beach hut. 'For old times' sake,' she said out loud. It wouldn't be long, and it would be on the market and sold and she wanted something to remember it by. She liked the idea of having some photos as a keepsake.

Clara joined the promenade at the bottom of the path and continued walking until the concrete path which gave way to sand. She stepped on to the beach and making her way toward the beach hut, spotted someone sitting in a deckchair on the small veranda outside. Clara whispered, 'Tommy? It can't be!'

Clara shook her head at such a ridiculous thought. As she approached, she could see it was her good friend Henry, the man from the outhouse.

Clara tiptoed up to the beach hut. He was sound asleep, and she didn't want to wake him. She watched him sleeping wondering what had brought him down here this early. She raised the camera and took a few shots.

'What are you doing?'

Clara lowered the camera. 'Sorry, I didn't mean to wake you.'

He sat up in the chair with a start and seemed to take a moment to orientate himself. 'Forgive me. I didn't mean to snap at you. I must have dozed off.'

'What are you doing here at this time in the morning?'

'I wanted to get down here early for a dip in the sea.' That wasn't the real reason he was down here on the beach at the crack of dawn, washed and dressed, and sitting in a deckchair. Ralph was hoping she passed by on a morning walk with Bailey.

He couldn't wait until later in the day to meet her. It's what got him through the interminable nights on the camp bed in that damp, draughty outhouse – that and his half-burnt painting of Mallorca. He still lay awake, late into the night, studying that picture until he fell into the same dream; the two of them walking along a Mallorcan beach, hand-in-hand, together again. He looked away, embarrassed.

Clara studied him thoughtfully. Her face reddened when she realised what he was doing here.

Ralph raised his eyes and said in a small voice, 'I wanted to see you. I… I was hoping you might be up early walking Bailey on the beach.'

There was an awkward silence as his gaze shifted to the camera in her hands.

'Oh, don't worry about your photograph. I expect it won't be any good.'

The words had barely passed her lips when she realised what she'd said. She hoped he didn't think that comment was a reference to his facial disfigurement and guessed that's why the black look. How could she be so thoughtless?

Clara tried to backtrack. 'What I meant to say was it would be out of focus.'

'I doubt that. You were holding the camera confidently. I bet you know more than you think.'

'Funny, someone used to tell me that, a long time ago.'

He looked away, casting his gaze down the beach recalling those happy, carefree days when they met at the photography club.

'But it was nice of you to say so,' Clara added. 'The truth is I have taken no photos with a camera like this in years. Not since—' Clara stopped short.

His eyes were on her again, searching her face. 'Not since…?'

It was Clara's turn to look away. 'It's been such a long time that I can't even remember,' she lied. Clara knew when she stopped taking photographs. It was the day she left for London, leaving behind the camera her father had bought her, and the boy she'd fallen in love with.

Clara glanced at him and couldn't get over how much Henry reminded her of the eighteen-year-old boy she once knew; older of course, much older – and slimmer – but even so, it was how she imagined Ralph would have aged if it had been him and not his doppelganger.

Ralph rose from his seat and stepped on to the beach in front of her. 'Would you like to have breakfast with me this morning?'

Clara hesitated. It wasn't a question of whether she'd like to, but if they had time; she had a taxi to arrange to take them all to the station. She glanced at her watch. It was still early. If they went back to the house now, would there be time for breakfast before anyone woke up and discovered them eating together in the kitchen?

He caught her hesitating, and added, 'We don't have to go back to the house if you don't want to. There's a nice little café on the pier if you don't mind the walk. I used to go there with—'

Ralph stopped short, the thought of his late wife making him feel guilty even though she was dead and buried. Perhaps the pier wasn't a good idea. They used to have breakfast together up at the house every morning, but something had changed. He couldn't figure out what. That's why he was down here instead hoping to see her, hoping it wasn't something he'd said or done.

Ralph frowned. He guessed she was going to decline breakfast again.

'I've got a better idea.' Clara looked at her watch; to hell with it, she'd call for the taxi to take them all to the train station when she got back. 'Come with me.'

'Where are we going?'

Clara grinned. 'Back to your place for breakfast.'

'My place?' Ralph said slowly. 'You mean at The Gables like we used to?'

'That's hilarious,' Clara laughed.

Ralph didn't get the joke.

Clara looked at him and nudged his arm playfully. 'No, silly, I mean the outhouse. It's just that the way you said it made it sound as though "your place" was The Gables.'

Ralph raised his eyebrows. 'Oh, I see what you mean.'

'You don't mind – do you?' Clara was worried he thought she was being too forward inviting herself round his.

'Do I mind?'

'That I'm inviting myself to the outhouse for breakfast?'

'No, of course not.' *After all, I own the place.* Ralph breathed a sigh. It was just as he feared. There was no way she'd believe him if he told her that he owned The Gables.

Clara smiled in relief. He might think she did not wish to spend time with him if she declined. It wasn't that at all. She did not want to suggest a little café along the promenade as she had no money and assumed her down-and-out friend had none either. However, the one thing she could guarantee was that he seemed to have a ready supply of bacon back at the outhouse.

'Come on,' she took his hand. Ralph closed his hand around hers and grinned. Together they set off along the beach.

'Why are you grinning like a mad hatter?'

Ralph couldn't help it. He was thinking about his reoccurring dream. Apart from the one small detail that they were always walking hand-in-hand on a Mallorcan beach, this was his dream come true. The fact that it wasn't in Mallorca did not bother him. Since when were dreams an exact science, anyway?

70

Clara was standing at the little window in the outhouse checking there were no lights on up at the house when she heard him sigh. She turned around. 'What is it?'

'I can't get the stove working. The gas bottle is empty.' Ralph sat down on the camp bed and frowned. Of all the days, why did it have to run out just when he was ready to cook her the best English breakfast she'd ever tasted?

Clara walked over and looked at the contents of the large saucepan. Bacon, sausages, hash browns, black pudding, mushroom and tomatoes were in the pan. He even had bread and a packet of eggs. She'd already put in her order for two fried eggs along with eggy bread.

She picked up the loaf of bread and carton of eggs and thrust them into his hands. 'Come on.' Collecting the saucepan, she left the outhouse. 'Follow me…'

Once again, Clara took his hand. They walked up the cobbled path.

Ralph expected Clara to turn toward the house. To his surprise, she went in the other direction. 'Where are we going?'

'Can't you guess?'

'Are you walking down to the shore carrying a saucepan?'

'Yes – watch me!'

Ralph laughed. 'This is insane. The lengths you'll go to, to have breakfast on the beach!' Clara pursed her lips. In part, it was to avoid bumping into anybody up at the house. But if she had a choice, she preferred to do this even if it meant attracting some quizzical stares from early morning dog-walkers passing a strange woman marching along carrying a saucepan full of uncooked food.

'We could have just walked up the garden to the house.'

'I know, but what fun is that?'

Now, this was the Clara he remembered; spontaneous, surprising and at times quite bonkers, but never boring. Ralph shook his head smiling at the beautiful woman leading him by the hand. Oh, how he wanted this perfect moment to last forever even if it was comical.

When they reached the hut, Ralph set up the small portable cooking stove they used to make that delicious stew. There had been plenty of other times they'd eaten in the evening down on the beach, but breakfast was always up at the house.

He lit the stove and remarked, 'I haven't had breakfast on the beach since…' He stopped short staring at Clara kneeling on the sand beside him.

Clara looked at him. 'What's the matter?'

Ralph was debating whether to tell her who he was, but there was something stopping him; afraid of losing her again he bottled out. 'Oh, nothing. This just reminds me of a time in my life when things were…' Ralph was searching for the right word.

'Simpler?' offered Clara.

He managed a smile. 'Yes.'

They both stared at one another, lost in a single thought: if they could turn back the clock would they have done things differently?

Clara snapped out of it first. She got up from the sand. 'I'd better find some plates.'

'Oh. Yes. Right.' He stared after her as she disappeared into the beach hut. Ralph wondered whether the more time they spent together; it wouldn't be a question of *if* she guessed the truth but *when*.

He put the pan over the heat. 'I'll cook breakfast,' he called after her, doubtful she'd hear him from inside the hut.

Clara heard him. He didn't just remind her of Ralph, he sounded like him too. Unless that was her imagination. Would she remember his voice after all these years? It still didn't change the uncanny resemblance she saw in the man before her to the boy she once knew.

Clara returned with two plastic plates and did not have to wait long for him to dish up.

'I cooked too much.'

'Oh.' Clara glanced at the leftovers in the pan.

'Well, I guess there's seconds.' He tucked into his meal and Clara did the same. 'That's some camera.' He pointed at the Leica balanced on her lap.

Clara followed his gaze. She'd left the camera locked in the beach hut when she went to have breakfast in the outhouse. Clara retrieved it when she walked into the hut to find the plates. She looked up at Ralph. 'You know something about photography?'

'A little,' he said modestly. Ralph didn't want to get into a conversation about work.

'I'm sorry I took a photo of you while you were sleeping.'

'It's all right, honestly. I'm sorry I woke up in a bad mood and snapped at you.'

'Don't be.'

They fell silent. Ralph looked up and down the beach and turned to Clara with a question. 'Where is the dog?'

Clara rolled her eyes. 'I asked him to come for a walk this morning, but he wanted a lie-in.'

Ralph burst out laughing. 'He wanted a lie-in?'

'I think so. He seemed to consider it before deciding walkies could wait until later.'

Ralph remembered his wife doing the same thing; asking Bailey if he wanted a walk. He glanced at the stove. 'Shame he didn't come. I'm sure he would have had a field day with all that leftover bacon.' He grinned at Clara.

'I see what you mean. Bailey would be cross if he knew what he was missing.'

The words were barely out of Clara's mouth when she heard a dog barking. She spotted Bailey racing across the beach, the smell of bacon guiding him straight to them. He launched himself at her companion first. 'He likes you,' said Clara watching Bailey muzzle his hand.

'That might have something to do with all the bacon I gave him when he was ferrying the basket between us with those notes – remember?'

Clara giggled. 'Oh yes, I remember.'

'All right, all right, enough already.' Bailey was attempting to lick Ralph's face. He didn't push the dog away because he didn't want to offend Clara and he was genuinely pleased to see Bailey.

It wasn't until he'd come face-to-face with the dog again that he realised how much he'd missed the fella. It had been a spur-of-the-moment decision to find him a new home. Except as soon as the dog was gone, he realised it was another heartrending regret he'd have to live with for the rest of his life.

'We both know why you're pleased to see me,' said Ralph giving him an affectionate scratch behind the ears, 'because I cooked bacon this morning.' He glanced at Clara and they exchanged a smile.

'Here you go, fella,' he said dishing some bacon on to his empty plate and putting it on the sand for Bailey. Ralph was enjoying their peaceful haven on the deserted beach with nobody else around when he spied two girls in the distance running along the shore. He frowned

Clara saw him frown and wondered what had caught his attention. She turned around and recognized her grandchildren.

Before she warned her new friend that he was about to come face-to-face with one precocious nine-year-old-going-on-thirty and an argumentative fifteen-year-old, they'd arrived outside the beach hut.

'Bailey!' Mia shouted at the dog. 'You are a very naughty dog. You are not to run off like that.'

Clara rolled her eyes. Sometimes Mia sounded just like her mother.

Bailey ignored Mia. He was busy polishing off his bacon, although his ears twitched at the sound of her cross voice.

Clara was just saying, 'Henry, meet Mia,' when Sophie arrived out of breath. She pointed at Bailey. 'What the hell…?'

'Language, please young lady.'

Sophie turned to her grandmother. 'He ran off. I thought the dog was trained. I kept calling him and he ignored me.'

'What were you doing out with the dog, anyway?'

'Mum said we were getting under her feet, so she sent us out to take him for a walk.'

Clara narrowed her eyes guessing that wasn't the truth. She knew what had happened. Sophie told Mia about the apartment. They ventured up there and let themselves inside, only to discover Bailey. That's how he escaped. Then they had to find the dog before they got into trouble.

Ralph looked from one girl to the other. 'I'm sorry, excuse me, but who are they?'

Clara took a deep breath, wishing she'd mentioned her family were staying at The Gables. Things were about to get very awkward. 'Oh, these are my grandchildren.'

'You have grandchildren?' Ralph stared at Clara. He shifted his attention to the two pretty girls standing beside her glaring at the dog.

'I told Mum the dog had taken off.'

Clara bet Sophie hadn't told Tamsin where she'd found Bailey.

'Mum suggested I should go down to the beach and look for you because that's where I'd most likely find Bailey. She said you would be at the beach hut.'

Clara pursed her lips. She knew what was coming next.

Sophie folded her arms and cocked her head to one side. 'Grandma, why didn't you tell us you had a beach hut?'

Ralph shifted his gaze to Clara wondering what she was going to say to that.

'Is this it?' Mia ran up to it and poked her head inside. 'This is sooo cool. Can I go inside?'

'Mia, why don't you help me wash up the plates?' Clara got up. She threw her breakfast companion an apologetic look suggesting breakfast was over.

He stood up and brushed the sand from his jeans hoping they could do this again; meet up for breakfast on the beach. He was about to walk over and ask her what her plans were tomorrow morning when Sophie stepped in front of him, blocking his way.

In typical blunt teenage fashion, Sophie gave him a wary look as she said, 'Who are you?'

'I'm Clara's friend.' He wanted to be something more, much more. Ralph looked at her grandchild. It should have occurred to him that she'd have a family to complicate matters. But sitting there on the beach he was lulled into a fantasy that all he had to do was win her heart and nothing else mattered.

Despite their arrival he managed a smile. Sophie had that steely determination he recognised from Clara's youth. He wanted to tell her how much she reminded him of Clara when she was young. Instead, he said, 'I see you like photography.'

Sophie had forgotten all about the camera she was holding in her hands. There was no point in trying to conceal it now. She glanced at the beach hut and noticed Grandma still washing up the plates with Mia. At least she hadn't spotted it. She would have gone up the wall catching her with another camera from the apartment. Like the one Grandma confiscated, Sophie discovered this also had film in it, so she'd borrowed it.

'I take a photography class at school. I'm practicing during the summer.' It wasn't far from the truth if she left out the part about borrowing the camera.

'Are you creating a portfolio of work to take back after the holidays?'

Sophie hadn't thought of that. 'Yes, that's what I'm doing. I want to travel the world as a photojournalist.'

'Really?'

Sophie nodded; surprised she'd told a perfect stranger. She hadn't informed anyone about her plans – not even Grandma. Although she did mention it to Dot. But then that didn't count because having dementia she wouldn't remember the conversation, let alone tell anybody else.

'Have you thought about joining the photography club?'

'There's a photography club here?'

He nodded. 'A famous photojournalist once joined many years ago when he was a boy.' Ralph neglected to mention that the boy he was referring to was him.

'Really?' Sophie's face dropped. 'I'd love to join, but I'm only here for the summer.'

'You could still go along.'

'You think so?'

'Uh-huh. It is a friendly club. They welcome new members all the time. It's where I met your grandmother.' The words were out there before he knew what he was saying. He stared at Sophie wondering if she'd taken in what he'd just said. She was busy fiddling with the camera in her hands. He glanced over at the beach hut. 'Well, I'd better get going. It was nice to meet you, Sophie.' He slipped on his shoes hoping Sophie didn't repeat what he'd revealed.

He was about to leave when he had a thought. 'Are you serious about becoming a professional photographer, Sophie?'

She looked up, her expression intense. 'Yes, I am.'

'Do you want a piece of advice?'

Sophie nodded enthusiastically.

'Take photos, experiment, learn and be creative. Now is your time to do just that. Find the artist within. Later, will come the hard part when you have to turn your art into a business to make a living.'

He smiled as he recalled those heady days when he was young, and it was all about the art of photography, before he had to grow up and earn an income.

'The most important thing to remember, Sophie, is that photojournalists tell other people's stories through their photographs.' He glanced at the camera in her hands and for the first time in months the urge to snap a picture returned. He knew who his subject would be. Oh, how he yearned to capture the moment when Clara stepped out on to the shore; he wanted to get a photo of her outside her beach hut.

Ralph lowered his eyes and caught Sophie staring at him. He looked at her grandchild and thought, I'm too late. It's not just the two of us anymore; they're here for the summer, and that changes everything.

He swallowed a lump in his throat and said, 'Sorry, I've got to go.'

Sophie stared after him as he walked briskly toward the promenade. 'Hey!' she called out.

He stopped some distance away and glanced in her direction.

'You never told me what it is you do.'

Ralph smiled. 'Can't you guess?' And with that, he turned on his heel and continued on his way.

Despite appearances, Sophie had been listening to every word he said. She wasn't stupid. 'You're him aren't you,' she said under her breath, 'you're the boy who became the famous photojournalist.'

She swung around and stared at her Grandmother. What was

it she said when she'd caught her upstairs in the apartment, something about having an interest in photography, once upon a time? Perhaps that's where they'd first met; at the club. She frowned. But when was that?

The old photograph from years ago of a young woman linking arms with two young men came to mind. Was this the beach where it was taken? Was he one of those guys?

Mia ran out of the hut straight up to her sister. 'You've got to come and see inside.'

Clara emerged, drying her hands on a tea towel, disappointed to discover he'd left without saying goodbye. She spotted him in the distance walking toward the promenade. She looked over at Sophie. 'Did he say anything before he took off?'

Sophie edged the camera behind her back. 'No.'

Mia grabbed her arm and pulled her forward. 'Come on, Soph!'

'Not now, Mia. I'm hungry. I'm going back to the house for breakfast.'

Clara's gaze shifted to the stove, and the cooler box where she'd put the remaining eggs, bacon, sausages and waffles. She looked at the girls. 'How about breakfast on the beach?'

Sophie had to cover her ears when Mia squealed with delight.

71

'You could have invited me,' said Tamsin as she approached.

Clara looked up at her daughter. She was not surprised Tamsin had made her way down to the beach. Clara guessed she would come looking for the girls, eventually.

'Here, take a seat.' Clara pointed to a spot on the sand beside her in front of the stove.

'I passed that man walking along the beach,' she added as she sat down. 'Did you meet up with him again?'

Clara frowned and felt she was being given the third degree. It was none of Tamsin's business. Nothing was going on between them of a romantic nature. A little voice in her head spoke, *don't you wish something was?*

'For your information,' replied Clara indignantly, 'I did not meet up with him. We merely bumped into each other again.' She left out the part about finding him sitting on the deckchair on the porch of her beach hut, along with the countless other times they had "bumped" into each other in the garden for breakfast over the last few weeks.

'I see,' Tamsin said flatly. The tone of her voice suggested she didn't believe her. Clara let it go. She did not want to argue in front of the girls. They were enjoying themselves.

'This is *way* cooler than going on holiday abroad and getting breakfast at the hotel bar,' said Mia.

'*Way* cooler,' repeated Sophie, surprising Clara by agreeing with her little sister.

Sophie glanced around the deserted beach. 'Shame Elliot isn't here.'

'No, it isn't,' Tamsin said.

Sophie threw her mother a sullen look.

'Anyway he was too busy putting that car back into the garage,' commented Tamsin.

Clara was pleased to learn about the car. It had been playing on her mind. She gave Tamsin a plate heaped with a cooked breakfast.

'Aren't you having any?'

'I've already had mine.'

Tamsin glanced down the beach. 'I see.'

Clara pursed her lips.

Mia looked at her mother. 'What about Evie? Shall I fetch her? I'm sure she'd like to eat breakfast on the beach too.'

Tamsin shook her head. 'Grandma wasn't the only one on a date this morning.'

Clara glanced at the girls. Neither of them was listening, she could tell. They were too busy tucking into their meal. Mia was also feeding Bailey bacon from her plate. Sophie was fiddling with something in her bag on her lap. Clara narrowed her eyes. Had she taken another camera? Making a mental note to have words with Sophie when they returned to the house. Clara thought of the camera *she* had borrowed and stowed away in a cupboard in the beach hut while washing up the plates. Perhaps she'd leave Sophie be. As long as she took it back in one piece what would be the harm?

Tamsin said, 'That police officer – Paul I think his name was – paid a call this morning.'

Clara's face went bright crimson. 'What did he want?'

'To take Evie out, I guess.'

Clara breathed a sigh of relief. All the same, she knew this could not go on – squatting in someone else's property. Clara looked from Mia to Sophie and finally at Tamsin, all eating their meal with no clue what dire straits their grandmother had found herself in. Which reminded Clara to ask, 'Tamsin, what time are you setting off home?'

'Who mentioned anything about going home today?'

Mia looked delighted. 'I don't want to go home – *ever*.'

'Me neither,' said Sophie casting her empty plate aside. She picked up her bag with the camera inside.

Clara's head swivelled from Tamsin to Sophie. Just how long did they think they were staying?

'Mum, can I join the photography club in town?'

Clara turned to her granddaughter. 'Where did you hear about the photography club?'

'From that man…'

Clara looked at Sophie. How on earth did he know about the club? It was not generally advertised but very much word of mouth. Despite spending so much time together over the last few weeks, it was surprising how little she knew about her friend.

'What else did he say?'

Sophie got up from the sand and shrugged at Grandma's question. 'Is it all right if I go back to the house?'

Tamsin looked up at her daughter. 'Yes, but I want you to stay away from Elliot.'

'Okay.'

Tamsin did a double-take, surprised Sophie had agreed. She expected some resistance and was ready for a full-on teenage rant about the unfairness of having her life dictated by her mother. She narrowed her eyes. Sophie was up to something. 'What are you going back to the house to do?'

'I'm taking some photos for my portfolio?'

Tamsin had no clue what she was on about. If it did not involve Elliot, she was happy.

Sophie gave her mum a sly smile feeling she'd got one over

her regarding the camera. She clutched the bag tightly and couldn't wait to get back to the house.

'Just one moment, young lady,' said Clara.

Sophie rolled her eyes and turned to face Grandma. If there was one person she couldn't hoodwink, it was her grandmother.

Clara glanced at Bailey. If Sophie had been in the apartment this morning, which Clara imagined she had – Bailey couldn't have opened the door himself – Clara bet she had walked out with something else besides the dog. Her eyes drifted to Sophie's bag.

Clara looked at Sophie a long moment. 'Go on then but be careful not to break anything.' She raised her eyebrows at her granddaughter hoping she got her meaning.

Sophie stole a glance at her bag and grinned. 'Okay, I promise I will be super-careful.'

'Good girl.'

Tamsin knitted her brow at their odd exchange.

Clara smiled at her granddaughter. She couldn't tell her off for borrowing someone else's camera equipment when she was guilty of doing the self-same thing.

'Bailey – *stay*,' said Mia when the dog stood up.

Bailey turned to Mia, licked her face which elicited a giggle, and slumped back down on the sand.

'Good dog.' Mia offered him the last slice of bacon from her plate. She watched him wolf it down before she said, 'Come on, Bailey, let's play a game of fetch.' She got up from the sand and threw a ball.

'This is nice.' Tamsin was sitting on the sand outside the beach hut staring at the sea lapping on to the shore in the distance. She glanced at her mother. 'How long have you owned the beach hut?'

Clara saw no point in lying. 'Since my parents died.'

Tamsin frowned. 'How long ago was that?'

Clara looked at Mia running along the beach, throwing Bailey the ball. Tamsin followed her gaze, reading her mind. 'Since I was Mia's age?'

Clara nodded.

'Why did we never come down here for holidays when I was little? I would have loved this.'

Clara sat watching Mia, waiting for the inevitable questions she'd avoided all these years.

'Why didn't they want anything to do with me?'

Clara didn't have to ask whom she was talking about. 'It's not that your grandparents didn't want to see you.'

'Then what? Did *you* stop them seeing me?'

'My father didn't wish to see *me* – that was the problem. Joe didn't help matters because he didn't want them in your life.'

'Why?'

'He was afraid of what they might come out with in front of you.'

'What do you mean?'

Clara hesitated. Without meaning to, she'd said enough already. She'd waited years for the opportunity to tell her the truth. The problem was the right moment never seemed to materialize. Clara had to face the fact that there would never be a right moment to tell her she'd lied to her all these years.

It would have been easier to tell her when she was little, barely old enough to comprehend what it meant – that the man she called Daddy wasn't her biological father. But as the years passed, it was Joe who didn't want Tamsin to know the truth. He was afraid she would search for her real father and love him less as a result.

Clara's thoughts strayed to the mess her life was now in, all because Joe had kept the truth from her – that he was intending to leave. Clara decided the time for secrets was over.

She reached out and took one of Tamsin's hands in hers.

Tamsin didn't flinch, but she threw her mother a questioning look as though Clara had lost her marbles.

Clara squeezed her hand. 'I don't want you to make any promises, but will you at least try not to hate me when I tell you what your father and I have kept from you since you were—' Clara swallowed, '—a baby.'

'Oh, my god,' said Tamsin, 'are you going to say I'm adopted? I always wondered why I had no brothers or sisters.'

'Er no, that's not it.'

'It's not?' said Tamsin studying her face.

'Not exactly,' replied Clara.

Tamsin let go of her hand. 'What do you mean – *not exactly*?'

Clara took a deep breath.

'Well?' Tamsin folded her arms and stared at Clara, unblinking.

'I just need you to know that this changes nothing, Tamsin. You're my daughter and… and Joe's still your father – kind of.'

72

'Is something the matter?'

Clara looked at him. 'Why do you ask?'

He brushed some sand off his trousers. 'Oh, I don't know. You seem quiet this morning.'

'Don't be silly, nothing's the matter. I was just thinking – that's all.'

'About what?'

Clara didn't want to spoil another glorious morning.

Every day this week she had ventured down to the shore with Bailey on the pretext of taking him for a walk. If Bailey still had reservations about his early morning walkies, the word *bacon* seemed to do the trick.

She looked forward to meeting him at the beach hut first thing in the morning. Now, she left it unlocked so he could cook breakfast. It was ready when she arrived. This morning was no exception. He didn't question why she no longer wanted to meet up at the house. And if he'd seen other people in and out of the property, he hadn't mentioned it.

Clara glanced his way, avoiding his question. She didn't want to tell him she'd been thinking about Tamsin and her reaction to finding out Joe was not her biological father. That was a personal matter which she could not talk about with him.

Far from being angry and resentful over what Clara and Joe

had kept from her all these years, she was empathetic when Clara told her the truth; Clara had run away to London when she found out she was pregnant, unable to face her parents and Tamsin's father. It was all too much after losing Tommy. Not that Clara told Tamsin about Tommy. That would be another soul-searching decision to enlighten her about the uncle she never knew.

She guessed why her daughter wasn't being judgemental; Tamsin had done a disappearing act herself, running away from Kevin and their financial problems. She'd then begged Clara to allow her and the children to stay on at The Gables just for a few more days. How could Clara refuse, even though she still hadn't put her in the picture? She had no business inviting her family to remain. But the upside for Clara was that she could spend more time with her friend before they cajoled her into returning home.

She'd expected Tamsin's next question – who was he? Who was her real father? A local boy she'd met, Clara told her. How could she tell Tamsin the whole truth; he wasn't just any boy – he was her one true love. Pregnant and in a fix, this meant that she had married Joe for reasons other than love.

Clara may have had her issues, but she would never have tricked Joe into believing Tamsin was his child. He was a good man, and it meant Tamsin would grow up with a father-figure in her life. How could she tell her that?

'Penny for your thoughts?'

Clara smiled. It would take a lot more than that for her to fess up about her past to a virtual stranger. Even though it seemed the more time spent in his company, the more she felt as though she had known him for years, not a matter of a few weeks over the summer during which their friendship had blossomed.

Clara put all thoughts of Tamsin and the past out of her mind – for now. She wanted to enjoy the moment before reality encroached on these perfect mornings. At some point soon she would sell the beach hut and leave Southwold; she couldn't stay squatting in The Gables forever.

Clara didn't want to think about that. She was thankful she had got to spend another week with him.

She looked across at Henry sitting the other side of the stove turning over the bacon. Bailey was close by watching his every move. Clara smiled. She couldn't express how she was feeling.

For the first time in years, she was where she wanted to be; she wasn't thinking about the beach or The Gables or Southwold but who she was with. Enjoying the company of somebody whom she'd just met without the added complications of a history or family or anything else that tethered her to the past. If she had her wish, this perfect moment together would last forever.

'Oh, no.' Ralph looked up at the dark clouds that had amassed overhead.

'We should—' she was about to say *take the breakfast inside* when out of nowhere a crack of thunder was followed by a torrential downpour.

Ralph took off his jacket and rushed over to Clara. He held the coat over them as they raced up the steps on to the veranda and dived into the hut. Despite Ralph's attempt to shelter them from the worst of the rain, they were both drenched.

'Oh, no!' exclaimed Clara when Bailey followed. She imagined what was coming next. He did what all dogs do when they get soaking wet; gave himself a good shake. A spray of water flew from his thick coat and pelted Ralph and Clara.

'Just great,' said Clara frowning at Bailey. 'As if I wasn't wet enough already!'

Bailey barked and wagged his tail.

Her breakfast companion laughed.

Clara joined in and laughed too.

As they both stood there soaking wet, smiling at one another, it occurred to her that for the first time in years she felt alive.

Their laughter subsided. In the confined space, as they were facing each other staring into each other's eyes, Bailey bumped into Clara and sent her forward into his arms. It was almost funny. She felt like a teenager meeting her sweetheart in the beach hut hoping her parents wouldn't discover them.

They didn't pull away, instead, they moved closer, much closer, and before they realised what was happening, were kissing like teenagers, urgently and passionately, as though they had to grab the moment.

Clara's eyes went wide. *Kissing like teenagers.* She broke free and took a step back.

He was standing there staring at her not saying a word.

Clara raised her hand and touched her lips with her fingertips. The only boy she had ever kissed in this beach hut was Ralph.

He reached for her. 'I'm sorry, I shouldn't have done that.'

Clara pulled away from his reach, backing towards the door with one question on her mind: why – why would he lie?

She stared at Ralph. All the while, she hadn't recognised him, but he must have remembered her the first time they met. But why not tell her the truth? Why did he say his name was Henry? What was he hiding?

Clara shook her head. This was all too much. She had to go. She opened the door and ran out into the torrential rain.

Ralph rushed to the doorway. 'Clara!' He called out. He saw her glance over her shoulder. She must have heard him calling out her name, but she kept running. Ralph stared after her with one thought on his mind – she knows.

Bailey padded over and stood at the door whining. He looked up at Ralph.

Ralph rolled his eyes at Bailey. 'What do you expect me to do? I can't go after her, not in that weather, not with my constitution. I'm likely to come down with pneumonia and snuff it before I make it right. You wouldn't want that – would you?'

He looked at the dog. Perhaps Bailey wouldn't mind if he

snuffed it, as he kicked him out of his home and sent him to live with strangers. That's when Ralph had an idea. 'Bailey, fetch her – go on.' It was stupid; Bailey would not understand—

Ralph watched in astonishment as Bailey bounded out the door and raced along the shore toward Clara. The dog circled her barking, and ran back toward the hut, stopping about half-way to see if she was following.

Hopeful she would get the message Ralph saw her stop and turn around. He held his breath. She seemed to be considering it. He closed his eyes and prayed that when he next looked, she would be making her way back to him.

He stood in the open doorway, the wind and rain lashing his face, and thought he heard footsteps on the wooden veranda. Ralph opened his eyes and saw Bailey, ears drooped, looking up at him. Ralph heaved a sigh. 'Well, at least you tried. Come in.' He moved away from the doorway and let the dog inside out of the rain. He glanced down the beach. Clara had reached the promenade. Without a backwards glance, she continued walking.

He turned around and got a spray of water for his troubles. Bailey was giving himself a good shake. Ralph glared at him. 'Thanks a bunch.'

Ralph found some matches and lit both rings of the portable gas hob. He thanked his lucky stars it wasn't empty. 'I'll have this place warmed up in no time.' He put the kettle on to heat up water for tea. A quick rummage around the hut unearthed two clean beach towels. Ralph looked at Bailey. 'Come here.'

Bailey lowered his head and put his tail between his legs, looking at Ralph as if to say *am I in trouble?*

Ralph reached for the dog, spread the towel over his back and rubbed him dry.

Bailey licked Ralph's hands and face and rolled over.

'You silly dog, don't think I will tickle your tummy.' Then he sneezed. 'Oh dear, it's time I got out of these clothes before I catch a cold.'

Ralph left the towel on the floor.

Bailey rearranged it before he settled down on his make-shift bed.

'That's damp, you know,' said Ralph as he pulled off his wet clothes.

Bailey didn't seem to mind.

Ralph found a small clothes airier and hung his wet garments up to dry. He wrapped himself up in the other large beach towel and sat down with a hot tea and a biscuit from a packet he found in the cupboard.

Ralph stared forlornly into drink and frowned. 'I should have told her. Why did I say my name was Henry?' He glanced over at Bailey. 'Don't answer that.'

He knew why he did it; she'd left him once before, years ago. He did not understand why. Did it have something to do with losing Tommy? Did she blame him because she was with him that night and not at the party? That's what he believed.

All these weeks since her return he'd wanted to ask her why she fled to London, but he was afraid. Afraid if he told her who he was, she would leave him again. He couldn't risk it. But it had happened anyway.

Ralph sat there shaking his head at Bailey. 'What's a man to do – eh? You're damned if you do, and damned if you don't.' He knew eventually she would guess the truth. He just hadn't expected it to happen in the very beach hut where they had their first teenage kiss all those years ago.

Ralph downed his tea, broke his biscuit in half and tossed a piece at Bailey. He watched Bailey sniff the cookie and then wolf it down. Ralph's eyes drifted to his wet clothes. He reckoned he would still be here for a few hours until the rain subsided.

Ralph got up, pulled the beach towel around him, and shuffled over to the kitchen area. Depositing his mug on the worktop he turned and caught his reflection in a small mirror hanging on the wall.

'Good God!' Ralph stepped closer and peered at his reflection. 'Is that what I *really* look like?' He tugged at his beard and lifted a lock of his grey hair which almost reached his shoulders. It was one thing resembling a homeless squatter, but after that kiss, when she realized he was Ralph…

He shook his head. What must she have thought? Was she so disgusted by what had become of her teenage sweetheart she fled in horror? He wouldn't be surprised. He tried to imagine if the boot had been on the other foot; if it was Clara who was homeless, penniless and down on her luck. It raised the question: what was she doing squatting at The Gables? And did it have something to do with her husband – but she had family and a home to go back to. He understood the time they had spent together over the past few weeks couldn't last forever – or could it?

He stared at his reflection. She didn't know the *real* Ralph; all she knew was the homeless squatter who lived in the outhouse at the bottom of the garden. She had no idea he was the famous photographer who had travelled the world and owned The Gables. He could offer Clara a good life, a comfortable life -- if she'd only give him a second chance. He wanted, more than anything, to rekindle their teenage love affair.

If someone told him he'd meet Clara again years later and there would still be that spark, he would have scoffed. They were just kids back then; their lives had barely begun. What would they have known of love? But if these last few weeks meant anything, it was that when it came to affairs of the heart, time was of no consequence. She was his first love, the love of his life, and always would be. If only he had a chance to tell her.

Ralph nodded his head. It was time to come clean – about everything.

'Come clean!' Ralph's eyebrows shot up. He turned around and looked at Bailey. 'I know what I need to do.'

Baileys ears twitched, listening to Ralph's voice.

He gathered his clothes together. They were still wet, but that didn't matter. 'I need to clean myself up,' he said as he pulled on his jeans, 'have a good shave,' he did up the buttons on his shirt, 'and get rid of this!' Ralph swept his long hair away from his face as he grabbed his trainers. 'And these!' He grimaced as he slipped them on. His trainers stunk. He looked down at Bailey. 'Then I will tell Clara she can stay at The Gables as long as she likes.'

Ralph hadn't factored in her family turning up. When he first saw them up at the house and guessed who they were, he had not let on that he'd seen them. He was afraid if he made a fuss, they would all pack up and leave – Clara included.

'I must tell Clara I own The Gables.' Ralph was striding to the door when he came to an abrupt halt. He shook his head. 'Well, isn't that the mother of all bad ideas. If she wasn't mad at me already for not telling her who I am, imagine how pissed off she will be when she finds out I've been pretending to be a squatter.'

Ralph frowned. It wasn't his intention to lead her down the garden path, so-to-speak. It wasn't his fault she'd turned up out of the blue and discovered him living in the outhouse. She'd just assumed he was squatting, but he hadn't corrected that misconception. Ralph brushed that thought to one side. All he wanted to do was show Clara he wasn't the man she thought he was – and that started with his appearance.

He stood there in his wet clothes and recalled the two suitcases packed with laundered clothes and his toiletry bag the hotel staff had brought up to the house and left in the apartment above the garage. He'd told them about the key above the door to the studio and asked them to deposit his stuff in the walk-in wardrobe.

Ralph smiled. 'Shall we go home, Bailey? What do you think?' It was a funny thing to say. He'd been home for months – in a manner of speaking. However, Ralph knew it was time to leave the outhouse. He had something to live for, *someone* to live for. He couldn't move back into the house. That's where Clara and her family were staying. He wouldn't dream of intruding. Besides, the last thing he wanted was for his squatters to leave. He smiled when he thought of his apartment over the garage, his own private space all set up for his return.

'Come on, boy, let's go home.'

73

Ralph was on his way home with a spring in his step and a squelch in his trainers when he slowed. The rain had subsided although he was not bothered now. It wouldn't be long, and he would be dressed in freshly laundered clothes. The reason for his reticence as he approached the house was the looks he was getting from passers-by.

He stopped at the gates to his property. What if he bumped into Clara before he cleaned up his act? What if she caught him looking like this? What if her grandchildren bumped into him? He had visions of them all packing up and leaving. Perhaps that's what they were doing right now.

Ralph still did not make a move to open the gate. If he tried to explain that he owned The Gables, he doubted she would trust him. He'd done that once before when he first discovered her on his property. She didn't believe him then, why would she accept that now?

He felt embarrassed by his appearance. That hadn't bothered him before. So what had changed? It was the fact that now he was aware she knew who he was. The thought of her staring at him, wondering what happened to that young man she once knew when all she saw was this tramp, was humiliating. Ralph backed away from the gates realising he couldn't risk it.

He wanted to walk up to his house like the person who

arrived back in Southwold six months ago, not the man who'd by all-intents-and-purposes had some sort of breakdown. But how was he going to get round the fact that his laundered clothes and toiletry bag were in *there?*

Ralph slapped his forehead when he remembered. 'Of course!' He put his hand in his wet trouser pocket and brought out his sodden leather wallet. There was no cash, only his bank cards. He looked down at Bailey. 'This is all we need. Come on, we've got some shopping to do.'

Before Ralph even stepped into one of those independent boutique clothes shops in the town, he had to visit the barbers. His first stop though was a cash machine if he didn't want to risk being escorted to the door.

Two hours later, Ralph stepped out of a clothing shop near the hairdressers a new man. He stood in the doorway. Nobody batted an eyelid as they passed a man in his sixties dressed in dark blue chinos and a light blue shirt. He had a cream suit jacket casually draped over one arm.

For the first time in months, Ralph blended in although, strangely, he felt self-conscious. He put it down to the fact he was no longer hiding behind his beard and long hair. Ralph rubbed his chin. He didn't remember the last time his face felt this smooth to the touch.

He'd never visited a barber to have a shave before. Then there was his hair. They'd done a marvellous job. Although it did not start well. They'd sat him in a chair and done what he imagined they did with all their customers, had a chat about what Ralph was looking for regarding a hairstyle. He'd been rude, and just told them to get on with it. Ralph didn't have time to discuss it. He just wanted it washed and cut.

Then as they were cutting his wet hair, it occurred to him he could end up with a crew cut for all he knew. When they finished blow-drying, styling and spraying, which he thought was a bit excessive, they revealed the new Ralph.

He'd sat there staring at his reflection and had no idea what came over him. Ralph burst into tears. A cup of tea and a digestive biscuit later, delivered from the manager who was getting in a flap because he assumed his new client hated his hairstyle, Ralph calmed down. He told the manager that the young man had done a brilliant job with his thick, grey hair, layering it and adding some highlights. It took years off his face.

The stylist slipped in a comment about how it was such a transformation that whoever he was doing this for – he'd guessed there was a woman – she would be one surprised lady. That did it. Ralph thought of Clara and broke down.

Standing outside the clothes shop, after seeing himself in the long mirror inside, his confidence was growing by leaps and bounds at the prospect of turning up at the house looking like this. He just hoped he wasn't too late, and she hadn't packed her bags and left. Ralph looked down at the plastic carrier bag containing his old clothes. He intended to dump them in a bin, the first chance he got. In the other hand was a new Panama hat. The hat wasn't essential, but he'd always wanted one. Ralph placed it in on his head and set off.

He walked along the street about a hundred yards before he remembered something. 'Crap!' He did a quick about-turn and strode back, breathing a sigh of relief when he saw Bailey still sitting outside the shop. He frowned at the dog as he neared. Why didn't Bailey follow? It wasn't as though he was on a lead and tied to a post.

'Bailey?'

The dog didn't run up to Ralph as he had expected. It took a moment for Ralph to realise what was wrong. He lifted his Panama hat and knelt. 'It's me – you silly dog.' Ralph looked different. He smelled different. That's why he'd walked straight out the store without Bailey noticing.

Bailey's tail wagged furiously as he rushed over and licked Ralph's face.

'That's quite enough of that!' Ralph got out his new handkerchief and wiped his face. 'Come on.' He stood up, his new shoes squeaking as the leather stretched. He looked down at the dog. 'Henry is gone, old boy. Let's go home and introduce Clara to Ralph, the man I hope she can find it in her heart to forgive for that little deception.'

Ralph knew it was no small thing to lie to someone like that and was not malicious. He wasn't trying to hoodwink her when he told her his name was Henry. It's just that when he realised she hadn't recognised him, he didn't want the past to rear its head.

In hindsight, it was a stupid thing to do. But then there were other things he'd done that, in retrospect, he wished he hadn't. Tommy came to mind. He should have told her the truth. He should have broken his promise to Tommy, but to his lasting regret, he did not.

As he walked along the street thinking about his best friend, Ralph's newfound confidence slipped. What if she found out? Ralph shook his head. How could she find out? There was little point dwelling on a problem that would never come to pass, so he dismissed that anxiety and quickened his pace.

He couldn't wait to get home and see the look on Clara's face when she met the famous photographer who owned The Gables. He could only imagine what she would say when she discovered the truth.

74

Ralph had rehearsed several possibilities for the first words out of his mouth when he returned home. *What the hell* was not one of them.

He had turned up at his property to find the gates wide open. As he walked up the drive, surprised no one had bothered to shut them, he was confronted by the sight of four police cars parked on the driveway, their blue lights flashing. 'What the hell—!?'

Ralph didn't have time to finish the sentence when a hand slapped his back, sending the wind right out of his sails. He turned around to find his next-door neighbour standing behind him. 'Ah, you're back!' He exclaimed. 'And just in the nick of time. I thought you would never return!'

'What is going on?' said Ralph.

'I called the police.'

'You did what!' Ralph shook his head. 'Why – what's happened?'

'Over the last few months, since you've been away, there have been some strange goings-on at your property.'

Ralph groaned. That's all he needed. A nosy, busy-body neighbour.

'I was walking out of my house and glanced through the iron gates into your grounds and spotted something. Well, *someone* actually.'

Ralph stared at him.

'I thought it was just my imagination. It was after I bumped into you that one time before you left on your last assignment abroad. You told me you had instructed an estate agent to find a house-sitter who would mind your home while you were away because you were afraid of squatters.'

Ralph vaguely remembered that conversation. Now, he wished he hadn't spoken his mind.

'I thought nothing of it until I noticed someone in the grounds of your property. But I didn't want to jump to conclusions. Maybe you had found a gardener. That was until I saw him this morning.'

'Who?'

'The squatter.'

'What are you talking about?' Ralph said, trying to remain calm.

'The man who I suspect has been living in your outhouse.'

'What do you mean?' Ralph intoned.

'I was pulling my curtains when I noticed him standing outside the gates.' He smiled. 'My wife kept telling me he was just a figment of my imagination until she spotted him too. To my knowledge, he'd never used the front entrance before. I reckon he found the gap through the hedge into your back garden. Why he was using the main entrance, I do not understand. But there he was.' He grinned at Ralph. 'I could see him as clearly as I see you now.'

Ralph could feel his face growing hot with embarrassment beneath his Panama hat as his neighbour peered at him. He cleared his throat. 'What was he like?'

'He was tall, about your height, with a beard and long, straggly hair. His clothes looked wet as though he had got caught in that thunderstorm this morning.'

Ralph moved the carrier bag with the dirty, sodden clothes inside behind his back.

'When I looked away to pull the other curtain, he was gone. He must have whipped inside and closed the gate. So, being a concerned neighbour, and a founding member of the neighbourhood watch, I did what any good friend would do – I called the police.'

Ralph looked at his neighbour. Since when had they become good friends? He hardly knew the man. Trust him to have one of those neighbours who couldn't keep his nose out of other people's business.

Ralph stepped forward, intending to sort out this misunderstanding, but his neighbour caught his arm. 'Let the police do their job.'

Ralph was about to tell him where to go, when he added, 'Just as well they sent *four* police cars.'

Ralph looked at him quizzically.

'The homeless tramp wasn't the only one living here. It turns out you had a house-full.'

Oh no. Ralph raised his eyebrows. *Everyone was home.*

'It's what we were afraid of…'

Ralph glared at him. 'We?'

'Well, this is a nice, quiet area with retired people or those with second homes. We don't want, you know, common riff-raff taking up residence in our street – now do we.'

Ralph looked at the man's hand holding his arm. 'Get off me.'

'Oh, pardon me.' He let go. 'Ah, is that the front door opening?'

Ralph's head swivelled toward the house.

'While we've been having a nice little chat,' said the neighbour, 'they've been rounding them all up. Oh, here they come.'

The first person to be escorted off the premises was a young woman; it was Evie.

Evie was pulling on her coat. 'I'm telling you, officer, I have done nothing wrong. Where's Paul? I want to speak to him.'

Ralph watched her being bundled into the back of a waiting squad car. His eyes shifted to the front door. A policewoman stepped out of the house escorting two more women. They were arguing.

'Mum, what in god's name is going on?'

'Look, Tamsin, I didn't put you in the picture.'

'Put me in the picture? What on earth are you talking about?'

'Ladies, can you step this way, please,' said the police officer motioning towards the car.

Ralph's eyebrows shot up the moment he saw her. 'Clara!'

Bailey raced over to greet her.

Clara looked up but didn't recognise him. Ralph knew why. She was looking for the vagrant, not the man dressed in smart-casual attire, wearing a Panama hat.

The neighbour had hold of Ralph's arm again. 'Where are you going?'

Ralph seethed. 'I am sorting this mess out.'

Once again, he let go of Ralph's arm.

Ralph overheard Clara talking to a police officer, 'I can explain…'

'You can explain down the station, Luv,' said the officer as he opened the car door. Tamsin and the two girls were being escorted to another vehicle.

He stepped forward and was stopped by a police officer. 'There's nothing to see here, Sir. Go home and take your neighbour with you.'

Ralph looked at the officer blocking his way. 'But I *am* home.'

For a split second he forgot about his transformation from homeless Henry this morning. The officer wouldn't believe he owned The Gables.

'Hey, you're that photographer that lives here. I've seen your photos on the front of National Geographic.'

Well, whoop-de-do thought Ralph. The famous

photographer has returned. He didn't give a fig about that. Next, he'll be asking for his autograph.

The officer produced a notebook and a pen. 'Would you mind…?'

Ralph gave him a cold, hard stare. 'I want you to release—'

'Ah, no can do, I'm afraid. I've got my orders. You must take it up with my superior at the station.'

'But this is my house *goddammit.* I want nobody arrested.'

The female officer waved at the squad car to get a move on. He turned to Ralph. 'We have to go.'

'But—'

'Hey, what's that dog doing in the back seat?' barked the officer, marching towards the car. 'Where did he come from?'

Clara, sitting in the back, said, 'Oh, he's a stray. I found him—'

Ralph overheard Clara. He shouted out, 'He's not a stray. Bailey, *come*!'

Bailey put a paw on Clara's arm as if to say, *I'm sorry, but I can't come with you this time,* and then jumped out of the car.

Ralph stood on the gravel with Bailey by his side as the police cars disappeared down the driveway. Clara turned in her seat and glanced out the back window. Her eyes went wide when she realised who he was. 'It's Ralph!'

The officer who had been speaking to Ralph replied. 'Yes, he's the owner of The Gables. I really want his autograph. He's quite the celebrity in Southwold, you know. He's travelled the world and taken some amazing photos. They've been in the National Geographic. God, I love that magazine.'

Clara turned in her seat and looked at the officer. 'What did you just say?'

'I really want his autograph.'

'No, before that.'

'Um… he owns The Gables.'

'He's the photojournalist who lives in that house?'

'Yes. I said that already.'

She folded her arms over her chest and narrowed her eyes.

'Clara, are you all right?' asked Evie. She was sitting next to her on the back seat and had noticed her friend's black look.

Clara was *not* all right. She was fuming. She couldn't believe he'd strung her along and lied to her – about *everything*. Why didn't he tell her who he really was? Why didn't he tell her he owned the house?

All this time she'd been worried the owner might turn up and discover her squatting in his property when he was there all along, at the bottom of the garden, *pretending* he was homeless, penniless. She thought they were kindred spirits united in adversity.

She glanced over her shoulder at his sprawling house. What was he doing living in his outhouse like a homeless person when he was anything but?

'Kindred spirits?' Clara said under her breath. She snorted. 'Not anymore.'

75

Ralph looked at Bailey. 'Right, let's sort this mess out.'

The dog barked and wagged his tail.

Ralph was standing on the gravel driveway. The police cars had left. He reached for his phone to call the station and speak to the officer in charge. He was dropping all charges and wanted them released as soon as possible.

'Oh, damn and blast it!' He'd forgotten how iffy the reception was here. 'Seriously – at a time like this?' He frowned. 'Okay, we will go down to the station in person.'

Once again, Bailey barked and wagged his tail.

Ralph turned toward the garage, hoping the keys were still in the ignition after Clara's little jaunt down the driveway the other day, when he thought he saw someone in the garden. 'Hey – you!'

The older man paused at the sound of Ralph's voice but didn't turn around.

'Yes, you,' he shouted after him. 'Stop!'

The stranger picked up his pace.

'Wait!' Ralph called out, following him. Through the trees he spotted him again at the bottom of the garden.

Ralph ran down the narrow path beside the vegetable patch. The track only led one place – the outhouse. He stopped in front of the door. The man he had seen a moment ago must be inside. Against his better judgement, he decided to confront him. Ralph couldn't fail to see the irony. He'd only just moved out of the outhouse. Did he have a squatter for real?

Ralph barged into the outhouse. 'I don't know what you think you're doing here but—' He stopped dead. There was nobody else there. He shook his head. 'I could have sworn…'

He knelt and looked under the camp bed. Standing, he glanced at the window with the make-shift curtain. It was too small for a man to climb through. 'Where the hell did he go?'

Stopping in front of the easel he stared at the oil painting of Pollensa old town in Mallorca with its honey-coloured villas and orange and lemon groves. He knew every inch of that picture, every brush-stroke. He remembered Clara and Tommy showing him photographs of the place where they took vacations before he visited on their eighteenth birthday.

He slumped down on the camp bed and rubbed his forehead. For a moment there, he thought… Ralph shook his head at such an absurd idea. Tommy was gone, and he was never coming back. This whole business with seeing Clara again was playing tricks on his mind, that and his guilty conscience for not telling her what really happened the night of the party. Perhaps it was time he disclosed the truth.

He glanced at his mobile phone. There was still no signal. 'Right, the car it is then.' As he reached the door, it swung open and almost knocked him over. 'Tommy?'

The young man stepped back in surprise. 'Who's Tommy – and who are you?'

Ralph sighed. 'Elliot – it's me.'

Elliot looked at him warily.

'I helped you fix the roof on the beach hut, remember?'

'Bloody hell!' Elliot grinned looking him up and down. 'I didn't recognize you. Well, don't you clean up good. Did you win the lottery or something?'

'Or something…' He didn't have time to get into that right now. 'What are you doing in the outhouse?'

'Well, let's just say I'm *persona non grata* up at the house.'

Ralph arched an eyebrow.

'It's all because I wanted to take Sophie out in the car.' Elliot quickly added, 'but I didn't. Clara caught me and went ballistic, so I have been keeping a low profile. I came across the outhouse. As you seem to spend a lot of time down at the beach hut, I've been hanging around here. Hope you don't mind.'

'Look, I've got to go,' said Ralph.

'What's going on?'

Ralph sighed. Elliot had no idea what had gone on up at the house. 'I'll explain later when I have sorted things out. Hang tight and I will bring them all back, I promise.'

'What are you talking about?'

Ralph left Elliot standing in the doorway with a bemused expression on his face as he ran down the path toward the garage.

76

Elliot was sitting on the camp bed reading a book when Ralph returned. He'd found his car with the keys in the ignition, thanked his lucky stars he didn't have to search for them – and being conscious of the time spent wasted at the outhouse – sped down the drive. As soon as he was clear of the gates, his phone beeped. He had reception.

He had pulled over and rang the police station to drop all charges. He had also told them to give Clara a message that they were to stay put; he was on his way to collect them.

Ralph stood in the doorway to the outhouse feeling utterly miserable. 'They're gone.'

Elliot lowered the book he was reading. 'Who?'

'Oh, not your sister, she's with her fella.'

Elliot grimaced.

'But Clara and her family have left.'

He'd made it to the police station only to discover Clara had got his message but refused to wait. They were already on their way to the train station. When Ralph reached the platform, the train was disappearing in the distance.

'I guess the house-sitting job finished,' commented Elliot.

Ralph was surprised. He still had no idea what Clara had been up to or what had happened all because of that nosy neighbour.

Elliot sat up with a start. 'That means the owner will return.'

Ralph looked from Bailey lying at the end of the camp bed by Elliot's feet to the book he'd been reading by H. Rider Haggard. 'Have you been enjoying my novel, Elliot?'

Elliot glanced at the book. 'Yes, very much. I didn't think adventure yarns were my thing, but this is good. You should…. read… it.' Elliot stared at Ralph and swallowed. 'Oh crap. Look, I don't want any trouble.'

'Calm down, son.' He walked over, picked up the novel and handed it to Elliot. 'This is one of my favourites.'

Elliot took the book. 'You're him – aren't you.'

'Him – who?'

'The famous photojournalist who travels the world.'

'Not anymore.' Ralph couldn't call himself a photographer if he was incapable of taking photos. He looked at Elliot. 'Do you need a job?'

'Pardon?'

Ralph looked around the outhouse. It was gloomy and damp, and not fit for human habitation – he knew that. He didn't want Elliot sleeping here or down at the beach hut. But it wasn't just about altruism; Ralph needed someone to keep an eye on his house even though he was meant to be moving back in. 'I'm offering you a job.'

'Doing what?'

'House sitting?'

'You wish to pay me to live in your home?'

'Yeah – why not?' He wouldn't be moving back into the main house himself.

To his surprise, Elliot shook his head. 'I can't sit around doing nothing. I've spent the summer renovating the beach hut.' His face lit up. 'I noticed a drain pipe leaking. You need me to fix it?'

Ralph shrugged. 'Sure.'

'I could do a spot of gardening. I like to earn my keep.'

'Knock yourself out.'

Elliot's face dropped. 'Do you need references?'

Ralph smiled and shook his head. He'd always been a good judge of character. 'No, you're fine, but I'm afraid the job won't be for that long though. I am considering putting The Gables up for sale.'

'Oh.' Elliot had a question. 'Why would you give me a job anyhow – you don't really know me from Adam?'

Ralph walked to the door and turned around. 'Because you remind me of someone I once knew a long time ago.' He glanced across the room at the painting on the easel. It was still there. He hadn't imagined it. Except something was… different. He wandered over to take a closer look.

'Oh, about that…' began Elliot.

Ralph stared at him in surprise. 'You did this?'

Elliot looked nervously at Ralph. 'I realise I had no right to touch your things.' He glanced at the book in his hand. 'But it's such a beautiful painting I just felt compelled to do something. I cleaned up the canvas as best I could and set to work.'

'You paint?'

Elliot shrugged. 'Yep, ever since I was a little boy.' He pointed at the canvas. 'That side was so badly scorched that I had to make a guess from some unfinished villas what the painter was trying to say.'

Ralph looked at him. 'What do you mean – what the painter was trying to say?'

Elliot smiled. 'Well, every picture tells a story – does it not?'

Ralph nodded thinking of his own vocation – photography. He'd never seen the finished painting, only the half-burnt canvas the police had given him amongst his wife's personal effects after the explosion that took her life. He stood there admiring the scene. 'You're good – do you know that?'

Elliot shook his head. 'I can't really take the credit.'

'Don't do that. Always believe in yourself, because if you

don't no one else will.' Ralph had an idea. 'Have you got any of your own paintings?'

Elliot frowned. 'Back at my sister's boyfriend's flat in London. Or ex-boyfriend now. He's probably chucked them out.'

'Then paint more. I have contacts in the art world who could sell your work.'

'Sell my paintings?'

For a moment, Ralph felt Elliot would take offence at the mention of selling his art.

'You think I might make a few quid?' he said, surprised.

'You might make a lot more than just a few quid if I got you into the right gallery.'

'You'd do that for me?' Elliot's face lit up before his expression darkened. 'I can't.'

'Why not?' Ralph regretted that question. 'I'm sorry, it's none of my business.'

'No, it's fine. The problem is, materials are expensive – paints, canvas. I haven't got any money left to buy them. No materials mean no paintings – simple as that.'

'Tell me how much and I will write you a cheque.'

'I don't want any handouts.'

That's what Ralph expected him to say. 'Call it an investment. We can be business partners. I will take a percentage of your sales.'

'How do you know my paintings will sell?'

Ralph looked at the canvas. 'I'm no expert, but I bet you this cheque,' he held it up, 'that they will sell.' He stared at the painting. 'In fact, I'd very much like to buy this one.'

'It's not mine to sell. Hey, what are you talking about, you already own the painting.'

'I do.' Ralph rolled his eyes at his own stupidity. He put it down to the fact it had been one of those days; Clara had discovered who he was, and now she was gone. 'All the same, I should compensate you for restoring my painting.' He turned to

Elliot. 'I can't believe you did this from memory. When did you last visit Mallorca?'

'Mallorca?' Elliot walked over and joined Ralph in front of the painting. 'Is that where this is?'

'You're kidding! You've never been?' Ralph looked at him in utter amazement. 'The way you conveyed the light, the vibrancy of the colours.' Elliot had not only completed the canvas, but he had also touched up what remained of the original painting.

'The original was good, but you have the colours, the atmosphere, the light down to a *T*.'

'I have?' said Elliot in surprise. 'So you've been there?'

'Yes. A long time ago, but I still recognise it. There's a town at the foot of the Tramuntana Mountains called Pollensa.'

Despite the number of times he'd stared at the painting as he drifted off to sleep there was a detail in the picture that had eluded him – until now. High above the rooftops in the mountain range in the distance, Ralph spied what appeared to be a building. He turned to Elliot. 'What is that?' He pointed at it.

Elliot stepped forward. 'It was the one part of the painting that was a complete mystery when I first set eyes on it. I call it *the place in the clouds*. It is so faint you can hardly see it, but it's there, nonetheless. Then as I was painting, it came to me; I had an idea it could be a monastery high in the mountain range.'

'A monastery?'

'Yeah. If you look closely, I'm sure that's a bell tower.'

Ralph no longer had the eyesight of a young man in his twenties. He whipped out his glasses and put them on. He studied the small almost imperceptible building peeking out from the clouds. 'Yes, you're right.'

Elliot turned to Ralph. 'You said you've been there, to Pollensa.'

Ralph nodded. 'It was a long time ago.'

Do you remember something like that in the… what did you call them, Tramuntana Mountains?'

Ralph took off his glasses. He tried to think. The road up the Serra de Tramuntana mountain range back then was treacherous. It wasn't somewhere you ventured unless you were a local and familiar with the terrain. But was there a monastery up there? It was possible, but he wasn't sure.

'I'll google,' said Elliot getting out his phone. A moment later he held up the phone and grinned. 'It exists,' he said triumphantly.

Ralph stared at the photo of a honey-coloured monastery obscured by cloud cover high. His eyes shifted from the image to the painting and back again. 'Well, I'll be…' he said before he realised, 'You've got reception!'

'Oh, yeah. Weird – huh. Who would have thought you'd get mobile reception at the bottom of the garden?'

Ralph rolled his eyes. He hadn't thought to check his phone in here. Not that it would have made any difference. She would still have left – he knew that now.

Ralph tossed Elliot the keys to the house. 'Just in case Clara has walked out with the key and forgotten to leave it under the flower pot.' It was a distinct possibility. He didn't add the part about her being bundled in the back of a police car and escorted off his property. Doubtless, Elliot would soon find out about the whole sorry episode from his sister.

'I'll have some canvas and paints delivered to the house.'

'I rather fancy painting here, if you don't mind.'

'Not at all.' Ralph cast his gaze around the outhouse. It would make a nice, quiet studio if they fixed it up with heat and light. He turned to go.

'Don't you need these?' asked Elliot looking at the keys in his hand.

Ralph shook his head. 'I'll be in the apartment over the garage if you need anything.'

77

Ralph walked up the garden and put his phone back in his pocket. He wasn't paying attention to his footing when he heard a yelp. 'What the…!' It sounded like a dog. It wasn't Bailey because he'd left him with Elliot. He glanced down and noticed a small dog licking his tail. The dog looked up at Ralph and growled.

'How in heaven's name did you expect me to see you lying in the long grass,' exclaimed Ralph, staring at the little dog.

'Winston! Where are you?'

Ralph turned around at the sound of a woman's voice and saw the dog running off toward the house.

He followed. Up ahead, was an elderly, overweight woman wearing a wide-brimmed straw hat. She was kneeling in the garden by one of his flower beds with a trowel in her hand.

Ralph came to a halt in front of her. 'Who are you?'

She stopped what she was doing, looked up and wiped her brow. 'I'm Dorothy.'

'What are you doing here, Dorothy?'

'Clearing the borders of weeds – what does it look like?'

Ralph was about to rephrase the question when she said, 'Why – who's asking?'

He sighed. 'Never mind.' Whoever she was, it looked as though Clara had left one of her party behind. Ralph's eyes went wide. Wasn't this the perfect excuse to contact her?

He was ready to make the call when he realised he did not have her number and had no idea where she lived in London. Ralph looked at the elderly woman called Dorothy. She would know how to get in touch with Clara, but right now she was happily digging away in his flower bed. The trouble was he didn't want her packing up her stuff and leaving. He wanted Clara to come back. Or he could take Dorothy to her. What a stroke of good luck because this meant, one way or another, he hadn't seen the last of Clara and, whether she liked it or not, she hadn't seen the last of him.

Dorothy looked up. 'Are you still here? What do you want?'

He doffed his Panama hat. 'I'm Ralph, can I get you anything? A cup of tea? A glass of cold lemonade?'

Dorothy put her trowel down. 'Now you mention it, I am parched.'

'Why don't you take a seat,' Ralph pointed at the garden chair, 'and I'll bring you out a drink. What would you like?'

Dorothy thought about it. 'I would normally go for a nice cup of tea…'

Ralph smiled. That was good news because he didn't have any—

'But a cold glass of lemonade sounds just the ticket.'

Ralph kept the smile plastered on his face. 'Lemonade it is, then. I'll be back in two ticks.' He put his Panama hat on, strolled into the kitchen, and then raced through the hall and out the front door. Hot-footing it to the garage he jumped into his car. It would take him five minutes to nip to the high street and grab a bottle of lemonade. Ralph put the keys in the ignition, and it roared into life.

'What in God's name—?' Something appeared from under the car and pounced on to the bonnet. It peered through the windscreen at Ralph, eliciting one almighty hiss.

'Where did you come from?' He guessed it was a neighbour's cat who had run into the garage and found a quiet spot beneath his car. He put his hand on his chest. 'Good grief, you gave me quite a fright.'

Ralph tapped the accelerator and the engine roared, sending the cat fleeing in fright.

'Good riddance,' said Ralph as he spotted the cat's tail rounding the garage door before disappearing. He moved the car out of the garage and slowly glided past his front door. He did a double-take when he saw the cat sitting on the doormat as though it lived here.

'Oh, come on! Not you as well!' Ralph rolled his eyes and caught the cat in his rear-view mirror curling up in a furry ball going to sleep. Did the cat belong to Dorothy? Ralph rolled his eyes at the irony. He remembered when he first returned from abroad and checked into the hotel in town. He'd wished he wasn't returning home to an empty house.

His thoughts turned to Clara. He couldn't help it. As usual things in his life never played out quite how he would have envisaged. Ralph tried not to think about that, but the scene at the police station kept replaying in his head…

❖

'What do you mean she's gone? What – all of them?' Ralph glanced around the empty reception area and turned back to the desk sergeant. 'But I told the captain I was coming to pick her up?'

'Unless we charged her with something, she was free to go. We couldn't hold her here and if I remember rightly, someone,' glaring at Ralph, 'decided not to press charges.'

'But . . . but where did she go?'

'Paul gave them a lift to the train station.'

'The train station?'

'Oh, there he is now.'

Ralph's head swivelled around as a police officer strode in. 'Where's Evie?' he asked the desk sergeant.

'She's gone to powder her nose.'

A young woman walked out of the ladies toilets. It was Elliot's sister.

Paul said to her, 'Right, I will give you a lift to mine and make up the spare bedroom.'

'I've got to find Elliot. He won't know where I am.'

Ralph stepped in. 'Elliot is back at the house.'

'Who are you?' Paul and Evie said in unison.

It was the desk sergeant's turn to step in. 'This is Ralph Halstead. He's the owner of The Gables.'

'Did you have us arrested?' said Evie, looking cross.

'Look, I'm sorry for the misunderstanding. You're welcome to stay on at The Gables—'

'No, thank you,' said Evie standing beside Paul. She put her hand in his.

'Fair enough.' He got the distinct impression that, by the looks of things, Paul probably wouldn't be making up the spare room tonight. 'Well, you know where to find Elliot.' Ralph turned to the young police officer. 'Did you take Clara to the station?'

He nodded.

He was about to hot-foot it to his car. If he could catch her before she boarded a train, perhaps he could apologise and persuade her to stay. 'You're too late,' the police officer said looking at his watch. 'The train has just left.'

Ralph stopped at the door and turned around. 'Did she say where she was going?'

'London – I think. She mentioned something . . . what was it now? Oh yes, I remember. She got a phone call. It was strange.'

'Why, what was it?' said Ralph.

'Apparently, her husband has woken up from his coma.'

78

Clara hesitated. She looked up and down the platform.

'Mum, what are you waiting for? The train is about to depart.'

Clara tore her eyes from the platform and looked up at her daughter standing in the open doorway of the train carriage motioning her to climb aboard.

Clara held out her suitcase.

Tamsin grabbed it and then offered Clara her hand.

After one last look down the deserted platform, she grasped Tamsin's hand and stepped aboard the train.

As they made their way down the carriage to find Sophie and Mia, Tamsin glanced over her shoulder. 'Mum, what are you looking at?'

Clara shook her head. 'Never mind. It's not important.' As she said those words, she was glancing out the windows seeing if she could spot any sign of him. This reminded Clara of a time in her life she would much rather not dwell on; the time she upped and left for London all those years ago. She told her parents where she was going and imagined it had got back to Ralph. Clara thought he would follow her to London, but he didn't. If he had, she might not be sitting here on this train about to see a man she spent the last forty years of her life with; a man she should never have married.

'We're lucky the train was delayed a few minutes at the last station otherwise we would have missed it,' Tamsin was saying as she hoisted their suitcases up into the overhead compartments. 'There, now we can sit down.'

Clara took a seat next to Mia who was miserable at the prospect of having her summer holiday cut short and returning to London. She had a book open in front of her, but she wasn't reading. Mia was staring out the window glumly. Tamsin sat down next to Sophie, looking equally miserable as her little sister. She was busy texting on her phone. Clara sighed. At least the girls got four seats together with a table for the journey home.

Home. Clara wasn't looking forward to it. The moment she was dreading had finally arrived. She should have been delighted that Joe had woken up and wasn't a vegetable. From what she could gather, apart from a burst eardrum, there had been no lasting damage. When Tamsin got off the phone with Kevin – he had been the only one the hospital had been able to contact – it sounded like he was back to his old self.

His old self. Clara frowned. Joe wasn't the man she thought she had married – dependable Joe who worshipped the ground she walked on. He was planning to leave her, but Tamsin didn't know that yet. And when she returned home, who did Joe think would take care of Dorothy while he and his lady-friend were doing their disappearing act? Clara's eyes went wide. *Dorothy*! She rose from her seat.

'Mum, what's the matter?'

'We've got to get off the train!'

Mia said, 'Grandma, the train is moving.'

Clara's head swivelled to the window. She watched the platform give way to open countryside.

'Mum?'

She sat down in her seat and looked across at Tamsin. 'We've forgotten Dorothy!'

'Oh, bloody hell!' Tamsin stared at Clara. 'I thought we'd forgotten something.'

Mia said, 'What about Winston, and Marley, the cat?'

Sophie looked up from her phone. 'It's all right, I texted Elliot.' Tamsin turned to Sophie. 'You and Elliot are texting?'

'Calm down, Mum, it's not like we're having sex or anything. It's just a text!'

Mia sniggered into her hand at hearing the naughty word.

Tamsin glared at them both.

'What did Elliot say?' asked Clara sitting forward in her seat.

Sophie was busy texting him back. 'He says Dorothy is fine. She's weeding a flowerbed, apparently. He will keep an eye on her. He's house sitting now.' Sophie looked up. 'That horrible man who made us leave offered him the job.' Sophie's eyes drifted to Grandma. 'What did you do to piss the owner off?'

'Language, please, Sophie.'

'It's all right, Tamsin.' Clara understood it upset Sophie they had to leave. They were all still under the impression she was genuinely house sitting.

Tamsin looked at her two daughters' glum faces. 'Come on, girls, it can't be as bad as all that. We're returning to London to see Grandpa, isn't that great?'

Clara turned to the window and kept her sullen expression along with a few choice words to herself.

79

The train journey back to London was a blur. All she had on her mind was Ralph. How could he lie to her like that? And why hadn't he told her he owned The Gables? It made no sense. What made less sense was why she was consumed with a man she had only become reacquainted with in the last few weeks and might never meet again.

Never meet again. Clara swallowed hard trying not to let her emotions get the better of her. She was angry with him because when she found out who he was, she realised something extraordinary; after all these years he made her feel the way Joe never could and still had hold of her heart. And there was nothing she could do about that.

Clara tried to put all thoughts of Ralph out of her mind as they drew up outside the hospital. She glanced at Tamsin and the girls. Having told her daughter that she wished to see Joe alone, she hoped Tamsin would take the girls to the café and get a bite to eat. It was a lot to ask, but Tamsin said she understood.

Clara guessed Tamsin thought her mum wanted some quality time with Dad. She was right, but not for those reasons. Clara did not want Tamsin and the grandchildren around when she finally had the chance to tell Joe what she thought of him.

'We're here,' the taxi driver said for the third time.

'Mum?'

Clara stared at the drab seventies building. Was it only a month ago that Kevin dropped her off and she discovered *that* woman sitting at Joe's bedside? Clara had the urge to tell the driver to take her back to the station. But where would she go? How could she head off to Southwold when there was nothing to return for? Clara thought about Ralph. He hadn't turned up at the station and asked her to stay. Why did she imagine, after all these years, he would still feel the same way about her? He had recently lost his wife and was still getting over that loss. That kiss in the beach hut was nothing more than a widower looking for some solace in his grief.

She recalled the breakfasts they shared together. He seemed to enjoy himself in her company. Maybe that was all there was to it. He'd found a familiar face with whom to spend a few hours each day to kill the boredom and take his mind off his late wife. Clara nodded. That must be it.

Then there was the issue of her squatting in his house. Why didn't he press charges? She guessed, for old times' sake, he wouldn't take it further. Besides, he realised what she was doing, but he had not factored in the nosy neighbour calling the police.

It was what she'd feared all along; that a neighbour would discover them. They were bound to get found out, eventually.

Why didn't turned he turn up at the train station? She mused. He'd phoned the police and told them to drop all charges and had a message passed on to Clara that he was on his way.

She was so angry with him that she left in a huff deciding if he was eager to meet her again, he would drive straight to the station and stop her boarding the train. But he didn't. It made her wonder. Was it possible after what she'd done – breaking into the house and squatting – he decided he didn't know her at all, and he was glad to see the back of her?

Before she knew what was happening tears rolled down her face. 'Oh, Mum.' Tamsin put her arms around her. 'Please don't cry. Everything will be all right now.'

Clara got out a tissue and wiped her cheeks.

'To be honest, Mum, I don't know how you've kept it together. If something like this happened to Kevin…'

That was the worst part. She hadn't cried once over Joe, but the thought of losing Ralph…

The tears welled up again. She wished events had not conspired to lead her back to Southwold and The Gables. Then she would have had no clue that he'd returned and that she had never fallen out of love with Ralph.

'We're here,' the taxi-driver said for the third time, adding, 'the meter's still running.'

Tamsin handed over the cash while Clara got out of the cab.

'Mum, I will take the girls home to see Kevin first and pop back later.'

'Oh, okay.' Pleased to hear that Tamsin and the girls were going home to Kevin.

She stood there on the pavement watching the taxi leave the car park. Mia and Sophie were waving goodbye through the window. She waved back. When the cab was out of sight, she turned around, took a deep breath, thought of all the things she was about to Joe – none of them very pleasant – and marched into the hospital.

80

Clara strode past the nurses' station on the ward as she headed for Joe's room. She walked straight in, before she lost her nerve, saying, 'Joe, I know what you were up to—'

Clara stopped dead. She glared at the person sitting at his bedside. It was the same woman she had seen before when she'd caught her talking to a comatose Joe about their future together.

Joe saw his wife standing by the door. 'Clara, darling—'

Don't you darling me. Clara fumed.

'I want you to meet someone.'

Clara stared at him in disbelief.

Joe was sitting up in bed with several pillows tucked behind his back. Apart from the fact that he had lost some weight and was looking a little pale, it was the same old Joe with the same old smile. He was acting as though nothing had changed. How could he be so cruel?

He beckoned Clara into the room.

She didn't budge from the doorway.

Joe smiled. 'This is an old acquaintance – Judy. Many years ago, before we married, Judy and I were…' he glanced at Judy, 'good friends.'

'I see.' She stared at the woman who had turned in her seat. She offered Clara a disarming smile.

Clara didn't return her smile. What was there to smile about?

Here was the woman who had stolen her husband. That wasn't completely true. Joe must have joined in the plan to leave too. Who knows, perhaps it was his idea all along?

Clara walked into the hospital prepared with all the things she was intending to say, but instead of letting rip, she was speechless.

'Judy read about my accident in the paper. She's been visiting every day.'

He said it so matter-of-factly it was all Clara could do not to fly across the room and slap that ridiculously sweet smile off the woman's face – off *both* their faces.

'Why don't you come in and sit down, Clara. You're making us feel uncomfortable, hovering by the door like that.'

'*I'm* making *you* feel uncomfortable?' She glared at Joe and had no desire to come in and sit down and be civilised. Instead she wanted to turn tail and leave them to it; their plans for their future together – whatever they were. Maybe Joe would get a pay-out from the insurance company if the other party was at fault. Perhaps he had received his big payday, just not in the way Joe, or Clara, had ever expected.

'Clara, I've got something to tell you.'

She rolled her eyes. As if he needed to spell it out. Still, she didn't leave or make a scene. Instead, she walked into the room and perched on the arm of a chair. It wasn't very comfortable, but then she had no intention of staying for long.

'Well?' She caught Joe throwing her a disconcerted look. He patted the bed beside him. 'There's a spot here.'

Clara looked at him. Did he imagine she would want to go anywhere near him? She remained where she was. She looked at the woman. 'Let's get this over with.'

Judy appeared surprised at her angry manner.

Clara frowned at her innocent expression as if she didn't have a clue what was going on here.

Judy glanced at Joe before she said, 'It all started when Joe came across this newspaper article about someone disappearing.' Clara gaped at her. Then at Joe. She never expected this. That they would tell her they were planning to run away together.

'That's when we found each other again.'

Ralph came to mind. Clara tried not to think about him.

Joe continued, 'It was when I discovered Judy's missing person's agency.'

Clara frowned. Did he just say, 'Missing persons?' She shook her head. 'I don't understand—'

'I run a missing person's agency now, but Joe and I knew each other years ago.'

Clara stared at the dark-haired woman with the large round face, hazel eyes and a ready smile. She looked familiar. Clara tried to picture her as a young woman. A memory surfaced of a nightclub in Soho back in the seventies, and a waitress. She searched her face and saw the woman in the baby boomer sitting before her. 'Wait a minute, weren't you and Joe…?'

Judy nodded. 'That's right, we dated. I thought we would marry – do you remember, Joe?'

'Of course I do.'

'Then you walked into his life, Clara, and *se la vie* – such is life. Imagine my surprise when Joe and I met up again after all these years.'

'Yes, imagine that,' Clara said sarcastically.

'Joe was looking for someone who went missing years ago.'

Clara rubbed her temples. 'I'm sorry, but you have lost me.' They were running away together – weren't they?

'That's how he came across my agency. So, he hired me to find them.'

'Wait.' Clara held up a hand. 'You mean you're *not* running away together?'

Joe and Judy exchanged a glance. 'What on earth gave you that idea?' they said in unison.

That's when it all came out. How she discovered the

newspaper article in his shed along with the search history she found on his laptop. Then that episode when she saw Judy at his bedside and overheard her saying that they had plans together. Finally, she told him about the money missing from their joint account.

When Clara finished, she took a breath and sat there waiting for them to stop bullshitting her and come clean. It was high time Joe admitted what he and Judy had been planning behind her back.

Joe stared at his wife.

'Well?' Clara folded her arms against her chest. 'Don't lie. You don't have to sit here concocting silly, far-fetched stories about agencies and missing persons or whatever you were on about. You were planning to leave me, disappear out of my life forever – admit it.'

Joe turned to Judy. 'Would you mind if I had a moment with my wife alone?'

Judy rose from her seat. 'Of course.' She walked out of the room, throwing Clara a confused look.

Clara watched her leave. She frowned at her back before she turned to Joe. 'How long has it been going on – you and Judy?'

'Almost six months.'

'Six months!' She didn't know what astounded her the most. The discovery her husband was having an affair or the fact that he was so brazen about it, telling her so matter-of-factly like he was just talking about the weather.

Joe sighed. 'I didn't want to tell you until the time was right, but I had the accident and it scuppered our plans.'

'Our plans?' repeated Clara glancing at the open doorway. She could see Judy milling about in the corridor outside.

Clara shook her head from side to side in dismay. How could she have lived with someone for so long and not know them at all? She stood up.

'Are you leaving?'

'What a stupid question, Joe.'

'I haven't finished.'

'Oh, I have. Next, you'll be telling me what you and Judy had planned.'

'I will if you just give me a chance.'

She gaped at him. 'You're unbelievable! 'There's one thing disappearing from my life, but I can't believe you would do it to Tamsin and the grandchildren.' She looked at Joe coldly. 'They deserve better.'

'What on earth are you going on about?'

She wouldn't even dignify that question with an answer. Although she added, 'I know what you were planning.'

Clara turned on her heal and headed to the door. She heard Joe say, 'But that's just it – there's no way you could have guessed.'

She paused at the door and turned around. Since the accident, all she wanted was for Joe to wake up and have it out with him. She expected Joe to feel uncomfortable being put on the spot and forced to confess. He might even show some remorse and regret or be ashamed of his behaviour. But not a bit of it. What astounded her was the way Joe was so blasé about it, as though he'd done nothing wrong. It was infuriating. Clara couldn't stand being in the same room a minute longer. She turned to leave.

'Did you think I was having an affair – with Judy? Is that it?'

Clara had stepped out of the room when she heard what he said. So did a group of medical staff passing by. They all looked over in her direction.

Clara slunk back into the room. 'Are you going to deny it?'

Joe's eyebrows shot up. 'The newspaper article you found about the bloke who disappeared and the search history on my laptop about people who disappear and start a new life. Then you mentioned the money missing from our bank account…' Joe laughed.

Clara's fingers curled into a fist. 'Are you laughing at me?'

She wanted to punch him. That would wipe that big, stupid grin off his face.

'Oh, Clara. I get it now. I can see what it all must have looked like when you saw Judy at my bedside. But it's not what you imagined.'

She couldn't believe this.

'It's not true. I wasn't having an affair.'

'Oh, yeah right.'

Joe studied her a long moment. 'I wouldn't do that. You know me.'

'Do I?'

Joe's smile faltered. 'I worship the ground you walk on.'

'I don't believe you.'

'But it's true. I wasn't having an affair, or planning, or even *thinking* about leaving you.'

'Then explain what that stuff in your shed was all about, and where have all our savings gone?'

'Come and sit down – why don't you.'

'No.'

'Please. I've got something to tell you. I think you might need to sit down.'

81

Clara eyed the chair beside his hospital bed. She didn't want to sit down to hear more bullshit. However, she'd known her husband for many years and something in Joe's tone told her this was serious.

She walked into the room and sat down in the chair furthest from his bed.

Joe looked at her for a moment. 'Tamsin said you've been away. You seem…' he paused '. . . changed somehow.'

'I don't know what you're talking about,' Clara answered, trying to brush the memory of Ralph aside. She pointed a finger at him. '*Don't* change the subject. You were about to tell me what you were doing before the car accident, and what happened to our savings.'

Joe nodded.

She leaned forward in her chair. 'Well?'

He took a deep breath. 'It all started when I was looking for the next Big Payday…'

Here we go. Clara rolled her eyes and had half-a-mind to walk out. If she didn't hear those three words – *The Big Payday* – ever again she wouldn't be sorry. When she fled to Southwold, she didn't miss Joe going on about ventures that never materialised. It had been a relief to escape from it for once. Throughout their marriage, it had hung around like a spectre ready to reappear at any moment and interfere with their lives. Why couldn't he be happy with what they had than pinning all his hopes and dreams on waiting for some dodgy pay off? How many times had she told him he would be better off saving over the long term, rather than staking everything on some new-fangled scheme that amounted to little more than a gamble?

Clara sighed. 'So that is where all the money went, on another bad investment hoping for The Big Payday.' She was not surprised. In fact, she would have been more surprised if Joe had done something sensible for a change.

Joe shook his head. 'I did not use the money in the way you imagine.'

Clara looked at him 'But you just said—'

'I said *it all started* when I researched the next Big Payday. That's when I hit on an idea for a business.'

'A business?' Clara couldn't hide her contempt. Her husband didn't have an entrepreneurial bone in his body. The schemes he invested in were always someone else's ideas set up to con naïve people like Joe out of their money. She didn't need to hear the details. She held up her hand. 'Don't tell me. I am *not* interested.'

'You will be interested in this.'

'Look, just get to the point.' She was losing her patience.

'It all started with an idea. I wanted to leave my job and do something different.'

That didn't come as a surprise to Clara. She knew this was what The Big Payday was all about – Joe getting off the treadmill as a taxi driver and following his dreams. She looked at him sitting in his hospital bed with a bandage wrapped around his head. Here was a man approaching sixty whose dream of sailing the med on his yacht was about as distant as the prospect of her and Joe getting back together. For a moment, she caught herself feeling sorry for him.

'What I wanted to do,' continued Joe, 'was become a private detective.'

'Oh, boy.' Joe – a private detective? She had the impulse to laugh. Instead, she said sarcastically, 'What sort of detecting were you hoping to do?'

'Missing persons.'

'Missing persons?' In her experience, Joe couldn't find his car keys unless they jumped up and hit him on the nose. How on earth did he expect to locate a missing person? But there it was, the same old Joe riding on the coattails of other people's ideas – in this case, his new girlfriend's business idea. As usual, he was living in a fantasy world. *A private detective?* Was he out of his mind? Who did he imagine he would get as a client? Clara asked him.

'Ah, well, that is an interesting question. My first client was, in fact, *you*.'

Clara stared at him. 'What in heaven's name are you talking about? I wasn't missing. I'd gone to Southwold.'

'Er… I didn't mean *you* were the missing person.' Joe dropped his gaze and studied his fingernails. 'I have a confession to make.'

Finally, the conversation was getting somewhere. She waited for him to admit what he'd been up to.

'Years ago, when we were first married, a postcard arrived on our doormat.'

Clara frowned at him. 'So what? We used to get postcards all the time from friends and relatives on holiday. I don't see what that's got to do with—'

'It was for *you* – not *us*.' He faltered. 'I realised that before we met, you had a history with someone, although you would never talk about it. So, I… I thought it was from a former sweetheart.'

Clara thought of Ralph.

Joe was studying his fingernails, avoiding her gaze. 'I don't know what came over me. It was inexcusable. But I never gave you the postcard.'

Clara rolled her eyes. 'You know what? I couldn't care less.

I'm not interested in the past; but would like to hear what is going on between you and—'

'Oh, but you will be when you find out who it was from. The thing is, Clara, I never knew – not back then.'

Clara was getting annoyed. 'What are you rambling on about?'

'It was only later when you told me you had a brother, I put two and two together.'

She stared at him. 'What are you saying?'

'The postcard. I'd forgotten all about it until I was having a little clear out in the shed and discovered it in the drawer of my desk. The peculiar thing is it coincided with picking up a fare that day which turned out to be my old friend, Judy. She talked about her work as a private detective – imagine that?'

Clara narrowed her eyes; she didn't believe in coincidences. *What would you call arriving in Southwold and finding yourself at The Gables at the same time as Ralph?* She dismissed that irritating voice in her head that kept steering her thoughts back to Ralph.

'So, when I realised my idea of becoming a private detective was stupid, I hired Judy to help me find—'

'Stop!' Clara was confused. 'What has this got to do with Tommy?'

Joe couldn't have looked more contrite if he tried. He mumbled, 'The postcard. It was from Tommy.'

She rose from her chair. 'What did you just say?'

'Clara, I'm so sorry. I did not understand what it meant at the time. I thought it was a former sweetheart getting in touch, and I did not want any chance you might leave me. So, I… I didn't give it to you.'

Clara stood there staring at Joe. 'A postcard from Tommy came *after* we married?'

Joe nodded his head. 'It's true.'

'You realise what that means?'

He looked at the floor and mumbled, 'Yes I do.'

Clara shook her head. 'No, there must be some mistake. We

hadn't long moved into the house. Perhaps it was meant for the people who used to live at the property from someone called Tommy.'

'It was addressed to you, Clara.'

'I don't believe you.'

Joe reached over and opened the cabinet next to his bed. He got out a file with some paperwork. He picked something out of the folder and held it out to Clara. 'Here.'

She looked at the postcard but didn't make a move to take it.

Joe waved it at her. 'Take it.'

Clara walked to the edge of his bed and took the postcard. She took a deep breath. Oh, how much she wanted it to be true that Tommy had written the card, but she would rather not look and find out it was not from her brother.

As if reading her mind, Joe said, 'I'm telling you, Clara, it's from him.' As she cast her eyes down at the postcard, Joe added, 'I was trying to make amends, don't you see? After I found it, I realised the enormity of what I had done. Tommy might have disappeared at your eighteenth birthday party, but according to the postmark he was alive and well a fortnight later. So, I investigated the scenario of people disappearing. I wanted to find him for you.'

Joe took a deep breath before continuing, 'Then I met Judy who traces missing people and together we planned to do just that. That's what all the research was about on my computer. I wasn't plotting to disappear. I was trying to discover what happened to Tommy. Judy has been visiting me since I woke up, to pick up where we left off.'

Clara looked at the dog-eared postcard in her hands. She recognised where it was from; the picture on the front was Palma in Mallorca.

Joe watched her studying the postcard. 'Judy and I were planning to go to Mallorca when I had the stupid car accident. I used our savings to book flights and a hotel for a few days and paid Judy for the time she'd spent trying to uncover the trail and discover his whereabouts.'

Clara glanced at Joe. 'So that's what Judy meant when I overheard her say you had plans together.'

'Yes.' He smiled at Clara. 'Despite what you think, we were not planning to run away together.'

'Why didn't you tell me all this when you found the postcard?'

Joe cast down his eyes. 'I just couldn't. Do you know how much I regret not giving you that postcard when it first arrived? It would have meant so much to you, finding out he was alive and well. I didn't know if you'd ever forgive me, and still don't. So, the only way to make amends was to find him.'

Clara stared at Joe. It all made sense now. Although she was aware relationships end, people drift apart, fall out of love, have affairs, she couldn't imagine Joe would ever do that to her.

There was something about all this she did not understand. 'What about Southwold? If you were intent on finding Tommy, why did you go to the seminar?'

Joe managed a smile. 'I attended because it was held in the town where you and Tommy grew up. You never talked about your past, your childhood, and I wanted to see it. Maybe it would help piece together some of his background. I thought that's what a real detective would do – gather as much information as possible. It was the perfect excuse to go.'

They both fell silent. Clara recalled that when he first told her he was attending the seminar in Southwold she had found out it was also being held in London. When she telephoned the hotel in London and learned there was still spaces, that's when she became suspicious about his motives for going. It was then that Clara suspected there was more to it than Joe attending another seminar. But never in her wildest dreams did she think it had anything to do with Tommy.

'Well, aren't you going to read it?'

82

She turned over the postcard and recognised the familiar scrawl on the other side. It *was* Tommy's handwriting. Clara felt her knees buckle when she read the date stamp. It was true. He wrote this *after* the party. She sat down on the edge of Joe's hospital bed. She saw his hand reaching for hers. He gave it an affectionate squeeze. 'Are you all right?'

Clara didn't flinch from his touch. 'I don't know.' She should have been furious that he had kept this from her. But that was years ago; how was he to appreciate the significance? It wasn't as though she had told Joe about Tommy. She could not talk about her loss. Not back then. That came out much later; years into their marriage.

Clara took a deep breath and read the postcard.

*Dear C...*Clara wiped away a tear. If Tommy ever wrote her name, it was always just "C". He hadn't written much. Only a few words; it was a postcard, after all. The problem was it raised more questions than answers.

Dear C, I'm sorry I had to do this, disappear for a while, but you are already aware what happened from my letter. I'm still here in Mallorca. I can't wait to see you again...

When she had finished reading the few words scrawled in his handwriting, she looked up at Joe. 'So, where is he now?'

'That's what I am hoping to find out.'

Clara studied the postcard. 'And what's this about a letter?'

'I have no idea – I swear.' Joe took a deep breath. 'It's all my fault – don't you see?'

Clara turned to look at Joe.

'All these years, you didn't know what happened to Tommy, whether he was still alive. It's haunted you all your life. But it turned out I had the answer all along in the drawer in my stupid shed at the bottom of the garden.' Then Joe cried. 'I'm so sorry. How will you ever forgive me?'

Clara stared at her husband. In all the years they were married, she had only seen him cry once, and that was tears of joy when Tamsin was born.

She tried not to think about that day when Joe, overcome with emotion at her birth, cradled another man's child in his arms. She stole a glance at Joe. Few men would have brought up another man's baby, let alone wept tears of joy at their birth.

This time it was Clara who took Joe's hand and squeezed it tight. If it weren't for him, she didn't know where she or her baby would have ended up.

Joe looked at her hand curled in his. 'I was driving along the motorway on the way home,' said Joe, wiping the tears from his eyes. 'I was distracted. My mind was elsewhere. All I could think about was the postcard. I didn't see the car coming on to the slip road before it was too late. That's how we collided.'

There was a long silence. Clara studied the postcard in her hand. That's when something occurred to her. 'It wasn't just down to you, Joe. Someone else must have known he was alive.'

Joe looked at her in surprise. 'How do you figure that?'

'Well, someone must have known Tommy's whereabouts otherwise how would he have found out I was married and the address where we moved to afterwards? It's not like I announced our engagement in *The Times*.'

'That's a good question, Clara.' Joe nodded his head. 'What about your parents? Do you think he contacted them?'

'No.' She knew this for a fact because, to his dying day, her father hoped that Tommy would turn up alive and well. Besides, if her brother were alive, he would try to reach out to her first – or that's what she thought until she got this postcard. Which begged the question: who else knew?

'Why do you suppose he never got in touch again?' Clara looked at Joe.

He frowned. 'That has played on my mind ever since I discovered the postcard. Because I didn't give it to you straightaway, perhaps when you did not respond he assumed you wanted nothing to do with him and he severed all ties.'

'Or perhaps something happened—'

'Yes,' Joe cut in, 'whatever his reasons for disappearing the night of the party, surely he would not have made just one attempt to contact you. Anything could have happened to this postcard on its' journey across the Atlantic.'

'It could have got lost in the post,' said Clara.

'Or in the back of someone's desk drawer,' Joe said. He eyed the old yellowed postcard. 'You were his twin. He would have tried to reach you again.'

'You'd think so,' said Clara, not bothering to hide the bitterness in her voice. 'But what of the letter I never received, explaining everything?'

Joe shrugged.

They both fell silent.

'Well, I for one want to find out what happened to your brother after he sent that postcard.' Joe looked at his wife. 'Are you in?'

'What about Judy? Were you going to Mallorca together to find him?'

'Together? Oh, goodness me no. Judy has a business and works from home in between the school run. She's a grandparent who takes her grandchildren to school and can't just drop everything and fly off to The Balearic Islands. Apparently, she spends a lot of time searching online for clues to the whereabouts of missing people, making phone calls and contacting various agencies. I was going on my own. Now, I don't have to.' He eyed her keenly.

She frowned. As much as she wanted to go to Mallorca to find Tommy, she couldn't just jet off either. But it wasn't responsibilities that were keeping her grounded, but lack of money. She said as much.

'Me too,' admitted Joe.

'But what about the flights and hotel you booked before the accident?'

Joe shook his head. 'The flight was non-refundable, and the hotel would be paid on arrival. The rest of the cash in our bank account went to Gerald to settle the bills while I was . . . sleeping.'

'Oh.' Her eyes drifted to the bandage around his head. 'Won't you get an insurance pay-out for the accident?'

'Chance would be a fine thing. I'm more likely to be sued by the other driver. It *was* my fault,' he replied.

'So, where does that leave us?'

Joe looked down at Clara's hand, still in his. *Us.* She had used the word *us.* That was music to his ears. He had been anxious when he woke up and discovered Clara was not at his bedside and wondered if she thought he wasn't going to make it. Had their newly divorced friends – Gerald and Debs – persuaded Clara to move on with her life? But what did that mean exactly?

Joe searched her face. It was something he was afraid of all their married lives. Deep down, he had always suspected Clara did not love him the way he loved her.

She had run away to London, pregnant with another man's child. She could have trapped him, pretended it was his, but she didn't. Joe admired her for that – her honesty. However, there was a flipside; sometimes he wished she had never told him. He would have gone through life believing Tamsin was his child. Joe wasn't just afraid Tamsin's father would walk back into his daughter's life, but his secret fear was that he would step back into Clara's life too, and that would be the end of their marriage.

When Joe looked at her, he still saw that amazing young woman he had first encountered getting into his taxi, with her blonde hair, beautiful brown eyes, and the plumiest voice he had ever heard. He remembered thinking this beautiful creature did not belong with the likes of him – an East End boy who drove a taxi for a living. The only thing he could think of was maybe she saw something special in him that no-one else saw.

That's why he'd spent decades looking for The Big Payday, not for the yacht – although living the high life sailing around the med would have been a wonderful by-product. But that wasn't his primary reason. All he ever wanted to do was show Clara that whatever she had seen in him all those years ago, he hadn't turned out a huge disappointment in her eyes. He assumed having more money was the answer. Then he found the postcard, and all that changed. If there was one thing he could do for Clara that he felt would cement their relationship until the end of time, it was to find her brother.

Joe squeezed Clara's hand. 'Don't you worry. We'll find him.' Or what happened to him after he sent this postcard.

'But how? You said it yourself there isn't the money to visit Mallorca.'

Joe's confident smile faltered. When all you did was make ends meet, everything in life boiled down to money. 'I don't know yet, but I'm sure something will turn up.'

Clara rolled her eyes at Joe. Didn't that just sum up Joe's philosophy in life? *Something will turn up*. 'Like another of your stupid ideas you believe will lead to The Big Payday?' Clara's voice dripped with sarcasm born of years of listening to the same old crap. This time she could not hide the contempt in her voice.

Joe looked at her in surprise. 'You were always supportive.'

'In the beginning,' Clara conceded. 'When we were first

married, I imagined it was harmless. But over the years, I realised you should have put all your hard-earned cash into a pension or perhaps bricks and mortar, or something that would eventually pay off.'

'Why didn't you ever tell me to stop?'

'Oh, it's my fault is it that there's nothing left, no pension, no savings – apart from the house?'

Joe shook his head. 'No, that's not what I'm saying. Look, I know you will not like it, but I am going to ask Gerald to lend me some cash. A short-term loan just until I get back on my feet and can go back to work. We could use the money to go to Mallorca together and search for your brother.'

'All right.'

'All right?' Joe repeated in surprise. 'All right you don't mind me going to our best friends for a loan, or all right meaning you will come with me to Mallorca?'

Clara sighed. 'All right to both. I want to find him, Joe.'

Joe's face lit up in a huge grin. He tempered his delight. 'I am so glad you're giving me the opportunity to make it up to you. You won't regret it.'

Before she responded, the consultant walked into the room. Clara stood up. Joe was still holding her hand.

'It's all right Mrs Delaney,' said the consultant. 'You can stay. I'm just here to give Joe his paperwork.'

Clara looked at Joe. 'What's that?' she said referring to the paperwork being passed to Joe. Although he seemed all right, did this mean he had to remain in hospital for more tests?

'Oh this?' said Joe holding up the paperwork. 'Didn't I tell you?' His face lit up as he said to Clara, 'They're discharging me. We're going home!'

Clara let go of his hand. 'Going home?' The word *home* conjured up The Gables, and Bailey lounging in front of the open fire, and a cranky disfigured man called Ralph falling asleep in an old deckchair outside a beach hut.

'You remember our little North London semi,' Joe said jokingly. 'God, how I've missed the place.'

Clara bit her lip. She did not share Joe's sentiments.

Joe turned to the consultant. 'How soon can I fly?

He considered this for a moment before replying. 'I'd give it three months.'

'Three months!'

'Now, remember you've had a clot on the brain. Although the swelling has subsided, and we are confident everything is okay, you will need a further scan for the all clear. So, in the meantime, we don't recommend you fly. Go by boat if you must travel – just no planes.'

Clara looked from Joe to the consultant. 'Is he all right to leave the hospital?'

'Yes. Here is an information leaflet. If he experiences any sickness, dizzy spells, fainting episodes, seizures—'

'Seizures!' Clara said in alarm.

'It's nothing to be alarmed about. Joe has recovered well. There are always risks with brain injuries that one may develop some residual side effects.'

Clara didn't like the sound of that. 'What do you mean?'

'So far, Joe has made a remarkable recovery but he could suffer with bouts of Epilepsy.'

'So far,' repeated Clara. 'Does that mean he could… relapse?'

'It just means for the next few weeks he needs to be kept a close eye on, but all going well no new symptoms should present themselves.' The consultant looked at Clara. 'You are not planning any more trips, are you?'

Joe reached for Clara's hand. 'She's not going anywhere – unless it's with me.'

'That's settled then,' said the specialist. 'As you will have someone at home with you twenty-four-seven, I am happy to discharge you today.'

'Twenty-four seven,' repeated Clara.

Joe grinned.

The consultant handed the nurse some paperwork and turned to Joe. 'You cannot return to work just yet. Plenty of rest. Do not over-exert yourself. Avoid stressful situations.'

Joe nodded dutifully.

The consultant seemed satisfied. 'Good. I'm sure you're both looking forward to things getting back to normal,' walking out of the room.

'Clara?'

She was sitting on the edge of the bed staring out the window.

'Is something wrong?'

Clara turned from the window and managed a smile for Joe's benefit. 'Not at all,' she lied. 'Let's go home.'

Joe beamed at her. 'That's music to my ears.'

83

Clara picked up a deflated balloon and put it in the rubbish sack along with the *Welcome Home* banner that Tamsin stuck on the front door ready for Joe and Clara's arrival yesterday evening. She was standing on the doorstep thinking of The Gables when she heard the phone ring.

'Oh, there you are,' said Joe as Clara stepped back into the house. He reached for the phone. 'Hello? Ah, Gerald, just the person…' Joe's eyes followed Clara as she walked into the kitchen. 'There's something I want to ask you—'

Clara closed the kitchen door on Joe's conversation. She knew what he was meant to ask Gerald: if he could lend him some money so they could take a trip to Mallorca. But what was the point? Joe could not fly, and she was unable to leave him and go on her own. There was nobody else to keep an eye on him. Clara didn't need reminding that she had to be there for him twenty-four-seven.

It crossed her mind to ask Tamsin to stay for a week while she did the trip herself. However, Joe needed to avoid stressful situations. Could she rely on her daughter not to tell him about Kevin's business folding and the dire financial straits they faced right now? They were barely holding it together. Although she thanked her lucky stars that, under the circumstances, Tamsin and the girls had moved back in with Kevin.

While this pleased her not having them under her feet when she had enough to deal with, running around after Joe, she was concerned how they were getting on. Her daughter had never experienced tough times. Now she faced most people's reality, that life wasn't always plain sailing. In fact, in Clara's experience, you had to treasure the moments when life *was* plain sailing.

'I've just got off the phone to Gerald.'

Clara turned around as Joe walked into the kitchen. She'd been staring out the window, her mind drifting to a faraway place; to a life she might have had if the unthinkable had happened and Joe hadn't woken up.

'Clara – is everything all right?'

'Fine,' she replied, avoiding his gaze. He did that a lot lately, asking her if everything was all right while she did her best to hide how she was feeling. Clara wiped the kitchen surfaces.

'It turns out Gerald called because he wanted to see me.'

'That's good then. After all, you *were* planning to see him about that loan. What was he calling about?' Clara asked off-hand. When he did not respond she turned around. Joe was frowning. She put the dishcloth down and sighed. 'What's the matter?'

'I'm not sure. He said he couldn't talk about it over the phone.'

Clara pursed her lips. She did not want to worry Joe, but guessed it was to do with the paperwork she gave Gerald soon after the accident. She bet he'd discovered Joe wasn't the only one in poor health; their finances were none too healthy either. If it was something he did not wish to divulge over the phone, that was not good.

'We will go together,' Clara announced, which is what she intended to do, anyway.

'I've already phoned for a taxi.'

'We're going right now?'

Joe nodded. 'Gerald said it couldn't wait.'

Clara stared at Joe. Their finances must be a lot worse than she envisaged. Either that or the other driver involved in the accident was suing them. 'I'll get my coat.'

A short ten-minute taxi ride later brought them outside the tall Georgian building in a leafy London square where Gerald had his legal practice. Clara was opening the car door when Joe caught her by the arm. 'I'd like to do this alone if you don't mind.'

'Whatever it is, Joe, we can deal with it together.'

'Yes, I know. I prefer to speak to Gerald, man-to-man. Perhaps we can sort it out, then you won't have to worry.'

Clara studied his face. This was the reason she married him and stuck by him. Whatever was going on in their lives, he always protected her. Even after the accident, he would do his best to protect her from any bad news lurking in Gerald's office.

Joe was old-fashioned that way. He was the head of the household, the breadwinner, the person who shouldered all the financial responsibilities.

Clara was not happy about this arrangement over the years, especially when he mismanaged their money in the pursuit of his fantasy – The Big Payday. However she did not try to become involved or get a job. It was easier having someone take care of all the mundane things in life like working for a living and paying the bills. Her attitude was not a surprise. That is what her upbringing and education centred on – becoming a housewife and mother.

Sometimes Clara wondered if Joe's pursuit of The Big Payday stemmed from the knowledge she came from a different social class and deep down he always thought she deserved more than he could give her on a taxi-driver's salary.

Clara didn't want super-yachts to travel around the med; only a place to call her own and a life of her own choosing. She should have found that for herself and knew why she hadn't; there was a baby to take care of. Back then, she needed him. Her eyes settled on her husband. Now he needed her, and the last thing she could do was walk away.

The consultant told her there was a possibility she would take Joe home and discover he had changed; apparently, a head injury will do that to a person. But his head trauma hadn't altered Joe, it had changed Clara.

During the summer they spent apart, while Joe was in a coma, she had the opportunity for the first time in decades to rediscover the old Clara. What the summer at The Gables taught her was that she was not that scared, lonely young woman any more looking for security and a haven with someone who would care for her.

She felt guilty for even thinking it, but the truth was she did not need Joe any more. What she needed was time on her own to figure herself out, to discover what she wanted in life and where she wanted to be. And who she wanted to be with. But that, she knew, was impossible. For now, the tables had turned; Joe needed her. She decided it was high time she reminded him of that fact.

'The consultant said about keeping an eye on you?'

Joe smiled at his wife. 'I am capable of walking into Gerald's office on my own, Clara. I am sure I will not keel over, although I might have a panic attack.'

She shot him a concerned look.

'I'll be fine. I'm only joking. Gerald will be with me the whole time.'

Clara was not convinced he *was* joking. The consultant had told them Joe was to avoid stress and overexcitement. If this wasn't stressful, she didn't know what was.

'Why don't you take the taxi to Kensington High Street and meet Debbie for lunch?'

Clara frowned at him. 'I couldn't do that. Besides, I have nothing arranged.'

Joe grinned. 'I took the liberty when I was on the phone to Gerald to ask if Debbie was free this morning to meet you and have a coffee or something. I understand the two of you have not been keeping in touch.'

Clara bit her bottom lip. There was a reason for that. She might spill the beans and tell Debs how she felt about Joe and their life together. Joe was in no fit state to hear the truth; if it wasn't for Tamsin and the girls, she might never have come back.

'So, Debs is waiting at Fortnum and Mason for you as we speak.'

'But—'

'No *buts* Clara. I've seen you moping about the house, staring off into space. You miss your friends and the shopping trips you girls used to do together.'

Clara looked at him. Nothing could be further from the truth. It was not her friends she missed.

'Have a good time.'

Against her better judgement, Clara stayed put in the back of the taxi while Joe paid the driver and gave him instructions to take her to Kensington. She watched him get out of the cab. Then she had a thought. 'Wait! How will I know when to pick you up?'

'There's no need. Gerald will run me home in his car.'

'Are you sure? I don't want you thinking you can hop in a taxi or take the tube just because you think you are better.'

'I am fine.'

Clara frowned.

'Okay. All right.' He held up his hands to forestall any further argument on the matter. 'If Gerald cannot take me home, I will call you – I promise. Have you got your mobile phone?'

Clara looked in her handbag. 'Yes.'

'Good. That's settled then. I'll see you later.' He leaned in the taxi and went to give her a kiss goodbye.

Clara turned her face away leaving Joe no option but to plant a kiss on her cheek. He didn't seem to notice her flinch. Either that or he was too preoccupied with why Gerald had summoned him to his office so urgently.

Clara looked up at the impressive building where Gerald

worked. 'I suppose you better get going,' she said, avoiding his gaze. She felt guilty about turning away from his kiss.

It was the same last night. It was their first evening together after they discharged him from hospital. Clara rejected his advances, reminding him that over the next few weeks he was not meant to exert himself. Joe had asked her if she was sure the specialist had told her that advice extended to no marital relations. The consultant had said no such thing.

'Good luck,' Clara said.

'Thanks.'

She watched him walk into the building and felt strangely detached as though he was just a friend or acquaintance, not her husband with whom she had been married for decades. The taxi set off. Fifteen minutes later, Clara arrived outside Fortnum and Mason. Sitting in the café, she did not spend her coffee morning worrying about what was going on in Gerald's office but how she longed for some peace. Surprisingly, Clara discovered she had not missed the city at all or her friends – or Joe.

She sat there sipping tea out of a fine bone china cup and thought of the mornings she had sat outside on the small veranda of her beach hut, with a cold sea breeze whipping around her shoulders and a builders mug of strong brew tea poured from a chipped, discoloured teapot. Clara didn't just miss the builder's cup or the chipped teapot, but the company; the absence of her new friends, Evie and Elliot, not to mention Bailey. And of course, Ralph.

'Penny for your thoughts?'

Clara turned to Debs wishing she hadn't used that phrase. It reminded her of someone she was trying to forget.

'I'm sorry,' Clara apologised. She had been sitting there staring off into space wanting to be anywhere but here.

'I was thinking,' said Debs, 'why don't we go shopping afterwards? It will take your mind off whatever is bothering you.'

Clara went to say *it's nothing* but caught Debs wagging a

knowing finger at her. 'I know something's up, Clara, even if you won't tell your bestie.'

'What's a bestie?'

'It's what my grandchildren call their best friends. Anyway, I think a spot of retail therapy will do you a world of good.'

Clara looked at Debs. She doubted that. It was not the lack of money that was dampening her enthusiasm; she'd bought stuff in the past even when they had no money.

'You're not coming shopping are you,' Debs said flatly.

Clara shook her head *no.*

Debs put her elbow on the table, rested her chin on her hand and studied her old friend. 'What's the matter, Clara?'

'Oh, I don't know.'

Debs shook her head. 'I do. You miss your life in Southwold, your new friends – Ralph? Was that his name?'

'Debs!' Clara wished she hadn't mentioned the old friend she had bumped into whom Debs guessed was more than just an old friend.

Clara glanced at the other women at their table. They were all acquaintances of theirs that Debs had invited along to celebrate Clara returning to the inner circle – meaning their coffee and shopping mornings. They didn't look as though they'd heard a word Debs said, too busy talking amongst themselves about their recent purchases and comparing notes about their new designer handbags.

'While we are discussing old friends…' Debs leaned in close and raised her eyebrows, 'or shall I say *lovers?'*

'Debs!'

Debbie laughed. 'Oh, come on, Clara. I see that look in your eyes whenever you mention his name.'

'I don't know what you're talking about.'

'Yes, you do.' Debbie smiled a knowing smile. 'Talking of old flames.'

Clara had it on the tip of her tongue to say *he is not an old flame* even though he most certainly was, when Debs said, 'I've met someone too, and you will never believe this…'

A moment later, Clara was sitting there staring at her best friend with a question she was dying to ask – well two, actually.

Debbie continued, 'You are not the only one with serendipity on your side. I walked into Gerald's office when the man in question was on his way out. Turns out, he is a new client and going through a messy divorce. I recognized him. He was the boy I fell in love with when we were fifteen. And he recognised me too.' Debs eyed Clara. 'What is it?'

Clara whispered, 'You've slept with him – haven't you.'

Debbie's naughty grin answered that question.

Clara was just about to broach the second question she was dying to ask when Debbie stepped in and said, 'If you are wondering whether you can rekindle a romance with an old flame, I can say quite emphatically you can. And I will tell you another thing. It is something special the second time around. I feel so…'

Clara was hanging on her every word. She had never seen Debs like this before – so alive, positively glowing. She looked so—

'… happy!' concluded Debs.

84

'Are you all right?' asked the secretary sitting in the reception room outside Gerald's office. 'You look as white as a sheet. Do you need to sit down? I can fetch you a glass of water.'

'No, thank you,' replied Joe shaking his head. 'I've just received some unexpected news that caught me off-guard that's all.'

Gerald came to the door and watched Joe gather his coat from the coat rack in reception. 'I'll have my secretary book another appointment. You will need further legal advice.'

Joe nodded.

'Well, good luck.' Gerald held out his hand.

Joe shook his hand in silence and walked out the door. He stood outside the office building and took deep breaths, his heart pounding in his chest. He glanced up and saw Gerald standing at the window staring down at him. Gerald offered to drive him home, but Joe needed time alone to digest the news. Instead, Gerald called a taxi.

He sat in the back of the taxi debating when would be the right moment to tell Clara the news.

❖

Clara arrived home in a taxi and felt a sudden sensation of déjà vu. She had a shopping bag in her hand, a treat from Debs.

'Lady, the meter's still running, so unless there's anywhere else you need to be…' the driver trailed off.

Anywhere else she needed to be. There was somewhere she'd rather be and wanted to ask him to turn around and take her to the train station. Instead, she sighed as she handed over her fare and exited the cab. Clara stood for some time on the pavement outside the house, staring into space, dreaming of another life.

'Clara, how's your husband?'

Snapped back to reality by a neighbour from down the street walking by with their dog, Clara wondered how long she'd been standing there. Her face coloured in embarrassment. 'He is much better, thank you. Well, I must dash,' she added striding up the path to the front door.

'Send Joe my best wishes,' the neighbour called after her.

'Will do,' replied Clara as she put the key in the front door only to find the door unlocked. Joe was already home. Clara's stomach churned. What bad news had he brought from his meeting with Gerald?

She stepped into the house and called out, 'Joe – I'm home.' She expected Gerald to be there too. Surely, he would have waited with Joe until she arrived.

She wandered into the lounge. 'Joe… Gerald?' There was no answer. Clara made her way upstairs. What if Gerald had dropped him off and Joe had had a seizure or something and was lying unconscious on the floor? She raced up the stairs and rushed into the bedrooms and the bathroom. There was no sign of Joe. 'The kitchen!' Clara raced back down the stairs being careful to mind her step in case she tripped over Marley, until she remembered her cat was still in Southwold.

Joe wasn't in the kitchen. She was staring out the window, wondering where on earth they had got to, when her eyes drifted to the shed at the bottom of the garden. Joe was sitting at his desk in his man cave. Putting the kettle on she wandered down the garden to say hello to Gerald.

Clara opened the shed door.

'Ah, I didn't expect you back so soon.'

She caught him cramming some paperwork away in his desk drawer. Clara frowned. The first thought running through her mind was *more secrets*. This did not bode well. He couldn't have made it more obvious; Joe was hiding something from her. Clara glanced around his shed. 'Where's Gerald? Did he just drop you off and leave?'

Joe looked sheepishly at Clara.

'Don't tell me he didn't drive you home!'

'It's not Gerald's fault. I preferred to get a taxi. I don't want to be chaperoned everywhere like a child.'

'But the consultant said—'

'Screw the consultant!'

Clara took a step back in surprise.

'Sorry. Look, I have a lot on my mind right now.' Before she could ask, he said, 'I want to finish up here and then I'll come inside.'

Clara stared at Joe. *What things?* She felt like asking. Instead, she said, 'So, how did the meeting go with Gerald?' She didn't want to hear bad news. They were not in a good place financially as it was with Joe unable to work at the moment, without finding out the other driver might seek legal advice to sue. Or perhaps there was something ominous on the horizon that Joe was keeping from her.

'I'll tell you in the morning.'

Clara folded her arms. She didn't budge from her spot standing in front of his desk. Whatever it was, she would rather know now than go through a sleepless night, tossing and turning, wondering what on earth was going on.

'I'm tired, Clara. It's surprising how much it has taken out of me just making that trip across London to see Gerald. I think I will finish up here and get an early night.'

Clara backed down. At least the one good thing that had

come out of it was that Joe appeared to be taking on board his limitations. The consultant's advice about taking it easy had sunk in. And whatever Gerald had told Joe, often the reality never turns out as bad as your imagination would have you believe.

Clara held on to that comforting thought as she left Joe alone in his man cave and walked back up the garden to make a cup of tea.

85

Clara was sitting on the small platform at the back of the boat dangling her legs overboard, the blue azure water lapping at her feet. She was staring at the sea. The bright rays of morning sunshine made it appear like a layer of glitter sparkling on the ripples of water as the yacht gently bobbed up and down.

She recalled that meeting Joe had with Gerald about their finances. Every time she had tried to broach Joe with the subject of that meeting, he became evasive, refusing to answer her questions, avoiding eye-contact.

All that time she'd been having sleepless nights about the money when it turned out Joe knew all along he'd become a millionaire. He was holding out telling her while he organised a big surprise. Clara glanced about her. The surprise was this yacht he'd bought himself and a trip to the Mediterranean.

All these years he was on track for the big payday – he just never knew it. Gerald found some old share certificates amongst the paperwork she handed to him when Joe was laid up in hospital. Joe had invested in some Microsoft shares when it was just a start-up company. The consensus being that investing in these new software companies would eventually net huge dividends. And, as everyone knows, it turned out they were right.

Joe gave Tamsin and Kevin the house and some money to tide them over until Kevin found a job.

With further legal advice from Gerald he put the house in trust for the grandchildren, allowing the family to live there rent free for as long as they needed. He paid off the mortgage and after purchasing the small yacht, invested the remainder in a pension. Joe was finally living The Dream, *his* dream.

'What are you doing down here, darling? I couldn't find you anywhere and thought you'd gone into town to do some shopping.'

Clara snapped out of her reverie. 'I don't want to go shopping.' Clara glanced at the people strolling along the palm-lined promenade where they moored their yacht. A walk along the promenade brought you to the beach and the honey-coloured Mallorcan town beyond. Clara knew it well. Port de Pollensa and the old town of Pollensa a short distance inland, where she spent her summers as a child.

She felt a hand on her shoulder and heard Joe apologising. 'I'm so sorry.'

She stared into the crystal-clear water and watched the fish swimming beneath her feet. Moored here for a month, they had exhausted all avenues and were no closer to finding Tommy than when they first arrived.

'I want to go home,' she told the fish.

Joe arched his eyebrows. 'What do you mean, you want to go home? *This* is our home.'

Clara sighed. She knew he wasn't talking about Mallorca. Joe was referring to the boat. While she had been dragging her heels, unable to get over the fact that this was it – her hopes of finding Tommy were dashed – Joe was itching to cast off. He wanted to make their way up the Mediterranean coast to their next destination.

Joe dismissed the crew. Their services were no longer required as he soon got the hang of sailing his own yacht. He was looking forward to spending some time together – just the two of them. Pity she did not feel the same way.

Clara got to her feet. It rocked making her nauseous. She turned around to look at Joe. 'Do you expect me to live on a boat for the rest of my days?'

'We always talked about our dream of sailing around the med.'

'That was your dream. I just didn't realise we would be living the dream permanently.

'Yes, great isn't it. You took the words right out of my mouth - *living the dream*. Judy thought it sounded like heaven.'

Clara gave him a look.

Joe shrugged. 'What?'

'Perhaps you should have taken Judy along instead.'

He said nothing.

She stared at him. Was that a guilty expression as though the idea *had* crossed his mind? It made her wonder what really went on in the few days between Joe waking up and her making it back to his bedside?

Kevin had been trying to contact them for several days. In the interim, Joe had been entertained by Judy and stories of her exploits running the private detective agency. She stared at Joe.

Joe was trying his best not to give away what he was feeling. They had been married for so long he would never put it past her to guess what was on his mind; he was recalling those long, interesting conversations with Judy. They had talked and talked like he never did with his wife. Judy was always more receptive to his ideas than Clara. How could he have forgotten what a good listener she was?

Clara eyed her husband. She knew what he was thinking or, more to the point, whom he was thinking about. She shook her head as she brushed past Joe and clambered up the short flight of steps. It was lovely up here with views out to the ocean and back to the town. It was breathtakingly beautiful seeing all this from the deck of a gorgeous yacht. Clara leaned on the handrail. It wasn't being stuck on the boat that was the problem. Perhaps if Joe had been the right person, she would have followed him anywhere.

She tried to put Ralph out of her mind, but he kept muscling in on her musing, refusing to let her be. Thoughts of Ralph reminded her of the time they spent at the beach hut.

At first, Clara needed to return to that one place where she was closest to her brother – Mallorca. She had amazing memories of magical summers spent with her family on the island. Now she discovered she would not find Tommy, and the search was over, Clara didn't want to be here.

Despite all Joe's financial resources at their fingertips, the trail had gone cold. What did she expect after forty years? Did she imagine some clue or someone who knew his whereabouts would miraculously turn up and lead her straight to him?

'What are you going to do?'

Clara turned at the sound of Joe's voice. She glanced around the yacht, her gaze settling on Joe. She knew even though he wanted to sail around the med, all this planning and thought had gone into one thing – finding Tommy for her. Although nothing had come of it, Clara couldn't fault him for trying. She looked at him apologetically at what she was about to say.

'You're going home – aren't you?'

Clara opened her mouth, about to correct him; how could she go home when Tamsin and Kevin were now living in their house?

As if reading her mind, Joe said, 'I don't mean to London. You're going back to Southwold.'

'I must.'

Joe stepped forward. 'I know.'

They stood there looking at each other, searching each other's faces, perhaps in one last effort to see if there was anything more they had to say and, for Joe, any possibility she might return.

'This is goodbye then?' he said.

'Yes.'

They still didn't move, forty years of marriage and all that shared history weighing heavy on such a momentous decision to call it a day. Clara turned away first. 'I will pack my things.'

She wiped a tear from her cheek as she headed below deck to pack the small suitcase and few items she bought during their trip. She spent little of Joe's money, only buying the essentials for her stay in Mallorca. She closed her suitcase and picked it up from the small cabin bed in the second bedroom. As she passed by Joe's suite, she caught sight of the walk-in closet. The doors were ajar. She felt sad for Joe. He went to all that trouble of having something fitted that he thought she always wanted.

'You never knew me at all,' she said sadly. Perhaps that was because you refused to open your heart to Joe, she admonished herself. She looked at the camera in her hands. This was the greatest gift he ever bought her and yet, if it hadn't been for Sophie, he would have no clue what was meaningful to her – what made her happy.

She walked into Joe's cabin and shut the closet doors. Perhaps someone else would appreciate all this. Judy came to mind. The woman he was poised to marry all those years ago until she climbed into the back of his taxi one rainy afternoon and turned his life upside down. But it wasn't just his future she changed forever that day but Judy's – and Ralphs.

Clara turned around and stared at the king-sized bed. She held no animosity towards Joe, quite the reverse. She hoped he found happiness with someone else – he deserved it. Maybe he could rekindle his relationship with Judy. She saw how relaxed and happy they were in each other's company. Even in that brief exchange with both in the hospital room, Joe and Judy had some connection that had not been lost in the intervening years.

It reminded her of herself and Ralph, how they fell back into that easy familiarity after so many years apart; it was as if the years between then and now melted away, and they were teenage sweethearts again. She was thinking of that kiss in the beach hut. *Sweethearts?* Clara shook her head. She was still mad at him for not telling her who he was. That was reprehensible. What was his game? Why did he lie to her? *But then why did you* a little voice in her head said?

'Oh, piffle.' She would rather not think about that squatting business. Besides, what did it matter now? She did not expect to see him again. It made her cringe with embarrassment. He knew all along who she was and what she was up to.

In hindsight, there was plenty about "Henry" that gave him away, but Clara was just too preoccupied with her own situation to discover what was right in front of her nose – Ralph. She hoped they didn't bump into each other when returning to Southwold because if they did, she had no idea what she would say to him.

I've missed you.

She shook her head. *Stop thinking about him.* No good ever came from digging up the past. That's what Dorothy used to say.

Dorothy!

'Here – let me take that before you have an accident.'

Clara was struggling to get her suitcase up the narrow flight of stairs. She looked up to find Joe standing at the top. He leaned down, reached for her case and said, 'There was something I wanted to have a word about before you leave.'

Clara stepped up on to the deck.

Joe caught her expression. 'What's the matter?'

Clara planned to return to Southwold and check into that nice hotel for a few days while she figured out what she would do next. She had the proceeds from the sale of the beach hut so she could afford to spend a few nights in the lovely hotel. However, there was a problem.

From what she'd gleaned from Sophie's texts, Ralph had moved into the apartment above the garage. Elliot and Dorothy were staying at the house. That was perfect. Clara didn't mind looking in on Dorothy and catching up with Elliot if she could avoid Ralph. She just realised the fly in the ointment. What about Dorothy? She could not remain there forever.

Clara frowned at Joe, and said, 'What about your mother?'

'Ah, that's what I wanted to have a word about. As you will be in that neck of the woods, I wondered if you could do me a huge favour.'

Clara realised what was coming next.

'She cannot stay on indefinitely at—'

'The Gables.'

Joe nodded. 'That chap was kind to let her hang on. Who did you say he was?'

Clara bit her lip. She didn't want to get into that, especially with Joe. 'Just an old acquaintance.'

'Really,' Joe said flatly, the tone of his voice suggesting he was under no illusion that there was more to it than that.

'So, about this favour…?' said Clara.

'Sophie's friend, Elliot, says Dot loves it in Southwold.'

'For someone who refused to venture outside of the East End all her life, she's certainly taken to the English coast.'

'Yes, so I've heard. So, I was wondering what you thought about her staying there.'

'But she can't stay on at Ralph's house for the rest of her—'

'Ralph?'

Clara looked at Joe. 'He's the owner of the house.'

'I see.'

Clara looked away wishing she hadn't let slip she was on a first name basis with the owner.

Joe was still studying her intently.

She stole a glance at him. She wanted to tell him that if he thought her motives for returning to Southwold was bound up with seeing Ralph again, he was wrong. Clara said nothing. This was her life now to do with as she pleased. She didn't have to explain herself to anybody.

When Joe realised she wasn't giving anything away, it only confirmed what he suspected all along – that she *had* met someone else. He'd been waiting for this moment their whole married lives; preparing himself for the inevitable – that she would leave him.

He always wondered where his life would have led if fate hadn't stepped in on that rainy afternoon. He'd been driving his London taxi when their paths crossed. She was standing on the pavement in the pouring rain and he stopped to ask her if she needed a cab. If he took a different route home, or passed by a minute sooner, he would have missed her, and they would never have met. Would he have married Judy?

He didn't really believe in fate. However, over the years, it occurred to him whether they were not meant to be together, and that something would happen, and fate would step in once more – this time to take her away.

If he had one regret, it was wasting all that time in pursuit of The Big Payday rather than being satisfied with what he had – *who* he had. He stared at Clara. If he'd spent more time with her instead, would that have changed where they were now? He doubted it. It's just maybe he would have enjoyed the moments they shared than always looking to the future.

Joe managed a smile. Perhaps fate had a hand after all. If it wasn't for finding that postcard from Tommy, and the events thereafter, those share certificates might have languished in his desk drawer until he popped his clogs. He would never have known his retirement dream was right there under his nose.

His smile faded as he glanced about his yacht.

'Joe – what is it?'

It wouldn't be the same sailing around the Med unless he had someone to share the adventure with. Judy came to mind.

He looked at Clara. If I have been married to the wrong person all these years, then what about Judy? Did she feel the same way? She *had* been spending a lot of time with him and held a bedside vigil day and night when he was in a coma. Shouldn't that have been his wife holding his hand, talking to him and willing him to wake up? But it wasn't.

It surprised him how quickly they picked up where they had left off considering they had not seen or spoken to one another for years. As much as he didn't want to admit it, this past month away in Mallorca he had missed Judy terribly. Until he bumped into Judy again, he always thought Clara was his one and only.

'Joe?'

'Ahem.' Joe cleared his throat. 'Um… yes, about Dorothy. I know it's a lot to ask, but could you visit some care homes in the area and pick up the details? I will make it back across the channel to the East coast so can sort out the arrangements, but in the meantime…'

Clara nodded. With all he had done for her trying to find Tommy, it was the least she could do. 'Of course, I can.' She smiled at him realising it was nice to end it on this note – friends.

86

'Now, about money…'

Clara was itching to get off the yacht. 'I am sure you can sort out the financial side with the care home once you have decided—'

Joe interrupted her. 'I wasn't talking about that, Clara. I was talking about you and me. Now I've come into all this money—'

It was Clara's turn to interrupt him. 'I do not want any of your money.'

'But I signed over the house in trust to the grandchildren. You will have nowhere to live. Besides, we have been married all these years, it is fair you should have half.'

Clara looked at Joe. He'd been a good husband and taken care of her. Even now, when she was leaving him, he still had her best interests at heart. He was the kindest soul.

Some people in her shoes might take advantage and neglect to mention the quarter of a million paid straight into her bank account from the sale of a little beach hut on the Suffolk coast, but she wouldn't do that to him. He waited all these years for The Big Payday. If she took half his money, then he would have to sell his boat to have a decent pension to live off.

The house wasn't the only thing he'd given away. He also provided Tamsin with a lump sum to cover Sophie and Mia's school fees, plus money for Kevin to invest in another business.

She would not be surprised if he had given his only child half of what he came into when the shares were sold. That left him with the yacht – his new home which she estimated set him back around the cost of her beach hut – and the rest for a decent pension pot. He would need that to cover the running costs of his yacht and living expenses.

The fact was if she took half of what Joe had left sitting in a bank account, he would have to return to work or sell his yacht; either way, his retirement dream would go out the window. He would do it though. Even though she was leaving him, he would still put her first.

Clara smiled. For the first time, she was putting Joe's needs before her own. How ironic that she should do it now when they were no longer together. Even though the money she had wasn't a huge amount when she factored in somewhere to live and money to live on, but for his sake she would make it work.

'My answer is still no.' Clara told him about the beach hut and the money in her bank account.

Joe looked surprised. 'I had no idea a beach hut could be worth so much.'

'Neither did I.'

'I didn't know you were left a beach hut.'

'It was so long ago I'd forgotten about it.'

'But that's your inheritance. I still want you to have—'

She wasn't at all surprised Joe was still insistent she had a share of his good fortune. Just to make him feel better, she added, 'If I ever need anything, I'll let you know, all right?'

'Yes, I suppose so.'

Clara walked over and gave him a kiss goodbye on the cheek.

She had butterflies in her stomach; anxious about whether she was doing the right thing – walking away from a man who, generous to a fault, would always care for her. She wasn't making this decision lightly, but after Southwold something changed. Clara knew what that something was – Ralph.

Even though it was a brief encounter, and she would most likely never see him again, Clara realised it was time to grow up and take responsibility for her own life. It started with deciding, for both their sakes, to go their separate ways. She looked at Joe. He deserved more. Perhaps a relationship that wasn't all one-sided, with a woman who loved him as much as he loved her. Clara could never be that woman.

'Will you be okay?' asked Joe.

'I'll be fine,' she replied, although she was already feeling some trepidation at going it alone.

'I'll phone for a taxi to take you to the airport.'

Clara got out her mobile phone. 'I'll do it.' This is where it began, doing things for herself, learning to stand on her own two feet. Perhaps like Joe, she would arrive at a place where she was living the dream; *my* dream thought Clara. She was optimistic that everything would turn out all right in the end. It's just, unlike Joe, she wasn't sure what her dream life would turn out to be yet. *But won't it be fun finding out?* the little voice of optimism said.

She stepped off the boat with her suitcase. She stood on the promenade looking up at Joe on the open deck of his yacht. He held up his hand, the little finger and forefinger imitating a phone. 'Call me. Let me know when you have arrived in Blighty.'

'I will,' she called back.

'Safe journey.' He waved.

Clara smiled and waved back.

Anybody walking by seeing this friendly exchange – a slightly overweight man on the yacht wearing a Panama hat and a loud Hawaiian shirt, waving goodbye to the slim, blonde-haired, sophisticated woman in a cream linen trouser suit – might assume they were good friends parting ways, and not a couple who just split up after forty years of marriage.

Clara turned from the boat and walked along the promenade toward the beach-side shops and the taxi ranks. After losing Tommy and walking out on Ralph all those years ago, Clara had never been very good at endings. She smiled at the thought that for once in her life something finished well. Nothing else in her life ever had. Meeting Ralph again did not end on a positive note.

She glanced at Joe's yacht bobbing gently in the water and hoped he felt the same way. It might not have been what he wanted – his wife leaving him – but he wasn't racing down the promenade begging her to come back, trying to persuade her to stay. Judy came to mind. Perhaps in those few days when Joe had awoken from his coma, he'd had time to reflect on his life and to reconnect with another woman; someone more on his wavelength than the girl he had married.

This did not upset Clara. People change. Joe had come to the realisation he had changed. He wanted more than *a looker*, as he used to call Clara. He wanted someone who he could connect with in a different way – perhaps that was Judy, or maybe not, but either way the person he was looking for wasn't Clara. She knew that, for she had connected with Ralph the way she never had with Joe. If someone asked, she couldn't explain it because it wasn't something you could put into words – it was just something you felt.

Clara's smile faded at the thought of Ralph. Was it possible she might still be in love with him after all these years? She walked along, trundling her wheelie case behind her. Every time she thought of him, her stomach did somersaults. She had never experienced that with Joe. In fact, after all these years, she'd forgotten what it was like to be so in love with someone that just the mere thought of them sent your pulse rate soaring.

Clara took some deep breaths and tried to convince herself it wasn't the thought of Ralph that was sending her pulse rate soaring as she climbed into the taxi. After she returned to Southwold, intending to stay in the hotel for a few days and visit Tommy's grave to say a final farewell, she had to face the big unknown – what was she going to do with the rest of her life?

87

Clara was staring out of the taxi window hoping there was an available seat on a flight home, when the traffic ahead came to a standstill. They had driven out of Pollensa on the main road that led to the motorway and still had a good hour's journey to the airport.

Clara leaned forward, wondering if the driver spoke English. 'What's the hold-up?'

He turned in his seat. 'Roadworks.'

'Ah.' She sat back in her seat. She had no idea what the departure times were, so it wasn't as though she was in any hurry. If there were no available flights today, she would book into an airport hotel and catch one tomorrow.

Clara sat in the back of the taxi recalling the trips in a hire car from Palma airport with her brother and her parents, driving this same route. She tried not to think about the last time she made the journey to the airport years ago without Tommy. It was the saddest day of their lives.

Clara was shaking her head, trying to dispel that memory, when she spotted a handwritten notice on the edge of the road by a dirt track. Clara spoke a few words in Spanish. *En venta.* She leaned forward and asked the driver, 'That sign over there. Does that say, *for sale?*'

He cast a glance over where Clara was pointing and nodded.

'Can we drive up there, please?'

'You want me to drive you up there?'

'If it's not too much trouble,' Clara replied.

The taxi driver smiled at the polite English lady asking him that question as if he would be doing her a big favour, even though she was paying the fare. 'Of course.' He turned out of the queue of traffic and up the dirt track.

Clara leaned forward with her elbows resting on the front passenger seat. 'Can you see any more signs?'

'Are you looking for the property for sale?' asked the driver.

'Yes.'

They travelled along a single track for about half a mile with a grove of olive trees one side and orange and lemon trees on the other. At the end of the narrow road was a large honey-coloured villa with green shutters and double gates with a driveway beyond. Clara couldn't see a *for sale* sign.

'Shall we carry on?' asked the taxi driver.

'Yes, please.'

They turned sharp left in front of the villa, and then the single-track road climbed. 'Oh, goodness,' exclaimed Clara when she saw the views to her left. She spotted the sea, the water shimmering in the distance, and the valley of olive groves, still and quiet in the haze of the hot afternoon sun.

'Stop the car!'

The taxi driver skidded to a halt on the unmade gravel road.

Clara opened the car door and stepped outside. She stood there in the sweltering sun, a white straw hat and a linen scarf protecting her from the afternoon heat, staring at the view.

The taxi driver seemed to understand and killed the engine. He turned in his seat and glanced through the open window at the English lady.

Clara held on to her hat as a welcome breeze brushed her face. She stood there for some time drinking in the views, marvelling at the peace and tranquillity of the area. It was a mere couple of miles from the beautiful Pollensa old town and yet it seemed a world away from modern civilisation. Now she understood why people often remarked that Mallorca reminded them of the South of France fifty years ago. This was what stepping back in time felt like. A horse and cart wouldn't have been out of place here.

She turned around and was about to get in the cab when she saw it. 'Oh, there's the sign.'

The taxi driver craned his neck. It was on a wooden telephone pole. They would have missed it if they had just driven past. A hundred yards up ahead was a driveway.

Clara got back in the taxi as he switched on the engine. 'Let's take a look, shall we?'

Once again, the taxi driver smiled at the polite English lady being very… well… English.

This time Clara got in the front seat. 'You don't mind – do you?' she asked.

'It's my pleasure,' he replied.

Clara was so excited at the prospect of what she might find for sale at the end of the driveway she had to temper her enthusiasm with a reality check; it will either be some large, expensive villa – similar to the one they had passed – that she could never afford. Or some hovel that was a total renovation project, complete with no roof, vines growing through the windows and a dirt floor; none of which was at all appealing even if she managed to do it up.

What appeared at the end of the driveway was just that. Clara sighed. 'You might as well turn the car around. I've seen enough. Let's head back to the airport.'

The taxi driver slowed. 'But you have come all this way. Don't you want to look at the property?'

'I thought that was it?'

'I think that's just some outhouses.'

'What makes you say that?'

'The driveway continues up ahead.'

'Oh, I see what you mean,' Clara said flatly, her enthusiasm waning after seeing the state of the outbuildings.

'Why don't we find out what's at the end of the drive – eh?'

She looked at the outhouse with its missing roof and vines growing through the windows. Her first inclination was not to bother, but the taxi was already on the move, continuing up the track. Clara sat back in her seat. She was still enjoying the views just not looking forward to what she imagined was up ahead – if the outhouses were anything to go by.

'Now, I'd call that worth the detour,' remarked the taxi driver drawing the vehicle to a halt outside the property. He switched off the engine guessing his passenger in the front seat would jump out of the car with delight after setting her eyes on the villa.

The property, surrounded by orange and lemon trees, was set back from the driveway with pretty terraced gardens leading up to the villa. If she was looking for the real authentic Mallorca, away from the touristy town of Pollensa or the even more touristy resort of Port de Pollensa, then he didn't think she would find a better situation than this. The views were stunning with the backdrop of the Serra de Tramuntana Mountains behind the villa and across the rolling countryside to the sea at the front. But it wasn't as though she was miles from anywhere. A five-minute car ride, or fifteen minutes on a bicycle if she did not want to drive, and she would be in Pollensa old town.

The driver turned to his passenger wondering why she hadn't got out of the car. 'Aren't you going to take a look?'

'I don't think so,' said Clara, her eyes never leaving the property.

'Oh,' he said in surprise. He glanced at the villa. 'It looks nice though, don't you think?'

How could she tell him it was everything she had ever dreamed of. She just hadn't realised this was her dream come true until she'd set eyes on the single-storey honey-coloured villa with its shuttered windows and shady veranda under a sloping pitch-tile roof.

It's as though it had been waiting for her all her life – right here on the hillside above the town of Pollensa. Afraid to get out of the car and explore in case she fell in love with the place even more. One glance and she felt this was it; this was the place she could happily spend the rest of her life.

'We better go.' Clara was gearing up for the huge disappointment that the villa might already be sold or beyond her price bracket or not as nice inside as outside. Or any number of frustrations that meant her dream would not become a reality. It couldn't be that easy, could it? People spend months searching for their dream home; they do not get stuck in traffic, happen upon a *for sale* sign, drive up a dirt track and discover Shangri-La.

'Stranger things have happened.'

Clara looked at the taxi driver. She didn't realise she'd just spoken her mind.

The taxi set off. She willed herself not to turn in her seat. It would only make her feel worse. At the bottom of the drive, Clara asked the driver to stop the car while she jotted down the phone number on the *for sale* board. Perhaps she might make the call, anyway.

He knew it; she'd fallen in love with the place. 'You could arrange a viewing.'

'What – *now*?'

He shrugged. 'There's no time like the present.'

Clara eyed the taxi driver. *There's no time like the present.* She smiled at him. 'You are absolutely right.'

Clara made that call.

88

Clara woke up with a strange sensation that her bed was moving. For a moment, she thought she was still on Joe's yacht and that leaving him had just been a dream.

She rubbed the sleep from her eyes and peered around her room. Little wonder she was groggy with tiredness. She got the last flight home from Mallorca but did not arrive in Southwold until two in the morning. Thank goodness the hotel had twenty-four-hour reception.

'What time is it?' Fumbling for her wristwatch on the bedside table, she looked at the watch. It was still early, but she had a busy day ahead of her. She wanted to lie-down again but promised Joe she would pay a visit to the local residential care homes in the area, collect their brochures, and gather information to pass on. She didn't mind in the least doing this for Joe – and Dorothy.

Dorothy couldn't stay living in The Gables forever. Ralph probably assumed someone would turn up to claim the old lady, eventually. Clara just did not want it to be her. She hoped to avoid the house – and Ralph.

❖

Clara thrust another brochure in her handbag as she walked out of yet another residential care home. There were quite a few in the area. She glanced over her shoulder at the tall, imposing Victorian building fronting the sea. It had spectacular views of the coastline from each bedroom, but it wasn't right for Dorothy. Clara knew what would be ideal, but she still hadn't come across a place with extensive grounds that offered Dorothy the chance to continue her new hobby – gardening.

Clara felt a pang of sadness about the rather British institution of care homes for the elderly. When Joe brought Dorothy home with him before his accident, she didn't want her mother-in-law moving in with them; perhaps visiting some care homes would have given her pause for thought before showing her the door. What choice did she have? Tamsin, Kevin and the girls had moved into their three-bed semi, and Joe was living on a yacht. There was no room for her with the family.

Out of nowhere she had the most absurd idea; *she could come and live with me.* 'Oh no, absolutely not!' Clara shook her head.

Clara paused, reflecting on the enormity of the situation but determined not to get involved. Dorothy was not her problem. She is Joe's responsibility. He should have considered his mom before he bought a yacht. A little voice in her head said, when has Joe ever put himself first? He deserves his boat.

Even so it was up to Joe to tell his mother she would spend the rest of her days living in one room in a residential home, miles from family. Thinking of family, Clara stopped in front of the gate and took a deep breath. Back once again at the little churchyard in Southwold, this was the reason for her return; to say a final farewell to Tommy. And she had some news she couldn't wait to tell him.

Clara opened the gate with a tinge of sadness and regret that, despite Joe's unfailing optimism, she realised the search for her brother was futile; too many years had passed since that postcard arrived from him.

'Hello, Tommy.' Clara reached out and touched the headstone. 'I'm back.' She smiled when she imagined what he would have said to that. She nodded. 'Yes, you are right: *two* visits that's some record considering I haven't visited in almost forty years.'

Clara's smile broadened when she recalled what she had come to tell him. Was it just two months ago she imagined her life was over? Now here she was, and everything had changed. Well, almost everything. She was still on her own, but this time things were different; she was no longer afraid of being alone. In fact, if anyone had told her she would discover she could manage fine relying on herself, she would have scoffed at that. She had always needed someone to take care of her; not anymore.

And the other thing? Clara laughed. 'I'm still broke, Tommy. I know what you're thinking: how could I have blown my inheritance so quickly? Well, that's what I came here to tell you. I didn't fritter the money away.' She remembered her life with Joe and all the cash she had wasted on stuff that was shoved at the back of a wardrobe and meant nothing to her.

'No frittering this time, I swear. I spent it though – *all* of it. Well, almost all of it. I paid for my hotel room last night and a return air ticket home.'

Clara smiled when she imagined his reply. Did you say home? I thought you were home?

'No, this isn't home anymore, Tommy. Both you and I have always known where that is. I blame it on our parents, making us fall in love with Mallorca as children – you could almost say it was our first love affair – Mallorca.' She smiled at that.

'And you know what else, Tommy? I received your postcard. Now I know you didn't take that boat out and drown on our eighteenth birthday. I may never learn what happened, but I like to imagine you stayed in Mallorca, led a full life and…' Clara trailed off.

She pushed to the back of her mind that after making all those inquiries about an Englishman approaching sixty living on the island, her and Joe's search had unearthed nothing. But Clara could console herself with the thought that Mallorca is not small; it's the largest island in the Balearic Islands and the perfect place to disappear – if one so wished.

Clara smiled. She imagined him living out his latter years in a little villa somewhere in Mallorca. Clara rummaged in her bag and produced some photographs. 'I came back to show you these Tommy. It is what I bought. This is home.'

Clara showed the headstone the photos taken of her new home in the foothills of the Serra de Tramuntana Mountains, with the stunning vista through the orange and lemon groves down to the sparkling blue Mediterranean Sea. 'I've made a lot of impulsive purchases over the years, Tommy. You have no idea. But this is the only one I will *never* live to regret.'

After the viewing, Clara recalled writing out a cheque for the full asking price there and then, to the surprise of the estate agent and the taxi driver. Once they got back to the office, they contacted the vendor who accepted the offer and drew up legal documents – late that afternoon. Clara then waited for the vendor to arrive. They both sat down and signed the contracts. Clara handed over the cheque. They had already done background checks to ensure she was good for the money and the cheque wouldn't bounce.

It had to be the fastest sale in the history of that estate agency. Clara dangled the keys in front of the headstone. On the keyring was engraved *Casa La Buena Vida*. 'I considered changing the name. It's long winded – don't you think?' Clara looked at the keyring. 'But it is kind of fitting. *La Buena Vida* – the good life.'

Clara put the keys back in her purse. 'The problem is, now I'm broke again. But you know what?' Clara was still smiling. 'I'm not bothered. Joe bought me this ridiculously expensive camera.' She was going to sell it but had a better idea. 'Maybe I'll earn some money from photography. I used to be good at it. I could sell my photographs to newspapers or magazines.'

She also had other ideas. 'Perhaps I could teach English as a foreign language to students, or work freelance as a tour guide in Mallorca for all those cruises that come into Palma.'

Clara clapped her hands together in excitement. 'Oh, Tommy, I feel so optimistic. For the first time in… well… ages I understand life is full of endless possibilities.' Clara's beaming smile faded. It was a shame her optimism did not extend to the possibility of finding Tommy anymore. The only good thing that had come out of all this was because of the postcard, she had been right all along: Tommy had not drowned the night of the party.

Had he faked his own death to lead a life of his own choosing from under the scrutiny of their overbearing father? Or had he suffered an accident soon after sending that postcard, lost his memory, and gone through life never knowing who he was and that he had people who cared about him and were looking for him. Whatever the case, perhaps now, all these years later, he was at peace.

She stared at his headstone. Maybe he *was* here – in spirit. She would like to think he *had* returned – in some form or another.

In the hushed silence of the graveyard a dog barked making her jump. Clara turned around to see a large yellow dog bounding towards her.

'Oh my!' exclaimed Clara, taking a step back in surprise. She stopped her retreat. Is that…?' 'Bailey!'

A moment later, Bailey skidded to a halt on the wet grass in front of her wagging his tail, trying to contain himself from jumping up at Clara, although he managed to lick her face several times as she crouched down to give him a fuss.

'Oh, I've missed you too, you silly dog.' She wiped her face with the back of her hand. 'Now, that's enough kisses, thank you.' She patted his head. Bailey reminded her she missed her pet cat, Marley, and ought to return to the house to collect him. While she was there, she would say hello to Dorothy and Elliot.

But the one person she did not want to see was Ralph. If she could avoid him—

'Clara?'

She froze. As she turned around, she threw Bailey a cross look and thought *bad dog, very bad dog.* If it wasn't for Bailey, she might have spotted Ralph first and sneaked out of the graveyard undetected.

She turned to face him. Ralph was right behind her. 'What are you doing here?' they both said in unison

'I came to visit Tommy,' said Clara, her tone of voice civil but business like, making it crystal clear she had not come back to see Ralph. He was standing there holding flowers. She looked at the flowers. Ralph followed her gaze. 'Oh, I never come empty-handed.'

Clara frowned. *Just great.* Ralph made her feel guilty and a little embarrassed about turning up empty-handed. 'Right, well I'm done here.' She glanced at Tommy's headstone. 'He's all yours.' She was desperate to get away and avoid Ralph's gaze or any unpleasantness regarding the subject of her and her family squatting in his property.

Ralph glanced at the headstone but did not step aside to let her pass.

'If you wouldn't mind letting me pass, *Henry*.'

He didn't budge. 'I can explain…'

Clara was trying to avoid those eyes, those lips, and the desire to throw her arms around him and kiss him again. *Get a grip,* thought Clara, *walk away. You've got a new life now with endless possibilities – remember.*

She tried to side-step around him and felt her shoe slip on wet grass. 'Oh, no,' She slid down on to her bottom. 'Now, look what you made me do!'

'Are you all right?'

'Do I look all right?'

Ralph reached out a hand to help her up.

Her first impulse was to slap it away, but any attempt at getting up by herself was futile. Clara took his hand.

Ralph attempted to pull her up but the next thing he knew, he was lying on the damp grass next to her.

'Oh, for goodness sake!' she hissed. 'Fat lot of good you are.'

When she didn't get a response, she turned and stared at him. 'Ralph? Ralph!' His eyes were closed. He was completely still.

'I was thinking…' Ralph opened his eyes and turned his head.

'You were *thinking*?' Clara fumed. 'I thought you'd hit your head and were…'

'I was thinking,' continued Ralph, 'that this takes me back.'

Her heart was still racing at the prospect he was hurt.

'Remember when we used to do this?'

'Do what – fall over in cemeteries?' she said sarcastically.

'Now that's plain silly. No, I'm talking about when we used to lie side-by-side looking up at that vast sky, watching the clouds float by. This will always be my favourite part of England – Constable Country.' Ralph was staring at the sky.

She lay down on her back next to him, her head resting on her bag. Clara looked up. She loved Constable's landscape paintings of Suffolk, the way he captured the soft rolling countryside, the light, the big expanse of sky.

'It's a funny thing isn't it – *time*.'

She turned to look at Ralph.

'Despite all the intervening years since I saw you last, it seems like it was only yesterday we were lying in the grass together, holding hands, just watching the clouds pass by overhead without a care in the world.'

Clara felt his hand reaching for hers. She didn't flinch, she let his hand envelope hers, their fingers intertwining. She looked up. It was as though the clock had swung back and they were teenagers again staring at that never-ending sky that hadn't changed from that day to this.

Clara smiled. 'Without a care in the world.'

'Are you all right?' A stranger walking through the cemetery had, to his surprise, come across two people lying by a gravestone on the damp grass with a yellow dog at their feet.

Ralph turned to Clara and squeezed her hand. 'I think we will be okay.'

She caught his meaning and gave his hand a gentle squeeze as her heart leapt. 'Yes, I guess we are.'

89

'Clara – is everything all right?'

She turned around and glanced across the room at Ralph. Propped up on one elbow in the king-size bed, his bare chest tanned he looked fit for someone approaching sixty. She smiled at him in answer to his question. She knew what he was asking: *After last night, are we still okay?*

He was so happy when she agreed to stay the night and accompanied her to the hotel to collect her suitcase and check out. Ralph couldn't wait to show her his apartment over the garage. Clara didn't have the heart to tell him she'd seen it before. Dorothy and Elliot were in the main house across the drive.

She smiled at him in answer to his question. 'You don't mind – do you?' She'd slipped his shirt over her bare shoulders when she got out of bed. The little black negligee Joe bought her, which she swore she would never wear, was the first thing she reached for last night to feel and look sexy for Ralph. She was never self-conscious about her body with Joe, but then he had seen her age and gain a few pounds over the years. But with Ralph it was different. She hadn't been with him since they were teenagers. What would he think of her now beneath her clothes, her makeup, and her coiffed hair? Clara stood there and pulled the shirt around herself.

Ralph smiled at her. 'You look adorable.'

'What – in your shirt?'

'My shirt, your negligee – nothing at all,' he added cheekily.

'Oh stop, you're just being kind,' she said blushing.

'Not at all,' he said in all seriousness. 'You are beautiful.'

Not convinced, she tried to smooth down her hair. She imagined what she looked like with smeared makeup and a mass of tangled hair. Clara hadn't removed her makeup last night; she only had time to slip on the negligee before he slipped it off. Her cheeks were burning again at the thought of how much Ralph wanted her, so unlike Joe after years of marriage where she often felt they were going through the motions – there was no urgency, no passion – no stamina. Clara was back to eyeing Ralph's physique wondering where he got the energy from.

'You like it – don't you.'

For a moment she wondered what he was referring to; all that was on her mind after last night was a sex life she never thought she would have again.

He pointed to her left.

'Oh, you mean the picture.' Clara turned back to the painting sitting on the easel in the corner of the room. She was standing staring at it when Ralph woke up.

'It's Pollensa old town isn't it.'

Clara didn't just like the painting, she adored it.

'When I was working on an assignment in Mallorca, my wife wandered around the market and fell in love with the picture. A local artist painted it.'

'I'm sorry, I didn't mean to—'

'It's fine. I can talk about her now. I'm in a better place, thanks to you.' He held out his hand.

Clara walked over and took his hand as she climbed back into bed next to him.

'She'd been carrying this painting past the restaurant when the bomb blast went off.'

'I'm sorry about what happened to her.'

Ralph squeezed her hand.

Clara turned her attention to the picture.

He could tell there was something on her mind. 'What is it?'

'It's nothing, honestly.'

'Tell me, please.'

'Well…' Clara was trying to find a tactful way of asking how come the painting was unharmed when his wife was blown to smithereens. She gave up.

Ralph followed her gaze. 'You're wondering how the painting survived intact.'

Clara nodded.

'It didn't. The canvas was scorched. About a third survived.'

'Then how—?'

'Elliot.'

'Elliot?' Clara threw him a questioning look.

'They returned my wife's belongings to me and among her effects were what remained of this canvas. God knows why they bothered. It really needed to be dumped, but I could not bring myself to get rid of it.'

Ralph didn't tell Clara about the nights he laid awake on the old camp bed staring at what was left of that painting and falling into a blissful dream; in that dream they were back together walking hand-in-hand along a deserted Mallorcan beach.

'You were saying something about Elliot…?'

'Oh, yes. Elliot discovered the canvas, and this was the result. I have to say, he did something extraordinary. You couldn't tell how badly it was damaged.'

Clara agreed. 'I think he's talented.'

'So do I. That's why I approached contacts in London. Elliot has been working on some paintings of his own. I wangled him a spot in a gallery to exhibit his work. We will see how it goes.'

Clara climbed out of bed to have another look at the painting. It is a wonderful thing what Elliot did by restoring it. I imagine your wife fell in love with Mallorca too. That is why she bought this painting. Which reminded Clara about her new home. 'Ralph, I have something to tell you—' She turned around and discovered his eyes were closed.

She wasn't surprised he'd drifted off to sleep and was intending to return to bed after she nipped to the loo. Then she got side-tracked by the painting. She hadn't spotted it last night. They'd been up until the early hours, not having sex *all* night – although they couldn't seem to get enough of one another – but eventually, they snuggled under the covers, nose-to-nose, and Clara told Ralph about Tamsin.

'I do not want any secrets between us,' she'd said. 'But if it turns out when I've had my say, you wish me to pack my things and leave, I will not blame you.'

'I don't want you to go,' Ralph had said.

'Just hear me out – then decide.'

Clara told Ralph what happened when she fled to London; she was pregnant with his baby. She'd been afraid to contact him in the aftermath of losing Tommy because he had seemed so distant since his best friend's disappearance. It was as though she had lost them both. If he couldn't handle losing Tommy, how would he cope with finding out she was pregnant with his child?

Clara stared at him across the room. She didn't ask him to explain himself; why he acted as though he did not want to know her on their return from Mallorca. Why he didn't come after her when she fled to London. That was all water under the bridge.

At first, he had been silent after her confession. She was not surprised. It was a lot to take in to discover that not only did he have an adult child, but two beautiful grandchildren too – all by the woman he loved.

Finally, Ralph had told her, 'It was the biggest regret of my life, not following you to London and trying to find you. The next thing I knew, I heard you got married. Then I thought I couldn't have meant that much to you if you met someone else so soon after you left me.'

I left you? she wanted to say, shaking her head, but she didn't. Clara recalled the rest of that conversation as she stood there watching Ralph sleeping…

'I met Joe on the rebound. I felt he was a good man who would care for me and my baby.'

'Does he know that Tamsin isn't his child?'

'I wouldn't have done that, trick a man into making an honest woman of me. He knew before we dated. He has been a good father, Ralph. The best.' Clara had to clarify that, 'He might not be her biological father, but he'll always be her Dad. Do you understand?'

Ralph had nodded, full of regrets he had missed those years and that relationship with his child. As much as he wanted to be her father, Clara was right: he would never be her dad. The man who raised her would always claim that right.

She had told him, 'I looked for you at the station before we boarded the train back to London. I thought—'

'You thought I'd come. I did. Even though I knew your husband had awoken from his coma, and I had no right to ask you to leave him, I turned up to beg you not to go. But I was too late. The train was disappearing in the distance. I'd just missed you.'

Clara remembered she had kept looking out for him as she boarded the train.

'I thought about following you to London, but what was I going to do? Walk into your husband's hospital room and tell him I wanted his wife to be with me instead? I had no right.'

'You had every right,' Clara had said, surprising him.

'I don't understand.'

'Because you love me, and I love you.' Clara smiled at him as she recalled that conversation before they fell asleep.

She was wide awake now, but she would let him sleep. Clara washed and changed in the en-suite bathroom. She was intending to slip out with the new camera and do the other thing she had returned to Southwold to do: take some photos of the beach hut just for old times' sake with her new camera. She wanted to get down there early while the beach was still deserted.

Clara stepped out of the bathroom and caught sight of the old camera belonging to Ralph that Sophie had discovered with a reel of film still inside; it was the one she had used when she slept here before. She'd taken it down to the beach with her early the next morning and taken photos of Ralph sleeping in the deckchair outside the beach hut.

She picked up the camera. Rather than slipping out with her new one, Clara had a better idea. Why not give develop that film? She didn't know what else was on it, but if her photos of the beach hut – and Ralph – came out okay then that would be preferable to the possibility of bumping into the new owners; something she would much rather avoid.

Although without the sale of the beach hut she would never have been able to buy *Casa la Buena Vida,* Clara still couldn't help but feel a pang of regret at severing that last link with Tommy.

Clara picked up the old camera from Ralph's desk and opened the door to the darkroom.

90

'What are you doing in there?' Clara turned around at the sound of Ralph's voice. He was standing in the doorway to the darkroom slipping on a robe over his silk pyjamas. She stared at him a long moment, enough for Ralph to notice. He said, 'What is it? What's wrong?'

What's wrong? She didn't know where to begin or how to put into words what she felt right now. Instead of uttering a word, she stepped aside.

Ralph furrowed his brow, switched on the light and caught sight of what was amiss. His eyes shifted to Clara. 'Where did you find those?'

She thought he might attempt a grovelling apology even though she knew the minute she saw what was on that film that nothing, *nothing* he could say would make things right. Clara snatched the photograph that was hanging up on a little peg drying. It was a picture from the reel of film she had just developed. It wasn't a snap taken of the beach hut, but a photo that must have sat in the camera undisturbed for decades. She thrust it at Ralph. 'Why didn't you tell me?!'

Ralph tried to look anywhere but at the photograph of Tommy. He shook his head as if to say, *please don't make me look at it.* She realised someone took it *after* the party because there was a newspaper on the table in front of him, in one of the old photos.

When she had got over the initial shock of discovering there were pictures of Tommy on the reel of film taken by Ralph *after* he'd supposedly drowned, she studied the photographs carefully. She saw the date on the paper, leaving her in no doubt Ralph knew Tommy had not taken that boat out and drowned.

There were other images too. One was of a lady she recognised. It looked like the young woman from the travelling circus. She read her palm many years ago and told her she would lose someone she loved.

'He was never in that boat,' whispered Ralph.

'I'm aware of that,' Clara said with an edge to her voice. She told him about the postcard Tommy sent; the one Joe discovered on their doormat one morning soon after they married and assumed it was from Clara's first love – and the father of her unborn child.

Joe wasn't aware at the time that it was from her long-lost brother, missing presumed drowned. How was he to appreciate the ramifications when, in the heat of the moment – afraid he would lose her – he'd stuffed that postcard out of sight at the bottom of a drawer? When he found it years later, it set a chain of events in motion that had led here, to Clara falling in love all over again with her teenage sweetheart – only to discover *this*.

'How could you!' All these years Ralph had kept something from her – from her parents. 'They planned it – Tommy's disappearance. And you knew all along. Why didn't you tell us?'

'He made me promise, Clara.'

'Promise?' she scoffed. 'Why? What on earth caused Tommy to keep a secret like this from his parents and his own sister?'

'He'd fallen in love.'

She thought of the young woman from the travelling circus who had come to town. She remembered her sultry Mediterranean appearance with her dark olive skin, black hair down to her waist, and a strong foreign accent. 'It was the woman from the circus.'

'You remember her?'

How could Clara forget? She was the medium who had forewarned Clara she was about to lose her brother, her twin.

'But why did he have to fake his own death? What was he afraid of? Was it that father wouldn't give him his blessing and try to stop their relationship? Is that why?'

Ralph shook his head.

'Then *what*?'

When Ralph didn't answer, Clara stormed over, thrust the photograph into his chest and walked out of the dark room. 'And before you ask,' she threw over her shoulder as she reached for her suitcase, 'it did not surprise me he hadn't drowned. I would have known. I would have felt something if he had died that night. He sent me a postcard some months afterwards, but then you knew that – didn't you. You were the one who got hold of my address in London and gave it to him.'

Ralph continued to stare at the floor in silence.

'I only received the postcard recently. There was no return address.' Clara stopped halted when something occurred to her. She turned around. 'Do you know where Tommy is now?'

Ralph looked up. 'I swear I have no idea what happened to him after we took those photos. I meant to develop the film and give you the pictures when you returned from Mallorca, but then you fled to London.'

'Oh, so it was payback for me leaving you.'

'No, not at all. I… I wasn't well. When I lost you, I tried to contact Tommy to tell him I had changed my mind. I wanted to tell you what happened. But when I tried to find him, that's when I discovered he'd disappeared for real. He was gone, Clara. I'd lost him, and I'd lost you. What was the point of sending you the photos if I couldn't tell you where he was?'

Clara stared at Ralph. Out of all this there was still something bothering her. Why Tommy didn't confide in her about his plans to elope with this girl. Why had he confided in

Ralph and not her? They were twins, best friends. He was always the one she turned to if she had a problem.

She guessed he did not want to face their father and tell him he'd fallen in love with a gypsy and wanted to marry her and lead an alternative life. He must have known father would not give his blessing. Perhaps she might have told him and softened the blow. She was always his favourite. Then again maybe it was the case that Tommy didn't want to involve her in his plans if it meant she had to take sides.

As if reading her mind, Ralph said, 'You asked me why he went to great lengths to disappear to be with her – what was he so afraid of?'

Clara stopped at the door with her suitcase.

'It was you, Clara.'

'What are you talking about?'

'He was afraid of *you*.'

'*Me?*' Clara shook her head. 'That makes no sense.'

'It does if he thought you might talk him out of it.'

'Talk him out of *what*?'

'Of leaving you – for her.'

Clara stared at Ralph. 'What are you saying?'

'He was afraid you would make him choose. He couldn't live with himself if that turned out the case. Twins – it's a complicated relationship.'

'What would you know?' She was trying not to think about that selfish, self-centred young girl who, in hindsight, always seemed so much younger and so immature compared to her twin, even though he was only older than her by four minutes.

'You have no idea what you're talking about,' Clara added defensively.

'Yes, you're right, but I think *you* do.'

Clara picked up her suitcase and opened the door.

'Where are you going? Are you going back to Joe?'

Clara stepped out on to the porch. 'I'm going home.'

91

'Are you all right, Dorothy?' whispered Clara.

'Shh, I'm trying to pay attention. I suggest you do the same. I think it's important.'

Clara didn't have to pay attention. Like most people waiting for take-off she'd heard it all countless times before. She turned to look at Dorothy sitting beside her and couldn't help but smile when she saw her expression. Here was an eighty-four-year-old great-grandmother who seemed as excited as the six-year-old across the aisle from them. Clara guessed the little girl was also on her first flight.

After checking Dorothy's seat belt was fastened, Clara sat back and watched the flight attendant going through the safety drill before take-off. As Clara's eyes glazed over, her mind wandered back to that morning a week ago when she stormed out of Ralph's place having collected Dorothy, Winston, and Marley her cat on the way. She didn't know what she would do with them all, but they were not staying with Ralph a moment longer.

Clara had already spoken to Joe about the different options regarding residential care homes in the area. He'd looked online and agreed with her which one he thought was right for Dorothy. A two-storey former gentleman's lodge on the outskirts of the town that wasn't that dissimilar from The Gables.

It didn't have views of the sea like some other much larger residential places, but it had a garden in which Dorothy could potter. That's where, with Joe's consent, she took Dorothy that morning.

She and Dorothy followed the care home manager along the hallway, passing two communal lounges on a tour of her new home. They arrived at a small room with a single bed overlooking the garden. Clara drew the net curtain to look at the view while the care home manager, a middle-aged lady with a kind disposition, placed Dorothy's suitcase on the bed.

Clara remarked what a lovely view Dorothy had from her window and how lucky Winston was to have a garden to run around in.

That's when the care home manager looked at her with a bemused expression and asked, 'Who's Winston?'

Clara recalled holding up the small dog she'd been carrying in her arms.

'I let you bring your dog as a one-off because Dorothy is moving in today, but on future visits I must insist that you leave your—'

'Oh, this isn't mine,' Clara corrected her as she placed Winston on Dorothy's bed.

Five minutes later they were standing outside the care home.

Dorothy wasn't apologetic. 'You cannot expect me to live somewhere if they won't let me keep my dog.'

Clara had picked up her suitcase and walked Dorothy and her dog back into town to find a taxi.

'Are you going to take me someplace else that will let me bring Winston too?' she had asked. Dorothy knew the score. Her son had bought a yacht. She couldn't live with him.

After spending time at The Gables with the space and grounds, and the smell of salty sea air through her open bedroom window, the truth was Dorothy did not want to return to her dingy flat in East London. That's when she'd looked at

Clara as they waited for a taxi to take her to goodness-knows-where and asked: 'What if you cannot find anywhere that will let Winston come too? Where am I going to live?'

With no family nearby, Clara realised if Dorothy was to stay in Southwold on her own, she could not be parted from Winston. That's when Clara caught her anxious expression, and blurted, 'Don't you worry, I know just the place.'

Dorothy's next adventure began with a pleasant, but temporary, sojourn in a local Bed and Breakfast that accepted pets. This gave Clara a chance to sort out the practicalities of getting Dorothy and the pets – Winston and Marley – their passports. And now here they all were, the pets in the cargo hold and Dorothy seated next to her taking a three-hour flight to Mallorca.

'Is everything all right?' Clara asked again, still conscious of the fact that Dorothy had never flown before. Would she have a panic attack as soon as the plane took off? Not that she'd ever had one before, but there was a first time for everything. Or would she come over faint or have a heart attack or stroke mid-air? All these most worrisome possibilities were running through Clara's mind when Dorothy turned to her and replied in her usual abrupt manner, 'Stop fussing. I'm fine.'

Dorothy picked up a newspaper as soon as the safety drill finished. The flight attendant asked them if they wanted any refreshments. Dorothy got out her purse.

'It's complimentary, Madam.'

'Complimentary,' repeated Dorothy in high spirits. 'Well, isn't that marvellous. I'll have a nice cup of tea, dear.'

Clara opted for a Gin and Tonic. She'd never been a good flier. The worry over Dorothy wasn't helping. Had she done the right thing by deciding, on the spur of the moment, to bring Joe's mother home with her? Clara glanced at Dorothy stirring her tea as she settled back to read her paper; she looked so relaxed anyone would think she was a seasoned flyer. For someone in their eighties who had never in their life ventured far outside Peckham, Clara was astounded that she was taking all this in her stride.

Dorothy folded her newspaper. 'I'm worried about Winston.'

Clara turned to Dorothy. Even though they had been through all this before they left, Clara explained again that, 'Winston and Marley are fine in the hold. Remember the nice vet gave them a tranquiliser? They will sleep the whole way. When we all arrive, they don't have to go into quarantine because they have pet passports, so they can come with us to our new home.'

Our new home. Clara gulped down her gin and tonic. This was not how she envisaged her twilight years – living with her mother-in-law. How ironic that a few weeks ago she didn't want Joe inviting his mother to live with them and here she was insisting Dorothy did just that – and Joe wasn't even around.

As if Dorothy could read her mind she brought up the subject of Joe. 'When did you say Joe would visit?'

Clara fancied another gin and tonic. That was the other thing. As Dorothy was moving in with her, it meant Joe would come to visit – often.

She'd sent Joe an email and told him she was bringing Dorothy to live with her in Mallorca. Clara didn't have the heart to leave her in what was, despite appearances, an institution. He'd emailed back and been honest enough to admit that he couldn't do it either but didn't know what else to do. It's not as though she could live on his yacht.

He emailed from his laptop while sitting on the deck of his yacht, sipping a margarita and enjoying the splendid views of the Italian Riviera. Moored off the Island of Capri, he had written all that in his email too. Joe enjoyed lazing around doing nothing all day save for a dip in the ocean – followed by a meander around the local town, and an afternoon lounging in the sun on deck reading a book. With his new life on the ocean waves, Dorothy would be a huge problem if she came to live with him.

It was not that she had dementia and might wander off in unfamiliar surroundings, getting lost and confused, or forget she was on a boat and fall overboard. The fact was Dorothy did not have any problems with her memory. A local G.P. in Southwold discovered her so-called dementia was in fact depression.

A change of scenery, getting out of Peckham and staying at The Gables with the space and the garden and the sea air had done the trick. Dorothy was back to her usual on-the-ball, sharp-as-a-pin, self. And that was the problem. Unlike Joe, Dorothy would be bored out of her mind living with her son in his retirement dream. Dorothy was a doer – much like her soon-to-be ex daughter-in-law, Clara. She needed interesting things to occupy her time. When her husband passed away, she was lost. They did everything together and she didn't know what to do without him. The spiral into depression began, leading to a misdiagnosis of dementia.

Clara knew there would be lots of things to do in Mallorca. Gardening, and fascinating places to visit. She just hoped Dorothy wasn't lonely moving to *Casa La Buena Vida* when she was used to all the friends and family who had been staying at *The Gables* over the summer?

Clara wondered if it wasn't Dorothy she was concerned about. Was there some trepidation on her part about returning to Mallorca? It had been a spur-of-the- moment decision to buy the villa. It was love at first sight, but would she feel the same way on her return?

Thinking of love at first sight, Ralph came to mind; although he was never far from her thoughts. It felt like love at first sight when she first laid eyes on him as a teenager and she had been shocked to discover all these years later, that special connection was still there. She was mystified that decades on, they picked up where they left off as though it was only yesterday, even though they had both met someone else in the intervening years.

Her thoughts drifted to the other man in her life – Joe. He'd been over the moon and taken aback when he heard what Clara was doing; bringing Dorothy with her. He had no idea his wife could be so… *selfless* was the word he used. After years and years of selfish, self-centred Clara, Joe was honest enough to say he did not know his wife had it in her.

Clara was worried he might wish to get back together, now he was seeing another side to his wife; a side she imagined he would rather like. As much as she did not want to be alone, after rekindling her relationship with Ralph, albeit briefly – she could not go back to a man she did not love the way she had loved Ralph. If that meant she had to spend the rest of her days alone – then so be it.

She glanced at Dorothy. She was not the easiest person to get along with, but Clara knew she would not be lonely. It wasn't the reason she'd brought Dorothy with her. If she had not developed that old film and discovered the secret Ralph kept from her, that he knew Tommy hadn't drowned that night, then Ralph might be sitting on this plane. But that wouldn't have changed the fact that Dorothy would still be here too whether Ralph liked it or not.

Clara had plenty of room to accommodate her new guest. *Casa La Buena Vida* wasn't small. Although it was a single-storey villa, was built in an interesting 'U' shape. The lounge, kitchen and hallway were in the centre of the property. There were two wings off the main hall both with two bedrooms and a bathroom, one of which was perfect for guests – or a permanent house guest called Dorothy.

They could use one of the bedrooms in Dorothy's wing as a lounge if she did not want to join her in the main sitting room. Clara was already thinking through the practicalities, trying to ignore that little voice in the back of her mind saying, *well that sounds fine, but will you still feel the same way about the villa when you arrive?* Isn't that why you are advised to do a second viewing, thought Clara getting herself worried and worked up over nothing – she hoped.

'More refreshments?' asked the flight attendant as she passed back through the cabin. 'Tea, coffee, alcoholic beverages?'

Clara's hand shot up at the mention of alcoholic beverages.

92

'Yes, you can put it down over there.' Clara pointed at a free space on the tiled floor in front of the fireplace. The delivery men rolled out a huge mat covering a large proportion of the tiled floor in the centre of the lounge. It made the room feel cosy.

She was just going to sit down on one of the sumptuous sofas when the delivery men were back again with something else. Clara rolled her eyes thinking *what now?* She watched them unpack another item. All this arrived a week after Clara, Dorothy, Winston, and Marley the cat settled into their new home. Clara bought the villa as is. A former holiday rental, the property was part-furnished. Although it was sparse and the furniture old and well used, there were beds to sleep in, chairs to sit on and some white goods in the kitchen. It meant she could jump on a flight with Dorothy and move straight in.

While Clara would have liked to equip the villa out in new furniture she chose herself, she was content to make do. This was just as well because she didn't have the money. At least she was here; that's what was important; she reminded herself.

It turned out Joe had other ideas.

Clara watched the delivery men unpack a flat-screen television and mount it on the wall in the lounge. It came with satellite TV; a local company would come around and set it up for her.

It was not something she would have bought. Clara didn't expect to be watching that much television. Her eyes drifted to the double doors leading out to the patio in the back garden. It was where she spent the warm evenings sitting with a book by the pool. When the sun went down the solar lights hanging from the orange and lemon trees in her garden came on, emitting a soft, comforting glow. She could still read by the electric lantern-style lights under the pagoda that ran the length of the back of the villa which provided welcoming shade on her patio during the day.

With year-round sunshine and Mallorca's mild climate, it meant being stuck in, in the evenings, was a thing of the past. Glancing at the television she imagined the grandchildren would appreciate satellite TV, along with Joe when he dropped by to visit Dorothy.

Clara appreciated the oak side table; it matched the coffee table that the delivery men placed on the rug in front of her. Then there were the small side tables that appeared along with the lamps. The room looked different from when they first arrived. In fact, the whole villa resembled something out of a magazine. She guessed that's where Joe came up with the idea. She couldn't have chosen better herself. Although she was still cross with him for spending all this money.

One thing Clara purchased before returning to Mallorca was a laptop so she could keep in touch with friends and family. Sophie set her up on Facebook. She soon discovered that Sophie had set up Granddad Joe on Facebook too and made him a 'friend,' which was fine by her – they *were* friends. Clara posted photos of her villa online when she arrived, using the new camera Joe bought her. Everyone was dying to see what it looked like before they visited. That included Joe.

Joe messaged her on Facebook to say he wanted to provide some "odds and ends" to make Dorothy's stay more comfortable at Clara's villa. Although Clara messaged back telling him that wasn't necessary, he insisted. A week later, two large delivery vans negotiated the single-track road up to her villa.

She did not expect Joe to re-furnish her entire home. He'd even included garden furniture and sun loungers for the pool. Clara wasn't pleased, but she couldn't turn them away. It should have occurred to Joe that perhaps over time she would have enjoyed furnishing her own place, although she could not envisage when that would happen.

However, she soon changed her tune when she saw what they were unloading. She was pleasantly surprised that Joe had such good taste. The more they unpacked, the more Clara had a sneaking suspicion he'd had help to choose all this; some things felt like a woman's touch, the vases of dried flowers and the useful odds and ends for the kitchen. Simple things like an egg timer and weighing scales she guessed wouldn't even cross Joe's mind.

Finally, after half a day of back and forward to the vans unloading and unpacking the items, the drivers loaded up their trucks with the old furniture from the villa that Clara didn't want to keep. Clara wandered outside to see them off. She felt something soft and furry brush her leg and looked down to find Marley, her cat, had come out from his hiding place in the garden to say hello. She bent over and scooped him up as the two men climbed into their vans. Clara waved a friendly goodbye although she whispered to the cat, 'Between you and me, I'll be glad to have the place to myself again.'

She looked at Marley purring in her arms. 'Well, you are a lot happier now – aren't you. As I recall, you didn't much care for the bumpy ride down the lane to your new home.' Clara smiled as she recalled her arrival here in the taxi; it was the same driver who had driven her here the first time around, except this time she wasn't on her own. She remembered the taxi-drivers expression when he arrived at the airport to pick her up and take her home. Clara was no less surprised by her little entourage.

Who would have thought the next time she laid eyes on the villa she would be accompanied by a lady of advancing years, one dog, and a very grouchy cat.

The taxi driver's wife who cleaned holiday rentals in the area asked if she would like a cleaner, and they had a neighbour who knew a pool man.

'A what?' Clara had said. When she viewed the property, she was so keen to get back to the estate agent's office and sign on the dotted line he had only done a whistle-stop tour of the inside. Somehow, she did not register the fact the villa had a pool. She recalled that the estate agent couldn't find the outside switch which lit up the back garden. It would have illuminated a lot more besides if he had.

It would have delighted most people, but Clara was less enamoured; her first consideration when she found out, having already bought the property, was how much would it cost to run and maintain? The cost of the pool man – apparently.

The pool man and the taxi-driver's wife, Maria, weren't the only ones in her villa at the moment helping get things ship-shape. Residents in the neighbouring villas dotted along the road had popped in over the last week to introduce themselves. They came with friendly advice too about the locality. She had appreciated the gesture even though she was not new to the area.

They had also turned up to help with the unpacking and rearranging of her new furniture. Dorothy was busy in the kitchen preparing a meal for their guests. Clara, with the help of the pool man, set up a long folding table and plastic chairs on the patio. It seated twelve and was one item that came with the house which Clara kept. She was glad she did. Dorothy and Maria were busy putting bowls of salad and bottles of wine on the table.

Clara glanced over her shoulder at the villa. She heard corkscrews popping as she stood outside the front with the cat.

There was a brick-built barbecue in the garden which Dorothy spotted. She thought it would be a wonderful idea to cook al fresco. Clara sighed. It was ridiculous, but cooking outside reminded her of Ralph, and the times she used to meet up with him outside her beach hut for breakfast. She wanted to put that episode behind her.

Watching the two large vans making their way down her driveway until they disappeared round the bend out of sight, she sighed in relief. It had been a long day. She didn't know what she would have done without her neighbours giving a hand and was thankful for the help. Now she was looking forward to an evening meal under the stars with her new neighbours. Clara frowned. The trouble was, all this – new acquaintances, a different house, a new beginning – was reminding her of The Gables – and Ralph.

She was just putting Marley down when she heard a car turning up her driveway. She waited until she saw it come into view. It looked like another delivery van. Clara threw her hands up in the air. 'God – what has he bought this time?' She'd already been online once today, soon after the delivery trucks arrived, logging on to Facebook and messaging Joe that while she appreciated the thought, he shouldn't have bought all this stuff.

Watching the delivery truck approach, she knew as soon as they left, she would be on Facebook again telling Joe that enough was enough, in case he had any more ideas for her villa.

Clara watched the small van stop in the driveway. A man stepped out, opened the back door of the van and got out a package. She rolled her eyes, and said, 'Follow me.'

He followed her into the villa and set the package down in the hall. She didn't know what it was, but by the shape and size guessed it was a framed print ordered straight from an online house-and-home catalogue. Until it was opened, she wouldn't know if she even liked it, let alone where it would go if she did.

Although his heart was in the right place, Clara would rather choose what *she* wanted to hang on her walls.

She thanked the delivery driver and turned to the package

sitting on the tiled floor in the hallway. The rectangular shaped item was in a slim cardboard box with plenty of *fragile* stickers stuck to it. Clara carried the package into the lounge.

Two of her neighbours were busy hanging a curtain pole up at the patio doors that led into the back garden. One of her neighbours, who spoke English, paused when he saw her walk in with the latest delivery. He asked her what else she had bought. Clara had neglected to mention that all this had come from her soon-to-be ex-husband. She didn't want to get into an awkward conversation about Joe and why he had bought her all this stuff for her villa when they had just split up; they might think he was moving back in with her.

Clara raised an eyebrow. She hadn't thought about that possibility – until now. She looked around her newly furnished lounge, her eyes drifting to the patio outside and the pool beyond with brand-new garden furniture. Perhaps that's what all this was about; maybe there was more to this than a generous parting gift for the years they had spent together. Hadn't she made it crystal clear she did not want a penny of his windfall?

She looked over at her new friends. 'Excuse me a moment.' She left the package unopened by the fireplace and disappeared along the hallway to her bedroom, where she wouldn't be disturbed. She sat down at her desk under the window overlooking the front garden with views of the orange and lemon grove. Clara switched on her laptop. Before she unpacked another item from Joe, she was going to message him on Facebook. This had to stop – along with any thoughts he might entertain about getting back together.

Clara called up his Facebook page and started by sending him a diplomatic message thanking him for the two furniture deliveries but clarifying she would much rather choose framed pictures herself to hang on her walls.

He was online because she got a message back. She read it. 'What do you mean you didn't send me anything of that nature?

It's sitting in my lounge!' Clara shook her head and opened *Skype*. She also switched her webcam on so she could not only speak to Joe over the internet but see him too.

'I only sent two deliveries, Clara, and that was furniture, curtains and blinds, and a television. Oh, and there might have been a few cushions, some throws, and a rug.'

Clara rolled her eyes.

'But nothing else – I swear.'

She could tell by his expression he was telling the truth.

'Perhaps it was delivered to the wrong address?'

'Oh.' Clara hadn't thought of that. At least she hadn't unpacked it.

'I think you should check the address on the package.'

Clara nodded at Joe. 'Good idea.'

There was an awkward silence. Clara was thinking *there never used to be any awkward silences between us before.* She hoped he would not ask her if there was a possibility of a reconciliation. Perhaps he thought the fact she had provided a home for his mother; it was a sign they might get back together.

Clara wanted to nip that in the bud. She steered the conversation away from anything of a personal nature. 'So, how's life on the ocean waves?'

'It's fantastic.'

Although Joe's head took up most of her screen, she could see a picturesque Mediterranean bay in the background. Last time they spoke he was moored off the Island of Capri in Italy. Ever since they arrived in Mallorca on Joe's yacht to look for Tommy, he had been itching to pull up anchor and head off to his next destination. He had it all planned. Clara knew he would be back though; he was planning to come and visit Dorothy in a fortnight. 'Where are you now?'

'Sorrento. We are having such a great time in Italy.'

We. She stared at Joe's tanned beaming face. 'Did you just say *we?*' She couldn't imagine who—

'Me and Judy. I er I hope you don't mind, but I invited Judy to come along.'

Clara was about to tell him he didn't have to ask her permission. That's when Joe turned the laptop around and there was Judy, relaxing in a sun lounger on the deck, wearing nothing but a swimming costume. She had a paperback novel in one hand and a glass of something in the other. She smiled and waved her book at the laptop.

Clara felt a pang of regret; but *I* left *him*, remember. She suspected it was more to do with envy that Joe had rekindled his romance with Judy and it seemed so easy, so effortless, so uncomplicated. For the umpteenth time Clara tried not to think about Ralph.

Joe had turned his laptop around so Clara could see his huge smiling face once more. It was the happiest she had seen him in a long time. She recognised that look; Joe was in love. She was back to thinking about Ralph – who else. Joe interrupted her thoughts, telling her he had to sign off. 'Judy is going to prepare the meal. We're dining al-fresco tonight,' he said excitedly.

Clara smiled. Joe was acting like an over-excited schoolboy. It was all still very new, every day bringing with it the dawn of another adventure. She knew how that felt; she was still pinching herself about waking up in her villa in Mallorca. The only difference was she had nobody to share her dream with – Dorothy excepted.

'She's such a great cook,' he added.

Clara frowned.

'Not that you weren't a good cook, Clara,' he said, sounding flustered.

'It's okay, Joe.' She knew she wasn't a great cook. It's something she never enjoyed doing; hence Joe lived off TV dinners. By the sounds of things that was a thing of the past too. Clara signed off. 'I'll see you in two weeks. Dorothy can't wait to see your yacht.'

'Great, oh got to go. Judy wants me to open another bottle of bubbly. See you in a fortnight.' The screen went blank.

She sat back in her chair thinking of Joe eating his dinner al-fresco with Judy. She wondered if Judy was there on holiday or whether she would join him on his yacht permanently.

Clara shrugged. What did it matter? She was already a divorcee – she'd split up from her husband years ago. The ins and outs of how they would conduct their relationship was no concern of hers. But the fact was Joe and Judy *were* in a relationship – that much was obvious.

She stared out the window and watched the sun go down as she listened to the sound of crickets on the lawn along with the clatter of plastic chairs on the patio reminding her, she too was having dinner al-fresco. Unlike Joe, however, this wasn't a romantic meal for two under the stars. Clara didn't mind. She was looking forward to getting to know her new neighbours whom she hoped would, in time, become good friends.

93

The patio doors in the lounge were wide open. She could see lots of activity, people to-ing and fro-ing from the kitchen with an assortment of dishes, others starting to take their seats around the long trestle table. It was time she joined them. She smiled at her good fortune to have such lovely neighbours.

She walked past the fireplace and sensed something was different. Out of place. That's when she caught sight of the package. The box was empty, brown paper discarded on the floor.

Her gaze shifted to the mantelshelf. Clara stepped back in surprise. Above the fireplace was a framed painting she recognized. The one she had been admiring that morning she woke up with Ralph in Southwold. Her eyes drifted to something sitting on the shelf; an envelope with her name on it.

'We took the liberty…'

Clara turned around. Her neighbour spotted her standing in the lounge by fireplace. He'd been passing the open patio doors with a dish and poked his head inside. 'We unpacked your last parcel. We were hanging the curtain pole, so we thought we might as well hang the picture.' He nodded toward the painting. 'There was a note addressed to you. We left it on the mantelshelf.'

'Thank you.' Clara stood there staring at the envelope. She knew who it was from. Her eyes shifted to the picture. Was this an apology?

'It's quite something – isn't it?'

She turned around. The neighbour was back again; standing at the patio doors looking in. Him and his spouse were expats, like Clara, choosing to live out their retirement in Mallorca.

His wife appeared by his side adding, 'We thought it would be a lovely surprise if we hung the painting over the fireplace for you.'

Clara nodded. It was a surprise all right. 'They shipped it all the way from England.'

'Really? Are you sure about that?'

'Yes, my…' Clara stopped. *Did she say her boyfriend, ex-boyfriend, teenage sweetheart sent it?* She glanced at the note she had yet to read. 'It belonged to a friend?' Clara furrowed her brow and turned to her neighbours. 'Why did you ask if I was sure it came from England?'

'It's just that there used to be a local artist whose paintings were very similar – remember dear?'

'Oh, yes,' his wife nodded, 'But that was some time ago when we first moved here, at least ten years now. The best thing we ever did, take early retirement, sell everything and move out here.'

'Yes, yes,' her husband said sounding irritated. 'We're getting off track. We were talking about the painting.'

Clara tried to curb a smile at the two expats starting to argue. They had clearly been married years. She wished she was with someone she'd known years and years, bickering like an old married couple, but unable to imagine life without them.

'Didn't he sell his paintings at the local market?'

Her husband nodded. 'The paintings were popular with tourists because they encapsulated the essence of Mallorca; something to do with the vibrant watercolours he used or the landscape he captured so well.'

'I guess he loved his country,' Clara mused.

'Oh, he wasn't from Mallorca. He was an expat just like us.'

'No, he was not like us,' said her husband.

'Don't be so judgemental.'

'I'm not being judgemental. He was…'

'Different.'

'I was going to say s*trange.*'

She shrugged. 'Okay, he was a recluse. He only came to town to sell his paintings.'

Clara asked, 'Where did he come from?'

'Rumour has it he lived in a monastery high in the Serra de Tramuntana Mountains.'

All three turned to look out the patio doors into the garden and the mountain range in the background; a dark outline against the setting sun.

Clara looked at her neighbours in surprise. 'There's a monastery in the mountains, and people live there?'

'Oh, yes. Apparently, there is an old order of monks.'

'Was he a monk?'

They exchanged a smile. 'I don't think so, no.'

'Then what was he doing living up there?'

'Who knows? It might not even be true. You know what small towns and the rumour mill are like.'

Clara thought of Southwold. She guessed it was the same the world over – rumour and local gossip. She turned her attention to the painting. 'It was purchased at the local market in Pollensa.' Clara didn't mention what happened to Ralph's late wife and the part Elliot played in restoring the canvas.

The couple stepped into the room to inspect the picture. They exchanged a glance as one said to the other, 'I swear it's by the same artist.'

They turned to Clara. 'We bought one of his paintings. The first purchase we made for our villa. There was nothing to sit on in the lounge, but hanging over the mantelshelf we had the most splendid work of art painted by that rather odd man.'

They told Clara, 'He was a fixture at the weekly market for

years then suddenly he disappeared. He hasn't been seen for months.'

The neighbour rubbed his chin. 'He might have been caught up in that terrorist attack. You remember, dear, when some device went off in a bar close to the local market. A lot of locals and tourists got trapped in it.'

'Yes, wasn't that awful?' They fell silent until he said, 'He might not have got caught up in that. Perhaps he returned to England.'

His wife looked at him as though he were mad. 'But *why?* Why would he leave all this to return to a cold, grey, miserable Blighty?'

'Perhaps he didn't have a choice. Maybe he had unfinished business back home.'

Clara's head bobbed from one to the other trying to follow their conversation but was preoccupied with some unfinished business of her own; namely, Ralph and the note in her hand she had yet to read. She was dying for some privacy. She glanced at the painting. 'Well, this is all very interesting, but I think our neighbours are waiting for us to join them.' She motioned at the garden.

They both nodded and stepped outside. Clara said, 'I'll be right out. I'm just nipping into the kitchen to fetch some… wine.'

She felt bad for telling a fib and had no idea whether there was any wine – her neighbours had supplied most of the food and the drink. Bypassing the kitchen, she walked straight into the downstairs cloakroom. Clara bolted the door, sat down on the toilet seat and opened the envelope. Inside was a pretty card with the words *New Home* on the front.

She felt hesitant about opening the card. What she wanted was an apology from Ralph, as grovelling as possible, letting her know how sorry he was for not telling her what Tommy had been up to the night of their eighteenth birthday party.

For the first time Clara wasn't just thinking about her brother but what had become of the young woman? They had fallen in love at the tender age of eighteen. What happened to them? Had they stayed together or despite trying to run away had something altered their plans? Unfortunately, she would not find the answers in this card.

Clara opened the card. *Was that it?* She stared at the message. *Am I missing something?* She picked up the discarded envelope thinking there must be a letter inside. But to her surprise there was nothing more.

She re-read the rather perfunctory note. All it said was *best of luck in your new home – Ralph.* Where was the apology? She felt so angry that she had half a mind to pack the painting up right now and send it back. Perhaps that's what she would do when her guests had gone.

Clara walked out to join her companions. She hadn't counted on just how late their meal, followed by copious glasses of wine and lively chit-chat, would go on for in the balmy evening of a Mediterranean climate. Clara collapsed into bed at two in the morning.

94

Later that morning Clara was standing on a chair, about to take the painting off the wall, when something caught her eye. 'What *is* that?' She squinted at the picture, then got down and went to find her glasses. She came back with Dorothy's magnifying glass she used to read the small print in her daily newspaper.

Dorothy walked into the lounge with yesterday's paper tucked under her arm. She was looking for her magnifying glass but stopped when she saw Clara standing stock on a kitchen chair. 'Clara?'

Clara jumped at the sound of Dorothy's voice and almost toppled off. She grabbed the mantelshelf and steadied herself.

Dorothy gave Clara one of her disapproving looks. 'What *are* you doing?'

Before she responded, Dorothy said, 'Is that my magnifying glass?'

Clara got down from the chair and handed it over. 'Sorry, I just needed to borrow it.'

'What on earth for?' asked Dorothy looking from Clara to the painting above the mantelshelf and back again.

'There's a boat in that picture.'

Dorothy had taken a seat in the armchair, arranging her newspaper on her lap, her magnifying glass to the ready. She looked over at Clara and rolled her eyes. 'It's Mallorca. An Island surrounded by water, so it is no surprise that the artist added the sea in the distance and—' Dorothy squinted. 'I presume that speck is the boat?'

Clara nodded. 'It's red.'

'What's red?'

'The boat.'

'Hmm, is it?' Dorothy wasn't listening.

'My brother's boat was red.'

Dorothy lowered her magnifying glass and looked at Clara. In all the years she'd known her, Clara never once brought up the subject of her twin brother. All Dorothy knew was what she'd heard from Joe; that during a holiday here in Mallorca when they both turned eighteen, Tommy had taken a boat out alone and presumably drowned.

Dorothy's eyes shifted to the painting. 'What's this about?'

Clara sighed. 'I'm not sure. It's just seeing that boat in the picture. It was a shock. I swear it is a replica of the one Tommy took out that night. It wasn't Tommy's. It was a small sailing boat my father used to hire during our holidays. I would recognise it anywhere.'

Dorothy pursed her lips. She was not surprised that after all these years when Clara returned to Mallorca, it would dredge up the past – especially something as profound as losing her twin brother when they were on the cusp of reaching maturity. She must have felt so alone in the world. Dorothy didn't think the copious glasses of wine Clara downed last night was helping. She suspected Clara was still a little drunk. Dorothy, a teetotaller herself was suffering no ill effects. She also turned in much earlier than everyone else.

In her usual blunt manner, she said, 'Someone could do with returning to bed and sleeping it off.'

Clara gave her a black look. 'Are you saying I'm tipsy?'

Dorothy thought of Clara standing on the chair with her magnifying glass. 'Yes, that's what I'm saying.'

'What a cheek!' exclaimed Clara putting her hands on her hips. 'I'll have you know I am not in any way, shape or form, still drunk. In fact, I take exception that you are implying I was drinking too much last night.'

Up the dinner table, Dorothy watched with growing concern as Clara downed one glass of wine after another. It wasn't like her at all. She enjoyed the odd glass of wine, but she'd never known her to be a heavy drinker. At the end of the evening, when the last of their neighbours left, Dorothy – who had already gone to bed – got up to use the bathroom. That's when she discovered Clara standing in the lounge in front of the fireplace. She was staring at that painting with a bottle of wine in her hand talking gibberish. All Dorothy could make out was a name – Ralph. She helped Clara undress and put on a nightie then tucked her up into bed.

Clara continued, 'I am *so* not drunk.'

Dorothy raised an eyebrow. Clara sounded like Tamsin when she was a teenager.

'I'm going out, and you can't stop me!'

Dorothy shook her head. 'You're going out – like that?'

'Like what?' Clara peered at Dorothy.

Dorothy pointed.

Clara looked down at her nightie. 'Oh. I will get dressed then.' She swanned out of the room.

Clara didn't reappear. Dorothy didn't hear her leave the villa either. Eventually, she rose from her chair and wandered down the hall toward Clara's bedroom. Her door was ajar. She looked in. Clara was face down on the bed snoring. Dorothy crept in, gently pulled the covers over her, and crept out. She quietly pulled her door to and walked down the hallway.

Back in the lounge, Dorothy opened the patio doors and stepped outside. She glanced at the pool and the surrounding lawn with shady orange and lemon trees dotted around. She stood for a moment staring at the water glistening in the morning sunshine. The backdrop of the Serra de Tramuntana mountain range was stunning. She couldn't have asked for a more beautiful place to end her days; that was all thanks to Clara.

As Dorothy started to clear the trestle table of the plates and dishes from the evening meal, she was still thinking about Clara. She didn't imagine in her wildest dreams that her daughter-in-law would insist she came to live with her in Mallorca. Why did she do it?

Dorothy thought if she had been in Clara's shoes, she would not have invited her rude, overbearing mother-in-law to live with her. In fact, after splitting up from Joe, she thought Clara would have been over the moon to see the back of her too. That made it even more surprising she was here.

Dorothy knew the way she treated Clara over the years had been abysmal but felt it was justified; she thought Clara deserved it. Not because she was from a different background and acted like a snob who looked down on her kind, which Dorothy didn't believe at all. It was the fact she thought Clara had beguiled her son – with her plummy accent and those large, dark, sultry eyes – into getting her out of a fix.

She'd suspected something was amiss when she found out they were getting married so soon after they first met. Dorothy hadn't come right out and said it, merely hinted at her suspicions. She was shocked at Joe's reaction. Her easy-going Joe, who should have laughed at such a silly idea, went ballistic at the suggestion that Clara was using him and marrying on the rebound because she was pregnant.

Dorothy had never seen him so angry. That's when she realised he already knew the truth. What he didn't want was anyone else to know – especially the child. It was *his* baby; he had made no bones about that. Dorothy never broached the subject again. That did not stop her despising Clara and taking every opportunity to put her down. In her mind, she never doubted Clara was using him. But to her surprise she stuck by him, even when Tamsin had grown up and left home. Recently, Clara separated from Joe, as Dorothy suspected one day she would. But she hadn't left a broken man in her wake. That's what she was most afraid of; the effect on her son when the love of his life walked out. Dorothy had been surprised when she discovered Clara wasn't the love of Joe's life after all.

Through the computer she'd spoken to her son on some new-fangled device called Skype. Dorothy had never seen him looking so happy. She suspected it had less to do with his yacht and more to do with a lady named Judy. Her Joe was in love again, and the woman in question was the girl he had practically left at the altar to marry Clara.

She remembered her because they had been stepping out for some time and the kind-hearted East End lass told Dorothy they would be engaged before the year was out. What happened next was something neither Dorothy nor Judy foresaw; a young woman stepped into Joe's taxi one rainy afternoon and swept him off his feet. And the rest was history.

Now, forty years on, Judy was back in Joe's life and this time he would not let her go. Dorothy smiled. She knew Clara wished him well. She also knew Clara refused to take a penny of his windfall; she had even given him a ticking off for furnishing the villa.

Dorothy hoped she didn't send it all back. She loved her antique-style dark oak furniture and the soft furnishings in her bedroom and sitting room, especially all the little extras like rugs to cover the cold tiled floors, cosy throws and cushions for the beds and armchairs. She had no idea her son had such good taste. That's because he doesn't, thought Dorothy.

She suspected Judy had a hand in all this. There were yet more thoughtful touches in the shape of two floor lamps in the lounge and her sitting room in which to read by. Dorothy switched one as she reached for the novel she'd left on the coffee table.

She had cleared away the dishes and was settling herself in her favourite armchair to read before taking an afternoon siesta. Dorothy was enjoying the Mediterranean way of life. An East Ender through and through, Dorothy thought she would miss Blighty. She missed some things, but not those cold, grey, damp days that continued for months and made her depressed.

Dorothy often suspected she suffered from SAD, seasonal affective disorder. She read about it in a magazine. Over the years, she could guarantee she would always feel down and at a low ebb during the winter. It had got worse since her husband passed away; stuck in her flat with no one to talk to and no reason to go out. It was as though her life was on hold until the clocks changed and lighter evenings rolled around again.

Dorothy didn't have the time to wait around to live life to the full. What she loved about Mallorca was that every day – even come winter which would be pleasantly warm and often sunny – she could potter in the garden or have a dip in the pool or listen to the whirr of the fan overhead as it sent her off to sleep.

Thinking of which, Dorothy reached for the remote and switched on the ceiling fan. Marley, stretched out on the patio in the shade under the pagoda, stood up and stepped into the cool lounge. He then curled into a ball on the rug in front of the fireplace and fell asleep again. Winston, who had also been outside, scampered into the lounge and gave Marley a wide berth. He raced over to Dorothy and sat down at her feet.

Before Dorothy opened her novel, she looked around the lounge. This was her favourite room in the villa; the view out the patio doors to the garden and the Serra de Tramuntana mountain range in the background was beautiful. And the scenery inside the room was just as tantalizing; Dorothy was looking at the painting over the mantle shelf. She couldn't decide which was better; the actual view from the lounge or the picture depicting the mountains with Pollensa old town and the ocean in the foreground.

Staring at the painting, Dorothy noticed something. She glanced outside, her gaze shifting back to the painting. Dorothy got up to take a closer look. 'Well, I'll be…' she said to Winston who was at her heels. She turned around and headed for the patio doors where she stood looking up at the mountain range in the distance. It was another beautiful day in Mallorca, not a cloud in sight, just blue skies and spectacular views from Clara's villa.

Dorothy stared up at the mountains. 'Do you see what I see, Winston?'

It had become something of a habit when she was living on her own, talking to Winston. 'I know my eyesight is not what it once was, but I'm sure that's the bell tower depicted in the painting.' She pointed. 'I wonder what's up there in the mountains?'

❖

When Dorothy walked into the lounge the following morning, it felt like déjà vu. Clara was standing there in front of the picture; except this time, she wasn't tottering on a chair.

Dorothy coughed into her hand. 'Ahem.'

Clara turned around. 'Oh, there you are.' She waved her hand at Dorothy. 'Will you come over here for a minute?'

Dorothy joined her in front of the painting. She wasn't looking at the picture though but at Clara. Dorothy was wondering who Ralph was. She knew the canvas hadn't come from Joe. She had found a card on the floor by Clara's bed, picked it up and noticed the name *Ralph* as she put it back on her bedside table. Dorothy hadn't meant to pry. She had just been looking in on Clara while she was sleeping to check she was okay. She studied Clara's profile. The painting and the card could have just come from a friend, but something told her there was more to it than that.

'Do you see that bell tower?'

Dorothy turned to look at the painting. 'Yes.'

'According to our new neighbours that bell tower belongs to a monastery in the Serra de Tramuntana mountain range.'

'A monastery, you say,' mused Dorothy.

'I'm not sure if it is true, but I will visit the tourist information office in town and find out—'

'So, that's what it is.'

Dorothy was standing at the patio doors pointing at something. Clara joined her.

'Do you see it?' said Dorothy.

'See *what*?'

'Why – the bell tower of course.'

95

'Maybe we should phone for the taxi.'

'I'm quite capable of driving my car.'

Dorothy winced as Clara crunched the gears again.

'I am still getting the hang of it – that's all.' Clara tried to put it into gear again, adding, 'Remember, I have only had it a few days, and just ventured out twice to the supermarket in Pollensa.'

Determined to drive herself, this time she wasn't poodling down the road to the local shop. They were venturing into the mountains.

Clara's stomach was already churning, and she hadn't made it down the drive. It was the thought of that winding route up into the mountains. The trouble was she had spent years relying on Joe. If she didn't make herself do this, then how would she ever be independent?

'Oh, thank goodness,' exclaimed Clara when she finally got it into gear. 'Off we go,' she said, sounding chirpier than she felt.

'Are you sure about this – doing the drive yourself? We *are* going up there.' Dorothy pointed.

Clara gave her a black look. Dorothy wasn't helping. She didn't need reminding that they were driving up a mountain. 'If you have changed your mind about coming, I can pull over and let you out.'

'Oh, I wouldn't miss this for the world,' said Dorothy.

'Then just shut up and let me drive.'

Dorothy stared at Clara in surprise. No one had ever talked to her that way before – not even her husband.

Clara added, 'Please.'

Dorothy looked out the window giving Clara the impression she was having a sulk but smiling to herself. Finally, someone had the backbone to give her some lip. Despite her initial reservations about how this would really work, living under the same roof as her soon-to-be ex daughter-in-law, Dorothy was delighted to discover Clara had a backbone after all. If there was one thing Dorothy couldn't abide was a wilting wallflower. Clara was no such thing. She hadn't shied away from taking charge of her life or taking charge of her mother-in-law. Dorothy glanced at Clara and decided they would get along just fine.

'That's Pollensa over to your right,' said Clara as they approached the roundabout on the scenic single-carriageway road that bypassed the town. This was Dorothy's first trip out since they arrived at the villa a fortnight ago. 'On the way back we might stop in Pollensa for some lunch and I will show you the lovely old town.'

Dorothy was staring out the front window at the Serra de Tramuntana mountain range. 'Do you think we'll be back in time for lunch?'

Clara was thinking the same thing. Just how long would the drive take to reach the monastery with the bell tower – and how arduous? Her stomach was tightening in a knot again at the prospect of the difficult car journey ahead. She knew from experience, when she used to holiday here with her parents as a child, that some of Mallorca's highways could be little more than dirt tracks.

Pleasantly surprised by the drive from the airport this time around – they had developed the main roads since she was here last – she couldn't imagine the same would be true off the beaten track.

Clara furrowed her brow as she approached the second roundabout. From here she could turn right and drive to the pine-fringed beach in Port de Pollensa or go all the way round and return to Pollensa old town. The road heading into the Serra de Tramuntana Mountains was straight on.

Clara hesitated. She didn't have to do this. She could just have a pleasant morning wandering around Pollensa with Dorothy, followed by a spot of lunch in a café in the pretty square, before rounding off the day showing Dorothy the shady Pine Walk by the beach in Port de Pollensa.

Clara's mind drifted to the painting. Although having been worse for wear when she climbed on that chair, Clara wasn't that drunk she didn't remember the red boat she had discovered bobbing on the water. When she woke up the next morning the little vessel was still there.

Clara slipped the car into gear and joined the traffic on the roundabout. She didn't believe in signs and that kind of mumbo jumbo. Whatever she was reading into the painting – the red boat, the bell tower, the fact that she even had the picture in her possession hanging in a room overlooked by those mountains – it was all just a huge coincidence.

'You are meant to be watching the road. We almost missed our turning!'

Clara jerked the car to the right at the last minute, taking the exit for the mountains.

Dorothy turned to Clara. 'For a moment there, I thought you'd changed your mind.'

As she was driving around the roundabout, Clara decided she was going into Pollensa instead. It's just she couldn't get the little red boat in the painting out of her mind. Something was drawing her to that monastery in the mountains.

Dorothy chirped up, 'Perhaps the monastery will have a cafeteria if we feel peckish when we arrive?' Clara took her eyes off the road for a moment and glanced at Dorothy.

Dorothy caught that look. 'What did I say?'

Clara tried to be diplomatic. 'I don't know what you're expecting, Dorothy, but we *are* going up in those mountains. It's off the beaten track.' Clara was relieved to discover the road remained nice and wide and tarmacked. If the monastery was inhabited, would the monks welcome people intruding on their privacy?

'Somehow, I don't think they will be expecting tourists, so they won't be rolling out the red carpet when we arrive.'

'What's that supposed to mean?'

Clara sighed. 'All I'm saying, Dorothy, is there will be little in the way of facilities when we get there.'

'Lucky I packed some sandwiches.'

Clara glanced at the large shopping bag on her lap. 'I was wondering what was in the bag.'

'I like to come prepared for all eventualities.'

Clara smiled. She could see where Joe got some of his habits from.

Dorothy looked in the bag. 'I also packed some fruit, yoghurt, crisps and…'

Concentrating on the road ahead, Clara wondered when the wide tarmacadam road would narrow, and the treacherous climb would begin. She wasn't looking forward to it.

'… and I remembered the jar of pickles because I do like some pickles.'

Up ahead, Clara saw the road climb. *Here we go.*

To her surprise, although the route was not straight, and they *were* climbing, the gradients were gentle. It looked almost new, reasonably wide, with safety barriers on the side that dropped down the mountain. Clara started to relax.

Dorothy glanced at Clara when she heard her sigh in relief. 'Like most things in life, they never quite turn out the way you expected.'

'And never a truer word was spoken,' said Clara, enjoying the drive. Before long they reached a sign for the monastery. Clara turned off the main road down a lengthy drive.

'This is nice,' said Dorothy, admiring the views. 'I wonder where the monastery is?'

To their surprise, they arrived at a large pay-and-display car park set in woodland with picnic benches and a little wooden information hut. 'Are we in the right place?' Dorothy asked.

'Let's find out.' Clara parked the car in a shady spot. The lady in the hut at the entrance to the car park gave them a map of the complex outlining the rooms in the monastery they could visit, along with directions for the waymarked walks through the extensive grounds. 'Look,' said Dorothy when they stepped outside, 'there's even a café for refreshments.'

Clara was studying the map, quite stunned. 'It looks as though there's three.' She had no idea this was a major tourist attraction in the area. But it wasn't just a visitor attraction. There was still an order of monks in residence. It was also an oratory music school. The helpful lady in the information hut mentioned a choir of schoolchildren who sometimes sing in the chapel which visitors could attend.

They passed by a pretty restaurant at the head of the car park with terraces and garden furniture for dining al fresco.

Clara glanced at the map and turned to Dorothy. 'It might be rather a walk to the Monastery.'

Dorothy waved her walking stick at Clara. 'I'm fine, thank you.'

She smiled at her soon-to-be ex mother-in-law. When Clara decided to take Dorothy with her to Mallorca, she thought she would live to regret. In all the years she had known her, barely a civil word had passed between them. However, in the fortnight since they moved into the villa, Clara had seen a side of her she never knew existed. Underneath that brash exterior, Dorothy was a kind and generous soul. She just didn't want all and sundry to know it.

For someone who hadn't ventured that far outside Peckham, Clara assumed she wouldn't find it easy adapting to a new culture and getting on with its people – locals and expats alike. Oh, how she had proved her wrong on all counts. Dorothy, it turned out, was quite the adventurer; despite her advancing years, she was game for anything. Clara smiled at her and decided they would get along just fine.

Past the restaurant the path curved to the left, and they found themselves on a wide straight boulevard bordered by tall pine trees. There was a cool mountain breeze which made for a pleasant walk. Clara and Dorothy stopped mid-stride as they caught sight of the stunning monastery founded in the thirteenth century.

'My goodness,' exclaimed Dorothy, 'that's a sight to behold.'

Clara read the pamphlet she had picked up in the information hut. 'This is the most important pilgrimage site in Mallorca.'

'What is the name of the monastery?'

'Lluc.'

'What else does it say?' prompted Dorothy interested to learn more.

'It's also famous for its boys' choir founded in 1532. The choir holds concerts and, according to this, if you are lucky, they will do a performance in the chapel during your visit.'

'How wonderful it would be to hear the children sing,' remarked Dorothy.

'Indeed.' Clara continued reading as they made their way along the wide boulevard towards the monastery in the distance. 'You can even stay here for a night or two. There are rooms that tourists rent – former monks' cells.'

Dorothy wrinkled her nose. 'Hmm, well each to their own.' It didn't appeal to her. She much preferred returning home to her comfy bed in her furnished wing of Clara's villa.

They arrived at a large paved plaza in front of the monastery.

Dorothy lifted her walking stick and pointed. 'There's the bell tower.'

Clara looked up. 'So it is.'

Dorothy glanced at her. Thinking back to when she found Clara in an inebriated state yesterday morning, talking some gibberish about the boat in the painting; the one she was convinced belonged to Tommy. Although not touching on that topic during the journey, it didn't stop Dorothy wondering just what she was hoping to find here.

Clara studied the map. 'According to this, we go under the arch over there into an inner central courtyard and the entrance is—' Clara stopped when she realised Dorothy had wandered off.

'Dorothy?' Clara spotted her. She was standing outside a small parade of shops. There was a baker, a café and a gift shop.

Clara folded the map and walked over. Something seemed to have caught Dorothy's attention. She was staring at a painting for sale in the gift shop. She thought it looked like the one over Clara's mantelshelf. Although this was a different street scene of Pollensa, it was by the same painter. There were the mountains in the background with a bell tower on the mountainside. But it wasn't that, that had caught her attention; it was the little red boat bobbing in the sea in the distance. The difference this time was that there appeared to be someone in the boat. Dorothy wished she had her magnifying glass.

Clara approached. 'We can visit the gift shop afterwards, Dorothy, but I was rather hoping we could see the monastery first before more tourists arrive and it gets busy…' Clara trailed off when she saw the painting.

'Yes, let's go,' said Dorothy linking her arm in Clara's and attempting to steer her away from the window. Dorothy was of a mind that nothing good ever came from dredging up the past.

'Wait. Isn't that a red boat bobbing in the water?'

Dorothy sighed.

'It's by the same artist – it must be.' Clara saw the bell tower.

'Look, there's a bell tower.'

'I know,' said Dorothy flatly.

'There's someone in the boat.'

Dorothy thought so too but hoped Clara didn't make a thing of it. 'If you like the painting so much, you could buy it. Why don't we wander around the monastery first, then you could always come back and decide if you want—'

Clara walked past Dorothy into the shop.

Dorothy rolled her eyes. 'Or we could go into the gift shop,' she said as she followed Clara inside.

They discovered a side room with more paintings for sale on display. Clara studied each while Dorothy sat down in a window seat by a fan.

She turned to Dorothy. 'There's a little boat in each of these pictures.'

'You don't say.'

A young lady who worked in the gift shop walked into the room. 'Hola. You like the paintings?'

Clara turned around and said hello to the sales assistant. 'Hola. Yes, I do like them. In fact, I already have one by this artist. Can you tell me anything about the person who painted these?'

The sales assistant shook her head.

Dorothy rose from her spot with the help of her walking stick. 'Right, well unless you are going to buy another one, why don't we go for a wander around the monastery?'

The young lady added, 'Mi Madre, excuse me, my mother knows something about him.' She pointed at the older woman standing behind a counter. 'Would you like I ask for you?'

Clara nodded as she followed her into the main shop.

Dorothy shook her head from side to side. She was wondering what it was Clara hoped to gain by this line of enquiry.

By the time Dorothy had made her way across the room she heard Clara saying to one of the ladies, 'That's interesting, thank you so much. I mean *gracias*.'

Dorothy followed her out the door and caught up with her outside the gift shop. 'What was that all about?'

'It turns out the painter was an artist in residence, lived here for years – decades. She said he would sit in this courtyard and paint. He used to take his completed works into town to sell them at the local market, but just recently he hasn't been well, so they have been displaying his pictures in the gift shop.'

'I see.' Dorothy's brow furrowed. 'But does that mean he's still alive – this artist?'

Clara nodded.

'And he's still here at the monastery?'

'I think so.'

They both fell silent. Finally, Dorothy had to say it. 'Clara, I don't want you to get your hopes up that the artist might be—'

'Let's go for a wander around the monastery, eh?' Clara was already striding off in that direction. Dorothy was afraid Clara was on a wild goose chase still looking for Tommy.

Dorothy was aware of Joe's not-so-bright idea to take Clara off to Mallorca on his yacht in search of her brother. What did he imagine they would find forty years after Tommy's disappearance? False hope, that is what Joe had offered her; it was what he'd given her most of their married lives with his silly dreams of The Big Payday. Dorothy was thinking of Joe sailing around the Med. She never thought she would see the day that Joe's dream would come true.

'Are you coming, Dorothy?'

Dorothy was intending to sit this one out. However, she changed her mind. 'I'll be right with you.' She quickened her pace and joined Clara at the entrance to the monastery.

'Shall we?' said Clara.

Dorothy looked at Clara. What has anyone got to lose chasing a dream? After all, who knows – it might come true. Stranger things have happened…

Clara and Dorothy stepped through the doorway.

96

'I'm afraid he is not well. He's not up for receiving visitors.'

'But he's here isn't he – the artist?'

Dorothy laid a hand on Clara's arm. 'Perhaps we should come back another time.'

The older man with the thin face, dark eyes and weary stoop smiled at the two tourists who had stopped him on his way to cloisters and asked after the artist – his good friend. The monk said, 'If you told me your business, I can pass on a message.'

'I would like to see him.'

The monk raised an eyebrow at the tourist's insistent tone of voice. 'I understand, but as I said before he is not well enough to receive visi—'

'Not even his own sister?'

Dorothy stepped in. 'Clara, please, this won't do. I think you ought to give it a rest. You're jumping to conclusions when you do not know his name!'

'But the boat, Dorothy. It's a message – don't you see? The boat, the bell tower…'

'What is this about?' asked the monk.

The words tumbled out of Clara's mouth before Dorothy could stop her. She told the friar about Tommy disappearing on his eighteenth birthday in Mallorca and pretending to take his father's red boat out when it turned out that's not what happened at all. He'd fallen in love with a girl from these parts and they planned to run away together – elope. Her name was Gabriella. She'd visited England one summer with a travelling circus.

Clara got the old letter out of her handbag. It was before they set sail on Joe's yacht, Sophie had given her grandmother something which astounded her. It was a note from Tommy. He wrote it just before he disappeared, informing her what he was intending to do.

It was Paul who found the letter lost in the lining of her old suitcase, the one Tommy had given her on her eighteenth birthday. It was an odd gift, but little did she know his reasons; he had slipped a note inside telling her his plans.

The trouble was she never got it. There was some stitching loose and, unbeknown to her, the envelope had dropped behind the lining. And there it would have remained if it wasn't for Clara's trip to the police station with Paul when arrested outside her beach hut. He had searched her bags, found the letter, put it in his desk drawer for safekeeping and then forgotten all about it. When he came across it, he had entrusted it to Sophie who promised to give it to her grandmother.

Sophie had slipped the note into a pocket of her jeans. There it stayed until Tamsin had had words with Sophie about the state of her bedroom and ordered her to tidy up and leave out any washing. Sophie dug out the jeans she had worn on holiday in Southwold. That's when she'd gone through her pockets and found the letter. She didn't know if it was important. It looked so old.

She could have just binned it, but then she had made a promise. 'Don't you see?' said Clara waving the letter at the man. 'The boat, that little red boat is in all the paintings – at least the ones I've seen. Then there's the bell tower. It's as though Tommy is trying to send me a message he's here.'

Dorothy stood there wiping her brow with a handkerchief and casting a furtive glance at the monk. She was waiting for him to escort them out of the building. Clara, the poor dear, sounded stark raving mad.

The friar was looking gravely at Clara

'Did you say, *Gabriella*?' he asked.

Clara nodded.

'When was the last time your brother made contact?'

She told him about the postcard from Mallorca which through a silly misunderstanding she had only just received. 'And that was the last anyone heard from him.'

The monk stood there rubbing his chin staring at Clara. Finally, he said, 'Come with me.' He took off down the corridor, his long black robes billowing behind him.

Clara and Dorothy exchanged a surprised look and set off to catch up with him.

Clara fell in step with the monk. 'Is it him do you think? Is it Tommy?'

He glanced at Clara. 'The man I am taking you to see goes by the name of Tomás.'

'Tomás?' Clara responded. 'Isn't the English equivalent Thomas – Tommy?'

The monk stopped in the corridor and turned to Clara. 'I don't want you to…what is the English phrase? To get your hopes up?'

Dorothy had caught up to them by then. She overheard the monk. 'I agree.' She turned to Clara. 'You can't get your hopes up.'

'I know, but if there's even the slimmest possibility, however remote, that the artist might be my brother…'

Dorothy turned to the friar. 'What makes you think this Tomás might be her brother?'

'Because of the year Tomás came to us.'

'It's when we lost contact isn't it,' said Clara excitedly?'

The monk nodded. They continued along the corridor as he told them how he first met his dear friend. 'We were working on the plateau behind the monastery, planting seeds, harvesting a small crop. You may be aware, we are self-sufficient.'

Clara responded. She had gathered from the pamphlet that the monks of the Sacred Heart were self-sufficient and that the only income they have comes from the shop, pharmacy, restaurant and museum. They had also visited the museum and read a little of the history of the monastery. A large rectangular complex nestled in the mountains, still hidden from the world even today.

'I was in the mountains behind the monastery when I saw him. Back then the mountain road was treacherous which meant we were almost cut off from the outside world. Few locals ventured into the Serra de Tramuntana Mountains. They had the sense not to. That's why I assumed, when I first set eyes on him, that he must be a tourist walking a trail who had got lost.' The monk shook his head. 'That's when it happened. He lost his footing and fell.'

'He fell?' Dorothy and Clara said in unison.

The monk nodded. 'When we reached him, he was in a bad way. We could not safely take him down the mountainside to the local hospital, so we nursed him back to health here at the monastery. In his delirium he talked of a woman. He said he couldn't live without her.'

'You mean to say he tried to do himself in?' asked Dorothy.

The monk nodded. 'At first, we thought that was it. After all, why would anyone go walking in the Serra de Tramuntana Mountains without a map or a guide? It's not like it is today with tarmacadam roads making it more accessible, not to mention mobile phones, cars, sat nav, and a plethora of walkers and tourists of all nationalities. Back then it was quite remote.'

Clara was hanging on his every word.

'But later, when he was recovered, he told us he wanted to get away, find somewhere peaceful, secluded. He'd certainly come to the right place. He just hadn't accounted for how treacherous the Serra de Tramuntana mountain passes could be. It was lucky we were around when he slipped on some loose stones underfoot and fell.'

The monk stopped in front of a door. He put his hand on the doorknob and turned to Clara. Lowering his voice, he continued, 'We pieced some things together. In his delirium he spoke of a girl, something about her family keeping them apart.'

'How sad,' said Dorothy.

'Did he mention the name of the girl?' asked Clara.

The monk nodded. 'It was Gabriella.'

Clara was silent as she turned toward the door. After all these years apart, was it possible her long-lost brother, her Tommy, was right there behind that door?

'What happened after he recovered?' Dorothy asked.

'He spoke some Spanish, but he wasn't from Mallorca. German we thought or English. Only tourists go walking in these parts. Later we realised he was British although he couldn't tell us where he was from because the head injury sustained during the fall had affected his memory. To this day, he still has problems with his short-term memory. He called himself Tomas, so that was the name we went by. He couldn't remember his last name.'

'Did you try to find out who he was, where he came from?'

'Of course, but all those years ago we had no internet or social media, so we put adverts in newspapers. We didn't have much money, I'm afraid. We did the best we could, but no one came forward who claimed to know him. He stayed on at the monastery as a handyman. In his spare time, he started to paint. When they constructed the road up the mountainside, making it more accessible, he would venture to the local market down in Pollensa to sell his paintings. That little red boat was, as far as I can recall, in each one.'

He continued, 'Sometimes there would be a young woman standing on the shore with a long mane of dark hair and a man alone in the boat. I asked him once what it meant, whether it might be something his subconscious was bringing to the fore like a memory from his past, but he didn't know. I seem to recall that in some paintings there was a blonde-haired woman.'

Dorothy looked at Clara.

The monk paused before he opened the door. 'I have to warn you, he is not a well man. I'm afraid he's had a stroke. The doctor thinks it is related to his head injury years ago from the fall, an aneurysm that's sat there undetected all these years. He refuses to go to the hospital. He keeps saying he's waiting.'

'What does he mean, he's waiting?' asked Clara.

The monk shook his head. 'Last time I visited he said, "I can't come with you just yet, there is something I need to do first." Or words to that effect. He wasn't talking to me. I don't know who he thinks was in the room with him. There was no one else in the bedroom besides the doctor, the nurse or me.' He looked at Clara. 'Are you ready?'

She visibly shook.

Dorothy found Clara's hand and gave it a reassuring squeeze. 'Come on, pet, what have you got to lose?'

Clara kept hold of Dorothy's hand and looked at the monk standing in front of the door. She took a deep breath and nodded. 'I'm ready.'

The monk opened the door.

97

Clara didn't know what she expected; a small austere monk's cell with a single bed, perhaps a chair and table beneath a small window. What Clara and Dorothy stepped into was a room of apartment-sized proportions. At the far end was a double bed positioned near double-doors on to a balcony with an incredible view of the mountains. The place was pleasantly cool despite the afternoon sun streaming in through the doors. She could see a man propped up on pillows on the bed.

The monk looked over at Tomás and whispered to them, 'This is one of his better days. He has less and less of them now. His time is drawing near.'

Clara held on to Dorothy's hand for support as they made their way across the room. A part of her hoped it wasn't Tommy. She didn't know how she would deal with finding him, only to lose him again.

The monk held out his hand motioning them to step forward.

Clara looked at Dorothy.

'Go on now.' Dorothy let go of her hand. 'It's time to lay the ghosts of the past to rest.'

Clara understood. Whether this was Tommy it was time to let him go. With each tentative step she drew closer to the bed.

Passing an easel on which was a canvas with an unfinished

painting she glanced at it. The picture was reminiscent of the one hanging in her lounge, except this canvas was unfinished; some of it was still in pencil outline waiting to be completed.

Dorothy stopped in front of the unfinished painting. She turned to the monk and asked in a low whisper about the picture on the easel.

'He was working on it when he took sick.'

Dorothy got out the small magnifying glass from her bag. Leaning on her walking stick she bent over and scrutinised the painting. It could have been a carbon copy of the one hanging over Clara's mantelshelf but for two things. Firstly, it was unfinished. That was the obvious difference. Dorothy held up her magnifying glass studying the little red boat bobbing in the water. Unlike Clara's painting, in this one there were two people in the vessel; a blonde-haired man was sitting next to a young dark-haired woman.

'What do you see?' asked the monk.

Dorothy stood up and put her magnifier away. She glanced over at the man in the bed. 'I think I know who he's been talking to,' replied Dorothy.

The monk was about to ask *who* when Clara, who was standing at the end of the bed staring at the man, said 'I knew it!'

Dorothy marched over. 'What's the matter, Clara? Is it Tommy?' He opened his eyes as soon as Clara spoke and said in a hoarse whisper, 'Clara?'

Clara drew closer and took his frail hand in hers. 'I knew you weren't dead, Tommy,' she said to him. All these years, she was convinced she would have felt something if her twin had died.

The monk continued. 'He had the stroke and has been at death's door ever since.'

Clara took a seat by his bed and stroked his forehead.

'At death's door,' muttered Dorothy.

The monk glanced at Dorothy. 'Nobody knows what happens when we are about to cross over. It is one of life's mysteries. Two weeks ago, we thought it was his time.' The monk looked at Clara before choosing his words carefully. 'We didn't imagine he would hang on this long. It's as though…'

'He was waiting for me.' Clara turned to look at the monk. So did Dorothy.

The friar nodded. 'He knew you would come.'

Dorothy frowned. 'But how is that possible?'

He looked at his good friend. The monk had lived in this monastery in the mountains many years, leading a simple but learned life of quiet contemplation and study. Old and wise, he could speak several languages. He taught music to the children in the choir school and lessons in Mathematics, science and the arts, and was an excellent raconteur. But if living in this most mysterious of places, high in the Serra de Tramuntana Mountains, had taught him one thing it was that no amount of study or advances in science and technology would ever unravel the mystery of the human heart.

He said, 'Who knows what supernatural forces are at work when we are in that in-between time – between life and death – and what we are capable of when it comes to matters of the heart.' He looked at Clara. 'I presume you and Tomas er Tommy were close?'

'We're twins.'

'Indeed,' said the monk, not at all surprised. He recalled the conversations Tomás had been having in his delirium with a woman called Gabriella, as though she was right here in this room. Was she too in that in-between time and had found her way back to him? Or perhaps she had already passed over and was awaiting him on the other side to be reunited in the next life.

He thought of the words Tomás had spoken, "I can't come with you, my love, there's something I need to do first." He looked at Tommy's twin. 'I think you're right; he has been waiting for you, Clara.' He believed Tommy needed to see his sister one last time.

'Clara,' he said again in a hoarse whisper.

The monk turned to Dorothy. They exchanged a nod in silent understanding; they should take their leave. Clara needed to spend some time alone with her brother before she let him go.

98

The easterly wind made her shiver. Clara pulled her cardigan around her as she stepped on to the beach. She hadn't realised how accustomed she'd grown to the Mediterranean climate until returning to Southwold. She looked at the urn in her hands. He said he wanted to come home. It's what their parents would have wished too.

Making her way down to the water's edge, she resisted the urge to turn around and look towards the beach hut he'd loved so much. Someone else now owned it. She tried not to think about the fact she had to give up her last link with Tommy to buy her new home. Then again, if she'd hadn't moved to Mallorca, perhaps she would never have found her brother. Clara smiled. Life had a funny way of making things right, even if it was in the most roundabout way.

She carefully unscrewed the lid. Tommy had always loved this stretch of beach. It seemed the perfect place to let him go. She took some handfuls of ash, opened her palm and the sea breeze carried him away. 'Goodbye, Tommy.'

Clara turned around and thought she might as well say goodbye to the beach hut while she was here. She couldn't envisage when she would come back to Southwold again. There was nothing to return for. This chapter of her life had finally ended.

As she was making her way up the beach, in the distance she saw a yellow dog. He was bounding towards her. 'Bailey?' The dog ran within a hairs breath of Clara almost knocking her over.

A woman with two children digging sandcastles called out, 'Sorry about that.'

'It's all right,' Clara replied noticing the dog was a Labrador not a golden retriever like Bailey.

She continued on her way only to discover there was someone sitting on a deckchair outside what used to be her beach hut. 'Oh, bother,' Clara said under her breath, not expecting the new owner to be down here this early in the morning. She was about to turn around and head back to the hotel when the person on the deckchair raised their hand as if in greeting. Clara glanced behind her at the young woman with the children who were still busy building sandcastles. The young woman didn't acknowledge the person outside the beach hut. Clara frowned and wished she had brought her glasses for it appeared they were waving at her.

Clara kept walking to see who it was. She stopped in front of the hut and looked at him in surprise. 'Did you buy my beach hut?'

'You're back! I thought it was you. Here, take a seat.' Ralph jumped out of his chair.

Clara rolled her eyes. Now she was here she might just as well take a breather before making her way to the hotel. She walked up the three wooden steps on to the little veranda, sat down in the deckchair and watched Ralph take his seat next to her. That's when Clara noticed the suitcase by his feet. 'Are you off somewhere?'

'I was going to Mallorca to see you. Fancy a brew? I've put the kettle on.'

'Anyone would think you knew I was coming.'

'Ah, the wonders of modern technology. Tamsin messaged me to say you were catching a flight home.'

'Tamsin?'

He nodded. 'The timing couldn't be better. As I was on my way to the airport, I asked the taxi to turn around and bring me to the beach, hoping you would come down here. I didn't want to miss you.'

'How long have you been waiting?'

'Oh, it doesn't matter. You're here now.'

'I er just came from the house.' Clara glanced at him sheepishly. She hadn't called at The Gables though; to avoid him. But she supposed he was aware of that. That's why he was here at the beach. 'I saw Elliot. He looks well.' Clara had looked in on Elliot in the outhouse where she guessed he'd be working on his next collection of paintings. She wanted to catch up with her friend before she left for Mallorca. 'I like what you have done with the outhouse. I didn't recognise it.'

'Yes, I had the three outhouses knocked into one and then converted into a cottage with a studio attached where Elliot can paint. He lives in the cottage now and keeps an eye on The Gables when I'm away.'

'You've returned to work then, abroad?'

'Well, there wasn't anything to stay for, was there.' He stared at her pointedly.

Clara took a deep breath. 'I was mad at you over Tommy, it was true. Then I found out he'd written me a letter. He didn't tell you that – did he?' She glanced at Ralph and could tell by his expression that was news to him.

She told him about the letter lost in the lining of her suitcase all these years. 'It wasn't your secret to keep Ralph. He just wanted me to read the note first – that's all.'

'Oh, I see. But why didn't you get in touch and tell me this sooner?'

Clara bit her lower lip recalling the painting Ralph had sent her and the note inside, very curt, written as if she was an acquaintance. She didn't know whether she had been reading too much into it, but it felt like goodbye. 'I thought you wouldn't want to see me again.'

'Whatever gave you that idea?'

'Perhaps it had something to do with the love child I'd kept from you all these years, and that I didn't tell you back then I was pregnant. To be honest, it surprised me you seemed to take it so well when I told you about Tamsin the night we slept together. But then I began to wonder what your attitude might be when it had sunk in, and you'd had some time to…' Clara trailed off.

Ralph raised an eyebrow. 'Yes, I had time to consider the reasons you did what you did. I always felt you left me because you didn't love me the way I loved you. But not now.

'After Tommy made me promise not to tell you he was planning to elope, I felt torn. Unable to tell you the truth was eating away at me. I wasn't myself. I kept you at arm's length. You must have thought I didn't want to be with you anymore and the last thing I'd want to hear is that you were pregnant with my child.' He sighed. 'I'm so sorry. It was all my—'

'No, I shouldn't have run away as I did. It was not your fault Ralph – any of it.'

'It wasn't yours either.'

They fell silent.

Ralph glanced down the beach. 'It was you down there at the water's edge?'

Clara looked at the urn cradled in her arms. 'I came back for Tommy.'

'I know.'

They fell silent again. Ralph said, 'Look, won't you stay for a few days?'

Clara started to shake her head. 'I can't. It's Dorothy. Joe won't be staying at the villa long visiting his mother before he sets sail again, and I cannot leave her on her own.'

Ralph held up his phone. 'She's far from on her own.'

'What are you talking about?'

Ralph was scrolling through some photos on his phone that Dorothy had put on her new Facebook page. He smiled. 'When the cat's away the mice will play – eh?'

'What do you mean?'

Ralph handed over the phone saying, 'The Cockney's call it *having a knees-up?'*

Clara scrolled through the photos, her eyes growing wide. She recognized the cleaner and the pool man. There were at least half a dozen other people, all around Dorothy's age, sitting along the trestle table in the back garden holding up glasses of wine for the camera and looking, quite sozzled.

'Well, I never!'

'By the looks of things,' said Ralph, 'she has made new friends. Good for her.'

Clara agreed.

'I still can't believe you've adopted your mother-in-law though.'

She gave Ralph a sideways glance.

'Oops, I meant your soon-to-be *ex* mother-in-law.'

'You make it sound like I've adopted a pet.' Thinking of which, Clara looked about her. 'Where's Bailey?'

'Oh, the little turncoat has moved in with Elliot. As soon as we finished the cottage, he decided he liked it so much that's where he wanted to live. I hardly see him.'

'Maybe if you were around more?' ventured Clara.

'Yes, if there was a reason for me to be around more….' he eyed Clara keenly. 'So how about it, are you going to stay on for a few days?'

'Why don't you make that cup of tea you promised me, and I'll think about it.'

'Well, don't take too long,' said Ralph as he stepped into the beach hut. 'I have to let everyone know your plans.'

'Pardon me?' Clara turned around in her seat, but Ralph was already inside.

'There you go, one builder's mug of tea from the chipped teapot – just how we like it.' He passed Clara a mug and sat down in the deckchair next to her.

'Ralph, what did you mean when you said you have to let everyone know?'

'Ah, yes, that. We were all hoping to meet up on the beach, just family and friends, a small get-together in honour of Tommy.'

'Oh, Ralph.' Clara placed a hand on his arm. 'How thoughtful.'

He looked at her hand resting on his arm. He tentatively placed his hand on hers wondering if she would pull away. She didn't. Instead, she curled her fingers in his. Ralph said, 'I take it you will be around for the next few days?'

Clara smiled at him. 'We've been apart long enough. It's time we got to know each other again.'

'I'll drink to that!' said Ralph holding up his mug.

They sat there on the deckchairs holding hands and drinking tea as they stared out to sea, both appreciating how lucky they were to have found each other.

Ralph's thoughts drifted to the painting he had sent Clara. Even though he no longer had that picture which used to be the last thing he'd see before drifting off to sleep, he still dreamt that same dream every single night. He smiled as they sat there holding hands. It wouldn't be long, and his dream would come true. Someday soon he would walk along a Mallorcan beach hand-in-hand with the woman of his dreams.

Epilogue

'Here they come!' Clara turned to Ralph. 'Is everything ready?'

Ralph double-checked. 'Yes, as ready as we'll ever be. Shall I dish up the food?'

'Good idea.' Clara passed him the plates. 'Have we got enough for everybody?' she asked as she watched them all walking along the beach heading in their direction.

Tamsin, Kevin, Sophie, Elliot and Mia were in front, followed by Paul and Evie. She knew her friends Gerald and Debs were also down from London for the small gathering on the beach at dawn, and Debs new old flame; she couldn't remember his name. The two stragglers at the end she guessed were Joe and Judy. They had crossed the Atlantic and moored somewhere in Southwold.

Judy, Debs and Gerald never knew Tommy. Neither did Debs boyfriend. But they were part of her story, and that made them all part of Tommy's.

'Well?' asked Clara looking worried.

'Relax. I've made more than enough. There will even be plenty of leftover bacon for Bailey.'

As if on cue, Bailey came bounding along the beach towards them. He stopped in front of Clara for a fuss, then Ralph, and finally settled on what he was after, sniffing around the pan for some bacon. 'Just because you got here first,' said Ralph, tapping his nose with a spatula, 'does not mean you have first dibs. You will have to wait your turn like everybody else.'

As the rest of the party arrived, Clara handed each of them a knife and fork wrapped in a serviette and directed them to the barbecue where Ralph was about to serve breakfast.

'Take a seat when you've got your breakfast,' said Clara.

They had bought some deckchairs from a local store and carried them down to the beach. As it was quite cool this early in the morning, Ralph had made a fire for them all to sit round while they ate and watched the sunrise.

Clara stood watching Ralph dishing up bacon, sausages, eggs, waffles, beans and fried bread on to the plates and handing them out. She then meandered past Sophie, Elliot, Mia and Kevin who were first in the queue, giving them each a kiss and a hug. She stopped beside Tamsin. 'How are things since you moved into the house?'

'You mean how are things between Kevin and me?'

Clara nodded.

Tamsin grinned at her. 'Better than ever. It's quite strange. We have less money than we've ever had in our lives and yet we couldn't be happier.'

Clara was relieved. She remembered wishing she'd asked Joe to take down that wretched man cave at the bottom of their garden before he'd handed over the keys. The one thing that concerned her about Tamsin and Kevin moving into their house was the thought, however ridiculous, that Kevin would morph into Joe and think up all these outlandish get-rich-quick schemes. She knew that was absurd. Kevin wouldn't be so stupid – would he?

'So, everything's fine with you and Kevin?'

Tamsin replied, 'It most certainly is.' She wasn't about to sound ungrateful and tell her mother it wasn't to begin with when they first moved into her childhood home. She'd wished Dad had never signed the house over to the children in trust and given them the option to live there. It almost turned out to be the unravelling of their relationship and the end of their marriage for reasons she would never have envisaged.

It all started when Kevin took his laptop down to the shed at the bottom of the garden. She thought nothing of it at first. It was just somewhere he could get away from three women in the small North London semi and have some peace and solitude to investigate a business venture.

What Tamsin soon discovered was that Kevin hadn't come to terms with their new circumstances even though they were much better off than most people. He wasn't accepting this was their life now, living in an ordinary semi, his wife doing a part-time number at a local café while he looked for a job.

Even though everybody else was happy, she suspected Kevin missed his old life, living in a large detached house and running a successful business. She started to worry he was morphing into her father – always living for the future, The Big Payday, rather than accepting his lot and making the most of what he had today. Tamsin, on the other hand, couldn't be happier. It made her wonder whether a big payday would change their lives for the better.

Tamsin glanced at her mother greeting everybody as she made her way down the breakfast queue. It hadn't done her and Joe any favours – his pursuit of The Big Payday. They weren't together any more. The same couldn't be said for her and Kevin because her husband had realised there were more important things in life than the pursuit of money. Tamsin remembered that day…

The girls had come home from school, and she had returned from working in the café. Kevin wasn't in the house. She knew he'd be at the bottom of the garden working on his next venture. However, that day something was different. That day, he'd invited them all down to his man cave. Except it wasn't Kevin's man cave any longer.

While they were out, Kevin had had some of his old work pals in to do a job. He had ripped out all the office furniture and transformed the shed into what looked like a Scandinavian lodge. There were rugs on the wooden floor and a stove and books lining the bookshelves along with the board games they used to enjoy playing. He'd transformed Joe's man cave into a den.

Tamsin remembered verbatim what Kevin had said to her. "If the past few weeks have taught me anything, it's making the most of what we have."

"No more chasing dreams?" Tamsin had asked.

He'd shook his head. "My dream life is here – with you."

Tamsin would never forget that afternoon she discovered they would be okay. She took his hand in hers as they waited in the queue for breakfast.

Kevin asked, 'Is everything all right?' He glanced at Ralph serving up the breakfasts.

She knew what he was referring to. 'I told you,' she whispered, 'I'm fine.'

'Yes, I know things are going well between you and Ralph, but still, it's not every day you find out that your dad isn't—'

'Shh!'

'Oh, sorry.' Kevin turned around and glanced over people's heads at Joe at the end of the queue. 'He can't hear me.'

'I want to tell him myself so he knows that although I'm getting to know my father, he will always be my dad. Does that make sense?'

Kevin nodded.

'That's why I haven't told the girls yet.'

Mia turned around and eyed her parents. 'Told us what?'

Tamsin exchanged a glance with Kevin and rolled her eyes at her youngest. Mia had always been the more inquisitive of her two girls.

'Ralph wants you and your sister, well all of us, to spend the holidays down here at The Gables.'

That wasn't strictly true. Ralph had asked Tamsin if she and her family would like to move into The Gables – permanently. Ralph was no longer living in the main house; he'd told them the apartment over the garage was ample accommodation for himself and Clara when they were visiting from Mallorca.

No one was surprised when they announced they'd moved in together. That's when Ralph had finally retired and left Southwold with Clara for *Casa Buena Vida* where they were now living the good life along with Dorothy, Winston the dog and Marley the cat. He told Tamsin he'd always thought The Gables deserved a family with children and laughter, as he remembered it when Clara and Tommy lived there growing up.

Although Tamsin would love to move there, the girls were settled in their schools, she was enjoying her new job in a café, and Kevin had more work opportunities in the capital. But despite those practicalities, there was still the matter of when their family of four became five.

They would soon outgrow the three-bed semi when their third child came along. Tamsin's hand moved to her small bump. She hadn't broached it with Kevin what she'd been thinking. Despite all the sound reasons they had discussed for staying in London, Tamsin just wanted to throw caution to the wind and move down here and start a new life on the Suffolk Coast.

She glanced at her Mum who was her inspiration. Clara had done the same, thrown caution to the wind and moved somewhere else. She was doing many new and exciting things with her life because of a fresh start in Mallorca.

Tamsin had heard all about her budding photography business, taking photos of the stunning Mallorcan scenery and sending them to be published in magazines and newspapers. She also acted as a guide taking groups of tourists from cruise ships on tours of the island. And she'd started cookery classes – which was a first. It's something she and Dorothy enjoyed doing together.

Tamsin's hand moved to her bump. Maybe it was that nesting instinct kicking in because of being pregnant, but she couldn't help it. Tamsin had already decided she wanted to bring up her new baby here.

'Mummy – what were you saying?'

Tamsin looked at Mia. For now, the birth was months away. If Mia had an inkling there was the option to live here all year round, they'd never hear the end of it, so she said, 'I like the idea of coming back here during your school holidays – don't you?'

'Oh, yes!' Mia turned to her sister.

Tamsin smiled. 'I don't think you need to ask your sister if she likes that idea too.'

Mia looked at Elliot standing there with a protective arm around her sister and frowned.

Tamsin put an arm around Mia's shoulders. 'It won't be long and there will be boys beating a path to your door.'

Mia shrugged off her mother's arm. 'I don't want a boyfriend! Boys are stupid.'

Kevin and Tamsin smiled at their little girl. Their attention shifted to Sophie who had transformed from their other little girl to a blossoming young woman. A lot had changed during one summer, although nothing had turned out quite how anyone would have envisaged – even Elliot.

It turned out their daughter was dating an artist who was making quite a name for himself on the London art scene. Tamsin and Kevin were in the throes of deciding whether to let her accompany Elliot to New York in the spring. He was debuting his new collection of paintings at a prestigious New York gallery.

Tamsin took her cooked breakfast and sat down in a deckchair by the warming fire. Family and friends in the queue soon joined her. At the end of the line Bailey was rewarded with some streaky bacon before Ralph switched off the barbecue and discarded his apron.

When they were all seated, busy eating their breakfast and talking amongst themselves, Ralph turned the Clara. 'I made a new sign for the beach hut – I hope you don't mind.'

'It's *your* beach hut, Ralph, of course I don't mind.'

'It's *our* beach hut.'

Clara glanced over at the hut.

He smiled at the new sign. '*The Rekindlers* – that's us.'

Clara looked at Ralph. 'The Rekindlers?'

'Well, I guess it's not just you and me.' He motioned at Joe and Judy, and Debs and her old flame.'

'Oh, I see what you mean.' She grinned.

'I hope Tamsin and Kevin, or Sophie and Elliot never become rekindlers, but for the rest of us,' he held up his mug and said, 'it's never too late to rekindle a lost love.'

'Here, here,' said a spectral figure up on the clifftop as he turned to his love before they floated away together on the sea breeze.

Clara had the sudden urge to turn and look up at the cliff top. She thought she saw a couple sitting on the wooden seat above the promenade and wondered what had got them up so early, but when she blinked, they were gone.

'What's the matter?' Ralph followed her gaze.

'I thought I saw—'

'You thought you saw…?'

'Do you believe in the afterlife, Ralph?'

He took her hand. 'Are you thinking about Tommy?'

Clara shifted her gaze to Ralph and nodded.

He smiled. 'If by an afterlife you mean eternity, then I'm bound to say yes. Now we've found each other again, I'm never leaving your side. I'm afraid you're stuck with me.'

'For eternity?'

'Oh, yes.'

Clara smiled back at him and squeezed his hand tight. 'I'm never letting you go either.'

She raised her mug of tea and took a moment to look at the small group. 'To friends and family – and Tommy.'

'To friends and family,' everyone echoed, 'and Tommy.'

Ralph smiled as his gaze shifted around the campfire, finally settling on his beloved. Things don't always go to plan, that's for sure, but life has a funny way of setting the record straight – in the end.

'Has everyone seen my new beach hut sign?' Ralph pointed. He raised his mug for another toast. 'To the rekindlers.'

Everyone turned to look at the sign as they chanted, 'To the rekindlers.'

'To the rekindlers,' whispered Clara, glancing up at the wooden bench on the clifftop. 'Wherever you are.'

Dear Reader

If you enjoyed A Mallorcan Affair I would be extremely grateful if you'd leave a brief review on Amazon.

For further details about the author and her novels visit the author's website:

www.elisedarcy.com

Please feel free to add your email to the mailing list for updates on forthcoming book releases, special offers, and book recommendations in the author's e-newsletter.

Also by Elise Darcy

The Living Apart Together Series

Living Apart Together

It Takes 2 to Tango

Dear John

Love on the Rooftop

Standalone Novels

Lola & The Man

The Villa in Sicily

Printed in Dunstable, United Kingdom

69007021R00336